Pinned to the ground with the priest's knee on his chest, Peter looked back at his enemy calmly. 'Father Simeon will hunt you down,' he said. 'He will find me.'

'He will find your wretched corpse,' de Figham sneered, then clamped his hands around the slender neck and pressed his thumbs over the soft flesh of Peter's throat. 'I will choke the life from you this time, ditcher's whelp. As God is my judge, I will not be cheated a second time of the privilege of killing you.'

The priest grabbed the dazed boy by an arm and a leg, hoisted him chest high and, with a bellow of triumph, tossed him into the mouth of the derelict well.

MASTER OF THE KEYS

Domini Highsmith

WARNER BOOKS

A *Warner* Book

First published in Great Britain in 1996
by Little, Brown and Company
This edition published by Warner Books in 1997

A CIP catalogue record for this book
is available from the British Library.

ISBN 0 7515 1843 3

Typeset by Hewer Text Composition Services, Edinburgh
Printed and bound in Great Britain by Clays Ltd, St Ives plc

Warner Books
A Division of
Little, Brown and Company (UK)
Brettenham House
Lancaster Place
London WC2E 7EN

ACKNOWLEDGEMENTS

The author would like to thank the following for their support, advice and encouragement, and for the loan of books and Church records from private collections:

The Reverend Peter Forster of Beverley Minster
David Thornton, Verger of Beverley Minster
Pamela Martin, Head of the Reference Section, Beverley Library
Librarian Jenny Stanley and staff at Beverley Library
Julie Hicks, Martin Gobbi and staff at The Beverley Bookshop
Father X
Clifford Evans
Pauline Brown
Peter and Edith Webster
Melodie Richardson
Kerina Richardson
My daughter, Tammy
Sophie Oyston
Dale Oyston

And for retrieving and unscrambling lost work from a rogue computer, special thanks to Andrew Coverdale and Oliver Oyston.

North Bar

St Mary

Hengate

Archbishop's House

Town ditch

Town ditch

Bar

Corn-market

Bar

Westwood

Butcher Row

Fish-market

Hyegate

Eastgate

Lairgate

Minster
St Martin

Minster Moorgate

Town ditch

Keldgate

Landing & Drawbridge

Keldgate Bar

Lake

Copyright
Domini Highsmith, 1992

St Anne's Convent

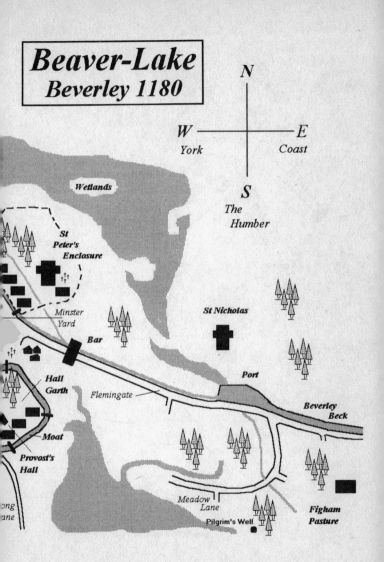

Beaver-Lake
Beverley 1180

N

W ——————— E
York   Coast

S

The Humber

Wetlands

St Peter's Enclosure

Minster Yard

Bar

Hall Garth

Flemingate

Moat

Provost's Hall

Long Lane

St Nicholas

Port

Beverley Beck

Meadow Lane

Pilgrim's Well

Figham Pasture

And again, my book is dedicated to the Unknown Priest, whose tomb now lays in the North Transept of Beverley Minster

CHAPTER ONE

January 1191

The bustling town of Beverley, set in the eastern reaches of Yorkshire and subject to the powerful see of York, lay paralysed by snow and ice and choked by freezing fog. Its people were hungry, its port brought to a standstill. Only the rats and the scavenging crows prospered; all else merely clung to life and hope, and waited for the turning of the season.

King Richard, the Coeur de Lion, was on the throne, an absent king more concerned with his inglorious foreign crusades than with the heavy burden of his sovereignty. While he slaughtered and plundered in distant lands with the blessing of his pope, Clement III, no king in Christendom dared to make war on his neglected England. The Holy Catholic Church offered God's own protection to the lands of its Royal Crusaders. England was safe, for no monarch found the prize so tempting that he would risk the wrath of Rome for its taking. The best of kings, Henry Plantagenet, was dead of a broken heart, and the sons who had driven him to turn his noble face to the wall were now his legacy to his beloved England. Richard the Warrior, John the Schemer and Geoffrey the Disappointed; three hostile and rebellious brothers divided by a throne, all burning in their hearts for

1

fame and covetous of their father's hard-won glory. Three sons and but one England. Three brothers to keep the invader out whilst stirring up the menace that brewed within.

Thirty miles east of York, where Geoffrey Plantagenet, King Henry's bastard, still laid claim to the archbishop's title and resources, the fire-crippled Minster church of St John presided over Beverley, the blessed *Beaver Lake* of centuries past.

Simeon de Beverley stood on Figham Pasture, his eyes half closed and his muscular body braced against the scythe edge of the north wind. He was a tall man, with hair the colour of ripened corn and eyes of a startling blue. The wind flapped his cloak about his legs and stung his exposed skin until his fingers, nose and ears were raw with cold. Down there in the town, this gifted scribe of St Peter's walked with a crippled gait and sought to live a life of studious humility. Up here, beyond the prying eyes of his enemies, he could abandon all claims to lameness and become for a while the true Simeon de Beverley, warrior priest.

This was as bitter a winter as any he had known, and yet so little time ago he had prayed for summer's end. The dry months had lingered too long, scorching the fields and turning the crowded timber-and-thatch town into so much kindling any stray spark might ignite. Late crops had shrivelled in the fields and fresh water had been scarce. Now the year had turned and winter had them in its grip, as harsh a winter as Nature could inflict. Below the pasture, in the troubled town of Beverley, the pace of life had slowed to a shivering, sombre struggle for survival.

Osric the infirmarian blew on his hands and grumbled at the severity of the weather. He was clad in a leather hood, with a fur-lined cloak reaching to his knees, and his temper was as brittle as the wind that searched out every gap in his clothing. His beard was streaked with silver and his temples patched with grey, but this surgeon and herbalist was still a soldier at heart, with nerves of steel and the instincts of a fighter.

'Damn it, this wind gnaws like a horde of hungry rats at my

2

ears.' He glanced at his companion, noted the lowered hood and the flapping cloak and wondered how Simeon bore the cold so well.

'A few short weeks ago we dreaded drought and summer fires,' Simeon observed. 'Now men fear to sleep at night lest they freeze to death in their beds.'

'Nature is cruel,' the older man replied, stamping his feet and wincing as his numbed toes ached in protest. 'When was she ever otherwise?'

'God guides her with a kind hand, when it suits Him.'

'Aye, and like a mean beast when it doesn't.'

Simeon nodded his tonsured head. Beyond the pasture, the half-ruined Minster stood like a solemn sentinel over the town, its windows as white as milk with reflected snow. If he had one real ambition in life it was to see that Minster church restored, and to have the hidden relics of St John returned to the shrine intended as his last resting place. Now Simeon signed the cross and briefly lowered his head in silent prayer, then whispered into the wind a soft, 'Amen'.

Osric followed his friend's gaze to where the house of Cyrus de Figham huddled against a bank of driven snow, its chimneys stopped and its windows safely shuttered. Nothing moved beyond the great barred gates. No tread of boot or track of cart marred the smooth carpet of snow laid on the surface of the courtyard. The house was deserted save for the hounds that howled beyond the barn and the vagabond who kept a half-hearted watch in the absence of his master.

'The priest is dead,' Osric said. 'You brood without cause, my friend. It's all over.'

Simeon turned his head and drew his pale brows down in a frown. 'How can it be over?' he asked. 'Rome demands an investigation into the death of Cyrus de Figham. When the facts are known, Thorald will be charged with his murder.'

Osric shook his head. 'No sane man will call it murder when the truth is out in full.'

'He knifed de Figham in the back,' Simeon reminded him. 'He pursued him through the streets and knifed him before scores of witnesses. I fear the papal legate will feel obliged to

3

deal harshly with him, if only to dissuade other men from following his example. They will not condone the murder of a canon by a priest, however complex the circumstances.'

'It was a justifiable killing,' Osric protested. 'The man deserved to die.'

'*We* believe that, my friend, but will the court? The law is clear and its servants must be seen to observe that law to the letter. God said, "Thou shalt not murder." No papal legate, no learned stranger dispatched to us from Rome, will disregard God's law for Thorald's sake.'

'Then the truth must be used to protect him,' Osric answered, infuriated by the injustice of so-called law.

'The truth will condemn him,' Simeon said. 'He's guilty. We know that's so.'

'But he can plead that he acted in your defence.'

'He ran down a fleeing man, Osric, intent on killing him.'

'Aye, and with good reason,' Osric remembered. 'He was provoked. Father Thorald is beyond reproach.'

Simeon glanced at his companion, his features grave. 'Osric, he knifed de Figham in the back.'

The wind howled over the pasture, driving snow into their faces. Simeon lifted his hood and wrapped his billowing cloak around him, then turned towards the town and strode away.

'It is not over,' he called out in a grim voice, and Osric, following behind with his head bent into the wind, was tempted to ask, 'How can it ever be for you, Simeon de Beverley?'

In a hovel lit by a crackling fire of twigs and slow-burning ox dung, an old woman with a crooked hand dipped into a sack and withdrew a square of ivory with coloured inlays. Carved around its edges were Hebrew, Greek and Roman markings entwined with many Christian symbols dating back into antiquity. The woman was Hannah, revered by many as a prophetess, and when she cast her runes she offered, for a price, a glimpse of the future for men to interpret as they

4

might. Her voice was as hoarse as a man's as she muttered and murmured over her ivories.

'He's coming. The runes have spoken. He is on his way.'

Old Hannah had not always shared her life with scuttling rats and the stink of poverty. Once a lady of extraordinary beauty, her preoccupation with the darker arts had prompted her God-fearing family to have her confined in an isolated convent. From there she had been driven onto the streets when visiting priests had denounced her as a witch. No kindness had ever come her way and now, in advanced age, she lived no better than an animal. She spent her waking hours roaming the streets and alleyways of Beverley, begging scraps of food and animal bones, selling her prophecies for a portion of bread or merely scouring the ground for any waste that would help keep the fire burning in her grate. Her rasping voice and constant chants gave warning of her approach, so that those who feared her tossed out a few twigs of fuel or scraps of food to hasten her passing. Now, as she named the rune drawn from her pouch, she knew that evil forces were once again being drawn to Beverley like moths drawn to a flame. 'Fortune's Fool!'

The fire flared and spat and crackled in the grate as a frosty wind blew in from the door where a tattered leather hung. She returned the rune to the sack, shook the contents gently, muttered an incantation and dipped again. Once more she lay an ivory on the table and watched the firelight flicker across its surface.

'Fortunes Fool! Twice in succession. He's coming, Simeon de Beverley.'

Again she dipped into the bag and again the pawn of fortune was lifted into the gloom inside the hovel. Hannah leaned into the hearth close to the fire, her old bones comforted by the meagre blaze. Her voice was a hoarse and brittle whisper as she rocked her body to and fro, muttering all the while, 'A stranger is coming, Simeon de Beverley. Beware the Fool of Fortune, *beware*!'

Fresh snow had been falling steadily for days. The sky hung low above the town, sombre and grey by day, leaden and starless by night. The Westwood and other common pastures wore a soft white mantle through which the frozen streams were interwoven like so many narrow silver threads. The wide marshes to the east of the town lay concealed beneath drifts of snow, their dangerous pools and gaps covered over so that the land appeared as innocent and inviting as a pretty winter meadow. Beyond the hovels, the town gates and the tangle of narrow streets, the stark profile of Beverley Minster stretched upward to a sky misted with snowy tears. The year had reached its lowest ebb, that season when meat and fuel were scarce, when travel was made so difficult that traders and pilgrims, on whom the town depended for its survival, were rarely seen. During these long and hazardous weeks the old and the weak would not be fed at the expense of the young and strong, nor the sick be given priority over the healthy. It was a time of natural pruning, when only the hardy would survive to carry the town into another year.

A scratching at the door told Hannah that someone had come in search of her special skills. She neither turned from the fire nor raised her head, for the shape of a youngster clutching a bundle of twigs was reflected in the polished copper belly of her cooking pot.

Her visitor was Edwin, a brave, intelligent fifteen-year-old who suffered a serious disorder of the nerves. Although not prone to those sudden, ugly seizures known as the jerks, feared by the superstitious as possession by the Devil, he could drop like a stone without cause or warning and sleep as if half-dead wherever he fell. He had lived with his twin sister inside the walls of St Peter's enclosure for the better part of a year. His friend and confessor was Father Daniel, priest to the canon of St Matthew, but his hero and mentor was Simeon de Beverley.

'Speak, boy. Or has the Devil got your tongue?'

Her question caused the boy to start in alarm, for her face was fully turned from him and he believed she could neither see nor hear him there. He swallowed the apprehension in his throat and asked, 'Will you take faggots for your fire?'

'I take no gifts.'

6

'An exchange,' he told her. 'A payment.'

'For what?' she demanded in a rasp.

The youngster stepped nervously from one foot to the other. This single, low-roofed room was alive with shadows, its rafters hung with bunches of herbs and dusty rags, its dirt floor spread with filthy rushes that belched foul smells when disturbed. He knew he should not be here, in this stinking dark hole where mysterious arts were practised, but his fears for the priest had driven him to seek a warning of dangers yet to come. He gathered up his courage and found his voice, then fixed his gaze on the ragged figure huddled close to the fire. 'I've come to buy a prophecy.'

Her voice seemed to reverberate in the chimney. 'So, you seek to glimpse the future in exchange for a few small twigs?'

'I have a white rabbit's foot here in my pocket.'

'Then you're a wealthy man,' she mocked, and laughter rattled in her throat as she tossed a handful of herbs on the fire and watched blue sparks dance in the sooty chimney. She turned to him then, her haggard features so oddly lit by the flames that her eyes and toothless mouth appeared as blackened holes in her face. She saw a tall, slender youth with brown hair and a gentle face. His fingers trembled but his gaze was steady.

'Who are you, lad?'

'I'm Edwin, from St Peter's.'

'Edwin from St Peter's,' she repeated, nodding her head as if the news was no surprise to her. 'You serve the Special One?'

Edwin licked a dryness from his lips and nodded. 'I serve Father Simeon.'

Hannah lifted her shoulder to wipe a dribble of spittle from her mouth. 'Come closer, lad, What do you want from me?'

'I want . . .' he stepped as far from the curtained doorway as he dare, 'the runes.'

Hannah stretched her empty mouth in a crooked grin. Even as she shook her head as if to deny his request, her gnarled

7

fingers were reaching for the pouch of ivories. 'Fools,' she muttered. 'All men are fools. Why can you not be satisfied to live the life you have and be glad of it? Is today not hard and cruel enough that you must always seek to burden it with tomorrow's ills?'

'I don't ask it for myself,' Edwin told her. 'I ask it on Father Simeon's behalf.'

'Ah, for the Special One.'

'On his behalf,' Edwin repeated, stressing the words. 'He must not know I'm here.'

The woman chuckled again, then coughed to clear the rattle from her throat. 'All men are pagans in their souls,' she told him, and Edwin shuddered to hear Father Simeon's own words on her lips.

'Will you tell the runes?' he asked, setting down the bundle of wood and stepping back to draw the rabbit's foot from his coat. 'These are all I have.'

'An hour's warmth,' she grumbled, nudging the bundle of sticks with her foot. She snatched the rabbit's foot, gnawed on it with her blackened gums and dropped it into the hearth with a scornful snort. 'No meat. What use is a bone that has no flesh?'

'It's all I have.'

'What is it you seek here?'

'I need to know if he's safe.'

'Safe?' She barked the word, her dark eyes glinting as she eyed the boy. 'Safe? What living man is ever *safe*?'

'I need to know,' Edwin persisted.

Nodding her head and muttering words that made no sense to him, Hannah handed the pouch to Edwin and indicated, by gesticulation, that he should turn it over several times to shuffle the contents. This done, she unfastened the drawstring at its neck and thrust her undamaged hand inside. She repeated Simeon's name as she set an ivory on the table and, when she removed her hand, the inlaid figure seemed to spring to life.

'Oh, Lord!' Edwin stepped back and instinctively signed the cross, then edged a little closer with his head cocked to

8

one side, the better to examine the small rectangle of ivory. What he saw was an image of a fair-haired man in princely robes, crowned and seated on a throne, a dagger in one hand and a sceptre in the other. Protruding from a wound in his side was the gilded blade of a sword. A pauper knelt at his feet with a begging bowl held out to catch the dripping blood. 'Is that him?' he asked, unnerved by the resemblance between the ancient picture and the living man. 'Is that Father Simeon?'

'The Apostle.' She nodded. 'He represents high office gained through torment. See how he sits enthroned yet sheds his royal blood to fill the cup of lowly men.'

'They hurt him,' Edwin muttered, feeling the sudden sting of unwanted memories. The imprisonment, torture and subsequent stoning of Father Simeon during the Beverley riots had left such vivid images in his mind that the smallest reminder still caused his flesh to crawl. 'They turned against him and they hurt him.'

'Aye, it is their way.'

'But it wasn't fair. He was innocent.'

Hannah cleared her throat and spat on the rushes. 'These so-called Christians will murder the best of men, then repent the deed and worship him as a martyr to their folly. It is their way, lad, fair or not. Here on the ivory he sits revered, yet still they seek to drink his blood. He knows the path he walks. He accepts the burden.'

'Draw again,' the boy urged.

Hannah drew another rune and set it down. 'The Serpent.'

Edwin stared at the ivory, where a black snake was depicted rising from a pool of its own blood, leaving its severed head on the ground while a new one sprang intact from its mutilated throat. 'What is it? What does it mean?'

'It means that an enemy is not truly overcome. He lives to grow another head, to fight another day, to strike again.' She aligned the ivory more precisely on the table so that its blacks and crimsons were set in garish contrast to the gentler colours of Simeon de Beverley's image.

9

Edwin shuddered. 'Draw again.'

This time the rune revealed the angelic figure of a child, his hair picked out in specks of gold, his eyes in brilliant blue. A sacrificial lamb lay in his lap. In his right hand was a golden casket held aloft, in his left a writhing snake gripped by the neck.

'The Cherub,' Hannah muttered, and Edwin, staring wide-eyed at the rune, whispered softly, 'Peter.'

He watched the woman place the ivory on the right of the Apostle, then stared from one to the other, struggling to grasp the meaning of what he saw. Here was Simeon with the Serpent on his left and the Cherub on his right, and this ghastly old woman held the key to his destiny. At last he shook his head and asked again, 'What does it mean?'

Hannah heaved a sigh, impatient of his ignorance. 'The Cherub reminds us that the weak may overcome the strong,' she told him. 'And that the most venomous viper, properly held, can be rendered helpless even by a child. See there, above his head, one star is rising as another falls, but which belongs to whom, my curious lad, and who is to be the sacrificial lamb?'

Edwin dared to reach out and touch the ivories. 'If this first one is meant to be Simeon and this last one Peter . . .' he avoided contact with the vivid image of the two-headed serpent, 'who, or what, is this?'

Hannah chuckled and wagged a crooked finger in his face. 'Every paradise has its snake and every rose its barb. Read as you will. Interpret as you must. I only draw the runes and name their purpose.'

'Another. Draw out another.'

With a chuckle that seemed malevolent, Old Hannah dipped once more into the sack. This time she grunted and sucked in her breath as the ivory was revealed. Three times already she had drawn this figure, as many times as she had spread the cloth and spoken Simeon's name. She set the ivory below the other three, then shook her head and drew her threadbare shawl more tightly over her shoulders.

'Beware the Fool,' she said at last. 'He brings two cups,

one overflowing with honey and one with poison; friendship in one hand, treachery in the other. Whatever ill or good Fate thrusts upon him, that will he serve. Fortune's Fool. He offers his cups according to Fate's whim.'

'But his cups are identical . . .' For a moment Edwin caught his breath and held it, fearing that he, a near-identical twin, might be the one depicted in the rune. He swallowed his dismay and muttered, 'Draw again.'

'No more,' Hannah told him.

'Another. I have to know. Draw out another.'

'No more,' she repeated sharply. 'Not for a bundle of kindling and a fleshless rabbit's foot. Come back when you have more to offer.'

'But I haven't seen enough,' he protested. 'It makes no sense. I don't understand . . .'

'Men are not meant to understand such things.'

The old woman turned her face to the fire and stared into the flames, her body rocking as before while she uttered strange, guttural noises that might have been a chant or an incantation. A rat scuttled in a corner, hunting for food, and the wind from the open doorway sent fresh sparks into the blackness of the chimney. After peering again at the four runes on the table, Edwin signed the cross over his chest, shuddered and slipped away.

When the boy was gone, Hannah groped for the sack and lifted out another ivory. She did not look at it but set it down, still staring into the flames, her fingers blindly caressing the inlaid figure of a grinning skeleton wielding a cruel scythe, and the tiny shapes of men falling like severed corn before the blade.

'And here's the Grim Reaper,' she told the crackling flames, 'come to cut and gather his rightful harvest.'

In the alleyway outside Old Hannah's hovel, Edwin hugged the shadows below the eaves and made his way to the wider Cobbler's Row. He was perplexed by the runes and deeply disturbed by the signs of treachery that seemed to mark the reading. Simeon's wounds were barely healed, his body scarcely recovered from the ordeals of recent months. He

11

had faced death and been spared, had passed beyond the help of men and somehow been restored. That the core of his torments should, like the Serpent of the runes, regrow its head to strike at him again, was more than Edwin's young mind dared contemplate.

'The dark priest is dead,' he told himself and, seeking to lift his spirits, he whispered aloud, '*The dark priest is dead!*'

He paused before entering the street, alerted by a clamour some distance off. Cautious for his own safety in this unsavoury district of the town, he drew back into the shadowed alleyway and waited for the disturbance to pass. He saw a small crowd moving swiftly at one end of the street, and a moment later the clamour was approaching.

Four clerks in holy orders strode ahead of their master and his personal priest, beating the townspeople aside with heavy clubs and staffs. 'Make way! Aside! Make way for the blessed canon of St Matthew's.'

The canon moved like a seagoing ship in full sail, awesome in his magnificence. He was a man of huge proportions, dressed in white and purple robes, his belly crisscrossed by a triple girdle of silver set with jewels, his crimson cloak billowing in his wake to reveal its yellow lining in brilliant flashes. Flanked by his handsome, darkly clad priest and two guards bearing flaming torches, he propelled his obese body along the narrow street with all the force and arrogance of a monarch. This canon wore the status of his office on his back. His pope demanded a clear distinction between the princes of the Church and the common people, and here was one who played his part as nobly as the pope himself might.

'Wulfric de Morthlund!' Edwin gasped the name as he edged into the deeper shadows close to the bootmaker's workshop. Apprehension stroked his spine with icy fingers. This man represented the Church and yet indulged in every worldly vice imaginable. He was a debaucher, a stealer of children, a spoiler of young boys. He took his pleasure the way dogs take their meat, with a savage and ravenous appetite. This man was everything the Church abhorred and

12

yet, while he prospered in his holy office, he paid in gold for his absolution and left no crime, no iniquity unbought.

A cart had pulled into the alley behind Edwin, and men were piling two bodies wrapped in sheets amongst its load of timber and turf. He could see Old Hannah rummaging beneath the ox in search of dung to fuel her fire. Several townspeople had been driven into Cobbler's Row ahead of the oncoming canon and his entourage. Others swarmed from their houses in the hope that alms were being distributed to the poor. When the two groups converged, a frightened Edwin found himself jostled roughly into their midst.

'Make way! Make way!' The holy clerks were enthusiastic in their duties. 'Get back! Allow your canon to pass unhindered.'

A flailing club caught Edwin on the shoulder with a blow that jarred the bone. He tripped and staggered, was shoved aside by a running man and then hoisted to his feet by one of the clerks. His hood was down, his hair and face exposed, when he met the fierce gaze of Wulfric de Morthlund. For a moment Edwin stood as if transfixed, gaping at the glittering eyes set deep in the fleshy face, at the rounds of fat hanging below the chin, at the soft, moist lips and darting tongue. He saw the eyes soften and the mouth curve in a smile, then he struggled free of the clerk's grip, turned on his heels and bolted.

'Stop him! I want that boy! Catch him! Catch him!'

With de Morthlund's voice ringing in his ears, Edwin raced down the alleyway and squirmed through a narrow gap between the ox cart and the wall. He had reached the far side of the obstruction when a strong hand grabbed him from behind and held him fast. He struggled wildly, kicking and yelling, only to gasp in relief at the sight of a familiar face.

'Father Daniel! Thank heaven . . . I thought . . .'

'Edwin! Why in God's name did you ignore my warnings? He saw you, and now . . .' Father Daniel shook the boy by the shoulders, exasperated and anxious for his safety. Tall and handsome, this priest was known as Daniel Hawk and was widely respected for his hunting skills. He was a priest without direction, an honest man swamped by corruption and tossed this way and that by the evils of his circumstances. He was an honourable friend to orphaned Edwin, and their friendship, though innocent, put both their lives at risk. Daniel Hawk would never be free to tread his own path, for his soul had ceased to be his own when, still a boy and subject to his master, he had become the catamite of Wulfric de Morthlund.

The priest set Edwin from him and snatched up the lad's hood to cover his face and hair. 'Run,' he hissed, 'and keep on running until you are safe inside St Peter's walls.'

'But Father, I must talk to you—'

'Go!'

As Edwin dashed away, Daniel Hawk turned back and was confronted by Old Hannah. She held a pile of steaming ox dung in her hands, and her eyes were glinting brightly when she told him: 'Beware the Fool.'

'Step aside, old woman. Let me pass.'

'Fortune's Fool is on his way. Beware of him.'

'Keep your prophecies to yourself,' he said sharply. 'Do you not see I am a priest? Get thee behind me, Satan's tool.'

So saying, Daniel drew the edge of his cloak over his nose and mouth to avoid inhaling her stench, edged through the gap and strode away, ignoring her taunting cries of 'Beware the Fool.'

Pacing impatiently before the bootmaker's shop, Wulfric de Morthlund threw back his cloak, placed his fists on his massive hips and glowered as Daniel Hawk approached alone. 'What, empty-handed, Little Hawk?'

'The lad was too quick for me, my lord. He must have ducked into one of those filthy hovels.' Daniel looked his master in the eye and lied without a qualm, then quickly added a second untruth to the first. 'And besides, he has some kind of pox. His body is alive with running sores.'

'Damn it!' De Morthlund heaved his great shoulders in a

sigh that caused his flesh to wobble. 'Damn it, he was a pretty lad – that tawny hair and soft eyes . . . a pretty lad.'

'Just a gutter wretch not worthy of your interest, my lord.' Daniel lowered his head in a respectful bow, then followed his master towards the door of the shop. At the sound of laughter he glanced back to find a grinning clerk observing him. This was Nicholas, once a weaver of cloth, now bent on ingratiating himself in the pursuit of better prospects. His face, neck and hands were deeply pitted with pox scars, a disfigurement that left him hideous to look upon but favoured in men's eyes. A man who had survived the pox was considered doubly blessed. Having once been afflicted and spared by God, he could neither suffer the disease again nor spread it.

'Out of favour, Father Daniel?' Nicholas asked in oily tones. 'Or are you no longer pretty enough to please your illustrious master?'

'My master pleases himself,' Daniel replied.

'Does he indeed? You let that lad escape.'

'I did no such thing. He was too quick for me. I lost him in this maze of alleyways.'

'You let him escape,' the clerk insisted. 'But no matter, Father Daniel. Our canon will no doubt pay me handsomely when I deliver to him the tasty titbit you so carelessly allowed to slip through your crafty fingers.'

'You'll never find him.'

'Ah, but I intend to make it my business to find him.'

'He's gone,' Daniel told him, 'gone to earth like a rat.'

'A clever man can entice a rat from its hole.'

'He was pox-ridden. I saw the sores for myself.'

'Did you indeed?' The clerk shook his head and offered a knowing smile. 'A jealous lover rarely praises a rival.'

'Guard your tongue, Nicholas Weaver.'

'Guard your livelihood, Daniel Hawk,' the clerk countered. 'A boy so pretty would surely rob you of it.' With a malicious chuckle, he brushed past the priest and swaggered, still grinning, into the bootmaker's shop.

Several streets away and running hard, young Edwin

15

scrambled through cluttered yards and dashed along winding alleyways as, taking his bearings from the Minster
bells, he hurried back to the safe haven of St Peter's
enclosure.

CHAPTER TWO

While Edwin crept unseen into the enclosure of St Peter's and went about his duties with a troubled mind, events were taking place a dozen miles away that would soon convince him of the ominous truth in Old Hannah's prophecy.

The isolated monastery of St Dominic the Mailed lay in virtual ruin in its bleak and marshy setting, abandoned by all but a handful of loyal monks. In recent years storms had ravaged its roofs, floods had undermined its foundations, drought had diminished its wells and destroyed much-needed crops. More recently a prolonged epidemic of the flux had claimed the lives of half the brotherhood, including its abbot. Many survivors had fled while the contagion was at its height, leaving behind those who either feared to make the journey or refused to carry the sickness beyond the monastery walls. The last donkey had vanished with Seth, a trusted brother who had slipped away in the night when his struggling patch of vegetables took the frost, too sick of heart to keep his pledge to stay and too ashamed to bid his fellow monks farewell. St Dominic's was a sorry place whose inmates endured a bleak, soul-testing exile. No wealthy nobleman offered gifts for its upkeep. No sympathetic church gave it support, and no generous benefactor helped replenish its failing stores and dwindling resources.

'The Lord will provide,' Abbot Aidan said, looking out across the snowy marshes and feeling the wind's chill right to his ageing bones. 'He is merciful.'

A monk was bending over a small desk in the corner, strips of cloth wound around his frozen fingers and hunger gnawing at his belly. He glanced up and dared to voice the question, 'When?'

'In His good time.'

'But we are dying, Father Abbot. We cannot wait.'

'You must have faith,' Aidan admonished.

'I must have food,' the clerk muttered in a miserable voice, and stooped once again over his cleric's work.

Father Aidan, still known and revered as Father Abbot, had left his abbey in Holderness when his superiors felt he had grown too old for the rigours of his office. A younger, more dynamic man was sent to be Father Abbot in his place, and Aidan's heart was broken in the process. He withdrew to St Dominic's, seeking isolation in his old age, but found instead a disheartened flock in need of leadership. Without official sanction, he slipped once more into the role of Father Abbot, shouldering the burden God had thrust upon him. For two years he leaned upon the strength of Brother Gerard, once a soldier under Henry Plantagenet and no stranger to the face of human suffering. But now, following both man-inspired and God-sent upheavals in the outside world, a force had found its way into St Dominic's that neither Gerard nor his abbot could control.

Below the half-glazed window of the abbot's quarters, partly concealed by the shadowed pillars of the cloister's covered walkway, two men were speaking together in lowered voices.

'I believe this stranger you house is the man I seek.' The soldier known as Chad was heavily cloaked against the cold, his rugged face protected by a hood. 'You say the wound in his back was caused by a knife blade?'

The monk nodded. 'Or a sword, perhaps.'

'And he has no recollection of his own identity, no memory of where he belongs?'

'None, if his protestations are to be believed,' Gerard said.

Chad sensed uncertainty in the monk's reply. 'Do you doubt his story?'

Gerard shrugged. 'I know nothing about him and yet, from the very first, I instinctively took against him. He was brought here by a family travelling from the south to the abbey at Meaux. They found him wounded and delirious by the roadside and assumed him to be the victim of wandering robbers. Good Christians that they were, and fearing to have his death upon their conscience, they carried him here to us. He was raving like a madman in his pain. I fear he rules our abbot as a master rules a serf. He claims everything we have for his own comforts, then sets one brother against another with his bribes and criticisms. His demands exhaust us and his rages disrupt our already troubled peace. Little by little, his presence here is destroying us. Forgive my outburst,' the monk said wearily. 'I am not an uncharitable man, but I speak as I find. The priest is dangerous.'

'If all you say is true, your fears are justified,' Chad told him. He was convinced that the man Gerard so feared was the very man who had vanished from Beverley after inciting the townspeople to riot. If it proved to be so, these gentle monks were harbouring a killer. He glanced at Brother Gerard's sandalled feet, through which his toes, discoloured by the cold, protruded onto the bare stones of the cloister. His robe barely covered his knees and his cloak and hood were threadbare. These servants of St Dominic the Mailed were bound by a solemn vow of poverty, and rarely had Chad encountered that lowly state more adequately demonstrated. Compassion stirred in his tough soldier's heart. His belly was filled and although he faced another lengthy journey in foul weather, he knew that here was human need far greater than his own.

'Here, take my travelling pack of salt meat, bread and cheese,' he told the monk. 'As much as I have is yours, and you may keep my pack donkey for the abbey's use. In exchange for these I ask that you send word to Jacob de Wold, Provost of Beverley, if the priest regains his memory or makes any plans to leave. Do you agree?'

'I do,' Gerard nodded, 'and God bless you for the gift. Will you inform the Archbishop of York of our plight? He's the son of our late king, who was generous to our order and—'

'Don't count on Geoffrey Plantagenet to concern himself with your needs,' Chad cut in sharply. 'He doesn't hold with charity unless it's politic. King Henry's son he might be, but Henry's likeness he most definitely is not. The Archbishop of York will not come to your assistance.'

'But as God's servant, surely he's *obliged* to help us?'

Chad grunted. 'Nothing obliges the Plantagenet. He serves no interests but his own. He'll see no profit in concerning himself with the needs of a handful of starving monks and their crumbling monastery.'

'Well then, this Provost of Beverley, this Jacob de Wold. Perhaps *he* can be persuaded to intervene on our behalf?'

Once again Chad dashed the hope aside. 'I doubt he will. He's a man of honour whose hands are tightly bound. Every penny he has he offers to the hungry of his own parish. He'll pray for you, but his prayers will neither warm your frozen toes nor fill your bellies.' He rested his strong hand on the monk's thin shoulder. 'Take heart, Brother Gerard, my young master is a man of many resources, and if that priest you harbour is who I strongly suspect him to be . . .' Scowling, he drew the flapping edges of his cloak across his chest and added grimly, 'Trust me to do whatever I can to help you.'

'I ask no more than that,' Gerard said with a bow.

'And now I must be on my way before what remains of the day is lost and we're forced to travel in darkness. My master will return with me to identify this priest and to ease your present hardship.'

Chad shook the monk's hand and, as he turned away, Gerard cleared his throat and spoke to his retreating back. 'I tried to warn our abbot from the start. Believe me, Chad, the man's rage is an unholy thing. I swear there are times

20

when I've glimpsed the Devil himself staring out from those eyes.' Gerard shuddered as he recalled the hatred that leaped and danced like flames in the dark cauldrons of the priest's eyes. 'I acted in good faith, and in the name of caution, when I did it.'

Chad stopped, half turned, and fixed the monk with a hard stare. 'When you did what?'

'That which was necessary to keep the viper checked.'

'What? What did you do?'

'I set his legs in iron splints and leather straps to confine him until we could judge for ourselves what manner of man had been brought into our company. Every day since then I've blessed God for the inspiration. I bound him in a curb brace.'

Now Chad turned fully round to face the monk. 'A *curb brace*?' he echoed.

Gerard nodded. 'The stoutest I could fashion.'

'What? Have you shackled up a healthy leg in irons, then bound it to the other so that the man believes his limb to be broken? Have you deliberately hampered him?'

'I have, and with good cause,' Gerard told him, relieved to clear his conscience of the deed. 'I too was once a soldier, Chad. I learned to tend a wounded stranger with caution, lest he recover from his injuries and massacre his rescuers.'

'But how on earth did you manage to do it?'

'It was simply done.' The monk shrugged. 'The right leg was damaged, the flesh torn and infected. It took no more than a small lie to convince my abbot that the bone was also broken.'

'By the gods,' Chad hissed. 'If he's the man I seek, he'll kill you for it.'

'Then take him from us before he discovers the truth.'

'God help you when he does,' Chad told him.

'Who is he? By what name do you know him?'

Chad shook his head. 'Let the name your abbot gave him suffice for now. Know only that he might be the worst of men.'

'Then I was right to suspect him?'

'Aye. The Devil must have jumped with glee when those travellers saved his life.'

The monk's face creased with concern. 'I fear also for the woman and child who are forced to lodge in the room beyond his door. At dawn he sent their man away on some secret and urgent errand, and now he has declared himself their sole protector. Are they safe?'

Chad scowled. 'Is the lamb safe with the wolf? Take my advice while you await my master, Brother Gerard. Tighten the buckles on that curb brace and pray we are not delayed. Goodbye, my friend.'

Gerard watched the soldier vanish amongst the cloister shadows. He heard the clatter of hooves as Chad mounted his horse, and the crash of wood on iron as the gate was closed and fastened behind him. 'God speed,' he muttered, then turned on his heel and started in sudden alarm. 'Father Abbot!'

The old man was standing by a crumbling pillar, shaking his head in consternation, his eyes wide with dismay. 'May God forgive you, Brother Gerard.'

'You heard?'

Aidan nodded gravely. 'I heard enough to learn from your own lips how you've abused your authority and your position of trust. You must release that unfortunate man at once.'

'I beg you to reconsider,' the monk pleaded. 'In two days Chad will return with his master to take the priest away. Did you not hear him say that the brace should be well secured until then?'

'He speaks as a soldier. We are monks. Those irons must be removed.'

'No, Father Abbot, the irons must stay.'

'*At once!*' the abbot insisted. 'Confess your error and set him free.'

'What, and lift the lid on his rage? Have a care, Father Abbot. Already he demands enough wine and food for the needs of four men, then throws it to the rats when it's not to his taste. While lying helplessly on his back he rules this order as a cock rules over a henhouse. Free him, and he will—'

'Do you forget that I am Abbot here?' the old man demanded.

'You are, my Lord Abbot, but only so long as my curb brace keeps that priest confined and his temper in restraint. Release him and he'll devour every man he encounters, including *you*.'

'Mine is the final authority here. Our guest will abide by my ruling.'

'Such a man abides by no rule but his own.'

'You exaggerate, brother. *You* are the one at fault here. That agonising contraption of yours is the source of his ill humour. He rages against his discomfort and long confinement.'

'Not so,' Gerard insisted. 'His rage is a thing of evil. It feeds on itself from within. I knew it from the moment he arrived here. He's dangerous. Let the brace remain for two days more, until we are safely rid of him and—'

'Enough!' Aidan declared. 'How dare you take it upon yourself to abuse the solemn vow of charity on behalf of every member of our brotherhood? I know the truth, Brother Gerard. I will not be compelled to shrink from God because of your misdeed, nor will I face Him with such a wicked secret in my heart. There can be no way but that which we know to be right. Remove that inhuman fetter.'

Gerard clasped his hands together in entreaty. 'Father Abbot, he has the young woman and her female child under his protection. He has sent their man away from here on an errand he will not explain, even to you. How can we leave them vulnerable by freeing him?'

'Vulnerable?' Aidan asked. 'Are you suggesting that he would harm them but for your cruel contraption?'

'The soldier is convinced of it.'

'Then the soldier should examine his own heart on the matter. The man upstairs is a priest in holy orders, that much we *do* know about him.'

'And you, Father Abbot, are an innocent,' the monk countered hotly. 'Too many years of humility have blinded you to the failings of those who rule outside these walls. When Satan goes abroad he travels tonsured and wearing the finery

23

of the priesthood the better to deceive the innocent. Be warned while we still have that priest in our power. While we house the woman and her child in isolation, too cowardly to rest our gazes on them lest we fall to temptation, that priest will defile them both and—'

'*Enough*! You compound your guilt by flinging such accusations at a servant of the Church.'

'Two days,' the monk insisted. 'Just two more days . . .'

The ageing Aidan raised his hand for silence. 'Brother Gerard, you have my final word. *Release the priest.*'

They had named him Roche, after the patron saint of invalids and plague victims, and they knew as much about him now as they had known the day he had been carried screaming and cursing through their gates two months ago. He was a man of letters and good breeding, with the smooth, clear voice of a choral priest and the accent of a gentleman. His stare was compelling, his manner superior and intimidating. Every item of comfort the abbey possessed had been made available to him. A constant fire burned in his grate while the brothers shivered for want of fuel. Heavy tapestries hung from his half-glazed windows to keep the draughts at bay, while the monks endured a chapel whose windows opened to the elements.

Father Roche had made a lackey of Benedict, a nervous young brother, uncertain of intellect and easily bullied into grovelling obedience. This cringing monk now hovered close to the crackling fire, stealing its warmth in payment for his servitude.

'I did not send for you,' Roche declared, fixing his visitors with a hostile gaze. 'What do you want here?'

Gerard bristled at his tone, offended on the gentle Aidan's behalf. 'Our father abbot is concerned about the man who brought you here,' he answered mildly. 'He wishes to know the nature of the errand you have now sent him on.'

'I see, and has he lost his tongue, this abbot of yours, that you are required to speak on his behalf?'

'Brother Roche, it is my duty to—'

'I am not your *brother*,' the priest replied in disgust, then fixed his gaze on the abbot and told him, 'nor am I obliged to answer to *you* for my actions.' He winced and shifted on his couch, easing his bound legs into a more comfortable position. 'Damn this contraption. The iron grips me like a vice and the leather chafes my skin. Bring me something for the pain. Bring balm for the irritation. And in the name of heaven find me some decent wine. Ye gods, I am tormented.'

'Brother Gerard will remove the brace,' the father abbot told him, waving the young man forward.

'What?' The dark eyes lit with a sudden glint of suspicion. 'Remove it? How so? Any fool is aware that a shattered thigh bone does not knit together in so short a time. Remove it too soon and the bone will heal askew.' He glanced from the abbot to the younger man. 'Damn you conniving monks to hell. I'll suffer the brace though it kills me before I allow you fools to make a staggering cripple of me.'

'There has been a mistake,' the abbot offered, and watched the long eyes narrow into slits as he spoke the words.

'A mistake?'

'The brace is not required.'

Father Roche glared at both men in turn, weighing and measuring each with his stare. Then he lay back on his couch and assumed a stillness peculiar to himself, a stillness Gerard likened to the calm before a thunderstorm. His voice was low and soft when he said, 'Explain yourselves.'

'I set the brace in error,' Gerard offered. 'The bone is intact.'

In the silence following the words, Benedict stooped and hoisted his robe to the welcome heat of the fire. His placid face registered no hint that he was aware of the sudden change of atmosphere in the room.

'A mistake?' the dark priest asked quietly. 'Are you telling me this brace was never necessary, that the bone is not broken?'

'I confess that to be the case, Father Roche.'

'Then I say again, explain yourselves.'

25

With sinking hopes, Gerard attempted to pacify the priest with reasonable argument. 'You must appreciate, Father Roche, that we monks are defenceless here, in this isolated place. You were found on the outside, bloody and delirious. We had no way of knowing if you were friend or foe, healthy or infected, sane or mad. We needed to protect ourselves.'

'And so you applied a curb brace for my disablement,' the priest responded. He extended his arm to beckon the monk to his bedside. When Gerard stepped forward, he grabbed the monk's robe by its neckfolds and yanked him downwards until his face was but an inch away from his own. With fury blazing in his eyes, he spat two words in icy tones: '*Remove it!*'

Gerard's fumbling fingers plucked at the thongs and straps and buckles that bound two healthy legs together between strong irons. As he bent over the contraption, the door beyond the couch clicked open and two pale faces peered through the gap. The woman was young and plump, with a fine cascade of red-blonde hair. The child, wrapped in a threadbare blanket, was a pretty thing who stood no higher than her mother's breast. Gerard's fingers trembled over the buckles as Chad's words echoed in his head: *Is the lamb safe with the wolf?*

'God damn you monks to hell,' the priest hissed, wincing as the irons came away.

The skin beneath them was discoloured, with bruising where the straps had gripped and there were swellings in the gaps between. The original wounds had healed, the cuts and gashes knitted into scars that marked the leg from hip to calf. Father Roche probed the thigh bone with cautious fingers, kneaded and poked at it, then raised his fist and brought it down with force to test the bone.

He reached for both Gerard and the abbot, compelling them to assist him from the couch. He tested his weight on his limbs; long confinement had weakened once-powerful muscles. He moved unsteadily at first, then with growing confidence, flexing his knees and testing his remaining strength. When he had his balance firmly in control, he shook off the helping hands and moved across the room without assistance, pacing this way and that until his hesitant shuffle became an acceptable stride.

'Unbroken,' he said.

'A simple precaution,' Gerard assured him.

'A soldier's curb brace, damn you.'

'For our protection. You would have done the same, if—'

'Come here, monk,' Father Roche ordered, standing in the centre of the room with his legs stiffened under him. He glared at Gerard, crooked his finger and beckoned him to approach.

As Gerard stepped closer, intending to lend assistance, the priest's arm swung up and caught him a vicious blow to his face. Gerard dropped without a sound and lay inert, blood gushing in twin streams from his nostrils.

'Father Roche! By all that's holy . . . !'

At the unexpected tone of authority in the father abbot's voice, and at the touch of a restraining hand on his arm, Roche's dark face turned, the features tight with rage and the mouth twisted into an ugly snarl. He swept his other arm upward in a back-handed blow that flung the frail old man across the room and left him, crumpled and moaning, in a corner. This sudden eruption of violence so terrified the hapless Brother Benedict that he fell to his knees with a cry and began to babble as if in fear for his very life.

'I'm innocent. I knew nothing of this. I believed it to be broken. I had no part in it . . . I swear before God and all His angels . . .'

'Get out, you snivelling cur,' the priest snarled. 'And take these . . . these *vermin* from my sight.'

He watched the terrified monk struggle to assist the two injured men from the room. Gerard, so dazed and confused that he could barely stay on his feet, did what he could to help drag the semiconscious abbot to the stair while Roche, venting his fury as he paced on unsteady legs, yelled after them, *'Out, you vermin monks! Out! Out!'*

The dark priest slammed the door behind them and dropped the bar with a clatter, then pounded the wood several times with his clenched fists, roaring like an animal. At last he rested his perspiring face against the door, exhausted but unsatisfied, still muttering in his outrage.

A soft click at his back brought him around with fire blazing in his eyes. One glimpse of the golden-haired woman was enough to send the heat of his fury rushing to his loins. For weeks she had kept herself apart from him, ignoring his efforts to lure her to his bed, refusing him the rights of a man to have his needs appeased. Someone must pay the price for what had been done to him, and that frightened woman, so long a torment to his shackled lust, would pay in full for both her own disobedience and the monks' iniquity.

'Come here, woman. Obey me or be damned. I said, *come here!*'

He heard the scraping of a heavy chest as it was dragged across the inside of the door. The woman's continued determination to withhold herself from his demands incensed him. He flung himself in an ungainly stagger across the room and shouldered the door ajar, then kicked aside the chest and other obstacles hastily placed behind it. Once inside he reached for her as she, fearing the worst, thrust herself between him and the child. As the bleeding Gerard, assisted by a gibbering Brother Benedict, half carried their abbot down the winding stair, they heard the woman's screams and knew the viper had been freed to do its will.

CHAPTER THREE

The soldier, Chad, reached Beverley as night was falling. He dismissed all but one of his men to an eating house, then rode for the North Bar to rejoin his master.

'Have you found him?' the young nobleman asked, the instant his grim-faced companion came into view.

'Aye, it can be no other,' Chad replied.

'I knew it. I knew in my bones that he was still alive. Did you see him?'

'No, but I'm convinced we've found our man. He'll remain confined until you can get to St Dominic's to make a formal identification. For pity's sake, Fergus, take all the provisions you can carry when you go there. Those monks are starving.'

One crooked mile from Beverley's ancient Minster, the solid barrier of the North Bar stood like a dark sentinel in the fading of the day. Two windows high in the wall were washed with the yellow glow of the watchman's lamp. The heavy iron-clad gates were lowered, the chains and pulleys resting in their casings. Predictably, the bad weather of recent weeks was tightening its wintry grip, leaving the Minster town cut off, its roads impassable. Travellers were few and trade was slack, but still the beggars came, leaving their farms and settlements to beg bread at the doors of Beverley's churches.

The town was locked each day at nightfall, but during the short, grey days of winter, the watchmen kept to their lamps and barred the gates well in advance of the curfew bell.

Chad and his young master were sheltering in a recess by the bar, their hoods keeping the icy wind from their faces. They watched the frozen wastes beyond the town, where hovels and makeshift dwellings hugged the steep banks of the Great Ditch. The sky was grey and heavy with unshed snow. From the east a mist was creeping in and this, too, had a sharp and frosty edge.

The two made an incongruous pair. Fergus de Burton, youngest son of a nobleman and out to make his own way in the world, had the look of a reckless rake about him. His smile was a little too quick and his manner impudent, and his laughing eyes were all too easily drawn by the glimpse of a pretty ankle or a coy female glance. By contrast, Chad was a big, sharp-featured fellow with a soldier's manner and a rugged, grim face that rarely bore a smile of any description. Seconded to Fergus de Burton from the archbishop's personal guard, he was tireless in his master's service and never for a moment forgot that he was a soldier. Right now he was cold and stiff and weary as he cleared his throat with a growl and spat on the ground.

'This is madness,' he complained, stamping his feet on the frozen ground and hugging warmth to his chest with his powerful arms. 'You've heard my report three times in all its detail, and still you insist on standing here while the cold bites at our bones. Give up this wild idea, Fergus, before we freeze to death.'

'I'll not give up until I've seen it for myself,' Fergus replied.

'Then we'll still be here at dawn,' Chad growled. 'It's nothing but a myth you chase, and Lord knows, this town breeds its myths as freely as it breeds its ditch rats. It's a fool's errand, Fergus, and a cold one.'

'Be patient, Chad,' Fergus de Burton told him. 'You should know by now that all myths contain a grain of truth for those with the will to sift for it. This Beverley intrigues me. We have here many rumours of a hooded figure with strange powers, and of a mysterious child with the reasoning of a sage. We have miracle cures, hidden treasures, an empty shrine where pilgrims kneel to be fleeced of their offerings by greedy priests. And we have a so-called cripple who was stoned to death and then returned to life. Yes, Chad, this ancient *Beaver Lake* is a nest of rumour and muddled legend, and each enigma centres around that single priest, Simeon de Beverley.'

'Aye, the lame scribe of St Peter's,' Chad nodded. 'The one men either love with a passion or hate beyond all reason. I never knew anyone who met that priest and was indifferent to him. He's a strange one, but I like him well enough. I believe he can be trusted, and that's no common thing, an honest priest. Do you believe he cheated death, as people say?'

'I believe it,' Fergus told him with sincerity.

Chad looked sideways at the man he served. Fergus de Burton was a slippery individual. Behind his ready smile and silver tongue, this likeable young man had but a single clear ambition: self-advancement. To that end he consorted with the princely and the poor, with friend and enemy alike, and performed a nimble, dangerous dance between the two extremes.

Chad shrugged his shoulders and blew into his palms. 'Some say he abandoned God and made a pact with Lucifer in exchange for his life. Do you believe that, too?'

'Of course I do.'

'Some whisper that he faked the stoning so that men would see a miracle and think him a saint in the making. Is that also to be believed?'

'Absolutely,' Fergus nodded.

Chad heaved a sigh of exasperation. 'But every rumour conflicts with the next.'

Fergus nodded his head and winked an eye, his grin as playful as a child's. 'And I believe them all.'

'Well then I can only judge you, Fergus, to be a liar or else a gullible fool.'

'I assure you I am neither,' Fergus chuckled. 'I rarely

question what people say or what they choose to believe. Truth is a slippery commodity, Chad. It alters its shape and substance according to each transaction. I simply use it to my own advantage. After all, my friend, every tale ever shaped by a man's mind or repeated by his tongue must hold a measure of truth in it for *someone*.'

The curfew bell began to toll and Chad blew into his hands again to warm his aching fingers. 'We're chasing phantoms, Fergus. We should go inside before we freeze to death where we stand.'

'Patience, my friend. He will come. When that bell's done with its tolling all the streets will be deserted and only the night creatures will be astir. Then he will come.'

A limping man dragged a wooden staff through the snow as he passed by the town's stout boundary with a clutch of ragged children in his wake. Hearing the men's voices, he cupped his hands as if offering up an empty bowl and opened his mouth to reveal a single tooth amid blackened gums. The children followed suit, their hands cupped in the beggar's pose, their mouths gaping open. Small dark shapes were scuttling at their heels, drawn from their lairs by the stench of human hunger.

'Beggars and rats,' Chad spat. 'And who can guess which brood outnumbers the other?' He dipped in his pouch for a coin, flicked it high in the air and watched it fall. The family fell on it, scrabbling on the ground until their father's staff across their backs reminded the youngsters that even the lowest of society had its pecking order. As they moved away with their miserable fortunes increased by a single penny, the rats followed behind, ever watchful of the smallest and weakest member of the group.

'Well, I'll be damned!' Both Chad and Fergus saw the slender figure of a boy with long black hair creep from the mist and collide with the beggar man as if by accident. A hand dipped into a tattered tunic, apologies were made and curses laid, and then the ragged boy, and Chad's alms penny, were gone.

'The survival of the slyest,' Fergus grinned. 'One begs and

the other steals, and who's to say which hand is the most deserving of your penny?'

The curfew bell ceased its tolling and the minutes stretched into an hour before Fergus became alert and whispered, 'Look, Chad. Over there beyond the gate.'

He urged the soldier back against the shadows of the wall. A man was coming towards them at a run, his light cloak flapping against powerful legs and his breath frosting the air about his face. He moved like an athlete, sure-footed on the treacherous ground, his strides perfectly coordinated, his breathing steady and even.

'I see him,' Chad hissed. 'But do I believe it?'

'Believe it. There is your man of myth, your crippled scribe.'

Concealed within the recess, they watched the priest pass by them on his way to the Eastern Pasture and the marshes. He left a trail of clear prints in the snow, as evenly spaced as those of any strong and healthy man.

'It's true then,' Chad declared. 'His foot is healed.'

'Aye, and has been so for a decade if my calculations are correct.'

'Are you telling me that leg of his has been healed for *ten years*?'

'Since the tempest,' Fergus nodded. 'When that babe was brought to Beverley and the whole place laid to ruin, Simeon's crushed bones were miraculously healed at the altar of St John. I've examined the records of his trial and the statements of many witnesses. He was tried for his part in Beverley's near destruction. Our Mother Church thinks ill of any priest whose devotees claim miracles in his name, thus attracting to him the fame of a living saint without the prior consent of Rome. They placed him on the horns of a dilemma and so, to save himself and the child left in his care, he remained evasive about the healing. I'm told he hobbled down the full length of the provost's great hall at the trial, flanked on all sides by the Church elite, dragging his foot along the boards and lurching with every stride. By God, I wish I'd been there to see it. What a performance that must

33

have been, to convince all those ecclesiastical notables that a hale man was still a cripple.'

'Did no one think to examine him more closely?'

'Why should they?' Fergus asked. '"I am as you see," was all he said, and they took him at his word.'

'We all believe what we see with our own eyes,' Chad told him, still peering into the misty darkness into which Simeon had vanished. 'And yet until this moment I was so sure, so heartily convinced, that he was lame.'

'And how did you suppose he managed to move so freely through those secret tunnels beneath the town if he was truly crippled?' Fergus asked. 'Believe me, Chad, he's every bit as nimble as that boy of his when it comes to scaling walls and chimneys and running with the sewer rats. He's a crippled scribe by day and, as you saw for yourself, an athlete by night.'

'He takes a terrible risk, crossing those lands in darkness.'

'No risk at all,' Fergus assured him. 'He knows every inch of Beverley as well as he knows the marks on his own palms, and I do not envy any robber who tries to waylay him. I have seen that quiet man when his fury's up. I'd not cross swords with him unless I had an army at my back.'

'But he risks being seen and brought before the court. He should guard such a dangerous secret with more care.'

'What, and waste God's gift of healing?' Fergus laughed with a touch of cynicism. 'He is too much a priest to be so ungrateful. He would rather risk his life twice a day than live as a cripple and show his God that His holy gift is superfluous to requirements.'

Chad turned and began to stamp his feet in the snow. 'Well, Fergus, you've had my news from St Dominic's and we've seen your Beverley myth for what it truly is. Can we go now? We've been standing here in the cold for two hours just to prove you right in your suspicions. What plan is stirring itself in your crafty mind?' He suddenly scowled again and added, 'Simeon's a good man. I'll not be part of any plot to harm him.'

'Nor will I,' Fergus assured him.

'So, what will you do, dangle the priest and his family as bait before the Plantagenet?'

'I will indeed, if it serves my ends.'

Chad bristled at his honesty. 'Then you'll do it without my help. I'll not seek to prosper at their expense.'

'Nobly spoken,' Fergus smiled, 'and exactly what I had expected to hear from you. Have no concerns on that score, Chad. If I can bring my new plan to fruition, Simeon de Beverley will make my fortune just as surely as I will make his. As he rises, I will rise. You saw the width of his back and the strength of his limbs. A man might become a giant simply by riding on his shoulders.'

'You tamper with innocent lives,' Chad grumbled. 'Geoffrey Plantagenet is out of favour with Rome and with his brother, the king. If he's relieved of his bishopric, as well he might be if King Richard has his way, then you'll surely fall with him and drag Simeon down with you.'

'Geoffrey Plantagenet will *not* be relieved of his bishopric,' Fergus told him. 'Admittedly, while neither pope nor king can subjugate him into accepting holy orders, his position, and therefore mine, remains uncertain. That's why he must be encouraged, by some incentive he finds irresistible, to cut his coat according to his cloth.'

'They'll not persuade him,' Chad insisted, shaking his head. 'He's a soldier, not a priest. He wants the wealth and power of his position at York, but he'll not shackle himself with ordination while his faith remains as fickle and as inconstant as his temper. No, Fergus, they'll never persuade him into the priesthood.'

Fergus grinned at that. 'No, my friend, *they* won't . . . but you can be sure *I* will.'

'The Devil you will!' Chad exclaimed.

'My silver girdle against your jewelled sword.' The young man smiled, extending his hand to seal the wager with a shake. 'I'll do it, Chad. You can depend on it.'

As the soldier studied the handsome young face with its disarming grin and laughing eyes, he did not doubt the determination behind the arrogance. What Fergus de Burton lacked in age and experience was far outweighed by his natural skills in the art of manipulating men and situations to his advantage. Once again Chad found himself wondering if he served a brilliant youth whose star was rising or a foolish upstart doomed to an early and inglorious end.

'Aye, you'll be a giant,' Chad concluded, pumping the young man's hand, 'or else you'll be a dead man. So, do we leave for St Dominic's at first light?'

'Of course not. You think like a soldier, Chad. You'd storm the monastery with your little band of men and drag the priest away by force.'

'Is there a better way?'

'There is, my friend. First we obtain an official warrant of arrest from the provost here. Then we present the abbot with the seal of my authority, *Geoffrey*'s seal. After that, no man will dare to stay our hand. Our prisoner must be taken legally and with the full consent of the Church lest he find a flaw of ours that can be cracked open for his escape. Then, and only then, may you storm the monastery.'

'I'd as soon do that with food and fuel. They're starving.'

'Then Fergus de Burton will feed them,' Fergus grinned, 'and bask in the credit of such a noble and charitable deed.'

Fergus was as good as his word. In the town was a certain carter who owned several pack beasts, all well fed and shod with iron, and the carter jumped when Fergus rattled his purse. Despite this season of want and widespread privation, every item he demanded would be provided, and the monks who served St Dominic the Mailed would have their empty bellies filled at last.

While the young nobleman sought his papers from the Provost of Beverley, and while Chad's soldiers guarded the growing supplies piled in the carter's yard, the barren wastes to the east of the town were no longer quite deserted. With the help of a small boy clothed in rags, a stumbling man was attempting to cross the treacherous marshlands lying beyond the boundaries of the settled areas. A high fever reddened his face in unsightly blotches. He was sweating profusely and his hands were shaking. He dreaded the hidden perils of these Beverley marshlands, but he also feared the brutal justice of those who kept the town gates. They would fear the fever he could not conceal, and those healthy, well-fed gate men would drive him off to die rather than risk admitting the pestilence to the town. So close to his objective, the sanctuary of St Peter's, he had decided to avoid the gates and stumbled hurriedly into the wilderness, braving the most difficult and dangerous of routes to the church. Blinded by the swirling, snow-filled mist, he struggled on, grimly determined to reach his destination at any cost. He must not fail, though he might die in the attempt. He must reach St Peter's enclosure and deliver up the gift entrusted to him. The future of his family depended on it.

'Keep moving, Tobias,' he told his shivering servant, and the eight-year-old boy who bore his weight could do no more than brace his skinny legs in an effort to keep himself, and his staggering master, upright.

Recent snowfall had given the area a deceptively smooth appearance, laying a soft carpet of white over deadly holes, gullies, ditches and frozen furrows. With his stick the man probed for the infamous marshland pools, those narrow mud-filled shafts that could suck an unwary traveller to his death in seconds. The cold gnawed at his fingers and toes. He sucked it into his lungs with every breath and despite the heat of his burning fever, he knew that he was freezing to death from the inside.

'Can you see it, lad? Can you see St Peter's Church?'

The boy pulled back his hood and squinted into the curtain of snowy mist, his eyes red rimmed. 'No, master. I see nothing but snow.'

'Have courage, Tobias. We're sure to find it soon.'

'Yes, master.' The lad looked back, his hood still lowered, and blinked at the acres of white-shrouded wasteland they had already covered. His gaze traced the twisting, looping patterns marked out in the snow by their meandering footprints. They

37

had been walking all day and yet had covered no more than half a mile in any one direction. Those footprints showed the futility of their efforts, yet he lacked the heart to tell his master they were wandering around in circles. More snow was gathering and the night was closing in. Without food and shelter, and already weakened by the long and arduous journey from St Dominic's, they were unlikely to survive those cold hours until dawn.

It was dark and snowing heavily when the man spoke again. He had been faltering for some time, barely gaining an inch with every painful step he took, and now his legs buckled and he sank to the ground with a groan. 'Just a small rest . . . a few moments . . .'

Hearing the soft, sweet chiming of a church bell in the distance, he looked to his left, then cocked his head and made a half turn to his right. In the eerie stillness, the mournful tolling of the bell seemed to come first from one direction and then another, now close at hand, now far away.

'St Peter's bell! I'm sure of it, but which way, Tobias?'

Tobias shook his head. 'I can't tell, master. The sound is everywhere. I think the east . . . No, it comes from over there, to the west . . . and yet . . . perhaps . . .' Defeated, he dropped to his knees beside the fallen man. 'I can't be sure.'

The weary Tobias knelt with his head bowed, knowing that their dark shapes were already whitening with snow and blending into the landscape. The notorious Beverley marshland was devouring them. He had heard of its swamps and mud pools, its sucking bogs and collapsing holes, its packs of hungry wolves and wandering hordes of goblins and evil sprites. They seemed the lesser evils now, for he had witnessed the worst of it for himself. This marshland drained the life-force from living creatures, sucked them dry and drew their empty shells into itself. Shrouded in white and softened by the mist, it was as beautiful as it was deadly, and it whispered and coaxed Tobias to lie down beside his master and sleep. Some instinct in the child made him resist that overpowering temptation to submit to his fatigue. He shook his head and wiped snow from his face.

38

'We must go on, master,' he muttered, managing the words yet making no physical effort to regain his feet.

'Soon,' the man promised weakly. 'A short rest, Tobias . . . a few moments more.'

'No, if we sleep we'll be swallowed up.' Tobias brushed snow from his master's clothes with distracted fingers, then tried to free his own rags of it. 'We'll be swallowed up . . . swallowed up . . .'

The man was curled in a shivering ball beneath his white-layered cloak when soft sounds drew Tobias reluctantly to his senses. Through his lethargy he became aware of the rhythmic breathing and steady footfalls of a running man. Forcing his eyes wide open, he peered into a misty veil of snow and saw a figure moving effortlessly across the ground, its breath blowing in frosty gusts and its aspect so pale it might have been shaped by the land itself.

'Master. Master!' He shook the prostrate figure, his mouth too numb with cold to shape the words in anything louder than a whisper. 'Look. Do you see it?'

'I see it.' The man had raised his head to squint into the snow. 'By God, I see it.'

The running man was dressed in linen breeches and a full white shirt, open at the neck. His boots were of stout, pale-coloured leather, his white linen mantle hanging in folds about his shoulders. He ran the way an animal might run, swift, sure-footed and easy, into the boy's limited area of vision and out again. He might have been an apparition or a marsh sprite, or an image conjured by a failing mind except that he left a track of footprints as straight as an arrow behind him in the snow.

'Wait! Please wait, sir! Help us!'

Tobias believed he yelled the words out loud, but a weak whisper, blown on the wind and cushioned by the snow, was the only sound that reached even his own ears. He saw the snowy curtain close and the figure vanish, and then he was scrambling to his feet, pulling and tugging at the resisting body of his master.

'No, I can't go on,' the man sobbed.

39

'You must,' the boy urged. 'It's a sign, master. We must follow him quickly, before the snow covers the marks of his boots. He knows the way. He'll lead us from this godforsaken place. Come, one last effort and we'll be saved.'

Encouraged, they struggled on together, groping through the snow where a trail of large, clear footprints marked out a sure and safe path across the marshes. It led them on a westward course, away from the eastern wetlands and the concealed banks of the perilous Old Beck. As they strove to keep each print in sight, the weather seemed to mock their efforts by blowing fresh snow across the ground, slowly obliterating the guiding marks.

They met the wall abruptly. It loomed before them out of the mist, a towering barricade of ancient stones hugged all about by thorn and creeper. Here the line of footprints ended suddenly, turning neither to the left nor to the right. They simply stopped, as if their owner had passed right through or over the great mass.

'Gone . . .' The man sank to his knees with a sigh of despair as Tobias, robbed of the last shreds of his courage, rested his head against the frozen stones and began to weep.

CHAPTER FOUR

B eyond the high stone wall of St Peter's enclosure, Simeon dropped into a crouch and sucked air into his laboured lungs. Tonight's run had been particularly strenuous, the four gruelling miles greatly extended by the demands of the season. The town boundary offered a less precarious route in better weather, but in this savage winter things were changed. Poor country people, ruined farmers, beggars and vagrants clung to the outer walls like flies around a carcass, driven to seek what ease they could for their hardship. These wretches in turn attracted thieves and cut-belts who would beat a man to death for the clothes on his back. Here, too, the wardens prowled, supposedly keeping order amongst the peasants and keeping campfires under control. They took their pay from the Church and their authority from the staffs and clubs they carried. Many were bands of ruffians no better than the destitute they harassed, and Simeon had run a wide course to avoid them.

Having rested for a moment to regain his breath, Simeon bent to offer a whispered prayer for the dead. Here, beneath a tangle of thorn and weed, a murdered canon lay at rest, his simple lead-lined coffin protected from looters and desecrators. Beside him lay a tragic young woman and her stillborn child, and close to them the tiny grave of a newborn babe whose death had helped reshape the course of Simeon's life.

Squatting beside the tangled overgrowth, the priest lowered his blond head and felt the cold wind chill his heated skin as he remembered those who lay in that safe and secret place.

'*In nomine Domini*, in the name of our Lord, be at peace.'

In the shelter of the trees Elvira hugged his big cloak to her as she watched him pray. She had seen him scale the wall as nimbly as a cat, then drop to the ground and squat before the graves, still panting after his gruelling run across the frozen marshland. His yellow hair was shaved to shape a crown around his head. Were it not for this voluntary observance of the preferences of Rome, no casual observer would have taken this handsome young man to be a priest. But priest he was, and celibate, and Elvira mourned that which his God denied her.

Simeon heard a soft tread on the ground and knew Elvira was, as always, close at hand and attentive to his needs. Still squatting, he closed his eyes as she draped his squirrel-lined cloak about his shoulders, allowing her hair to brush his cheek as she leaned against his back.

'You overtax your strength,' she told him. 'This icy wind will chill you to the bone.'

He caught her hands in his. 'I am recovered, Elvira.'

'So you insist, but only a few short weeks ago your life hung by a thread,' she reminded him. He felt her shudder as she added softly, 'I nearly lost you then, Simeon.'

Simeon rose to his feet and drew her into the warm folds of his cloak, where he held her close, her breasts against his chest and her small hands clasped around his body.

'You will never lose me, Elvira,' he promised. 'Never.'

For ten years their love had brought them joy, torment and sorrow in equal measure. It offended his holy office, outraged his enemies and tested his vows to their limits, and yet neither he nor she could set that love aside. He was a celibate priest and she a ditcher's wife, and their love endured every obstacle it encountered.

'Did you pray for the babe?' she asked.

'I did.'

'And for Alice?'

'And for Alice.' He felt her shudder again and knew she was remembering the innocent girl who had suffered such horrors in this life that she had used a rope to hasten herself into the next. 'She is at peace now, Elvira.'

'Is she, Simeon? Will your God forgive her, or will He weigh her faults against His laws and find her wanting?'

'Elvira, above all things God urges us to forgive. He would not set goals for mortal men that He, in His greatness, is incapable of achieving. He knows our hearts, our fears and our limitations. He is a loving God.'

She looked up at him, her eyes huge and dark in her pale face. 'And will He also forgive the beast who drove poor Alice to hang herself? Will He absolve Cyrus de Figham of *his* guilt?'

Simeon sighed and kissed her forehead. 'That is a question no mortal can answer,' he told her.

She lifted her face and he bent his head to kiss her. The touch of her mouth on his sent fires through his body and desire swept over him in a familiar wave. However hard he wrestled with his conscience, however sincere his prayers for strength in the face of this temptation, he lived with the knowledge that should God turn His head but for a moment, his solemn vow would die in Elvira's arms.

She drew away from him with a sigh as St Peter's bell resumed its mournful tolling. The squat stone tower was only a few yards away, yet the sound of the bell seemed to drift on the brittle air and reach their ears as if from a greater distance. Simeon signed the cross and turned from the weed-covered graves, his arm still about Elvira's shoulders. Flakes of snow had settled like diamonds on her thick black hair while others clung in imitation of tears to her dark lashes. She was as beautiful to him now as she had been a decade ago, when the dirt and grime had been cleaned away to reveal the flower that poverty had kept hidden from the world.

'I love you, Elvira,' he told her.

She smiled. 'I know you do.'

43

'Come, it will soon be dark and—'

'Hush, Simeon!'

'What is it?'

'I'm not sure. Did you hear a cry?'

'Only the bell,' he told her, 'and the whisper of drifting snow beyond the wall.'

Elvira rested her head on his shoulder as she fell into step beside him, only to stop and lift her head again, her senses straining. 'Listen. There it is again.'

'A night animal?' he suggested.

She shook her head. 'More like a weeping child.'

'There is no child here, Elvira.' He touched her cheek with the backs of his fingers. 'You still grieve for your dead baby. Perhaps in your imagination— ' He stopped abruptly as the soft sound came again, and now there could be no doubt that somewhere very close at hand a child was sobbing.

They found nothing among the bare trees and the creepers. Here the snow was undisturbed, the ground unmarked by any foot but their own. They stood together in the quiet and, when they heard the voice again, Simeon moved as close to the wall as the overgrowth would allow. Holding Elvira by the hand, he bent his head to listen. They heard the wind and the tolling of the bell and then, distinctly, the faint voice of a child imploring, 'Help us.'

'My God, can it be possible?'

'A child lost in the marshes,' Elvira said in disbelief. 'How on earth did he get this far? How did he reach the wall?'

'No matter. He is here and we must help him.' Simeon clambered up the wall, using the hidden footholds he had mastered years ago. 'Get Antony and Father Thorald. Tell them to go by the gate and meet me here, beyond the wall.'

Elvira caught at his flapping cloak. 'No, Simeon. Please don't go over there alone. It might be a trap. Your enemies are everywhere. Please, wait for the others.'

'Fetch them,' Simeon told her firmly, then smiled to reassure her as he hauled himself upward and vanished over the top of the wall. He landed lightly on its other side, and nearby found a small boy kneeling in the snow beside the still shape of a man. Both were covered by a thick layer of snow and were half-frozen in their inadequate clothing. Simeon drew the boy into his own cloak, wrapping the thick fur around him and feeling a deathly chill as the small form drew warmth from his own body. With his hand he wiped the man's face free of snow and frost and felt the heat of fever on his skin. The eyes flickered open, oblivious to the falling flakes as they struggled to focus on Simeon's face. The cracked lips twisted to release a weak and rasping voice.

'Who are you?'

'I am Simeon de Beverley.'

'Simeon? Of St Peter's?'

'The same.'

'Ah, then it is done.' The sick man sighed and allowed his head to fall back against Simeon's arm. 'God is truly merciful.'

Thorald, a huge, bearded priest of the home church, and Antony, a wiry Flanders monk, came running together from the gates of St Peter's, hugging the base of the wall where the ground was stable. At a curve in the wall they slowed their steps and moved as if on a narrow ledge, their fingers gripping the uneven stones, for here the ground fell away into dangerous hollows now concealed by drifts of snow.

'I have the child,' Simeon told them. 'Help the man.'

Antony removed the man's stiffened cloak and Thorald pulled off his own to wrap it tightly about the shivering body. Between them they hoisted him onto Thorald's massive shoulders and began to pick their way back over the slippery ground. Simeon was already striding for the gates, the boy concealed beneath his cloak, held fast against his chest. They found Elvira waiting in the infirmary, where a bed had been laid with fresh straw and a woollen blanket. Mutton broth had been ladled from the fire pot and bread dropped into a dish of milk to soften, then set by the fire to warm. When at last the two were stripped of their boots and outer wrappings and covered by warm blankets, Simeon sat between them on a stool, perplexed by their appearance at St Peter's. Those

45

marshes were virtually impassable in any season. That two strangers, one a mere child, had managed to cross them during this spell of biting cold and driving squalls of snow seemed little short of miraculous.

The boy was crouched on a bed on the floor, shivering as he cupped a bowl of soup in his hands. His gaze was fixed on Simeon, and the hardship of his journey was clearly etched on his ashen face. He sipped from the rim of the bowl, savouring the warmth and nourishment with every mouthful. Despite his ragged, underfed appearance, there was a hint of breeding in the boy. He did not fall upon his food and cram it into his mouth as poverty demanded but broke his bread in measured portions and chewed it without haste.

'Who are you, boy?'

'Tobias, sir.'

'Where are you from, Tobias?'

'Where?' The boy appeared to ponder the question carefully. 'I don't know, sir. From some other place. We are searching for a priest, Simeon of St Peter's.'

'I am he.'

Tobias looked at him gravely, noting the corn-coloured hair and deep blue eyes. Then he nodded, satisfied that it was so. 'I thought you were a marsh sprite,' he confessed. 'We saw you running in the snow when we were lost and my master could not go on. We followed your footprints as far as the wall and then they vanished.' A look of wonder lit his weary face. 'Did you fly over it?'

'I *climbed* over it,' Simeon assured him. 'Men do not fly, Tobias.'

'You saved us, Father Simeon. You left your tracks for us to follow and then came back for us. My master said it would be so. He promised you'd help us.'

'Does your master know me?'

The boy looked puzzled, then lifted and dropped his shoulders in a shrug and answered simply, 'You're Simeon de Beverley.'

'What's your master's name, Tobias?'

'His name? Why, his name is *Master*.'

46

Simeon caught and returned Elvira's smile. The lad was too young and inexperienced to know that the place in which he lived could be identified by name, or that his master bore a personal name like any other man.

'He ate bad bread,' the lad volunteered, his eyes half closed and his body no longer shivering. 'It cost him every penny in his purse, but it was bad. It made him ill.'

'Ergot poisoning,' Simeon told him. 'The bread was probably made from tainted rye.'

'Will he recover?'

Simeon nodded. 'With God's blessing, and our infirmarian's help, he will survive. Sleep now, Tobias. We'll talk again when you're rested.'

In the narrow bed the man had slipped into a light delirium. Elvira bathed his face with a cloth steeped in a warm herbal infusion. The woman who helped prepare and bottle the herbs had packed hot stones around the man's body to break the chill that gripped him. Their heat drew little clouds of steam from his clothes and helped reduce the swelling that trapped his frozen feet inside his leather boots.

Osric the infirmarian was two miles away at Wheel, tending a farmer badly trampled by an ox. In his absence the men of St Peter's did what they could to help the stranger who had stumbled into their sanctuary but, as the night drew on, his condition worsened. Simeon was dozing by the fire when he heard the anxious muttering of his name. He stooped over the bed to find the man awake, his eyes barely focused and his face dripping with perspiration. Frantic fingers grabbed weakly at the folds of Simeon's shirt and spittle bubbled from the man's mouth as he spoke.

'The holy water,' he rasped. 'For the wine ... the altar wine. Take it. Use it ... for her sake ... use it.' He pulled a capped horn from his clothes and pressed it into Simeon's hand. 'Blessed in Rome ... stirred with St Peter's relics. Take it ... use it.'

Simeon glanced at the horn, then asked the man, 'Did you risk your life and the boy's to bring this here?'

'I did ... for her sake ... for Alice.'

47

'For Alice? You know of Alice?'

With a groan and a muttered, 'Alice . . .' the man fell back on his pillow, too weak to continue. At the fireside, Elvira took the horn from Simeon and turned it in her fingers. The crossed keys, symbol of St Peter, were engraved on its silver cap. The angel, eagle, lion and bull, symbols of the four evangelists, Matthew, Mark, Luke and John, were beautifully embossed around its silvered point. Between its cap and its point hung a delicate silver chain and fixed to each link was a tiny pearl set in a silver cage.

'This is a treasure,' she breathed. She looked at the restless form on the bed and shook her lovely head. 'Simeon, what kind of man will suffer such hardship and eat bad bread when he might purchase a feast with this?'

'A man with a purpose, Elvira. Someone, somewhere, seeks to endow our altar with a blessed gift, and this poor wretch was determined to see it done. He says the horn was sent from Rome . . .' He paused, reluctant to repeat the name on the sick man's lips. 'He spoke of bringing it here for Alice.'

'Alice?' Her dark eyes looked at him with reflected firelight twinkling in their depths. 'This stranger knows of Alice?'

'It is a common name,' he reminded her.

'Not within these walls,' she said. 'The only Alice we know of lies mutilated and buried under the creepers. How could he know of her when she lived all her life in Beverley and never spoke of any living relative?'

'The poor man is raving with ergot poisoning. When Osric comes he will know what medicines to use to break the fever. Until then, until this wretch regains his full senses, we cannot be sure of whom he speaks.'

Elvira nodded and stroked the warm, smooth horn across her cheek. She shook it gently, close to her ear. 'There's liquid inside.'

'Holy water, blessed in Rome for our communion wine.' As Simeon seated himself beside her, she leaned her head against his chest and gazed into the flickering flames of the fire with heavy-lidded eyes. She felt his arm around her shoulders, his steady heartbeat beneath her cheek, and was already dozing when she heard his deep voice urge, 'Sleep now, my love.'

The fire had died to a crimson glow and the figures around it were slumped in sleep when the sick man resumed his restless tossing on the mattress. Nobody heard the whisper of his voice as he muttered desperate words in his delirium. 'Kill him. Kill Simeon de Beverley. Kill him.'

That night young Edwin's sleep was so disturbed by dreams that Simeon sat by his bed with a rush light burning. At the Dawn Mass Edwin dropped his candlestick with a clatter that caused old Canon Cuthbert to start in alarm. He was absent from the midday meal, choosing instead to dine alone on food brought by his twin sister, Edwinia.

'His conscience pricks him,' Antony guessed. 'He's an honest lad with an open face, but since yesterday he's avoided meeting anyone eye-to-eye.'

'Perhaps I should send for Father Daniel,' Simeon suggested. 'Those bad dreams worry me, Antony. They prey upon his mind and yet he is reluctant, or too afraid, to describe them. Whatever guilt he carries cannot be left to gnaw at him like this.'

The Flanders monk nodded in agreement, convinced that Simeon's protégé was troubled by some minor transgression. A man hardened to life and familiar with his own weaknesses made little of small sins, but a boy like Edwin, good hearted and keen to please, was likely to be less forgiving of his own mistakes.

'I'll send word to Father Daniel,' he said, then cocked his head on one side to study the face of his friend. 'What troubles you, Simeon?'

'Something Edwin was muttering in his sleep. He said, "The dark priest lives," and he awoke in terror, convinced de Figham was here, in this very room.'

'Nothing more than childish night frights,' Antony told him. 'He was terrified of de Figham and he believed, as all of us believed, that you'd been stoned to death because of that fiend in priest's attire.'

49

'No more than that? Bad dreams? Childish fears? I wish I could be sure of it, Antony.'

'The priest is dead,' the monk insisted. 'Thorald killed him.'

'So he believed.'

'There were witnesses to the killing, Simeon. Eight weeks have passed without word or sight of de Figham. He's dead. We're rid of him.'

'So it seems, and yet I wonder, Antony. Sometimes I feel him out there, watching and waiting, feeding on his own hatred and looking for another chance to strike.'

Antony touched Simeon's arm and looked into his troubled eyes. He was surprised to discover these fears in Simeon, for he himself was in no doubt that Thorald's aim had been true. 'Be at peace, my friend,' he told him. 'The Devil has Cyrus de Figham now.'

Simeon smiled down at the monk and shrugged his shoulders. 'If not,' he said lightly, 'we will know of it soon enough.'

Twelve miles away, the brothers who served St Dominic the Mailed were gathered in the crumbling chapterhouse, eleven men with heavy hearts and little hope with which to face this new adversity. The door of Gerard's cell had been chopped down to provide fuel for a fire. They huddled glumly around its flames, listening to the rasp of their abbot's breathing. Many feared that this latest disaster would mark the end of their small order.

'Pray for us . . . Open your hearts and minds to God . . . Pray that Satan has not been loosed among us. Pray for His mercy. Pray. God will provide.'

'God has abandoned us,' a monk whispered, and his shivering companions lacked the heart to contradict him.

Abbot Aidan lay on a bench beside the fire, his ribs so badly bruised that the very act of breathing had become a painful chore. Although his legs could still be made to bear his weight, no one doubted that his pelvis had been fractured. For a whole day he had lain thus, nursed through the night by devoted monks, warmed by a meagre fire and sustained by nothing save his faith and constant prayers.

Brother Gerard's face was swollen and discoloured. Blood caked his robes and stained his neck and hands, and he breathed through his open mouth because the bridge of his nose was broken.

Andrew, a calm and dedicated man who had been with the order since childhood, voiced his fears for all to hear. 'The priest has two daggers and a short sword in his possession, and his door is heavily barred from the inside. We are eleven men in all, and yet we cannot hope to overpower this monster. Nor can we starve him into submission while he holds the woman and the child as leverage. His demands must be met in full, for their sakes.'

'He's harmed her,' the father abbot muttered, and there was misery in his eyes. 'We hear her screams, even from here, and we know he does her harm.'

'And after her the child,' Gerard hissed. 'He will tire of the woman soon enough and . . .'

'Spare us the details,' Aidan pleaded. 'Dear God, I sought to discharge one sin and so provoked another.'

'My curb brace was the lesser of the two,' Gerard reminded him. 'If only you had not overheard my confession to Chad. If I'd but held my peace a short while longer . . .'

'The fault is mine,' Abbot Aidan told him. 'I should have sought God's guidance, but instead . . .' he paused, struggling for sufficient breath to form the words, 'I acted in the heat of my discovery. I was unwise. I should have waited.'

'Tomorrow the soldier and his master will return,' Gerard said bitterly. 'Two more days were all I asked.'

'And I refused. I denied you the time you needed.' Aidan turned his head to the others who were gathered in the chapterhouse. 'My brothers, your father abbot has failed you. Forgive me.'

In a draughty corner by the door, Benedict was on his knees, weeping as he stammered out his prayers. With a sudden cry he flung up his arms and began to crawl on his hands and knees towards the bench where his injured abbot lay. The other monks stepped back to allow him through, then clasped their hands in prayer as he prostrated himself, still sobbing, before the bench. 'Forgive me, Father Abbot. Brothers, forgive a wretch his folly. I've robbed our winter stores on his behalf. I've filched the communion wine on his instructions, and . . . and . . . Oh dear God, what have I done?'

Shocked by the man's admission, Gerard stooped to grab him by the folds of his robe, hoisted him to his knees and shook him roughly.

'You robbed the stores?' he demanded, barely able to believe his ears. 'While we're reduced to measuring every bite we eat, while we live in fear of starving before the winter has run its course, you snatch the food from our mouths for the sake of that . . . that . . .' He flung the man aside in disgust and demanded, 'What else? What more have you done to betray your brothers?'

'I acted in good faith,' the young man babbled. 'Father Roche is a wealthy man. He swore to fill our stores from his own storehouse. He promised bread and salt meat by the cartful, logs and peat for our fires, milking cows, laying hens—'

'In exchange for what?'

Benedict slumped over, covered his face with his hands and spoke through his fingers. 'I told him of our holy relic, how our abbot ordered it locked away in a stout chest in the crypt, forbidding any man to lay a hand on it.'

'What?' Aidan gasped from the bench. 'You *told* him? But you were sworn to secrecy . . . every one of you was sworn. You had no right—'

'I know, I know . . . and now . . .'

'Now he'll demand it for himself,' Gerard said, 'and how will we dare refuse while he holds two innocent souls to ransom?'

'You don't understand,' Benedict sobbed. 'I believed him when he said that God had chosen me as the saviour of our order. In exchange for all he promised . . . for all our sakes . . . I *gave* it to him.'

A stunned and fear-filled silence followed his confession, then Aidan struggled from his bench muttering, 'Help me up. I must go to the crypt and see for myself that St Bridget's horn is safe.'

'It's gone, Father Abbot. He has it.'

'No! It cannot be so.'

'He has it. Dear God, forgive me.'

Gerard placed his hands on the abbot's shoulders and tried, without avail, to calm him. 'Father Abbot, you must be still. Your chest is crushed and . . .'

Strengthened by his anxiety, the old man brushed aside those hands that would restrain him and reached instead for those that offered assistance. By an effort of will he struggled to his feet, fighting his pain as he fixed his gaze on the door and propelled his broken body towards it.

The brothers helped him through the sheltered cloisters and across the windswept grassland to the chapel, then down the twisting stairway to the crypt. A monk had lit a single torch, which cast their shadows like prancing demons across the walls and vaulted roof. Behind the tomb of some long-forgotten abbot, a small oak chest was pushed against a wall, its clasp burst open.

'Empty!' Abbot Aidan clutched Gerard's arm and struggled to fill his protesting lungs with air. 'St Bridget's horn is gone!'

That day and another endless night were spent in prayer as the brothers maintained their vigil at their failing abbot's bedside. By dawn they knew that God, in His infinite and unfathomable wisdom, had once again turned deaf ears to their prayers. Even as Gerard prepared to send his promised message to the Provost of Beverley, the donkey gifted by Chad was stolen from them. Wearing the abbot's warm cloak and carrying what food and wine was available, the man they knew as Father Roche left the abbey by its eastern gate, riding the docile beast at an urgent pace. He held the child before him while the woman, bruised and with her clothes hastily repaired, followed behind them at a stumbling pace with a heavy sack across her shoulders, her soft linen boots inadequate for the journey. She looked neither to the left nor to the right, determined to keep her innocent child in sight.

The penitent Brother Benedict had vanished during the night, too mortified by his guilt to face his brothers. The father abbot lay on the cold stones by the fire, his body chilled yet damp with perspiration, his breathing rapid and shallow. Because the brothers knew he was soon to die, they had stripped him of all his clothes and covered his naked body with a thin white shroud. Like all true Christians facing certain death, he had willingly abandoned every comfort, lest the good Lord reject him for his lack of humility.

'Our father abbot's lungs are filling up with mucus. He's drowning in it,' Andrew told them all.

'Someone must travel on foot to Beverley,' Gerard said. 'He must carry news of this to the provost there, Jacob de Wold. The soldier, Chad, was insistent that the Minster church be warned if the priest tried to leave. Who knows the way to Beverley?'

His question met with silence. Some shook their heads, but those who knew the way held back from saying so, lest they be chosen to make so forbidding a journey in bitter weather.

'Will no one go there?' Gerard asked at last.

'We have no beast to carry a man that far,' Andrew reminded him. 'Nor warm clothes for his back, nor food to sustain him.'

'The provost must be warned, nonetheless, before that priest wreaks havoc in the town as he has done within our brotherhood. You, Brother Giles. Did you not travel there two summers since? And you, Brother Mark, are you not familiar with the journey?'

The two monks bowed their heads without reply, and Gerard knew he had no right to press them further. 'Then I must go myself, and quickly, before—'

'You cannot possibly make such a journey,' Andrew protested. 'Your nose is broken and you have lost a great deal of blood. You will not survive, Brother Gerard.'

54

'It seems I have no choice. Someone must go.'

'I'll do it. I'll make the journey.' The man who spoke was Brother David, who had been a mason in Beverley before seeking refuge and seclusion at the abbey after his family had perished in the Great Fire. He knew the town, for he had lived and worked there all his life, and in its near destruction on the eve of St Matthew's feast, two years ago, he had been robbed of all that gave his life purpose. He had sworn never to return to Beverley, but within the hour he was ready to leave St Dominic's, armed with a scribbled note and a small wedge of salt meat, his sandals swathed in strips of cloth and his shoulders protected by a blanket.

'God speed, Brother David,' Gerard told him, and David, knowing he would never have the heart to return to this sad place, nodded and muttered, 'I'll speak to a good priest, Father Simeon, on your behalf. He'll help you, even if your God will not.'

'*My* God?' Gerard queried. 'David, my brother, He is your God too. Do not turn from Him now. Do not abandon Him in this dark hour.'

'*He* has abandoned *us*,' the man said grimly, then lifted his borrowed blanket over his head and set his feet for Beverley.

The father abbot died at noon when the thickened mucus in his lungs rose up and choked him. His humble flock heard the final words to pass his lips, words that could keep his soul alive no longer: 'God will provide.'

And so God in His mercy did provide, four hours too late to reward poor Aidan for the constancy of his faith. Fergus de Burton, as brash and self-confident as youth itself, rode through the abbey gates with Chad beside him and a half-dozen mounted soldiers at his back. They carried bulky saddle sacks and led six donkeys piled high with provisions. In addition to this, each soldier carried a bundle of sticks strapped to his back, fuel gathered on the journey for the abbey fires.

'You kept your word,' Gerard said in reply to Chad's gruff greeting.

'Did you doubt I would?'

Gerard nodded without apology. 'I kept mine, too, by sending word to Beverley, though I doubt my brave messenger will survive the marshland if this cold continues.'

'A message? Has the priest recovered his memory?'

'Worse than that,' the monk told him. 'The priest is gone. He left at dawn with your donkey and the last of our supplies'

'Left?' Chad echoed. 'How could he *leave* with both legs strapped into curb irons?'

'Our father abbot overheard our conversation in the cloisters two days ago,' Gerard explained. 'I was made to remove the curb brace and confess my subterfuge.'

'Damn! Damn his devilish tricks and damn your abbot's untimely interference.' Chad slid from his horse to inspect the monk's battered face. 'What happened to you?'

'The priest struck me. One blow was enough to shatter the bone.'

'Be thankful that you live to nurse your wounds,' Chad told him coldly. 'He might have killed you. What of the woman and her child?'

'He took them.'

Fergus de Burton, still mounted, had observed this interchange with a grim expression on his boyish face. Now he leaned down from his saddle and asked without urgency, 'Will you ask your father abbot to speak privately to me on this matter?'

'I can ask him nothing,' Gerard answered with a sad shake of his head. 'He, too, was struck by the priest, a cruel, merciless blow for a feeble old man to suffer. He died at noon.'

Chad glanced at Fergus, received a brief nod and so spoke less harshly to the monk. 'Your brotherhood has our sympathy, Gerard. You've paid a high price for your charity. Rest assured the priest will answer for it. Was the woman taken against her will?'

'She had no choice but to go with him, unless she was prepared to sanction the abduction of her only child. She

56

was ill-used. We saw as much from her appearance and we heard her screams from the chapel.'

Fergus dismounted and watched his soldiers help the men of the brotherhood to unload the horses and donkeys. The unfortunate timing of current events demanded his plans be altered. The priest had left the monastery at dawn, a full six hours before their arrival. They had not encountered him on the road, so Fergus guessed that he was planning to slip back into Beverley by a furtive route. He sucked air through his teeth and shrugged his shoulders, then smiled at Gerard and asked, 'Was the priest left-handed?'

Gerard shrugged his shoulders. 'He felled me with a single blow from his right hand and knocked our father abbot across the room with his left.'

'The man we seek is ambidextrous,' Fergus nodded. 'Describe his eyes.'

'Black, sometimes grey, depending on the light.'

'Did he wear a ring?'

'He did. An onyx stone in a heavy gold setting, worn on his index finger. His hair was long and black and he was as handsome as the Devil.'

Fergus arched a brow at that. 'An apt description.'

'Men are blinded by physical beauty, so the Devil holds it dear.'

'Tell me about his dagger.'

'He had *two* daggers and a double-edged short sword. The sword was unremarkable save for its silver trim and inlaid gems, but the knives were marked according to the Office of their owners.'

'Priests' knives? Are you sure of that?'

'I am.' Gerard nodded. 'One was engraved with the sword and the divided cloak of St Martin.'

'As carried by the missing Canon of St Martin.' The young man nodded. 'And the other?'

'It was marked with a ship's anchor and three golden orbs resting on the pages of a book.'

'St Nicholas,' Fergus said. 'Father Thorald's knife.'

'He must be stopped,' Chad said.

'Indeed he must. He can't reach Beverley inside two days on a single donkey and with a woman to slow him down. I suggest we leave our own donkeys here and ride for the town ahead of him.'

'Leave the pack animals?' Gerard echoed in dismay. 'But they carry only a single bale of hay. How will we feed six hungry beasts in your absence?'

Fergus de Burton rested his hand on the monk's shoulder and smiled into his eyes. 'Extra supplies are on their way here by cart, though they might well be delayed if the snow begins again or the wind increases. So, if no help reaches you by the time the hay is eaten, put your faith in God and—'

'And pray,' Gerard said wearily.

Young Fergus shook his head and reassured the monk with an amiable grin. 'By all means pray if you must, Brother Gerard, but if the carts are delayed I suggest you put your faith in God and eat the donkeys.'

Gerard nodded grimly. 'God speed, and if you should meet with Brother Benedict on the road, please urge him to return to us.'

'I will,' Fergus assured him as he strode away.

Outside the gates, the sky was lowering and the wind was blowing a fine drift of snow in every direction. Led by Chad and Fergus, the small company of soldiers skirted the high walls of the abbey and headed for the narrow road beyond the derelict gatehouse. They halted only once, to inspect the body of a man wrapped in a dark monk's robe lying broken beneath the highest portion of the wall. No wounds were on him save those he had sustained in his plunge from the highest corner of the abbey's roof.

'Brother Benedict?' Chad suggested.

Fergus answered with a nod, 'Who else but he?'

As they moved on towards the road, Chad squinted at the sky and scowled his dissatisfaction. 'We've lost our mules for sure,' he grumbled. 'I know the signs. There'll be a blizzard. We should stay for a share of the meat and take what shelter we can until the weather lifts.'

'There is no time to consider our own comforts,' Fergus

replied. 'Revenge is the strongest driving force of all, my friend. Once he's safely home in Beverley, this 'Father Roche' will head first for Thorald at the home church, and then for Simeon at St Peter's.'

'You're certain he's your man, then?'

'Do you doubt it?' Fergus asked, heeling his mount. 'No two men were ever cast in that same mould. St Martin has found his missing canon at last, God help us all. This priest is the one we've searched for all these weeks, Chad. I know it now without a doubt. He's Cyrus de Figham.'

CHAPTER FIVE

The many bells of Beverley were ringing in the dawn. It was another grey and chilly day, mercifully calm after two days and nights of snowstorms and howling gales. The wind had lost its biting edge, but the promised blizzard still hung above the town. More snow had fallen during the night, creating high, impassable drifts and leaving a thick, soft layer of white as far as the eye could see.

Peter, Simeon's ward and godson, had climbed the high wall surrounding St Peter's enclosure to sit astride its top. From there he could see that every bare tree was hung with layers of snow, every stone and rooftop capped with a bright, clean covering of white. The nearby Minister church, hastily repaired two years before, dominated the town and was, despite its dire need for proper renovation, magnificent. Its fire-blackened timbers were hung with snow and its windows twinkled in the feeble light. Behind the boy, towards the north, the timber-and-thatch houses of the town were crammed together beneath a glowing coverlet of white, with Beverley's many waterways threaded like bands of silver here and there.

Looking south towards the little port, where the water carried a sheen like that of highly polished metal, Peter watched a party of carts and riders heading for the town.

His eyes were large and very blue in a pale face topped by a crop of yellow hair. He was slender and delicately boned, a wily and intriguing ten-year-old who came and went according to his whim and whose identity was clouded with mystery. From this, his favourite vantage point, he observed the riders as they approached at a slow pace. He saw that the two men leading the group made a splendid pair. Of similar height and stature, one was dark and swathed in a full black cloak with a crimson-lined hood, the other fair and robed in burgundy beneath a paler cape. Both rode dark horses sporting silvered leathers, and both were tall and upright in the saddle.

'Two men are coming with a band of pilgrims,' Peter said. 'Two strangers, dark and fair.'

He neither expected nor received a response from his companion, who stood amongst the shadows of the wall, his face concealed.

Peter blinked snowflakes from his eyelashes, then swung one leg over the wall and dropped lightly down to the ground on its outer side. His companion met him there and the boy fell into step beside him, matching his child's pace to the longer strides, watching the rhythmic swinging of the long black cloak as it skimmed the snow, and the boots that made no sound and left no mark on the whitened ground.

The two riders had met, at separate points on their individual journeys, with a group of pilgrims travelling north to Beverley. For safety's sake each had chosen to join this company as it made slow progress towards their common destination. Some rode upon mules laden with everything they possessed. Others came by cart or on foot: two battle-weary soldiers, two orphaned sisters, a family doing penance for the transgressions of their son, a wealthy merchant bringing his daughter, deaf and mute from birth, to beg a cure at the sacred shrine of the patron saint of deaf-mutes, John of Beverley. They travelled together for mutual protection along these dangerous, bandit-infested roads, each with his heart closed off from his companions. The two who rode ahead were strangers to each other, and each came to Beverley with a private purpose. It was with lightened hearts and weary bones that they heard the pealing bells of the Morning Offices, then saw the mist-shrouded port and, beyond it, the Minster church of St John at their journey's end.

As was the custom of strangers on the road, these men had revealed little more than their names on the journey. The swarthy traveller in the crimson hood was Hector, a holy man from Lincoln. The other, a vigorous man nearing fifty, was Rufus, a northern man. Neither would offer or encourage a deeper intercourse than that.

'We have been fortunate,' Hector remarked. 'These roads are perilous during the winter months, when the rabble hungers.' He signed the cross over his chest and bowed his head in silent prayer, giving thanks for their safe arrival.

Rufus stroked his long moustaches where silver streaks gleamed in the thick blond hair. He was fifteen years his travelling companion's senior, a man whose sons were fully grown but whose powerful build and vigour were undiminished by middle age. He trusted not to God for his personal safety but to the strength of his fighting arm and the quickness of his mind.

'Amen,' the swarthy Hector said, emerging from his prayers, and Rufus, in respect, echoed, 'Amen.'

The two had travelled in silence for many miles, companions only in modest conversation and a mutual need to undertake this dangerous winter journey. They passed the port and the home church of St Nicholas and made their way along Flemingate, so named for its foreign traders and manufacturers. At Flemingate Bar, known also as the East Gate, they could hear the voices of the choral priests, uplifting and melodic as they drifted with the mist above the town. The blond man rapped his dagger hilt on the gate and roused the watchman with a shouted greeting.

'I am Rufus de Malham, father of Simeon de Beverley, your priest of St Peter's,' he announced, and at his words the rider beside him stiffened in his saddle.

'And you, sir,' the watchman demanded. 'Name yourself.'

'I am Hector of Lincoln, brother of Cyrus de Figham, your holy canon of St Martin's.'

As the gates were opened to admit them, the riders paused to survey each other in the full revelation of their true identities. The curate was the first to speak, his voice low and his features gravely set.

'Well, Rufus, it seems we visit opposing camps.'

'It seems we do,' Rufus replied.

'Then may God temper your purpose here with mercy and fair judgement.'

'And may He, in His wisdom, do the same for yours.'

Hector lifted his elegant fingers in salute, then turned his horse's head towards the Minster church. Rufus was scowling as he watched him go. St Peter's enclosure lay in the opposite direction, and as they parted company he felt that he had been misled into breaking bread with an enemy. Cyrus de Figham was the priest whose hatred had driven Simeon to the brink of death and whose evil schemes had brought him to disgrace. It troubled Rufus now that he had travelled so many miles in the company of that dark priest's closest kinsman.

He was about to heel his horse when he saw a small boy in a light grey tunic watching him from the slopes beyond the ditch. For a moment he was struck with memories as fresh as yesterday, clear images of a precious son and heir. So vivid was this impression that he glanced at the boy's feet, expecting to see one ankle crushed and deformed by the weight of a falling horse.

'Ye gods, I know you, boy.'

Everything he had heard, every rumour and report, came back to him now with startling clarity. Men whispered that the priest of St Peter's had sired a son despite his claims to chastity, and Rufus de Malham, staring at this yellow-haired child, was instantly convinced that it was so.

'*Peter!*' He spoke the name in a whisper and, although the sound could not have carried far, he saw the blond head lower as if to acknowledge the voicing of its owner's rightful name. A moment later the contact between them was broken as the boy moved off to join a dark-robed man who stood some distance off. He turned his head just once before the mist closed in around him, and Rufus said again, as if astonished, '*Peter!*'

Within the gates of St Peter's enclosure, Simeon had completed the Morning Office, removed his ceremonial robes and taken up his axe. When the message reached him of his father's unexpected arrival, he threw it down and came running from the wood where he had been chopping sticks for the fires. He was dressed in breeches and knee-high boots, with his shirt-sleeves rolled up over powerful forearms. From a neck-chain hung the golden brow piece of a warhorse, and from his waist a simple wooden cross bearing the figure of the hanged Christ.

Rufus de Malham stared as if transfixed as his son approached. The lame boy of St Peter's was no more. The crippled scribe of Beverley was forgotten. Here in their place was a man at the very pinnacle of his manhood; handsome, impressive, vigorous and *whole*. He slid from the saddle and hurried forward to clasp his son against his breast in a hearty embrace.

'By heaven it is true. Your leg is healed.'

'Aye, father, ten years ago. Can you forgive the secrecy?'

'My dear boy, knowing the facts that forced the lie, I can forgive it.'

'But why are you here?' Simeon asked. 'Are you mad to risk such a journey in the depths of winter? Is my brother . . .?'

'Thaddeus still lives, though his lungs are fragile,' Rufus told him.

'Then what brings you here?'

'Must a father explain why he seeks out his son?'

Simeon looked hard at the handsome face, so like his own save for the long moustaches and the grey streaks in his hair. He knew this man, despite their many differences and lengthy separation. Rufus de Malham did nothing without a purpose. He would not leave his estates to wardens and a sickly son while he travelled the breadth of Yorkshire in foul weather with no objective but to greet his absent son.

'You are heartily welcomed, Rufus,' he said at last, knowing his father would explain himself only in his own good time.

'And I'm heartily glad to see you again.' Rufus grinned. He held Simeon away from him and surveyed him with great pride. 'Who would have thought that my skinny boy would one day grow into such a man as this? Look at you! What father could wish for more? And as for that son of yours . . .'

'My son?'

'Peter. I saw him outside the gates, briefly and at a distance, but I'd know him anywhere. Where is he? Where is my grandson?'

The grin faded from Simeon's face and was replaced by a look of dismay. 'Father, you have had my letters these ten years past. You know the truth. Peter is *not* your grandson.'

'Aye, lad,' Rufus grinned, 'just as that crippled leg of yours was never healed.'

'I have never lied to you about Peter,' Simeon insisted.

'Where is he? Bring him here, so I can . . .' Rufus broke off with a gasp, for he had seen Elvira stepping lightly towards them, her long hair gleaming black, her face serene. 'Elvira? My God, she's everything men say of her.' He moved to take her hands in his and draw her fingers to his lips, enchanted. 'My daughter,' he said at last, 'I greet you with a full heart. I am Rufus de Malham, Simeon's father, and you, without doubt, are the lovely Elvira, Simeon's wife.'

Her glance was troubled as she looked to Simeon, who touched his father's arm for his attention. 'Father, you are mistaken. Elvira and I are not . . .'

The older man scowled and squared his shoulders, facing Simeon with a father's authority. 'Feed me no more of your fabrications, Simeon de Beverley. What lies you choose to live with here, in this troublesome little town, are your own concern, but do not attempt to deny what any man with half an eye can see. You have a wife and a son. To deny them is an insult to my intelligence.'

'Your intelligence is in no doubt, sir,' Simeon bristled. 'It is your obstinacy I question. You know the truth.'

'Only as much of it as you dare commit to paper,' Rufus

countered. 'You have deceived me, Simeon. Do you think me so gullible as to deny the evidence of my own eyes?'

'Father, if they were truly mine—'

'Aye, and if that leg of yours were truly healed.'

The two men locked gazes and, standing beside them, Elvira saw much more than a striking physical resemblance between the two. Here were men of equal strength and stubbornness, men who, once they believed, would stand their ground and shift not a single inch from their convictions.

'Come,' she said at last, drawing Rufus by the elbow as she smiled into his face. 'You must be tired and hungry after your journey. Let me show you our scriptorium, where you must lodge while you are here. We can talk there in private until Simeon is free to bring Peter to us.' She saw the thanks on Simeon's face and felt the tension ease from the situation. Despite their regular contact by letters, these two had met face-to-face on only a handful of occasions in eighteen years. Emotions too long suppressed were inclined to flare under diverse guises, impeding their talk with quarrels and transforming their rare encounters into confrontations. Too much alike yet divided by too many differences, father and son held back their hearts and so allowed their meetings to pass like skirmishes on a battlefield.

Elvira led Rufus by the arm to the large stone building that stood among trees beyond the main buildings of the enclosure. This was Simeon's scriptorium and library, where scribes worked every day of every year, and where books from every corner of the world were lovingly stored. For an hour they sat before the fire with a tray of food between them, their conversation easy but intense. Elvira told her story from its strange and frightening beginnings, sparing no detail. She told of the unholy tempest that had brought her into Simeon's life, of the wonderful horse that had burst its heart to bring Peter, then a tiny babe, to Beverley. She told of the evil men who had feared the child and sought to kill him, of the sacrifices made on Peter's behalf, and of the secret, fear-filled years before their town caught light and burned from end to end in the worst fire in its history.

And, without reserve, she told this quiet man of her love for Simeon, and his for her.

'He keeps his vow,' she confided softly, at the end. 'His God still has first claim on him. His vow of celibacy has not been broken.'

Rufus stared into her lovely face, seeing a woman of vital and passionate beauty. As Simeon's father, he found himself shamed by his son's unnecessary restraint. No pope in history had ever seriously demanded celibacy of his priests, nor did the Scriptures say it was God's will. If Simeon kept his vow it was through personal choice alone, and Rufus judged him less than a man for that.

'How on earth can you accept such a situation?' he inquired bluntly.

'How can I do otherwise?' Elvira said, with her small, sad smile. 'With or without my acceptance, things are as they are.'

'You could love another. You could find a man to offer what he withholds.'

Elvira smiled, untroubled by the suggestion. 'No, Rufus, *all* of me belongs to Simeon. If he must keep his vow then so must I. If, one day, his God releases him from it, and if my husband is proven to be dead, then I shall be his lawful wife and he my lawful husband.'

'Such a union is unnatural.'

'I have no quarrel with it.'

'I find that difficult to believe,' he told her bluntly. 'Can you really love my son enough for this . . . to live your life behind high walls, a wife yet not a wife?'

Elvira's gaze was steady and her smile content. 'I do,' was all she said, and he was convinced.

The boy came up by the covered well in the centre of the scriptorium, snaked his slender arm through the grid to slip the rust-encrusted lock, then sprang through the gap as nimbly as a hare. Elvira heard the sharp intake of breath as Rufus saw him at close quarters for the first time. His reaction did not surprise her, for the boy's uncanny resemblance to his foster father was a source of increasing wonder to them all.

'Peter, come close and greet Father Simeon's father.'

'Rufus de Malham,' Peter said, bowing his head and offering his small hand in formal greeting. 'I am honoured to meet you, sir. I saw you arrive.'

Rufus glanced from the boy's face to Elvira's. Despite the colour of his hair and the deep blue of his eyes, there was a look of her in this handsome, almost beautiful little boy. The delicate bones and graceful movements, the translucent skin and hesitant smile were not Simeon's but hers. This boy was a perfect blending of the two, creating a balance between the ruggedly attractive priest and his gentle lady. Doubts fell like ominous shadows across his heart, for what he saw in Peter rendered Elvira's story nothing but pretty lies.

'I cannot accept this fanciful explanation,' he confessed to Simeon much later, when the two were alone together in the quiet of the scriptorium. 'How can I when the passion between you burns as bright as a torch? How can I when that boy looks back at me with *your* eyes, *your* face and Elvira's smile? Looking at him, I see my eldest son standing before me as he was before he came here. He is created in your image, Simeon, yours and hers, yet still you deny that Peter is your son.'

'I did not sire him,' Simeon replied softly. 'He is my son in every way but that.'

Although fatigued by his long journey, Rufus paced the floor of the scriptorium for the better part of the morning, firing questions at Simeon, dispelling rumours, examining and evaluating everything he knew, or had believed he knew, about his son. His quick, inquiring mind vaulted from one point to another. Determined to put an end to all the privacies, and to close the distance that had grown between them, he probed his son in search of the truth behind the mystery of St Peter's. He had always believed that hearsay and common gossip were inclined to hang upon a single thread of truth. Those hours with Simeon taught him otherwise. Behind the myths of Beverley was a truth more complex and more intricately knotted than any man could ever hope to unravel.

'Accept it,' Simeon urged, 'and believe, as we do, that God moves in mysterious ways His wonders to perform. Open your heart and your mind, Father, and try to understand what simply *is.*'

'Accept what *is?* Simeon, Elvira has told me of Wulfric de Morthlund's part in burning your town to the ground and of de Figham's murder of his canon. Your holy canons behave like madmen. The very people your town depends on for its spiritual guidance, these so-called servants of God supposedly elected for your protection, not only milk your people of what little they possess, but are capable of destroying your whole town. In the name of Heaven, what manner of man do you breed here?'

'*Good* men,' Simeon said, his hackles rising in Beverley's defence. 'Brave men, dedicated men who are willing to risk their lives and livelihoods for the good of the people. How else would we survive but for the true believers, the genuine priests among us?'

'And what use is *good* if it turns strong men into cowards?' Rufus demanded. 'Any one of St Peter's priests is a match for your real enemy, Cyrus de Figham, and yet you balked at dealing with him as you should.'

'We balked at nothing,' Simeon corrected. 'Do not judge us, Father. You do not have the right.'

'I have a father's right,' Rufus countered, squaring his shoulders and returning Simeon's angry stare. 'You saved the life of an evil man who tried to murder Peter. In God's name, why? When you had him on that high parapet in the Minster, dangling over certain death, why did you not open your fingers and let the devil fall?'

'Thou shalt not murder,' Simeon quoted tightly.

'Priest's talk!'

'Father, I *am* a priest.'

'You are first a *man,*' his father growled. 'This Cyrus de Figham had made himself your mortal enemy. But for him, the trial, the carting, the stoning – none of those things would have taken place. Ye gods, if I could have one moment in your place, holding that devil's life by the strength of my fingers, I'd let him fall and never know a single pang of conscience.'

'Cyrus de Figham is dead,' Simeon reminded him.

'Dead? Who says he's dead? He was seen slipping off the landing by the hall garth and the flow of water carried him away. All else is mere supposition. No living witness has seen the body.'

A voice from the doorway bellowed in reply. 'I say it, Rufus de Malham. I killed Cyrus de Figham. Willingly and with no regrets, I ran him down and flung my dagger intending to take his life. My aim was true.'

Rufus turned to the priest who had entered the room, a giant of a man with a barrel chest and bushy beard. This was the priest of St Nicholas, the home church, the one who had kept the port alive when it seemed the very elements were bent on destroying it. By his courage and tireless labours he had kept that lifeline open and so ensured the survival of the town.

'Father Thorald.'

'Yes, I am he.'

'And here's another mystery for your store,' Simeon told his father. 'This one with Thorald is Antony of Flanders, a wandering monk whom Fate once brought to Beverley and shackled to our town. Ask him to explain his origins and he'll repeat a thousand stories others tell of him. Ask him for the truth and he'll disappoint you, because he himself is ignorant of that.'

His anger defused, Rufus shook the hands of both men, the towering, glowering Thorald and the diminutive, clear-eyed monk. His regular letters from Simeon had told him much about these two, and every word he read was to their credit. He nodded gravely, satisfied on at least this single point: his son had chosen strong and worthy men to be his friends.

'Will you share the Mass with us?' Simeon pressed, his own anger gone without trace, and Rufus answered, grudgingly, 'If I must.'

Tobias was sitting by his master's bed, watching the strength and the life ebb away and the troubled eyes cloud over. Three

70

days had passed since these good people had found him on the frozen marshes, but nothing they did could keep the flesh on his master's bones or the life light safely burning in his eyes.

Despite the kindness, the warmth and the regular food, Tobias was uneasy here in St Peter's enclosure. His own part in this unhappy errand still remained incomplete, and he knew that those he loved depended on him. He touched the damp brow of his master. The eyes flickered and twitched but did not open.

'You did your best,' he told the dying man. 'You did everything he asked of you. Rest easy, master, and let me do the rest.'

Just then another boy drew close to the bed, a tall youth with brown hair and gentle eyes. He carried a bowl of broth and a dampened towel, and he had come to tend the dying man.

'I am Edwin,' he whispered.

'I'm called Tobias.'

'Yes, I know. Brother Antony told me all about your brave journey and the precious gift you carried here for Simeon. He sent me to help until Osric, the infirmarian, returns.'

'When will he come?'

'Nobody knows. Blizzards and high winds shift the snow so that the roads are lost and the dikes concealed. Some ways are open, some are blocked with snow. And besides, Osric's skills are needed elsewhere.'

'They're needed here,' Tobias whispered, suddenly close to tears. 'Is my master dying?'

'Yes, I believe he is,' Edwin told him. 'His fever refuses to break and he's very weak.'

'Father Simeon says all men are given names,' the boy said sadly. 'He was my master and he was kind to me, but I don't know his name, and now he's dying. How can he die among strangers, without a name?'

'God will know it,' Edwin told him.

'But who's to tell Him?'

'He will know it. He knows *everything*,' Edwin smiled.

71

Tobias was unconsoled. 'Fortune has been unkind to him. Perhaps he was a fool to help the priest and then—'

Two words from Tobias's lips leaped out at Edwin with an ominous ring. 'Fortune?' he echoed. 'Fool? Dear God, the ivories . . . Fortune's Fool!'

'Edwin? Have I said something wrong? I only meant that—'

'Fortune's Fool,' Edwin repeated, and Tobias watched as the colour drained from his face and his limbs began to tremble.

For long moments Edwin swayed on his feet, his gaze unfocused. One hand came up to his brow and he uttered a sigh, and then his body folded and he fell to the ground with a crash.

Tobias leaped aside to avoid the overturned bowl of steaming gruel. 'Help! Someone help! Edwin's sick!'

It was Simeon who came to calm the boy. He and Antony had brought his father to the infirmary, hoping that by now Osric had returned from his task at Wheel. He stepped through the door in time to witness Edwin's sudden collapse. 'Calm yourself, lad,' he told Tobias. 'Edwin is no more sick than you or I. He has an affliction that is distressing but does no harm, so long as he falls among friends and on safe ground. He is merely sleeping, nothing more sinister than that. See, if I cover him with my cloak he will recover in a little while and be as hale as he was before.'

Simeon covered Edwin with his cloak and set his head at an angle so that his breathing was unimpaired and his tongue in no danger of being swallowed.

'He says my master will die,' Tobias muttered.

'Aye, I fear he might,' Simeon replied.

'Then I'll wait. I'll stay with him.'

'Of course you will. You are a loyal lad, Tobias. Your master will be glad of your company on his last journey.'

Tobias nodded gravely and positioned himself at the bedside, one of his master's limp, hot hands clasped tightly in his own.

The men were examining Osric's extensive store of herbs

and remedies when Edwin began to stir. Shaking his head and muttering, he reached for Simeon's arm and attempted to haul himself to his feet on shaky legs. Rufus stepped back a pace, unsettled by the sight of a falling sickness that came without a seizure and with no telltale foaming at the mouth to warn of its advance. Simeon, by now familiar with the nature of Edwin's malady, was concerned by the boy's unusually slow recovery.

'What is it, Edwin? Are you ill?'

'Father Simeon? Am I awake? The room is spinning . . .'

'Breathe deeply, lad. And slowly. Fill your lungs and your head will clear.'

Antony glanced up and scowled his concern. 'Something's wrong. He always comes awake on the instant, recovering as suddenly as he fell. This lingering confusion is unusual.'

'Fortune's Fool,' the boy muttered. 'Two cups . . . two identical cups . . .' He stared at Simeon as if seeing him for the first time. 'The Apostle, the Cherub, the Serpent. Are they all here? Has it happened already? Are they *all* here?'

'Wake up, Edwin,' Simeon said sharply.

'Fortune's Fool . . . Fortune's Fool.'

Simeon grasped the boy by the chin and spoke loudly into his face. 'Wake up, Edwin! Wake up!'

With a start he came to his senses and glanced beyond Simeon to where the traveller lay dying on his bed. Ill at ease but clearly recovered, he busied himself with clearing away the broken gruel bowl and its spilled contents. Simeon drew the others away, but his eyes were troubled as he watched the boy.

'Perhaps his condition is worsening,' Antony suggested softly. 'I have seen strong men bite off their tongues and rave like mad dogs when the falling sickness grips them.'

'I must get word to Osric,' Simeon nodded, then caught a clerk by the sleeve and whispered in his ear, 'Keep watch on Edwin and see he takes his medicine regularly. Do you know what to do if he should suffer a full seizure?'

'Yes, Father Simeon,' the clerk replied with a nod of his tonsured head. He lifted a palming board that was attached to the cord at his waist. 'This piece of wood will be wedged firmly between his teeth to protect his tongue, and my weight will pin him to the ground if the frenzy grips him. Don't worry, I'll keep watch on him.'

Simeon turned to Antony. 'He's sleeping badly and missing meals. Did you send for Father Daniel?'

'I did, but de Morthlund keeps him on a tight tether. He'll come when he can.'

Simeon was frowning over his clasped fingers. 'What was he muttering about? Fortune's Fool? The Serpent? The Apostle?'

'And the Cherub,' Rufus added.

'He spoke of these same things when the night frights gripped him. What does it mean, Antony? Is Edwin losing his mind?'

The little monk shook his head. 'I will send for Daniel Hawk as a matter of urgency. That boy needs to be confessed without delay.'

Much later in the day, Rufus joined Simeon and Elvira in the scriptorium, standing quietly at his son's side as he penned bright colours onto a manuscript. The priest's desk was set in a fork where two broad shafts of light from opposite windows met and blended. The bright colours of the inks were deepened and lifted, and the soft blond of Simeon's hair was touched with a halo of silvered light. Rufus saw the calluses on Simeon's palms, the healed scars on his knuckles and the rope marks on his wrists, and he wondered how those hands could execute so fine a task with such lightness, such delicacy of touch.

'Those colours are beautiful. What book is that?

'This is my life work, my Beverley chronicles,' Simeon explained. 'And this particular illumination marks the seventeenth chapter. I have compiled a detailed record of our history, and of the people and events that are helping shape it.'

'Ah, another so-called history penned by scholars but dictated and carefully edited by those who would have their memory glorified for posterity. You waste your talents, Simeon, on counterfeit things. You should leave such work to the flatterers and fawners who dare to call themselves historians.'

'Your assessment is hasty,' Simeon told him, penning a fine red line against a swirl of glittering gold. 'These chronicles of mine contain only the truth, however damning or unflattering. Where a man does good I record the deed, and where a man does ill I write that too.'

'You would never dare,' Rufus declared. 'No scribe in Christendom ever dared write the truth.'

Simeon turned his head to fix his father with a steady stare. 'Do you accuse me of falsehood, Rufus? Do you hold your son in such low esteem?'

'You are a priest,' the older man shrugged. 'You do as you must. You're subject to a higher authority, and so your words are tempered by the preferences and designs of those whose lives you record. Come, my boy, would you seriously have me believe that you commit to paper such things as we see around us every day, corruption and debauchery in the very corridors of the Church, abuse of power, theft and rape, even *murder*?'

'Where these things occur, I painstakingly record them.'

'What? I don't believe it!'

'But it's all here, Rufus, line by line and page by page, *all of it*. However men might wish to be remembered, posterity will learn the truth of these troubled years in Beverley.'

'Posterity has *never* learned the truth from history books,' Rufus insisted. 'It reads only what men want said of them and what the scribe is paid or bribed to write.'

'I am neither paid nor bribed. I write the truth, and if my chronicles survive, future centuries will know of us and how we kept St John's *Beaver Lake*, and his holy Minster, from sinking into the mire of corruption.' Simeon paused to rap the pages with his finger. 'In here also lies the secret of where St John's relics and holy treasures are hidden. Should I not live to see his church and his shrine fully restored, I hope some future priest will discover my secret and raise our saint to his proper place in Beverley.'

Rufus threw up his hands in exasperation. 'Are you determined to make a martyr of yourself?'

'Not at all,' Simeon assured his father. 'Like you, I am well aware that our scribes trim and copy their work according to the influences brought to bear upon them by others. They fill their pages with whatever truth is politic, then copy such inventions from each other. These books of mine will tell only the stark and honest truth, however unsavoury or shocking that truth might be.'

'Fool's work! Empty gestures! Worthless conceits!' Rufus declared. 'Some priest or canon, or your own archbishop, or the Primate of Rome himself, will have you tried for your candour and these damning pages consigned to the flames. Posterity will never know that you existed, Simeon de Beverley, and those Beverley chronicles of yours, *if* they survive, will be branded as a work of malicious fiction.'

'Father, why did you come here?' Simeon asked wearily.

'You know why I came. I want you to come home.'

Simeon shrugged his shoulders and returned his attention to his inks, leaving his father to pace the floor in his frustration. Rufus, as always, was spoiling for a fight. For three days they had sparred and parried thus. Their lives were divided by a chasm too deep to cross, and every bridge they tried to build was flimsy, so that they tore it down with hasty words. When Rufus spoke again his tone was sullen.

'These people of Beverley for whom you toil would have seen you hanged not many weeks ago.'

'Aye, they would, had it come to it,' Simeon agreed.

'Instead they tried to stone you to death.'

Simeon wiped his pen on a piece of cloth and drew fresh ink from a tiny bottle on his desk. 'Hysteria makes animals of even the worthiest of men,' he told his father.

'Worthy men do not turn their coats according to which way the wind blows. Worthy men are loyal. Worthy men don't take up sticks and stones against their proven friends.'

Simeon turned his head. 'It is over, Father.'

'And so you have forgiven them?'

Simeon nodded gravely. 'I am a priest. Should I preach forgiveness and not give it freely?'

Rufus raked his fingers through his hair in exasperation. 'Come home with me, Simeon. Come home before this *Beaver Lake* destroys you.'

Simeon met the hard encounter of his father's stare and, willing him to see and understand his heart, answered with a soft, decisive, 'No.'

'I need an heir, Simeon. Your brother, Thaddeus, will succumb to his diseased lungs before he reaches the age of thirty. I need a strong and capable son to share the burden of my wealth. Bring Elvira and the boy, and learn to live your life as a whole man. Give your wife and son a better life, a safer future. I need you, Simeon. Come home.'

The young priest set his inks aside and rose from his chair to embrace the father who had gifted his crippled son to the Church and then watched the health of his remaining son eaten away by lung disease. This man had made a grievous sacrifice, and now he sought to retrieve the best of it. 'Share Mass with us,' Simeon urged.

'Mass will alter nothing,' Rufus told him. 'I want my son returned, with his wife and child. No, do not contradict me, Simeon. Return to Malham Hall with Elvira and Peter, and no one will ever suspect that the boy is anything but my lawful, natural grandson. I offer you back your inheritance in full. If not for me or for yourself, then accept it for their sakes. Give up this thankless task, this foolish dedication to a cause and a town that offer no reward. Come home, Simeon.'

The single bell of St Peter's church began its long, slow tolling for the Mass. Elvira rose from her stool by the fire, set down her stitching and reached for a plain white cloth with which to cover her hair. Her eyes spoke silent volumes as she turned her face to Simeon. In their dark depths he heard the words as clearly as if she had spoken them aloud: *Do it, my love.*

He drew her aside when she would have followed the others from the scriptorium.

'Elvira, would you be happy to leave here?'

'I would,' she told him honestly. 'I would be happy to live in the open, without walls and guards, to feel safe and unafraid. I want to see Peter prosper where there are no enemies to harm him. More than that, Simeon, I want to see him laugh and play like any other child.'

'He is not like any other child, Elvira.'

'No, but perhaps he could be, given better circumstances.'

Simeon cupped her face in his hands and stooped to brush her forehead with his lips. 'If I could change things, Elvira . . . If I could make life easier for you . . .'

'Your God is a jealous God,' she reminded him. 'He allows me only second claim on you.'

'And I am blessed by your acceptance,' he said. Her eyes were veiled, her face closed, and he detected a shadow of doubt slipping between them. He recalled the handsome Jew who would have offered her a better life and a love that was not hampered by private vows, and as he drew her into his embrace, he was touched once again by a deep and painful fear of losing her.

As they left the scriptorium, a man in a rough woollen hood emerged from the trees and paused to bow his head in greeting. A thick layer of snow covered his shoulders, dropped from the branches disturbed by his passing. In his hands he carried four dead crows, all hanging by their feet from his fingers, their wings spread and their eyes veiled over.

'Who are you, brother?' Simeon asked.

'David.'

'Do I know you?'

The man turned back his hood and looked at Simeon with clear blue eyes and a sad expression. 'You gave me shelter after the fire,' he said.

'Ah, yes. You were a mason. You suffered burns. I believe your family—'

'They were lost,' the monk said sharply, and Simeon saw that, two years on, the man's wounds were still as raw as when he had first been carried to St Peter's.

He glanced at the crows, recalling how this man had slipped

away in the night, leaving a clutch of birds and a rabbit as payment for Osric's care. 'Stay with us for a while, brother David,' he said. 'Share the Mass with old friends and know that you are welcome here.'

The monk bowed again, his brows creased in a deep frown. 'The brothers serving St Dominic the Mailed have asked me to draw your attention to their predicament. They sent me with an urgent message to your provost, but that concerned another matter.' He shuddered and seemed uncertain. 'The brothers have neither food nor fuel for their needs.'

'They will be helped,' Simeon assured him.

'Their abbot is dead.'

'God rest his soul.'

David nodded. For a moment he looked as if he might say more, but then he shrugged and turned from them abruptly, strode along the pathway and stooped through the doorway of the bakehouse.

'Two years and still he grieves,' Simeon remarked.

'Some hurts go deep,' Elvira reminded him, and Rufus, falling into step behind them, said, 'Amen to that.'

CHAPTER SIX

Instead of going directly to the church, they crossed the bridge and passed through the wooded grounds to the farthest corner of the enclosure, there to stand for a while beside the secret graves, remembering their dead. Here, in the most secluded corner of St Peter's enclosure, beyond the woodland and the church and protected by the ancient boundary wall, they stood together in silence, praying in their hearts.

Simeon had obtained permission from his provost to hold this special Mass at the altar of St Peter. Many outsiders were eager to attend, among them four Little Sisters of Mercy who had left their convent to live within St Peter's enclosure. Their prayers would be for the tragic Alice, who had once been one of them. Several priests from diverse churches were here to pay their last respects to the murdered canon, Father Bernard, now safely laid to rest within these walls, a gentle man struck down by the priest who coveted his office and his church.

Only Simeon and Elvira prayed for the babe whose brief life and hasty death had changed the whole course and pattern of their lives. They believed themselves alone in their remembrance of Elvira's son, until Peter slipped between them to place a faded winter rose on the tiny grave. 'Sometimes I fear he understands too much,' Elvira whispered, and Peter slipped his hand in hers as if to offer comfort and reassurance. He felt a roughness on her palm and turned her hand to examine a cluster of blisters on the skin.

'It is nothing,' Elvira told him. 'Perhaps I hurt myself while gathering wood. Osric will heal it when he returns.'

Peter's brows were puckered in a frown as he looked from her hand to her face, and Elvira could see that the injury disturbed him. She smiled and squeezed his hand and said again, 'It is nothing.'

There was a young priest amongst the small group of mourners, a tense young man whose face was grimly set behind the growth of a splendid beard. Richard of Wheel had found the body of Father Bernard slumped and bleeding in one of the Minster stairwells. In the aftermath of the tempest of a decade ago he had slipped into that dark place to urinate, too nervous of the looters in the streets to go outside, too respectful of the Church to lift his robe amongst the rubble. It pained him still that such a man as Bernard could be struck down from behind and left to lie in the stream of another's piss.

'My hatred didn't die with Cyrus de Figham,' he confessed, and the bitterness in his voice confirmed the honesty in his words. 'It torments me still. It knows no ease.'

'Learn to forgive, for your own sake,' Simeon told him.

'Learn only to *accept*,' Rufus insisted. He glanced sharply at his son and added, 'Sometimes forgiveness is too much to ask of a man.'

As they left the grave side and made their way through the frosted, snow-laden trees beside the church, Rufus drew Simeon aside and slowed his pace.

'I travelled here with Hector, a curate from Lincoln, and only when we reached the East Gate did I discover that he is the brother of Cyrus de Figham. What does he want with Beverley that he risks his life to travel here in this foul weather?'

'I doubt his presence is any more sinister than your own,' Simeon offered. 'His brother has been missing for almost two

81

months, and Cyrus was a wealthy man with much property that must be properly apportioned. Thanks to the servants, and to the authority of Wulfric de Morthlund, the house at Figham has been protected from looters and seems to be intact. That house and its barns and cellars represent a prize for any who can prove he has a rightful claim to them.'

'Like crows to the carcass,' Rufus observed.

Simeon nodded. 'And the Church itself will claim a substantial share. Indeed, if the papal legate finds against Cyrus de Figham, the fines upon his estates might well exceed their value. Should it prove so, this Hector of Lincoln could find himself obliged to meet the excess. There is also the matter of Father Cyrus's church to be considered. St Martin's is now without a canon.'

'Aye, and a sorry church it is, so Thorald tells me. Its missing canon was guilty of gross neglect. What would this curate of Lincoln want with such an unprofitable place?'

Simeon smiled and offered what he believed to be the truth. 'Like all our churches, St Martin's offers the status and rewards of the canon's office,' he explained. 'The house at Figham was Cyrus's own, but a decent enough house goes with the church, along with a quantity of land and many profitable rights and privileges. Few men would choose St Martin's over a church more respectably supported, but few would turn it down if it was offered.'

'You are cynical, Simeon.'

'I am honest,' Simeon told him. 'Men are men.'

Rufus de Malham sighed and shook his head. He saw St Peter's as a quiet island in a stormy sea, a modest stronghold standing firm against petty rivalry and corruption. He was perplexed by Simeon's decision to be its helmsman and his dedication to those who looked to him for leadership. Most of all he was frustrated by Simeon's quiet determination to make a stand for right within a Church so rich in popish wealth and yet so poor in Christian virtue.

Peter was walking ahead of them, the hood of his robe lowered so that the puckered scar on his neck was visible. That scar was an ugly reminder of darker days, when those who ruled in Beverley would have cut a newborn's throat to preserve the status quo. It was also a dangerous mark of identification, for many were now aware that the enigmatic Peter de Beverley bore a would-be assassin's brand on his throat. He, too, lived on the edge of troubled waters, inviting persecution by his strangeness and his knowledge of secret things.

As if he felt the eyes of Rufus on him, young Peter turned his head and looked into eyes that were as blue as Simeon's, as blue as his own. His smile was brief and his expression said he knew the other's thoughts.

'A strange child,' Rufus muttered, and Simeon answered, just as softly, 'Aye.'

The communion wine for the special Mass was to be blessed by the addition of water from the sacred relic obtained from Rome. The horn that had been brought for Alice was safely in the church, set on a crimson cushion fringed with gold, and all would offer thanks in their prayers for the brave man who had willingly risked his life to deliver it to St Peter's. The Mass was to be performed a full two hours before sunset, a concession granted to allow attending priests to return to their own duties in time for the evening offices. The bell was tolled at two in the afternoon, and a slow procession of men and women filed into the church.

Father Cuthbert, Simeon's guardian and mentor, was waiting at the entrance to St Peter's. He was garbed in his canon's robes and a fur-lined cloak. His feet, always susceptible to the cold, were clad in boots into which Elvira had stitched warm squirrel pelts. Now in his eightieth year, Father Cuthbert had grown frail and slow in his movements. His thin hands trembled constantly and his eyes often shed unwanted tears that left their tracks on the delicate skin of his cheeks. Old age, and too many years spent poring over books or bent in prayer, had drawn his chin ever closer to his chest, fixing the bones of his neck so that he could no longer meet the gaze of taller men. His faculties were failing, his once-sharp mind inclined to lapse into periods of perplexity. Some said that his love for Simeon kept him alive, while others believed he clung to life in the hope of seeing Peter ordained into the priesthood.

'*Dominus vobiscum*, the Lord be with you,' he said in a clear, thin voice as he rested his trembling hand on Peter's head.

'*Et cum spiritu*,' Peter responded with a smile. 'And with you, also.'

The boy and the old man locked gazes for a moment, each aware of the other's thoughts and of the grave decision that would soon affect their lives and Simeon's future. It was time for the old and frail to step aside so that the young and brave could take full control. The boy and the canon had discussed the topic at length, and their conclusion was still a secret between themselves. Now Peter nodded knowingly and Cuthbert did the same, and then the boy stepped back to allow those behind to enter.

'God's blessing, Father Cuthbert.'

At the sound of a familiar voice, Cuthbert reached for Rufus's hand and shook it warmly. 'Has it really been eighteen years since you brought our precious Simeon to us?'

'It has,' Rufus confirmed, 'and I grudgingly admit you have made a fine man of him, Cuthbert.'

The old man chuckled and wagged a blue-veined finger. 'Much more than that, my dear Rufus. We have made a fine *priest* of him.'

Rufus stood back respectfully as Simeon, grandly robed in preparation for the Mass, and Peter, in his simple tunic of grey cloth, escorted their ageing canon into the church. He felt an unexpected and unwelcome sting of envy as he watched his son, and the boy who might yet prove to be his grandson, exclude him in the presence of their Church and their beloved canon.

Elvira's hand was light on his arm and her dark eyes filled with compassion as she smiled into his face. 'You are his father,' she said. 'Nothing changes that.'

'I gave him up,' Rufus reminded her. 'He was ten years old and crippled by a horse, and I gave him up in favour of his brother.'

'You did your best in difficult circumstances, Rufus. Your son is happy here. He does not blame you.'

'No, but I blame myself, Elvira.'

As Elvira walked with Rufus into the church, she felt the sorrow that weighed upon his heart and she hoped that, by seeing Simeon at his best, this man would be rewarded for his sacrifice.

Inside the church, candles and flickering torches played their light upon the walls, where brilliantly coloured paintings told the parables and gospels for all, wealthy or poor, educated or ignorant, to recognise with ease. Light fell in meagre measure from the high-set windows, barely dispelling the blackened shadows clinging to the rafters. As more worshippers entered by the door, the press of standing men and women moved closer to the dais on which the holy altar stood. Those too old or infirm to stand throughout the lengthy service were offered the benefit of stone slabs set into the ancient walls and pillars. Here in St Peter's church no priest's cry, 'Let the weak go to the wall,' was ever heard, for these people looked to their old and sick with a compassion that had no need of priestly prompting.

As Simeon took his place beside his canon at the altar, Elvira watched him with a solemn face. Here was her tall, broad-shouldered Simeon, the strikingly handsome man who could turn the head, and the heart, of any woman. She saw in him the love that gave meaning to her life, while all about her others looked and saw only Father Simeon, the priest.

'Where is Peter? He was here a moment ago.'

She glanced around in response to Rufus's whispered question, then shrugged her shoulders and smiled without concern. 'He comes and goes as he chooses,' she told him. 'Do not worry, Rufus. He will return for communion before the Mass is concluded.'

Rufus merely nodded, concealing his own concern. He would rather make a prisoner of the boy for his own safety than allow him to move at will about this fickle, unpredictable town where enemies and profiteers abounded.

*   *   *

85

Edwin and Edwinia stood by the wall of the infirmary until the last worshippers had gone in and the door of St Peter's closed behind them. Osric had trimmed their hair to matching lengths, and they were so alike that they could only be distinguished by the slight difference in their heights and the clothes they wore.

'I'm frightened,' Edwina told her brother. 'It troubles me when strangers come, nameless strangers out of nowhere.' She looked up at Edwin with accusing eyes. 'And when my brother proves himself a thief.'

'It's only a rabbit,' Edwin insisted, patting the bundle concealed beneath his coat.

'A *stolen* rabbit.'

He shrugged. 'I'll set a snare and catch another. I'll work beyond my duties, if I must, to make amends. And I'll make confession to Father Daniel. He'll tell me what to do.'

'Edwin, Father Daniel will only tell you what you already know. You should never have gone there.'

'I know.'

'And now you'll repeat your folly,' she said. 'Please Edwin, forget this plan. Return the rabbit and tell Father Simeon of your fears. Don't go there again.'

'I must,' he told her. 'Expect me back within the hour. I intend to take my place at Holy Communion with the others.' Then he kissed her cheek and hurried away.

He went by way of Eastgate, following the town ditch and the high wall of St Peter's enclosure until he reached the fish market, and from there through the maze of narrow alleyways to the Cobbler's Row.

As if no time had passed since his last visit, the old woman was sitting as he had seen her last, stooped over her table by the hearth. Something unpleasant was burning in the grate, giving off a dense smoke that met the roof and billowed back into the room with an acrid smell. As he stooped through the doorway, breathless from his dash, she saw his reflection in her copper pot and hastily covered her table with a square of dirty sacking.

'Edwin,' she said without turning her hooded head in his direction. 'St Peter's servant.'

He wiped the sting of wood smoke from his eyes. 'I stole a rabbit.'

'So, now you are a thief.'

'Men have come to Beverley,' he told her. 'The weather is closing in for miles around, but still they've come. Why are they here? Tell me the runes.'

'A little knowledge is a dangerous thing,' she tantalised.

'Tell me what's happening,' Edwin insisted. 'Is Simeon in danger? His father wants to take him away, the brother of his enemy is here, and now Simeon allows outsiders into his church for a special Mass and . . . and . . .'

She turned her ugly face and Edwin shuddered at the cold glint in her eyes. 'And?'

'I think the Fool is here, the one in the ivories. He brought a gift for Simeon, and now he's dying and no one knows his name or where he comes from, only that Fate has used him ill.'

'Ah, Fortune's Fool. I warned you, Edwin. I told you he would come.' She glanced at the bulge inside his coat. 'Pay me.'

He drew out the rabbit and watched her knead the limp carcass between her good hand and her claw. 'Lots of flesh. Nice plump flesh,' she muttered, drawing it to her nose and inspecting every inch of it with her nostrils. 'And fresh as morning snow. Fresh meat in winter. Good, good.' Her voice was suddenly sharper as she barked: 'He offers the poisoned cup.'

'What?'

'The Fool. Fate's instrument. His cup is tainted.' She chuckled as she lifted the cover from the table. In his absence she had added several ivories to the first, and now her filthy finger tapped the worst of them. 'Death. The Fool offers death. And here's the Emperor, prizing his gold above the lives of men. Here's the Janus, double-faced and slippery as an eel, and here's the Martyr, ready to sacrifice all, and the Jackal devouring its own young.'

87

Faced with so many brilliant images, Edwin felt his senses reel. The vivid inlays of the ivories seemed suddenly garish, their images distorted and monstrously pagan.

'I don't understand . . . there are so many . . .'

With a sweep of her hand the runes were scattered, to fall amongst the filthy rushes face down, with not a single pattern visible. 'Choose!'

The old woman rose from her stool and moved towards Edwin. In alarm he took several paces back towards the door.

'Come, lad. Be brave. Choose the rune that will determine Simeon's future. There's chaos coming, broken lives and mended fortunes, cruel endings and sweet beginnings, changes, sorrows, triumphs. Choose which is to be, Edwin.'

'No . . . I can't . . . I . . .'

Edwin glanced at the scattered ivories, then shook his head and shrank away, afraid to be made the instrument of Father Simeon's fate.

'*You* called up the ivories,' Hannah barked. 'You, Edwin of St Peter's, have paid the fee that lifts the veil. *Choose.*'

'I can't. I . . .'

'*Choose!*'

He jabbed a trembling finger at the pale rectangle lying closest to the door, and in desperation stammered, 'There! That one.'

She crouched, snatched up the rune and, without taking her eyes from his, revealed the pattern on its underside. 'The Grim Reaper,' she anticipated and, by some cruel play of firelight on shadow, the black-robed, skeletal figure seemed to pause in gathering its human harvest to turn its grinning face in his direction. 'He's coming, Edwin, and yours is the hand that drew him from the sack.'

With a gasp Edwin turned and fled from the smoke-filled hovel. In the alley beyond the door his racing feet slid and stumbled on the icy ground. The old woman's cackling laughter rang in his ears and the name of his chosen rune repeated itself in his ears with the rapid pounding of his heart: *The Grim Reaper . . . Reaper . . . Reaper . . .*

Although aware that his anxieties and exertions could induce another falling fit, he raced along alleyways, scrambled over walls and fences and scaled the gates of a carter's yard in order to reach the wider streets by the shortest possible route. At the fish market his haste directed him to the right instead of to the left, along the clutter of houses that was Hyegate, and from there to Moorgate, close by the Minster church. He skinned his knees on the wall of a splendid house, then crawled through a cluster of bushes to reach its rear door. By the kitchen wall a window glowed with lamplight, and beyond the glass a familiar figure stooped over a lamp, examining the pages of a book.

Daniel Hawk lifted his head at the sound of scratching on the glass. 'Edwin!' He rushed to the door to drop the bar across it, then threw open the window, grasped the boy by his shoulders and hauled him inside. 'Why are you here? I sent word that I would come to St Peter's as soon as I could get away without arousing Father Wulfric's suspicions. What in God's name are you doing here?'

'I had to see you, Father Daniel.'

'Here? In this house? Have you lost your senses, boy? Wulfric de Morthlund is asleep in the room above. If he catches you here, if he sees you again . . .'

'I had to come. Father Daniel, I've done a terrible thing. I've tempted Fate on Simeon's behalf, and now . . .'

Daniel drew the boy to the fire and bade him sit while he poured some wine into a modest pewter goblet.

'Catch your breath and calm yourself, or you'll fall into a seizure,' he said. 'Here, drink it slowly and let it still your agitation.' He drew up a stool and watched as the boy obeyed, his dark, aristocratic face unreadable. 'Now, Edwin, tell me what's happened, from the beginning.'

The priest looked on with kindly eyes as the boy related his story and his fears. Daniel Hawk had heard of the woman Hannah and her mysterious runes, and he knew that Simeon already figured in the secret, self-serving schemes of powerful men. This garbled tale revealed little that was new to him, or that he had not presupposed, concerning the ill-fated priest of St Peter's.

'And you say you saw them all in these pictures?' he asked at last.

Edwin nodded. 'Simeon and Peter I knew at once. The others were less certain, but their purpose was clear. Father Daniel, I think the dark priest still lives. I saw him as the Serpent, growing a new head and with his fangs bared. He's coming back to kill Father Simeon.'

'Cyrus de Figham is dead,' the priest reminded him gently. The boy was not convinced and nor was Daniel, for he had long suspected that Wulfric de Morthlund was making secret plans around the anticipated return of that missing canon.

'I saw him in the runes,' Edwin insisted. 'The woman spoke of chaos and broken lives, and I was the one who drew the runes. I did it. It's all my fault.'

Daniel Hawk leaned back on his stool and shook his head. His dark hair shifted with the movement, long and thick around his ears and shoulders, thinned above a noble forehead so that his hawk-like features were accentuated. Traces of scarring were still visible on his cheek and hands where the Beverley fire, and his own courage in his master's defence, had left dark stains and puckered scars to mar the beauty Nature had given him.

'You did nothing that was not already done,' he told the boy. 'God makes the future, Edwin, not foolish youngsters with more curiosity than common sense. You should know better than to dabble in such things. The dark arts are not to be trifled with.'

'I know,' Edwin admitted miserably. 'Tell me the runes lie and I'll believe you, Father Daniel. Tell me she uses trickery, that I didn't see what I saw.'

'What's done is done, Edwin. You should never have gone there.'

'Tell me the one called Janus, the one with two faces, was not myself. Dear God, am I to betray Father Simeon after all he's done for me?'

'Now that much I *can* explain,' Daniel assured him. 'Janus

90

was a minor god revered by the ancient Romans. His faces looked in opposite directions, so that no man could be sure where, or on whom, his gaze was resting.'

'And I'm a twin,' Edwin reminded him. 'I too have another face, worn by my sister.'

'You are not the Janus, boy. Your heart is good. Old Hannah toys with unsavoury things no Christian hand should touch. Her practices are forbidden by the Church.'

Edwin blinked and said defiantly, 'But our Church has signs and symbols of its own. It uses images and spells to conjure magic. It prophesies and predicts, and it offers what blessings and curses a man can afford to buy. Why should Hannah's be forbidden and ours allowed when so much of what we practise is the same?'

Father Daniel shook his head as he reached for his travelling cloak. 'Your reasoning is sound, Edwin, and your questions, as always, remind me of my inadequacies as a priest. I cannot answer such questions. I can neither measure nor comprehend the distinction between her faith and ours.'

'Then what am I to do?' the boy demanded.

'Come, we will go together to St Peter's and speak to Simeon while my master sleeps off the burden of his midday meal.'

'Father Simeon is at the special Mass for Alice and Father Bernard,' Edwin told him. 'Will you speak to the man who brought the holy gift? He will surely die unless the infirmarian has returned to save his life.'

'Expect no miracle cure from Osric,' Daniel told him. 'His skills are those of a military surgeon and a herbalist. He is no saint. If the man is truly dying, Osric's skills will alter nothing but the manner in which he passes.'

'Fortune's Fool,' Edwin repeated. 'I fear he's brought disaster with him. Old Hannah says he offers the bad cup, not the good.'

'Then perhaps she is mistaken,' Daniel smiled. 'You say he has brought a treasure, a precious relic, to St Peter's. How can a man be evil when he offers such a gift?'

'Perhaps he stole it. Perhaps it carries a curse.'

'Then we will find out for ourselves, Edwin. Come with me

91

now to St Peter's and we will settle the matter with Simeon's assistance. Use the window and keep yourself well hidden by the bushes. Meet me where Minster Moorgate meets St John's Yard, and lift your hood, Edwin.'

The infirmarian had indeed returned to St Peter's enclosure. When Daniel and Edwin arrived he was still with the gate man, dressed in his travelling leathers, his girdle hung with instruments and pouches of medication. He scowled his disapproval that the pair had allowed themselves to be seen together in the streets. However innocent their friendship, if Wulfric de Morthlund heard of it he would destroy them both.

'You play with fire, Priest, and you put that boy at risk,' he told Daniel with a scowl.

'Only because I must,' Daniel replied. 'Young Edwin has done a foolish thing and Simeon must be informed.' He lowered his voice and leaned towards the rugged Osric. 'He has discovered something that should not be disregarded, despite the circumstances. I need to speak to Simeon.'

Osric nodded grimly. 'Then you must wait until Mass is ended. I intend to join them in the church in time to share the wine. You are welcome to join us there, but first you must give your services to the needy. I am told we have a dying man among us.'

On his bed in the infirmary, the man who had braved foul weather and many dangers in his quest to reach St Peter's now lay on the slippery slope between life and death. His eyes were partly open but his vision clouded. He was lying still, save for the agitated movements of his fingers as they plucked at the blanket covering his body. A small boy kept vigil at the bedside, another pretty face with innocent eyes to be kept well hidden from men like Wulfric de Morthlund. A man in a modest monk's robe sat close by, his back against the wall, his knees drawn up and his folded arms providing a pillow for his head.

While Osric tossed a handful of herbs into a simmering pot hung over the fire, Father Daniel signed the cross and prepared to administer the final rites. As he touched his thumb to the feverish brow in blessing, the eyes flickered open and focused on his face.

'Hear my confession, Father.'

'I will. Prepare yourself,' Daniel told him.

'Father, I have sinned, but I had to do it . . . for Alice.'

'Simeon took care of her,' Daniel assured him. 'He gave her absolution and a Christian burial. Now say the words so that I might hear your confession.'

'No . . . no . . .' The man appeared bewildered. 'My Alice still lives,' he protested. 'She lives so long as I fulfil my part in this unholy bargain. My dear wife, Martha, and our little Alice are safe now that the deed is done. Dear God, forgive me . . . forgive me.'

Daniel felt the short hairs prickle at the nape of his neck. He waved the cup aside when Osric stooped to administer his stupefying brew. 'Let him speak,' he insisted, then leaned close to the man and told him, 'Confess your sins. Confess and be absolved before you die.'

'I've killed him. I've killed them all. I did it for them, for my Martha and Alice . . .'

'I knew it,' Edwin breathed. 'The poisoned cup.'

'Be still, Edwin,' Daniel snapped, then urged the man, 'What have you done?'

'Simeon,' the man replied, his voice fading to a whisper. 'Simeon will die . . . the holy water . . . the Mass.'

Perplexed by his words, Daniel lifted his head and saw the infirmarian shrug his shoulders. The singing of the Mass was clear and sweet on the crisp afternoon air as the service drew towards the sharing of the wine that marked its conclusion.

'St Bridget's horn . . .' the man on the bed was muttering. 'I know what it contains . . . why Abbot Aidan kept it hidden away . . . I did it for them . . . for them. Dear God, forgive me . . .'

'*Poison!*'

While the others stared without comprehension, Edwin saw the truth with sudden clarity. His confusion vanished, leaving his mind as clear as crystal.

93

'What is it lad?' Osric growled.

'The relic, the precious horn from Rome ... it doesn't contain holy water as this man promised. *It's filled with poison!*'

With a roar the infirmarian dropped the cup and made a dash for the infirmary door. Daniel and Edwin were close on his heels as he raced towards the church, his voice a bellow against the melodious swell of choral voices: 'Stop the Mass! In God's name, *stop the Mass!*'

Behind them, Tobias reached out to touch the feverish cheek of his master, then drew a roll of parchment from beneath his mattress and, amid the furore beyond the door, sniffed back his tears and quietly slipped away.

CHAPTER SEVEN

'Stop the Mass! Stop the Mass!'

As Osric sprinted for the church, men rushed from the gates and the other buildings in response to his alarm. Their footsteps pounded like thunder on the timbers of the bridge that spanned the centre drain, and in the crush its lamps were both dislodged. Those who had crowded outside the church doors for lack of space inside now fell back as the yelling trio bore down on them. Father Thorald had been standing by the door and, when it burst open, was almost felled as Osric cannoned into him.

'In God's name, stop the Mass!'

The worshippers and the choral priests fell silent. On the dais, Simeon stood before the altar, holding the gleaming communion chalice aloft. Father Cuthbert and Father Richard knelt before him, ready to follow Simeon in sipping the blessing from the holy cup. In the sudden hush another, less familiar voice was heard as Peter stepped out from behind the altar and said, 'Father, have a care. Set down the chalice.'

Simeon glanced from the boy to the four who were now pushing their way to the front of the church. Thorald was leading, with Osric on his heels and Daniel and Edwin close behind, and they came at speed despite the crush of people in the church. Simeon set the chalice down on the altar cloth, signed the cross and turned to face his godson.

Peter was standing calmly by the altar, holding a young goat in his arms. He had come by way of a sliding panel which led to the labyrinth of tunnels beneath the town.

'The Cherub,' Edwin breathed, clutching at Father Daniel's arm and feeling the colour drain from his cheeks. 'I saw him in the rune as I see him now, except that the animal he held then was a lamb.'

'He knows,' Daniel hissed in a whisper, loud enough for Osric to catch the words.

'By what emergency is the Mass interrupted?' Simeon asked in his deep yet gentle voice. As a man he trusted those who stood before him. As a priest he saw this intrusion as an offence. He pointed a finger at Osric. 'Explain yourself.'

'We suspect the holy water has been poisoned,' Osric said. His words were met by a gasp from all who heard them.

'Look at the cushion,' Edwin exclaimed.

Simeon looked and saw the ragged holes where the contents of the horn had leaked from the loosened cap and burned the fabric. His eyes went to Elvira, who was examining her blistered hand, then to the jewelled chalice with its innocent-looking contents.

'Let the goat decide the matter,' Peter offered, setting the bleating animal before the altar. He had tethered it to one end of the cord worn at his waist, and now he took the other end and dipped its tassel into the communion wine. Many drew their breath and crossed their breasts as he did so, for it seemed to them that they witnessed an act of sacrilege. The goat was young, not yet beyond its time of suckling. When the dampened tassel was dangled before its face, it took it readily and sucked it dry.

In the hushed church every eye was on the altar. Richard helped Father Cuthbert to his feet and Peter moved close to Simeon, who rested his hand on the boy's small shoulder. Long minutes passed and nothing seemed amiss, so that those who had forced their way inside began to wonder what hasty error of judgement had driven them here. As

96

the interval lengthened, those making up the congregation began to mutter amongst themselves and shift their feet conspicuously.

'It seems your fears are groundless,' Simeon said at last. 'I thank you, Osric, for your concern. However, as you can see, the animal suffers no ill effect.'

'The man who brought the horn is dying,' Osric told him. 'We all heard his confession, Simeon. He came to kill you.'

'And yet the wine is untainted.'

'But the cushion . . .'

'Damaged by some other means.'

'No, Father,' Peter told him. 'Observe the goat.'

The animal's body had begun to twitch and its eyes rolled in its head. A white froth oozed from its tightly clenched jaws and bubbled from its nostrils. Without a sound, it drew its head upward and backward at an unnatural angle that exposed its fleshy throat. Its agony was plain for all to see as it staggered in twitching circles before falling across the altar step, its spine arched and its eyes bulging. Its death was grotesque but mercifully short, and it left the observers stunned.

'Dear God in heaven!' someone exclaimed, and a soft voice answered, 'Lord be merciful.'

One of the Little Sisters of Mercy pulled off her linen wimple and stooped to draw it over the animal's body. Then she began to usher the congregation towards the door, her manner firm and her voice sharp with authority. Other sisters and several priests assisted her in the task, and those who now hastened to leave were in no doubt that they had looked death in the face. Had the holy wine been allowed to pass among them, the last participant in the Mass would have sipped the poison before the first one fell.

While the church was being cleared and the body of the goat carried out for burning, Simeon's friends gathered close around the altar.

'He called the relic St Bridget's horn,' Daniel explained.

'I know it by another name,' Antony said. 'In India it is

called Lucifer's trumpet. I didn't recognise it for what it was. Dear God, if I'd even suspected . . .'

Osric was turning the cushion on which the horn was lying. 'I have heard of it,' he said. 'It's said to contain the deadliest of poisons. They say it has a thousand deaths to its credit and that a single drop can destroy an army. It is thought to be the source of the poison in the deadly chalice once offered to St John.'

'Surely no poison is so potent?' said Simeon.

'Believe it, Simeon,' Osric told him. 'I have heard that the men of Arabia extract a fluid from the olive root that is said to be the most lethal poison known to man.'

'From the olive? The branch of peace and friendship?'

'Perhaps this venom is from that same source. You saw how a few drops added to the chalice destroyed the goat.'

When Simeon reached out to touch the horn it was Peter who stayed his hand. He was suddenly reminded of Elvira's injured palm. 'Osric, Elvira handled the horn. Her hand and fingers were hurt.'

The infirmarian examined the cluster of blisters on Elvira's hand. 'How did you treat it?'

'With an infusion of rue, as you did for young Michael when he was stung by bees,' Elvira told him.

'Good. It seems well enough,' Osric grunted, touching the blisters with his fingernail. 'Rue, though a poison itself, is an antidote to most other poisons when properly infused. The leakage from the horn would have been very slight until Simeon removed the cap.' He turned to his friend and his thoughts were clear on his face. 'Thank God for a steady hand, my friend. If you had spilled the poison when you uncapped the horn, or taken the blessing for yourself ahead of the others . . .'

'May God forgive him for what he meant to do,' the priest said. 'He told me the holy water was meant for Alice.'

'His daughter bears that name,' Osric told him.

'He also swore that the horn was doubly blessed for our special Mass and that he had travelled from Rome to bring it here.'

'Then he lied,' the infirmarian growled. 'He fully intended that the chalice used for the Holy Mass should be laced with that deadly poison.'

'At the risk of every worshipper in my church?' Simeon demanded. 'Was he insane? What on earth did he hope to achieve by such a wicked act, except a place in hell?'

'Your death,' Osric told him bluntly. 'He wanted you dead, Simeon, at any cost.'

'Damn him. *Why*? He knew me only by name and reputation. What have I done that a stranger wants me dead?'

'You must look to the craftsman, Father, not to his tool,' said Peter.

'The craftsman? Then you believe he was sent here by some other?'

'I know it,' the boy replied.

'And did you know from the start that the horn contained a deadly poison?'

'No, Father,' the boy replied, shaking his head. 'I am suspicious of all things reputed to be holy relics, and when I saw the marks and blisters on Mother's hand . . .' He shook his head again and a nearby torch tinted his hair with bronze reflections. 'If I had known, I would have spared the goat.'

The last members of the congregation were filing out through the door and Richard had settled Father Cuthbert on one of the altar steps when Simeon asked, 'Does anyone know why this stranger came to us with murder in his heart?'

'Who knows,' Osric shrugged. 'He spoke of his woman, Martha, and their child. He believed they would be safe from harm when you were dead.'

'Their lives for mine? So, someone else wanted my death and forced that unfortunate man to do the deed, but who? Who hates me enough to want me dead?'

Edwin stepped forward, his face pale and his brown eyes troubled. 'The Serpent,' he said, and Daniel, now convinced that he was right, gave the serpent of the rune its rightful name, 'Cyrus de Figham.'

'He's dead,' Father Thorald growled.

'He lives,' Daniel insisted. 'You botched the job, Thorald.

99

If you had but tipped your blade with St Bridget's poison, or followed the body downstream, or slit his evil throat from ear to ear . . .' He paused, then spoke the rest in less aggressive tones. 'The Devil takes care of his own. De Figham lives.'

'How is this possible?' Thorald brought his fists crashing down on the altar and ground out words between his clenched teeth. 'Damn him. I would rather swing for his murder than know that he still lives.'

Rufus de Malham had kept his silence until he could bear to hold his tongue no longer. 'Here in your own church?' he demanded of Simeon. 'Inside this fortress? Behind these guarded gates? You attend to your priestly duties as you should while someone tries to kill you *at your own altar*?'

'Satan gains entry where men are least vigilant,' Simeon told him. His voice and his gaze were calm, but a pulse throbbed visibly in his cheek, and those who knew him well could sense his outrage.

'Damn it! Do not feed me platitudes,' Rufus bellowed. 'Are you not safe in your own church?'

'No,' Simeon answered mildly. 'If Satan did not bother to attend our holy church, how would he procure the souls of our good Christian men?'

'Too slick an answer,' Rufus retorted, 'and so pious it sickens me. What more will it take to persuade you to walk away from this place, Simeon? Come home. Give up this defiant game with murderers and bring your family to a place of safety.'

'I cannot leave here, Father.'

'Cannot? Are you so obsessed with this Beverley that you defy your common sense even when death stares at you from your own communion chalice?'

'I cannot leave here,' Simeon repeated.

'Elvira can.'

'She is free to do as she wishes, but she will not go with you while I remain.'

'Then let me at least take Peter. Let me take him away from here and give him the protection he deserves.'

Simeon shook his head. 'Peter will not leave Beverley.'

'*Will not?*' Rufus demanded. 'Damn it, Simeon, he's only ten years old.'

'He is the Keeper at the Shrine.'

'What in heaven's name does *that* mean? He is a child. He needs protection.'

Thorald, still stunned by the certainty in Daniel Hawk's announcement that their enemy still lived, thrust his great bulk between father and son in an effort to defuse their simmering tempers. 'These matters are better settled in another place and at a more appropriate time,' he growled. 'For now we have more pressing things to quarrel over. A would-be murderer lies dying in our infirmary and, if Daniel Hawk is right, Simeon's deadly enemy has already taken steps towards exacting his revenge.' He glowered into the face of Rufus de Malham. 'Would you have your son desert his friends and flee while under attack?'

'I would have him safe,' Rufus countered.

'Then you do him a grave disservice, sir. He is no coward to turn tail and run when he is most needed.'

'Thorald! Rufus! Enough of this.' The little monk from Flanders pushed himself between them and, with a palm placed firmly against each of their chests, exerted pressure enough to ease the two apart. 'The Mass is cancelled, the altar plate will be removed and the church locked up until the evening service. Come with us to the infirmary, Rufus. When this issue has been settled, you will have every chance to speak to Simeon on family matters.'

Both men conceded grudgingly and followed the others, in silence, to the door. At the bridge Simeon paused very briefly to lay his palm on the bridge supports, a private ritual he never failed to observe. Behind him, Daniel fell into step with Thorald.

'If Cyrus de Figham still lives, Thorald, you will not be accused of his murder as we feared. We believe the papal legate has arrived in England. When the weather lifts, he will come here with his team of inquisitors and papers for your trial. In the light of what we now suspect, the charges against you will be dismissed and his journey will prove fruitless. Does that not please you?'

'It pleases me not at all,' the big man replied. 'Look at Richard. See how he churns inside to know that the killer of Canon Bernard does not fry for all eternity in hell's fires. No, Daniel, it does not please me at all. I would rather take my chances with the legate's court than have that snake-eyed priest still drawing breath.'

'Thorald, from now onward you must be extra vigilant. You too will become a target for his rage. He'll not forgive you for aiming that knife at his back.'

'I know that, Daniel.'

'What a pity for all that you did not succeed.'

'I will, the next time,' the priest assured him grimly.

Daniel was shocked at that. 'Do you intend to try again?'

'Aye, I must.'

Daniel dropped back and watched the brooding priest stride on ahead, his footsteps ringing on the timbers of the bridge. The young priest was shocked by the murderous glint he had seen in Father Thorald's eyes. Killing a man in the heat of a riot, with Simeon lying stoned and lifeless on the ground while his persecutor fled, was an act that could be argued before any court as justifiable slaying. Plotting the murder of a fellow priest, a high-ranking canon and a powerful figure within the Church, was more than even the most sympathetic consul would accept. Cyrus de Figham was missing, presumed dead, and yet his venom had reached St Peter's altar and was already creeping into the hearts of honest men. Even in his absence, old wounds were being reopened and old hatreds rekindled, and Daniel knew what he had always known, that Beverley would know no peace while Cyrus de Figham lived.

The man was dead when they returned to question him, and the stool beside his bed was empty. A search was made of the grounds for Tobias. Every building and every inch of the woodland came under the scrutiny of priests, clerks and labourers who feared the child had crept away to grieve in solitude. By now fresh snow was falling and it promised to be another bitterly cold night, too harsh for a poorly clad eight-year-old boy to spend out in the open.

Simeon and Elvira returned to the scriptorium for their early evening meal, both deeply concerned that Tobias had not been found.

'He told me he lived in a peaceful country house,' Elvira said. 'He was taken in as an orphan and treated well. Until he accompanied the family on their journey to the abbey at Meaux to visit a dying relative, he had never known real hardship or cruelty. He is an innocent, Simeon. He has no idea how to survive alone or how to judge a good man from an evil one. God forbid that he is on the streets alone, with no one to watch out for him.'

'He is no longer in St Peter's grounds, that much we know,' Simeon told her. 'When the Mass was stopped, everyone ran to the church and the gates were left unguarded. Even a child can open the little Judas gate with ease from the inside. He must have slipped away unseen in all the confusion. Perhaps he believed we would turn him out when his master died.'

Elvira sighed heavily and touched her brow with her fingers. 'Then we failed him, Simeon. Suppose he is trying to find his way back to St Dominic's to tell his mistress of her husband's death? The poor child might be out there right now, lost again on the marshes.'

'After the curfew bell, I'll take a lantern and search the marshes until I find him.' Simeon promised.

Rufus and Richard both agreed to join Simeon in the search. While they ate their meal they heard the distant calling of Tobias's name as other searchers still combed the grounds for the boy. When Simeon noticed that Rufus was staring at the golden brow piece which hung from his neck, he lifted it over his head and held it out for closer inspection. Rufus had heard its story from Elvira. She had taken it from the harness of the warhorse that had burst its heart to carry the infant Peter to Beverley, then offered it to Simeon, who had worn it now for a decade. It bore a neat round hole in its very centre, where the bolt from a crossbow, fired by a hidden bowman, would have killed Simeon but for the cushioning thickness of the gold.

'Solid gold,' Rufus observed. 'The animal that wore this brow piece was a magnificent beast, by all accounts. Is this its name, engraved here in the gold?'

'Cephas,' Simeon told him. 'Do you know it?'

'I have heard of it.'

Simeon glanced at Elvira and shared her smile. 'It is the same in Roman, Greek and Hebrew,' he explained. 'Cephas, the Rock; the name Christ gave to his own priest, Peter.'

'Peter?' Rufus echoed.

'Aye,' Simeon told him, 'and I swear I didn't know of this brow piece when I named the boy. My choice of his name at the baptism is just one more puzzle within the greater mystery.'

At Osric's signal – a brief, distinctive tattoo on the wood with the hilt of his dagger – the scriptorium door was unbarred and he was admitted. Thorald was with him, and both wore grim expressions.

'The man who died,' Osric demanded. 'Did no one think to strip him so that a search could be made of his clothes?'

'He was ill and half-frozen,' Simeon told him, rising from his seat, 'and no Christian should be stripped unless death stares him in the face. What is it, Osric? What have you found on him?'

Osric drew in his breath and shrugged his shoulders. 'He came to kill you, Simeon. He very nearly killed us all with that poisoned horn, and he might yet succeed in his unholy quest.'

'What? But how? What threat can he be to us if he's dead?'

'What threat indeed,' the infirmarian answered bitterly. 'He has brought a pestilence to us, Simeon. He has brought the spotted flux.'

The remains of the afternoon were spent locating and questioning every person who had tended the sick man. Elvira and Edwin were thought to be most at risk – Elvira

104

because of the open wound on her palm from the poisoned horn, Edwin because his falling sickness rendered him less robust than the others. Those who had bathed the man's head and changed his soiled linens were brought to the infirmary and exposed to Osric's scrutiny. Those who had given him food and water, or had merely kept him covered with a blanket during his fever, were dosed with a herbal remedy and made to scrub their hands with salt and beast fat. While these activies were at their height, Daniel Hawk drew Simeon aside and begged the priest's leave to return to his master's house.

'I must go back. If I am missed and discovered here . . .'

He left the rest unsaid, knowing that Simeon was familiar with this particular anxiety. Simeon had helped Osric tend the young priest's injuries when his master had last discovered him at St Peter's. Father Wulfric had kicked and beaten him without mercy, then turned him out, penniless and friendless, to reflect upon the folly of his ways. That which Father Wulfric owned, he owned exclusively. He shared with neither friend nor priest nor God, and that he owned his priest, body and soul, was in no doubt. The men of St Peter's had bound up Daniel's ribs, stitched his deeper wounds, massaged the swelling from his damaged muscles and managed to save the sight in his injured eye, and after all that, despite himself, he had been on hand in Wulfric's hour of greatest need. If love runs close to hatred, as some men claim, Father Daniel Hawk and his master gave of both in equal measure.

Now Simeon shook the young priest's hand and thanked him for his efforts at St Peter's. 'It was good of you to come, Daniel, and then to stay so long to help with the cleansing.'

'Osric believes he can keep the infection contained. Is that possible?'

'It is, if this is the common flux or the puking sickness, or any one of the wet distempers that come and go with the seasons. But if, as I suspect, it proves to be a pestilence, such as leprous flux or cankerous belly, this town of ours will have no hope of fighting it.' He spread his hands. 'There is little

105

any of us can do against such visitations. If we get it, we get it. If we die, we die. And if we live, we praise God for our deliverance.'

'God's will,' Daniel agreed without conviction. 'We priests teach that He gave free will to man, and yet we must accept all things, without complaint, as *His* will. Does that paradox not perplex you, Simeon?'

'My friend, we men are the strangest of all God's creatures,' Simeon smiled. 'Our faith is littered with inconsistencies and contradictions.'

'And yet we are made in His image,' Daniel added. 'Are we to believe that He, too, is as flawed as His own creation?'

'We believe as we must,' Simeon replied. 'We trust Him, and that's the essence of our faith.'

Daniel squared his shoulders and drew his cloak about him. 'I must be gone. Edwin and his sister are waiting to speak with you. Talk to them, Simeon. Listen to what they have to say.'

'About the dark arts? About babbling old women and painted ivories? Such things are best avoided, Daniel, even in conversation.'

'You are wrong,' Daniel insisted. 'How can you ignore what you have seen for yourself today. The Serpent is Cyrus de Figham. The Cherub is Peter with his goat. Fortune's Fool is the dead man with his poisoned horn. The Grim Reaper is Death, and the dead man brings the pestilence. Can you disregard all that and not even question what else is written there?'

'Painted ivories,' Simeon repeated. 'Pagan trinkets.'

'"All men are pagans in their souls." Your own words, Simeon. At least keep an open mind. Speak to the children.'

'Very well. If it puts your mind at ease, my friend. Now go, before Wulfric de Morthlund rouses himself from his bed and starts screaming for his priest. God's blessing, Daniel.'

Edwinia had been standing in the shadows with several sheets of paper hidden behind her back. When Father Daniel left the room and Simeon crooked his finger in her direction, she came shyly forward but did not raise her eyes to his face. She stood in awe of this charismatic priest, and she knew he could read what was written on another's soul. The priest's features softened when he looked at her. She had been close to death when Edwin had brought her to St Peter's, but now she was well and strong and, though much of her childish awkwardness remained, she was growing into womanhood without flaw. He still found himself surprised by her striking likeness to her brother, for he had always believed that twins of different sex were never identical, yet they shared the same features, hair and eyes.

'What is it, child?'

'Forgive me, Father. I have sinned. I used forbidden inks and paper and I . . . we . . . Edwin and myself, we want you to see them for yourself.'

'See what, Edwinia?'

'The runes.'

'Child, our Church does not allow its priests to dabble in pagan things.'

'We know that, Father. Edwin described the pictures so that I could see what he saw on the ivories. I've made a likeness.' She handed him the papers and stood aside while he examined them. 'Edwin says they're an excellent likeness of what he saw.'

Simeon spread the sheets on a table and studied them in turn. The drawings were excellent and the name of each was spelled out in letters worthy of any trained scribe.

'Edwinia, did *you* produce these drawings?'

'Yes, Father. Edwin tells me I have a talent.'

'You have indeed. Who mixed your colours and trimmed your pens?'

'I did, Father.'

'But who has been your tutor? Who taught you these specialised skills?'

'Nobody taught me, Father Simeon. Every day I fetch and carry for the scribes and copyists. I watch how they mix their inks and trim their quills, and I clean away the scraps and finished bottles at the end of their day's work.'

'Then in future you will be given a special tutor of your own and time to study every day. Such talent, such eye for line and detail, must not be wasted. To my knowledge no woman has ever been trained as a scribe, Edwinia. You will be the first.'

'But the pictures, Father. Edwin says you must study the pictures and—'

'Let me keep these for a while, Edwinia. Report to Father Horace to begin your training after Mass tomorrow. You are forgiven for using the inks and paper. Return now to your chores.'

'But Father—'

'To your chores, child.'

'Yes, Father.' As she turned away, Edwinia dared to look him in the eye. 'Father Simeon, when I become a scribe my name will not appear in any book. My benefactor will not dare flout custom by allowing his scribe to be identified as a woman. Perhaps I will not be the first. Perhaps there have been many women scribes before me and we simply assume them to be men.'

As Simeon watched her walk away, he regretted that her talents had not been discovered earlier, and he wondered how many women scribes had toiled over intricate drawings and never seen their names acknowledged by posterity. It was Antony who brought his thoughts back to the matter in hand. He was bending over the table with his gaze fixed on the drawings.

'You dismissed her without responding to her concerns,' he muttered gravely.

'I will not condone that boy's behaviour by word or by deed,' Simeon told him.

'But everything is here, in the pictures. We cannot ignore this.'

'Nor can we allow our children to think we might countenance such things. Our task is to keep them to the Christian way.'

'But this is prophecy,' Antony protested. 'What the woman foretold is happening, right here and now. Some influence beyond our understanding must have sent that boy to Old Hannah's house for these. We should interpret the rest and be prepared for whatever is to come.'

'I know that, but I do not want Edwin or his sister to know it.' Simeon looked at the empty bed and shook his head. 'It baffles me, Antony. Where is *the other*? Why did *he* not warn us of these events, instead of leaving us to stand or fall by chance? For ten years the Guardian at the Gate has come to us whenever some disaster has been about to befall us. Why did he not come this time?'

'He did,' Antony told him.

'What? *The other* was here? When did he come? Who saw him?'

'Speak to your father, Simeon. He saw him with Peter on three or four occasions and merely assumed him to be the boy's protector, one of our priests who chose to keep his hood well forward. Speak to Rufus, and then speak to Peter. Something is brewing.'

'Perhaps I was right to trust my instincts,' Simeon nodded. 'It is not over.'

'No, Simeon, not over. God forbid that I should be proven right in this, but I suspect the worst is only just beginning.'

CHAPTER EIGHT

The body of the dead man was covered with a sheet and carried out to a patch of frozen ground on the far side of the infirmary. A man was set to guard it from rats and other scavengers, and no one was to be allowed to touch it unless the infirmarian himself was present.

Osric threw back the sheet on Simeon's insistence. Viewing the body naked for the first time, he recognised at once the many signs that might have alerted them all, had they only taken the precaution of removing his clothes. To strip a sick man naked was to invite his death. True Christians came into the world and left it in a state of nakedness. In the span between they reserved the right to be clothed, and in so doing kept death's hand from reaching out to touch their vulnerable bodies.

'I believed his sickness to be ergot poisoning,' Simeon told Osric. 'The boy said he ate bad bread.'

Osric shook his head and adjusted the cloth that covered his mouth and nostrils. 'Ergot poisons the brain as well as the body. It causes its victims to see and hear terrible things, to rave like madmen, even to tear off their own flesh in an effort to dislodge monsters others cannot see. It confuses the eye and the mind. Remember that, Simeon. This was not ergot poisoning.'

'What then? The deadly pestilence?'

'Who knows? Green potato poisoning can produce these symptoms, so too can a number of other edible poisons. Those marks on his body might be infected vermin bites, or even frostbite turned wet and florid by the application of heat. I fear the worst, Simeon, that we have been visited by a pestilence.'

Simeon stooped to examine the body more closely, though Osric held him back when he might have touched it. 'His belly is swollen as in the leprous flux, and very hard, as in cankerous belly.'

'Aye, it could be either,' Osric agreed. 'Or perhaps it swelled because the wretch was starving. That could also explain the vomiting and flux. A belly too long without food often expels the very stuff it craves or else the bowel is too weak to contain it. That bloody flux could be an indication that his insides had begun to putrefy. Like the sweats and the swelling, the vomiting and the blotches on the skin, it could well tell us that he died of famine fever.'

'God spare us that.'

'If that proves so, we both know the extent of our problem, Simeon. It will spread from those who starve to those who don't, and within a few short days the dead in this overcrowded town might well outnumber the living.'

'This is an abomination,' Simeon said, his eyes dark blue above the stark white of his mouth cloth. 'How can we even begin to challenge an enemy we cannot recognise?'

'We make an educated guess and challenge it nonetheless,' Osric replied. He snatched up the grave cloth and drew it over the body with a flourish. 'Have the body tightly bound,' he told the two men who had carried it from the infirmary. 'Do not touch it with your bare hands and keep your lower faces covered until you are well away from it.' To Simeon he added, 'It must be burned.'

'What? Osric, we are not heathens here, we are *Christians*. We cannot *burn* a man. He must have a Christian burial. That much is his right.'

Osric turned and fixed his friend with a glare. 'Preach me

111

no sermons, Simeon de Beverley. He forfeited any rights he had to common Christian decency when he set out to poison a hundred innocent people in your church. And that body could well be the starting point of a plague. I will not allow thousands of people to be put at risk for the sake of our Christian observances. God is big enough to pluck a soul from the flames if He desires it. We burn the body.'

As Simeon moved away Osric held back, his brows drawn down as he stared at the body. He would not examine this corpse more closely, even with his mouth and nose covered, but something in the way it lay disturbed him. He had no doubt that his own diagnosis, limited though it was, touched on the truth. Some horrible disease or inner poison had brought this stranger to the very threshold of death, but the more he stared, the more he was convinced that the man had left this world by a different but equally sinister route. The head hung at a peculiar angle, even for a dead man, and the neck, though not discoloured, was oddly askew. As a soldier Osric recognised the signs. This man was dead because his neck was broken.

Two sisters from the convent beyond Keldgate Bar had stayed behind at St Peter's after the Mass. A priest brought them to Osric at the infirmary, one complaining of stomach cramps, the other of a constant desire to vomit. The priest was from St Anne's and also seemed unwell. His face was flushed and his hands unsteady, and there was a glint of fever in his eyes.

In Osric's absence, Elvira had questioned the women.

'I believe the younger one is approaching the onset of her courses,' she explained in a whisper. 'She believes her pains are due to the waxing and waning of the moon. She sweats, but only when the cramps are on her.'

'I'll give her an infusion for the pain,' Osric offered. 'But you, Elvira, can shoulder the burden of explaining to her the demands of Nature on a woman's body. What of the older one?'

Elvira smiled, though sadly. 'She vomits and staggers on rising, and her belly is swollen.'

112

Osric raised his brows. 'Then let her speak to a midwife.'

'She is an unmarried woman, Osric, one of the Little Sisters of Mercy.'

'Then someone should advise her that a woman's mercy should be tempered with restraint. I have no easy cure for the morning sickness. I can do no more than send her home to await her birthing time. That priest of theirs looks sickly. Bring him to me.'

Simeon helped himself to sweetened water from the pot Elvira had heated over the fire. He watched the priest protest as he was stripped and his skin examined, then saw the horror in his face as Osric led him, now robbed of all objections, to a bed in the farthest corner of the infirmary. 'He says he was served mutton stew from a badly damaged copper pot,' Osric confided. 'It could be the deadly copper poisoning. So, Simeon, do we pray for his sake that it is not so, or do we pray for our sakes that it is?'

That night two parties of searchers left St Peter's immediately after the curfew bell, one heading into the town to ask at every dwelling and campfire for Tobias, the other carrying lanterns on to the marshes. Of Simeon's group, only Thorald, Antony and Richard were allowed to venture far into the wasteland. The others were sent beyond the boundary walls to search amongst the destitutes and thieves. Their voices echoed on the crisp night air as they called out Tobias's name and strained their ears for the answering call that never came.

When the search was at last abandoned, Simeon resumed his daily chore of running around the boundary of the town. His thoughts were troubled and the steady, rhythmic pounding of his feet gave him some ease. He knew, now, of Cuthbert's intention to surrender his canon's seat in Simeon's favour. He knew that Peter had met that mysterious, black-robed figure they called *the other*, the self-styled Guardian at the Gate, whose presence always foreshadowed some disaster. He knew that Cyrus de Figham lived and planned his murder, and that one unfortunate man had been bribed to carry the poisoned cup. More than this, he knew that the prophecy in

113

the runes was already unfolding. There was more to come, and what he had seen in Edwinia's drawings was enough to strike cold chills into his heart.

'Tobias! Tobias!'

The distant calling of a single searcher was like the doleful hooting of an owl in the darkness. He squinted at the pale snow lying ahead of him as he ran, with half his mind intent on placing his feet where he knew there would be no hidden pitfall. For ten years he had run this course at dusk and dawn each day. For ten years before that he had prayed for a miracle to heal his crippled foot and make him whole again. Though circumstances forced him to live as the lame scribe he had always been, no force on earth would ever make him waste the gift God had given in answer to his many prayers.

As he ran he prayed for the lost boy who had not been taught to fend for himself and had not yet learned that children were a currency on any market. A sweet-faced child like Tobias could be bought and sold a dozen times by those who saw his worth, for the strength of his limbs, the ability of his fingers to lift a purse, or simply for his innocence.

'God keep him safe,' Simeon prayed, 'and if he is found alive, let it be by a good and honest man.'

It was dark when Tobias finally found the imposing house in Minster Moorgate. He had spent many hours in the Minster church, hiding in the shadows by the altar, hoping to see his master laid to rest in that fine place. He had managed to sleep for a little while in a corner, but cold and stiffness had eventually driven him out into the streets. At nightfall he knew the priests were searching for him. He could hear them calling his name and, sick at heart, he wanted nothing more than to be taken back to the shelter of St Peter's. Only his promise to his dying master kept him from running to meet those calling voices, that and the knowledge that his mistress and her daughter were depending on his faithfulness to them.

He came by way of gloomy alleys and crooked lanes to the canon's house in Moorgate, and when at last he saw it he knew that he had served his master well. It was like no house he had ever seen before. The main door, arched and set with iron stays, was raised well above the level of the ground and had a broad staircase of stone rising to its threshold. Its windows all had glass and heavy drapes. Every room, and there were many, had yet another room built over it. It had two chimneys and therefore many fires, and its roof was neither of thatch nor wood but of heavy, expensive slate.

'Oh yes,' he breathed, staring beyond the wintry garden to the lights behind the windows. 'Lady Martha and little Alice will be happy here.'

A priest in a long blue robe flung back the door as Tobias climbed the steps. His skin was grey in colour and every visible inch of it was pitted with ugly scarring. Tall and stern of feature, he looked down on the boy with his hands clasped in his sleeves.

'What is your business here?'

'I come in search of the Canon of St Matthew's,' Tobias told him, nervously twisting his fingers inside his coat.

'For what reason do you seek him?'

'I bring a message. My master died and I . . .'

'What message?' the priest demanded. 'Speak out boy, before this night wind freezes my bones.'

Tobias cleared his throat and quietly recited the words given to him by that other priest, the one he truly feared. ' "Hold not thy peace, O God of my praise." '

'Is that all?'

'Father Roche had me recite it many times. He said the canon will understand.'

'Wait here.'

The big door closed and Tobias hugged his arms across his body as an icy wind blew snow against the house. He remembered the fire in the great hearth of St Peter's infirmary, the warm bed and the mutton broth, and the body of his master, left unwatched. Soon his task would be completed and his duty done, and he would be free to return to that place until his mistress, relieved of her distress, came to reclaim him.

115

The message was repeated to the canon who was master of the house, and the shivering Tobias was brought inside.

Wulfric de Morthlund, Canon of St Matthew's, was lounging in princely comfort on his couch, his feet raised on a cushioned stool and his head supported by pillows. He wore a gown of bleached linen embroidered at its sleeves and lower edge, and an indoor coat of vivid purple silk. Beside him stood his priest, dressed all in black with silver trims, and his familiar, handsome face was firmly closed.

'Well, well, and what have we here?' Canon Wulfric struggled to his feet with the assistance of his priest. He stood before the couch with his fists on his hips. His ungirdled belly thrust itself before him in several rounds of bulbous flesh, and below his chin were rings of fat. 'Repeat the message, boy.'

'"Hold not thy peace, O God of my praise,"' Tobias recited.

'The cursing psalm.' De Morthlund's chuckle sent tremors through his flesh. 'This lad recites the opening line of psalm one hundred and nine, and I can guess who sent him here with it.' As he took a number of steps forward, Tobias shrank back, intimidated by the canon's great size. 'Come, lad, be brave. You are amongst friends.'

'Yes, sir.' Tobias bowed nervously and, seeking some common ground in his anxiety, looked to the canon's priest and bowed again. 'I know you, sir. I saw you at St Peter's.'

'What?' De Morthlund's voice had lost its gentle tone. 'What did you say? You saw my priest *where*?'

'At St Peter's,' Tobias answered in a small voice.

'*At St Peter's?*' the canon bellowed.

The young priest stepped forward, his smile no more than a stretching of his lips. 'My Lord Canon, the lad is mistaken.' He turned to Tobias with a strange, almost pleading look in his eyes. 'You are mistaken, child.'

'No, sir, you're Father Daniel, Edwin's friend.' He knew he was in error the moment the words were out, for the priest's face drained of colour while the canon's features reddened and he seemed to increase in size before the boy's very eyes. His voice was like thunder in the quiet room.

116

'Speak up, boy. Where and when did you see my priest? And who is this . . . this *Edwin?*'

'Sir, I think . . . I mean, I don't . . .'

'Well, boy?'

Tobias realised that in his innocence he had spoken out of turn. His master would not be proud of him for this. Here was the man who would provide for Lady Martha and her child, who would give them food and warmth and proper protection. Here was the man who would rescue them from their poverty at St Dominic's, as that other priest had promised, and yet somehow Tobias had caused him grave offence.

'Forgive me, sir,' he said, and made a show of staring hard at Daniel's face. The lie tripped easily from his tongue. 'I think you are Father Daniel, known as the Hawk, but I see now that you're not the man who tends the gardens at St Peter's. I was mistaken.'

'I am a priest, not a gardener,' Daniel told him with a smile that betrayed his relief. 'And I live here, in this house, not in that overcrowded rabbit warren called St Peter's.'

'Yes, sir. Er . . . The gardener looks a lot like you, I think.'

Wulfric de Morthlund was only half convinced. He glanced at Daniel through narrowed eyes, then glared suspiciously at Tobias.

'Look again at this priest and speak the truth, or I will have that miserable tongue of yours clipped. Did you ever see Father Daniel at St Peter's?'

'No, sir,' Tobias lied without a qualm.

'Then learn to guard your words,' de Morthlund snapped, 'before you take a priest for a common gardener and declare your error as fact.'

'Yes, sir.'

The fat man waved his heavily ringed fingers impatiently. 'Describe this other priest, this Father Roche who sent you here.'

'He's a tall man, sir, with long black hair. He wears a ring with a big black stone.' Tobias rummaged inside his coat and, eager to redeem himself, held out the letter. 'He sent this, to be handed to yourself and no other.'

The fat man watched the boy as he took the letter, his lips glistening with moisture and his eyes, set deep in his fleshy face, glinting like small polished beads. 'What is your name, boy?'

'Tobias.'

'How old are you?'

'My master told me I'm eight, sir.'

'Eight eh? That's a pretty age, Tobias, a pretty age.'

When the canon read the message from Father Roche he roared with laughter until his eyes grew moist and spittle glistened on his lips. 'So, that arrogant whelp suffers a broken leg and every small inconvenience known to man. He's cold and hungry and deprived of every decent worldly comfort. What's more, he's in the hands of *monks*.'

Daniel Hawk handed his master a cup of warmed ale. 'He hates monks even more than he hates priests.'

'Little wonder, then, that he quotes the cursing psalm through this delightful messenger. He's spitting venom!'

'So, he has survived?'

'Aye, Daniel, he's survived, and when he's fit to stand on his feet, this town will think the Devil has come to call. He sends me greetings and hopes I enjoy his gift.'

'His gift, my Lord Canon?' Daniel Hawk glanced at the boy and felt revulsion crawl along his spine.

'Tobias,' de Morthlund confirmed. 'This pretty child is my gift from Cyrus de Figham.'

Daniel cleared his throat to steady his voice. 'My lord, surely you don't intend to keep him?'

'Indeed I do. He's mine.'

'But if the Church should hear of it . . .'

'Damn the Church,' the fat man spat. 'I'll pay the fine threefold for him if I must, but by God I'll keep him.'

Unaware of the true nature of this exchange, Tobias swallowed his apprehension and dared to ask, 'Am I to stay here, sir? Are you to be my new master?'

Wulfric de Morthlund grabbed the boy and drew him

118

against his massive belly, pressing his small face into the mounds of flesh. 'Yes, my pretty Tobias, I'm your master now. And you, dear boy, will be obedient to *me*, will you not?'

'Yes, sir,' Tobias promised in his innocence.

'Excellent. Excellent. Leave us, Daniel.'

'But my Lord Canon, if I might—'

'Leave us, damn you.'

Daniel Hawk left the room without further protest. When the door was closed behind him, he leaned his back against the wood and pressed his clenched fists to his temples, helpless in his anger. That unprotected child, so keen to prove himself worthy of his master's trust, had carried out his duties to the letter and come like a sacrificial lamb to the man who would destroy him. And Daniel Hawk, sickened to his soul by this easy bartering of innocent flesh, was once again required to stand aside while his conscience raged against the crime. Wulfric de Morthlund was a law unto himself. The Church might fine him heavily for his sin, should it be discovered, but no purse of gold would buy Tobias back his innocence.

The wind blowing in over the marshes had a raw edge and carried swirling squalls. Cold stung Daniel's face as he strode away from the house. He would tramp the streets in sandals and without a cloak, if he must, but he would not stay to witness that small boy's ruin.

CHAPTER NINE

In the dead of night, when the midnight devotions had long been ended and the dawn Mass was still some hours away, those sleeping in the scriptorium were roused from their beds by an urgent rapping at the door. Seven mounted men were at St Peter's gate, all leather clad and weary from their journey. One of them bore the authority of the overlord of Beverley, Geoffrey Plantagenet, Archbishop of York. This man leaned from his mount to clasp Father Simeon's hand in a firm and confident grip. His face was shrouded by a snow-layered hood, but above the frost-whitened growth of stubble on his chin was a pair of sparkling light blue eyes which instantly revealed his identity.

'Fergus de Burton,' Simeon said, suppressing a smile.

'Greetings, Simeon de Beverley.'

'And which of your many faces do you offer us this time, Fergus? Is it friend or foe?'

The young man flashed a white-toothed grin, dampened his finger and held it high in the air, then answered with a mocking question of his own. 'Which way does the wind blow, Simeon?'

Edwin had hurried from his bed on hearing the commotion at the gate. He stood barefooted in the snow as the riders were admitted, his gaze fixed on the familiar laughing face of Fergus de Burton.

'The Janus,' he muttered, signing a hasty cross over his chest. He hurried after Simeon as the priest strode for the scriptorium. Edwin tugged at his sleeve and lowered his voice to a whisper, 'Don't trust him, Father Simeon. You mustn't trust him.'

'Edwin,' Simeon smiled, placing his arm around the shivering lad. 'You of all people must know how well Fergus has served me in the past, and yet he has warned me never to call him friend lest he prove otherwise. He will have my hospitality and my blessing, but he would be the first to call me a fool, were I to trust him.'

Fergus had joined them in time to overhear these words. 'Spoken like the wise man you are,' he announced with a grin. 'Take heed, young Edwin. Be sure you know the adder from the earthworm and you'll not be disappointed if he bites.'

'Not disappointed, perhaps, but dead,' Simeon replied.

'Probably. It's an uncertain world.'

Edwin stood back as the two smiling men walked on together. He liked Fergus de Burton. He would never forget his kindness, or the way he had led his army into Beverley to help save Simeon's life. Edwin was in his debt as many were, and yet he was convinced that here in their midst was the very Janus depicted in the runes. He had known it the instant he'd seen his face again and been reminded of the slippery, ambitious man behind the grin. He followed behind them, eager to warm his feet before the fire.

As the small group passed by the bridge, only Simeon noted the huddled figure of Brother David. He was crouched on the timbers between the two lamps, staring into the drain, and his reverie was not disturbed, either in curiosity or alarm, when the visitors clattered noisily through the gates.

On Simeon's instructions, food, warmed ale and blankets were hurriedly carried to the scriptorium, where the travellers were divested of their snowy cloaks and given stools by the fire. Stripped of his plain outer garments, Fergus stood beside the hearth in fine attire. The gems in his girdle were much increased in number, and his jewelled sword and matching dagger were enough to inspire the envy of

121

any man. In a few short months he had so ingratiated himself with York's archbishop that he had climbed ambition's hill with uncommon ease. Now he looked from Simeon to Rufus and back again with a twinkle in his eye. 'Like brothers,' he said with unconcealed admiration. 'Sir Rufus, I would have known you for his kinsman at half a glance. What brings you to Beverley in the depths of winter?'

'Personal matters,' Rufus told him in tones as frosty as his manner. He had heard too much about this silver-tongued charmer to be anything but uneasy in his presence. Any man who played the Plantagenet like a puppet without the other knowing his strings were pulled was too ingenious for Rufus de Malham's taste.

The young man sat back in his seat and gazed around him. 'I love this place,' he told his host. 'Even at night, when the torches and lamps are lit and the fire burned down, it has a charm that plays upon the senses. How many books are here? How many volumes?'

'Enough for any lifetime,' Simeon answered with a smile. 'Are you here simply to admire my scriptorium, Fergus, or have you some particular business in mind?'

Fergus allowed his smile to slip away. 'For many weeks, Simeon, I have been searching for the body of Cyrus de Figham, and now—'

'Why?' Simeon demanded.

'Why?' Fergus raised his eyebrows in surprise. 'Why? Because it was in my interests, of course.'

'Of course,' Simeon repeated with a smile. 'Go on.'

'If Cyrus de Figham is dead, Geoffrey Plantagenet has a strong claim on his wealth. If he lives, Geoffrey must be seen to act promptly in bringing him to book, and by that he will claim an even more substantial slice of the Figham wealth.'

'A two-pronged attack,' Simeon observed. 'Dead or alive, the Plantagenet will profit. And what, if anything, has your search revealed?'

'That he survived the knifing and the water. De Figham lives.'

'Aye, I believe he does,' Simeon replied.

122

'You knew it? But how?'

'Let us just say I read the signs,' Simeon replied.

'I think it likely that he is on his way here, to Beverley.'

Simeon felt Elvira's hand rest on his shoulder and saw the young man's eyes seek hers as if drawn there by some irresistible force. Beside him, Rufus was tense and wary. The others, Thorald and Osric, Antony and Richard, remained on their feet, conspicuously guarded. Together with young Edwin and those scribes who shared the scriptorium, they hoped to prove a match for the young man and his seven soldiers if this visit went against them.

'He will kill you, Simeon,' Fergus said without emotion, then turned to the glowering priest of St Nicholas and added, 'But first I think he might try to kill *you*, Thorald.'

'We thank you for the warning,' Thorald said, grasping the hilt of his sheathed sword. 'We are well prepared.'

'Are you? With swords and daggers at your belts and bars across your doors? Cyrus de Figham is no ordinary man, my friend, and his hatred is no ordinary hatred.'

'We know that,' Simeon told him, recalling the many who had hoped to drink from the holy chalice.

'He holds two hostages, a woman and her child.'

'We know that, too.'

Elvira closed her eyes against painful memories. 'Two more innocents for him to use as he did poor Alice,' she said. 'Where is your merciful God in all this, Simeon?'

Simeon reached up to cover her hand with his and said to Fergus, 'Tell us what you know.'

Little by little, the story unfolded. Fergus ended with Brother Benedict's part in it.

'One of their novices pilfered much-needed winter stores from his brothers to provide for Cyrus de Figham's every comfort. He even stole the precious relic from their crypt on his instructions. He was a cowardly, weak-willed man. We found his body as we left, lying broken and frozen outside the monastery walls. We think he threw himself from the chapel roof.'

'Killed by his conscience,' Simeon sighed. 'What relic did he steal?'

'A priceless horn decorated with silver and pearls.'

'St Bridget's horn.' Simeon nodded gravely. 'We have it here. It will be returned to the monks in due course. Tell me, Fergus, was the father abbot's death a direct result of the priest's attack on him?'

'Without a doubt. The fall from his blow was enough to shatter his ribs, his collarbone and his hip. He was old. His bones were thin. His lungs filled up with mucus and eventually stopped his breath. There can be no doubt that the blow caused his death.'

'This is de Figham's third deliberate murder that we know of,' Richard told their visitor. 'First his canon, Father Bernard, then the clerk who tried to keep the bell ringing and so prevent Simeon's carting, and now this unfortunate abbot. How many more will die before this monster is brought to book?'

When Simeon explained to his visitor that the stolen relic had contained a deadly poison and had been carried to St Peter's as a gift, the young man's sudden laughter startled them all.

'Poison? *Poison?*' He slapped his thigh with his palm and shook his head. 'And I had assumed he grabbed the relic *for profit!*'

Rufus de Malham was infuriated by this reaction. 'God's teeth! Are you amused by these events?'

Simeon raised a hand to ward off his father's sudden flash of anger. 'Calm down, sir. Fergus means no harm.'

'He mocks us,' Rufus insisted. 'A hundred innocent souls might have died today and all this impudent fool can do is guffaw in our faces.'

'I am not amused, Sir Rufus, merely struck by the irony of it,' Fergus told him amiably. 'Here is proof that swords will not prevent him seeking revenge on those he hates. We assume him dead and yet he lives. We think him a thief and he proves to be a poisoner. However harshly we may judge him, Cyrus de Figham will find a way to surpass that judgement. Hold back your temper, Sir Rufus. I may be outspoken to a fault, but be assured I am not your enemy.'

124

'I am assured that you are self-serving and devious,' Rufus told him bluntly. 'And as such you are not to be trusted.'

'Indeed, you judge me accurately, sir. I neither make pretence nor ask for anyone's trust, since I freely admit to serving others as a means of serving myself.'

'You condemn yourself from your own mouth,' Rufus stated with contempt. 'You are too glib, sir, in this admission of your failings.'

'I am honest,' Fergus said, and the mild-mannered smile slid from his face. 'And if you are as wise as you believe yourself to be, you will judge your *real* enemies with the same measure of hostility.' He turned to Simeon, effectively dismissing Rufus by that simple movement of his head. 'Simeon, your swords and bars will not keep de Figham from his solemn vow to kill you. There are better ways to rid yourself of vermin.'

'Such as?' the priest inquired.

'Use a more persuasive weapon.'

'I will, if one exists.'

'The solution lies at York, in Geoffrey Plantagenet.'

Simeon smiled and answered tightly, 'I would sooner deal with a venomous reptile.'

'Perhaps, but the archbishop's reach is long, and he wields more power than you can ever hope to muster in your defence.'

'And how is that power to be controlled?' Simeon demanded. 'Will you have me bed down with the snake and trust to chance that I am not bitten?'

'I can control his power,' Fergus declared.

'You? Control the Plantagenet? No, Fergus, don't be deceived by your recent success in winning his favours. Neither King Richard, nor his other brother, Prince John, nor even the pope himself would dare to make so grandiose a claim.'

'Because they do not have Geoffrey's measure.'

'And you do?'

'Absolutely.'

'Arrogant nonsense,' Rufus declared. 'The boastings of an upstart youth intoxicated by his own successes.'

125

'I find you quarrelsome, Sir Rufus,' Fergus told him with a smile that belied the hardness in his eyes.

'And I find you pompous, sir,' Rufus replied. 'Simeon, you cannot take his arrogance seriously.'

'If there is one thing I know of Fergus de Burton,' Simeon assured his father, 'it is that he can be trusted to keep his promises, however extravagant they may sound, so long as there is profit to be had in them for himself.'

'Then he is unprincipled.'

'Will you hear me out?' Fergus asked. When Simeon nodded his agreement, Fergus looked to the other men of St Peter's and, one by one, received their forbearance. Only Rufus made objection, but this he did without complaint, merely moving off to claim an empty stool, where he sat with his back turned towards the speaker.

Fergus leaned forward in his seat and voiced the thoughts that had been shaping themselves into a definite plan during the lengthy journey from St Dominic's. The seeds of the plan had been sown when he'd seen Thorald's knife strike Cyrus de Figham in the back, and the fruits of that seed had now ripened for the harvesting.

'I was never for a moment convinced that the knife, or the fall from the bridge, had killed de Figham,' he confessed. 'At first I might have been tempted to finish the job myself, had I found him alive, but I came to believe that others might be better served if he was spared.'

'Or else poisoned at their own altar,' Rufus interjected.

The young nobleman ignored the remark and continued. 'This brother of his, Hector of Lincoln, hopes to obtain what remains of Cyrus de Figham's accumulated wealth. Wulfric de Morthlund wants Cyrus's church for his catamite, Daniel Hawk. Geoffrey Plantagenet wants to be seen to take control and settle the Beverley disputes to the Church's satisfaction and, of course, to its profit. He also needs to make peace with Rome and earn the good countenance of the king. You, Simeon, want the freedom to live in peace.'

'And you?'

'I intend to offer each man his heart's desire, at a price.'

126

'How?'

'First we must corner de Figham and make sure he can do us no further harm. He must be stripped of his high position in the Church if we are ever to curtail, or even control, his power. If we can bring him under the tight jurisdiction of Geoffrey Plantagenet, and at the same time hold you up as the innocent scapegoat and faultless victim of his schemes, the rest will follow as easily as night follows day.'

'And just how do you propose to do all this?'

'By transferring power from him to you, with Geoffrey Plantagenet balancing the scales. When this is done, the Canon of St Martin's will be hampered more securely than any curb brace could guarantee. He will have no man's support, no money for bribes, no priestly robes to hide behind, and no power to bring God-fearing men to their knees in his service. He will be beaten, Simeon, and he will not dare to make a move against you.'

Simeon looked about him at the faces of his friends, then back at the young man with a doubtful expression. 'It is a fine plan, Fergus, and much to everyone's liking, but can it be made to work?'

Fergus nodded. 'It can, and with Geoffrey's blessing. De Figham offended him deeply when he by-passed his authority by writing directly to Rome in the hope of discrediting you, Simeon. Geoffrey still smarts from the sting of that, since it implied that he, our own archbishop, was either incapable of taking firm action in the matter or else reluctant to see true justice served.'

Simeon sat forward on his stool. 'Which in turn implies that he was bribed to stand aside, and since Rome is always swift to assume the worst of him . . .' He glanced at the others again and noted their growing interest. 'Continue, Fergus.'

'In those letters, Cyrus accused you of crimes that were later proved to be his own. His priest, John Palmer, was stoned by the crowd for carrying out his orders and leaving the townspeople to offend against God by executing an innocent man, yourself. De Figham wounded Antony here. Two witnesses to his murder of the clerk have fled to York, where they've been offered Geoffrey's, or, more precisely, *my* protection. More recently, he killed the father abbot of St Dominic's, raped a woman in his care and made off with her child. Need I go on?'

'When it comes to trial, they will have his word against that of lesser men,' Simeon reminded him, 'and we know how easily these learned men are swayed by a show of status.'

'But consider the numbers who will speak out against him, Simeon, once it is known that Geoffrey Plantagenet himself is ready to endorse the charges. His own notoriety will substantiate all the formal charges against him. Bring him to trial and he will be convicted by both his peers and the common people. The court will relieve him of his holy Office and force him to forfeit his wealth to the Church by way of atonement. And if his brother and his archbishop can reap the benefits of his downfall, you and I will become the princes of the day. You will then be free to live openly with your family, and I will have my lands and church at Ravensthorpe.'

'Can all this be achieved if Cyrus de Figham is already on his way here?'

'It can, so long as the papers for his trial are prepared and signed before the papal legate convenes his court.'

Simeon scowled, still searching for a flaw in the plan. 'Geoffrey's word might not suffice,' he offered. 'Rome might assume his interest is feigned in order to prove his own innocence. His enemies will call it a clever ploy to regain favour with his superiors.'

'No, Simeon, they will applaud his change of heart and believe God moves in him.'

'They will do no such thing. When was God ever allowed to share the same room as Geoffrey Plantagenet? He holds the see of York only because King Henry decreed it must be so. They will never be taken in by any so-called change of heart by that irreverent archbishop.'

Here Fergus leaned back in his seat and folded his arms across his chest. 'Oh yes they will, and they will trust implicitly, once I have persuaded him to appease both king and pope by submitting to the yoke of holy orders.'

Simeon looked aghast. 'Now *that* you can never hope to achieve,' he declared. 'He resigned as Bishop of Lincoln on that same point and neither you nor they will ever shift him from it. No, Fergus, Geoffrey Plantagenet will never take holy orders.'

Fergus grinned. 'He will if he thinks the Beverley treasure will come to him as reward, and if he hopes to return the holy relics of St John to his minster.'

The sudden silence around the fire was tangible. Simeon gave his answer in a single word: '*Never!*'

'I am not suggesting that we let him take the bait, only that we allow him to catch the scent. After that, his ordination and the prestige it brings will be their own reward.'

'I will not barter Beverley's treasures,' Simeon told him firmly. 'Nor will I use the relics of our saint to tempt this man. You ask too much, Fergus. I cannot agree to risk the confiscation of our treasure and our holy relics.'

'I know. That's why I would never ask it of you, Simeon.'

'Then how will you tempt the archbishop? With what authority?'

Fergus smiled and spread his hands. 'Authority? Since when does Geoffrey Plantagenet concern himself with authority? Hints and rumours are enough to stir him into action. Whispers of plots and hidden wealth are sufficient to heat his blood. A man needs neither genuine authority nor specific words to move the likes of him.'

'He will break you, Fergus, when you fail to deliver.'

'No, Simeon, he will enjoy the chase and revel in the approval of his monarch and his pope. Whatever the outcome, Geoffrey will love me for it.'

Simeon returned the young man's grin. 'My father sees you clearly, Fergus de Burton. You own the arrogance and the effrontery of the Devil. So, how can we be sure that de Figham is not in York at this very moment, bending the ear of your fickle archbishop in your absence, plotting against us while we conspire against him?'

'Because he left St Dominic's only six hours ahead of me, travelling on a donkey and with a woman and her child to slow his progress. He came this way by the roughest and most dangerous route. Like all wounded animals, he heads straight for his own lair. I believe his brother will keep him hidden until his defence can be prepared for the papal legate.'

It was Thorald who asked, 'How can you be so confident that this Hector, this obscure curate who now styles himself as a nobleman, will fall in with our plans?'

Fergus grinned and spread his hands in that familiar gesture of innocence so transparent to those who knew him. 'Why else would I have sent for him?'

'*You* brought Hector here?' Simeon asked.

'Of course. It was expedient, since there is much property and family wealth at stake. Hector has nothing of his own and is therefore keen to profit from his brother's fall from grace, if not from his death. He must also stand firmly with his Church in condemning his brother's more outrageous crimes lest he find himself discredited by association. Rome will expect him to bring Cyrus to heel, to help him see the folly of his ways and repent of his sins. What more worthy task could be undertaken by this pious man of Lincoln than to claim a kinsman's wealth as he saves his soul?'

'Fergus, do you sleep easy in your bed at night?'

'Like a baby,' Fergus grinned.

'And how fares your conscience amid all this elaborate double-dealing?'

'Well enough,' the young man told him. 'I do not create the ambitions and desires of others. I simply use what I find, and I use it well.'

For a long time they tossed Fergus's plan this way and that, sifting for every flaw and error, modifying this point, trimming that, until it seemed there was no better way. Only Rufus was reluctant to accept it.

'How can you trust the word of a man like de Burton?' he demanded of his son.

'Father, you view the world in black and white,' Simeon told him. 'For you a situation is either one thing or another, this or that, with a clear division between the two.'

'You either trust him or you do not,' Rufus insisted.

'There are shades and subtleties here that must seem strange to you.'

Rufus was exasperated. 'The wine is poisoned. Men drink from the chalice. Death occurs. What subtlety am I missing?'

Simeon chuckled. 'Fergus is right, do you know that? You *are* argumentative. You lead with your temper.'

'Aye, and there was a time when you were of the same mould. It seems to me that eighteen years of submission and obedience to the Church have reshaped your manly moods to priestly tolerance.'

Thorald answered that with his familiar deep-throated growl. 'Be warned by one who knows him well, sir. Your son's temper is a sleeping beast. When it stirs, no man is safe.'

'And glad I am to hear it,' Rufus nodded. 'Well, are you priests content that a man like Geoffrey Plantagenet might yet be fully ordained by Rome as your archbishop?'

'He holds the see of York, ordained or not,' Thorald reminded him. 'We live with such dilemmas where we must.'

'What hypocrisy,' Rufus retorted. 'An undeserving man takes holy orders to suit his ends, attends a splendid ceremony with only half a heart, and is henceforth revered by all.'

'God might surprise him, once he is ordained,' Simeon smiled. 'Remember that Beverley's one-time provost, St Thomas à Becket, was a worldly man while in his Office until he was persuaded to take the cloth. The taking of it made a saint of him.'

Rufus de Malham stared at his son, his features set and his blue eyes narrowed. 'You cannot possibly believe such a falsehood.'

'Falsehood? It is a matter of record, Father.'

'No, Simeon, it is a matter of record that Becket's ordination gave him what he wanted: *power*! He used that power to further his own ambitions and to bring his king to submission. It was power, not grace, that made him take such a stand, and he was killed so that his power could be curbed.'

'Thomas Becket was a *saint*,' Father Richard protested.

'Priest's talk! He was a man like any other. The people *called* him a saint to appease God for his murder. The Pope *declared* him a saint to show that priests who oppose the princes of the realm will themselves become the princes of the Church. Do not babble to me of *faith* when what you describe is lust for power.'

'Father, your words astound me.'

'I think not. You are a priest, Simeon. If you serve the Church then you must be aware of its hypocrisies. What astounds me is that you so readily accept them.'

Simeon offered a weary smile. His father's first visit to Beverley in many years had proved so eventful that he was left angry and frustrated by it all. In looking to let off steam according to his nature, he was spoiling for a fight on any pretext.

'I will not quarrel with you,' Simeon insisted, 'not on a matter we can neither prove nor disprove to anyone's personal satisfaction. Let us agree to a truce and seek our beds. We priests must rise again in an hour for the Morning Office.'

From the shadows by Simeon's corner shrine a small figure emerged and stepped into the light. Young Peter had missed no word that had been spoken in the scriptorium. He was a listener, an eavesdropper by inclination. His talent for stealing the secrets of others, assisted by his knowledge of underground tunnels and openings, made him privy to even the most clandestine of meetings.

'Were you listening to our conversation?' Simeon asked him.

'I was, Father.'

Simeon nodded. 'And in your opinion, should we trust our visitor?'

Peter looked solemnly at Fergus de Burton, then briefly bowed his head in greeting. There was a twinkle in his eyes as he shook his head and said, 'He does not ask that we trust him, Father, only that we believe in his will to advance in Geoffrey Plantagenet's service.'

'Ah, but will he succeed?'

'Oh yes,' the boy said lightly. 'He will succeed.'

While Simeon seemed content with the boy's assumptions, Rufus uttered a despairing groan, marched to the lower end of the scriptorium and flung himself down on his bed. He was too weary and too bewildered to argue that grown men were fools to seek the opinions of a ten-year-old child.

Exhausted though he was, Fergus de Burton slept for only an hour in his chair by the fire. As the prayer bell began its tolling to herald in the dawn, he sprang to his feet and stirred his men with his boot. Simeon, already robed for Mass, walked with him as far as the gate. From there they could see the great eastern window of the Minister, shining dully as it reflected a colourless sky hung low with unshed snow.

'One moment, Fergus de Burton.'

Father Cuthbert beckoned from the sheltering overhang of the infirmary roof where he had been sitting for the better part of an hour. He rose from his seat as the young man approached and pressed a roll of paper into his hand. 'For Geoffrey Plantagenet. Will you deliver it?'

'I will indeed.' The young man smiled.

'Say nothing to Simeon for now. He knows only that I am considering the matter.'

'He'll shoulder the burden willingly,' Fergus assured him.

'Ah, so you guess the contents of my letter?'

Fergus nodded. 'St Peter's needs a helmsman with a stronger arm, and Simeon needs the rank to match his enemies. It was only a matter of time before you stepped aside in his favour.'

Father Cuthbert strained his stiffened neck in order to

meet the other's gaze. 'You are wise, young sir, but are you to be trusted?'

'In this I am, Father Cuthbert. Geoffrey will have this letter as soon as I arrive in York. More than that, I feel I must urge him to act upon it promptly.'

'Thank you. You will be acting in Simeon's service.'

Fergus de Burton stooped to speak against the old man's ear. 'I'll be acting in *my own* service, Father Cuthbert, and for that reason you may trust me in this matter.'

'You speak against yourself at every turn,' Father Cuthbert smiled, 'but you have a good heart, Fergus, however loudly you profess the contrary.'

Fergus winked at the old canon. 'I, too, would like to see Simeon raised up beyond his present state.'

'I believe you would, since you obviously admire him, despite yourself.'

'Aye, I do. Your Simeon de Beverley is a worthy man.'

'Worthy indeed. Will you meet with the Jew while you are in York?'

'I may have business with Aaron,' Fergus replied.

'Then be so good as to convey my greetings and tell him it is time. He will understand.'

'I will do that, Father Cuthbert,' Fergus promised with a bow.

Cuthbert signed the cross and gave the young man his blessing. 'May God speed you on your journey, Fergus de Burton, and just as speedily bring you back to St Peter's.'

Two priests were hurrying to Mass. Simeon, who had stood aside to allow Fergus and Cuthbert to speak privately, stopped the priests and bade them assist their canon across the icy ground to his church, then fell into step with Fergus as he walked to the gate where his men were already mounted and hooded. As they passed the infirmary, a dark-haired ragamuffin emerged from the eaves and walked towards them with his head lowered. He collided with Fergus, who grabbed him by the hood and held him fast.

'Your pardon, sir. Forgive my clumsiness.'

'Clumsy be damned,' Fergus growled, hoisting up the boy

until his feet were off the ground. With his free hand he ripped open his struggling captive's tunic and shook him until his spoils dropped to the ground.

Simeon stooped to retrieve them. 'This is Osric's marble pestle,' he said in amazement. 'And Richard's crucifix, and Elvira's turtle-shell comb. And look at these ... salt beef and cheese and ...' He picked several coins from the snow and held them out. 'You wretched boy. Have you dipped your thieving fingers into our alms box?'

'This is as sly a thief as ever I saw in action,' Fergus told him, then grabbed the boy by the chin and looked hard into his sullen face. 'Mark his features well, Simeon. He will bear the thief's brand before he sees another year.'

The boy was of Norman colouring, with jet-black hair and dusky skin, a handsome, fine-featured lad beneath the grime. He stared back at Simeon defiantly, then bared his good, strong teeth in a fearless snarl and resumed his struggles to be free. Something in his eyes drew Simeon's attention, a subtle shift of colouring, a touch of grey within the darker depths. He was reminded of other eyes that had the same quicksilver shifts.

'What is your name, boy?'

The dark eyes fixed him with a glare and Simeon stepped back smartly as the boy cleared his throat and spat in his direction. He signalled to Osric, who had already missed his stolen property and begun a search for the culprit. The bearded man came running and took in the situation at a glance.

'Make sure his face is known to everyone here,' Simeon told the infirmarian. 'Then put him outside the gates and keep him out. St Peter has no need of a thief who would rob his modest alms box.'

The lad was energetic in his struggles to be free, but Osric tucked him firmly under his arm and carried him, wriggling and kicking, back to the infirmary. There he would be scrutinised by priests and labourers alike, so that all would

135

recognise him on sight, should he try to slip back into their enclosure.

At the gates Fergus squinted at the sky as he buckled his heavy cloak across his chest.

'We will have scant daylight again today,' he observed.

'Why not stay a while longer, at least until full dawn?'

'No, Simeon. Every hour that passes is one more hour in Cyrus de Figham's favour.'

'God speed you to York, then.'

'And God speed your father home to Malham,' Fergus grinned. 'His temper runs too close to the surface for my liking.'

'He does not like you, Fergus.'

'Nor I him. Does that trouble you?'

'Not at all. His back is broad enough to bear the consequences of his manners.' Simeon smiled and shook the young man's hand. 'God speed, my friend.'

'Friend?' Fergus feigned a dislike of the word, dampened his forefinger and held it high. 'It is a fickle wind,' he reminded the priest.

After Morning Mass Simeon hurried to the Minster to join those choral priests who were singing the dawn devotions. A robed priest spoke to the man who shared his choir stall and, after some whispering and shuffling of feet, he found Father Daniel standing beside him. The '*Te Deum*' filled the church, the rich male voices rising and falling in perfect harmony. It was a heart-lifting sound, enriched by hope and simple thanks for the safe arrival of another day. In the ebbs and flows of the chant, Daniel Hawk passed on his message to the man who was, in all but official sanction from his archbishop, the Canon of St Peter's.

'Cyrus de Figham is alive. He lies injured in a monastery near—'

'Near Meaux,' Simeon cut in. 'St Dominic the Mailed. He is recovered and is already on his way here. Your news is late, Daniel.'

'Wulfric has Tobias.'

136

'Dear God . . . How?'

'He arrived at the house with a message. He was sent there by Cyrus de Figham as payment for Wulfric's cooperation.'

'Is there no end to this?'

'He came like a lamb to the slaughter, and now . . .'

'And now Wulfric de Morthlund has him,' Simeon finished in an angry whisper.

Daniel leaned his back against the choir stall, waiting for the surge of singing to subside. He was a man whose faith was in confusion. He lived in sin and felt himself excluded from the presence of his God, and yet that same God touched his heart so often, and so painfully, that little in his life could offer peace or satisfaction. He turned to look at Simeon now, his scarred face a reminder of the deeper wounds that pained him in their rawness.

'Wulfric keeps him locked in an upper room, beyond anyone's reach. He is determined not to give him up. There is nothing we can do to help him now, Simeon.'

The voices swelled for the final, uplifting verses, and Simeon closed his eyes and felt the deep, familiar sounds wash over him. When he opened his eyes again, the stall beside him was empty and Daniel Hawk was heading for the door.

'God help Daniel in his turmoil,' Simeon breathed. 'And God help the innocent child in that debaucher's clutches.'

He clasped his hands together and began to mutter the Jesus prayer, that centuries-old prayer recited by monks and priests to induce a quiet euphoria through which they might commune more easily with God. The Jesus prayer was his spiritual balm, his mantra and his key to inner quiet.

'Lord Jesus Christ, Son of God, have mercy upon me.' His hands gripped each other so tightly that his knuckles began to pale. 'Lord Jesus Christ, Son of God, have mercy upon me.' His eyes snapped open, then narrowed into slits. 'Lord Jesus Christ, Son of . . . By all that's Holy, I will not sit still for this.'

The choral priests stood back in amazement as Simeon, always the calm and deferential priest, pushed his way from the choir stalls and strode in grim-faced fury from the church.

CHAPTER TEN

Hector of Lincoln rose soon after dawn. He had slept beneath covers of quilted silk, on a linen mattress stuffed with duck down, silken pillows for his head and hot bricks at his feet. A fire of peat still smouldered in the grate, and the room was warm and furnished with every possible comfort. One night was all it took to convince him that he, the humble Hector, curate of the modest church of St Mark's, Lincoln, was more than suited to the lavish lifestyle so long enjoyed by his younger brother.

Figham House belonged exclusively to Cyrus de Figham, but by rights it was Hector's inheritance. He would have been the master here, cradled in the lap of luxury, had he been blessed with but a fraction of his brother's cunning. It was to have come to him on his ordination into the priesthood, but while he had searched his soul and taken good counsel on the sincerity of his calling, Cyrus had hastily taken the cloth and, by his swift and calculating move, claimed the prize for himself. Thus their ageing grandfather had been offered the priestly grandson he desired, and he had rewarded Cyrus's cunning in fullest measure. Hector had been judged disobedient by comparison, and henceforth the favours of his grandfather had been withdrawn. He had paused too long to examine his conscience in the matter of his

138

vocation, and so had allowed a wilier man to prosper at his expense.

'Esau and Jacob,' he muttered now, pulling on a robe of wool half-lined with squirrel fur and slipping his feet into fancy linen slippers. 'The one robbed of his inheritance by the other. Never were the Scriptures more clearly illustrated. Cyrus, if you still live, God bids me bring you to account. You robbed me of my grandfather's love. You stole all that was to come to *me*, and you took the cloth for profit, not for the love of Christ or the Church.'

He rang the bell and his borrowed servants came running with food and good wine for his needs. This too was a new experience for Hector, so long accustomed to sitting down to modest fare with other hungry men.

After breaking his fast on excellent bread, cheeses and roasted meat, he passed from room to room with a critical eye and a deep sense of satisfaction. With the help of Fergus de Burton and York's archbishop, he would have this house and all that went with it. He would assume the status of his brother. These men of Beverley, peasant and priest alike, would offer him the fear and respect he craved. He would be raised from discontent to triumph, no more the lowly, hard-working curate but Hector de Figham, a man of power and influence.

Figham House was superbly set in its own grounds on the pleasant Figham Pasture, close to the moor. From its highest windows could be seen the ragged outline of the town. To its left was the Minster, with poor St Martin's set close by, to the right the gleaming waters and the congested mouth of the port. Between the two was a town packed with churches, schools and hovels, narrow alleyways and ditches, a town teeming with every level of humanity.

Here within the high walls of Figham House were three private wells fed by an underground spring of clear, clean water. Its attached barn was built of solid stone and heavily fortified, its courtyard smartly flagged, its rooms fully pan-elled, its windows glazed and set with ornate bars against intruders. A mere canon by office, Cyrus de Figham lived here in princely fashion, the favoured grandson enjoying the accumulated benefits of an old man's favours. His elder brother felt a hunger tinged with the disappointments of a lifetime.

'"Thou shalt not covet thy neighbour's house, nor his manservant, nor his ass, nor anything that is his."' Hector quoted the commandment softly as he knelt to recite the prayers of the Morning Office. 'And yet I do, I covet everything he has.'

By the time he rose from his knees he was convinced that Fergus de Burton had been sent to him by God. If the owner of this fine house still lived, he must be stripped of it. His brother had broken every holy law and used every vice to raise himself above his God-given status. The facts were indisputable, the solution crystal clear. Hector would be party to Cyrus de Figham's crimes if he kept his guilty knowledge to himself while Cyrus used his wealth to reclaim his high position here. It was Hector's duty, to God and to the Church, to relieve his brother of all these worldly riches so that his tarnished soul might be cleansed of all his sins.

'"Thou shalt not murder."' He tested the words out loud and found them comforting. Cyrus had murdered, not once but several times. A man may kill his enemy in his own defence, strike down his attacker or slay the perpetrator of serious crimes, but Cyrus de Figham had killed for profit and that, by any man's reckoning, was murder. If Cyrus was dead, as Hector believed he was, substantial claims could be made by an elder brother on his estates. If he still lived, as Fergus suspected, then only by his sincere repentance, and by the full rejection of his riches, could he hope to save his immortal soul from the eternal fires of hell.

Six clerks had been employed to make a detailed inventory of the Figham holdings, and every page condemned the owner as a lawbreaker and a thief. The archbishop's plundered wine was stored in his cellars, still with the seal of York on every barrel. Rare beaver pelts hung from the heavy rafters of his barn. Whole casks of precious salt stood one atop the other against the rear wall, much of it robbed from carters by de

140

Figham's hired men. Books and artefacts pilfered from the church filled several chests. In the upper room, where Cyrus kept his jewels and church vestments under lock and key, a cupboard fitted with metal locks and set in a recess held the relics of a number of minor saints. Here was the forefinger of St Hilda, the thumbnail of St James the Hermit, several hairs from the head of St Marius, a tooth of St Tuda, a vial of St Judith's tears. In Hector's youth there had been no cupboard here, only a robe chest and the loose stones covering a hide hole into which a small boy crawled to avoid the cruel teasing of his brother. Now he leaned his shoulder to the cupboard and, with no little effort, managed to work it, inch by difficult inch, from its deep recess. He crouched to lift the stones away until the childhood hide hole was revealed, and there he found evidence that Cyrus, too, had discovered this secret place.

'A treasure trove! God's teeth, this is where he kept his secret hoard!'

He groped inside and, one by one, withdrew four handsome caskets from the hole. Each box was a rarity in itself, with jewelled clasps and silver and copper hinges, panels inlaid with gold leaf and carved oak borders set with gems. One box was crammed with pieces of gold, another with pieces of silver, and two yielded a fabulous collection of jewelled brooches, rings, breastplates and girdles. In the dust in the farthest corner of the hole he found a leather pouch containing a collection of priceless gems no man of the priesthood could fail to recognise. Their exact duplicates, fashioned in brightly painted paste, now adorned the shrine of St John in the Minster.

For a long time Hector gloated over his find, his thoughts swinging back and forth until they settled at last on a simple, unavoidable truth. To his brother's crimes could be added sacrilege. Whether Cyrus had robbed or merely profited from the robbing of a sacred shrine, his possession of this pouch of gems was proof of his wicked crimes against the Church.

At last he returned to the hide hole behind the cupboard and, after lifting a few choice pieces from their contents,

141

returned the caskets to the dusty darkness. When the heavy cupboard was back within its recess, he wiped the perspiration from his brow and gave thanks that he had not forgotten the miseries of his childhood.

'I hated you, Cyrus de Figham,' he said aloud. 'Your lies and cruel torments made a misery of my life. You were my brother, and yet I *hated* you.'

He held the precious gems of St John before the light, marking their lustre and their flawless cut, then return them to their pouch. He carried the pouch downstairs to the tiny chapel that was a requirement of the Church in every priest's house and there concealed it behind the faded icon of the blessed Mary. Its future would be determined at a later date, when Hector had searched his conscience, fasted and prayed. That which was already done by a dishonest man might be as easily undone by an honest one, and yet even a man of honour, as Hector considered himself to be, should first ascertain God's will in these matters.

The clerks arrived two hours after dawn, when Hector had dined in luxury, dressed himself in his brother's clothes and selected a few choice items from his jewel caskets. He had the clerks lined up for his inspection, then passed a written sheet to each in turn.

'Which one of you is responsible for this?'

'I am,' a young man admitted.

'You have made errors.'

'But my lord curate, I have noted and corrected every one.'

'And I will pay no clerk for his errors and corrections. You are dismissed.'

'But if you dismiss me . . .'

'If?' Hector demanded. '*If?* Collect your quills and candles and leave at once.'

The unfortunate clerk left quietly, while the curate seated himself in a high-backed chair and allowed long minutes to pass in which the five remaining clerks could contemplate the penalties of careless work. He was savouring the moment. After years of being just another face in the crowd, a church man of the lower orders, he was suddenly lord and master of a fine mansion; honoured, respected, *feared*. He was *somebody*, and the confirmation of that left him with a sense of intoxication.

Among the clerks was Paul, once a sanctuary man and nervous that his past might be revealed. Five years ago he had been forced to flee to Beverley from York, accused of crimes his master had committed. Hotly pursued and unable to prove his innocence, he had reached the sanctuary chair beside the altar of St John and thrown himself on the mercy of Beverley's canons. When Cyrus de Figham had accepted a bribe to break the sanctuary pledge and hand him over to his enemies, Paul had fled to St Peter's and found true sanctuary there. He lived and worked within those walls and improved his skills under Simeon de Beverley, reputed to be the finest scribe in the country. In recent months Paul had left to become an independent clerk at the provost's court, no longer a hunted sanctuary man but a trusted servant of the Church with a new name and an unblemished identity.

'Your name, clerk?'

The voice and manner were ominously familiar to the clerk. 'I am Paul, sir, second clerk of the provost's court.'

'Are you ordained?'

'I hope to take my final vows this year.'

'Can you be trusted?'

'Yes, sir. My livelihood depends on it.'

'No, clerk,' Hector hissed. 'While in *my* employ your *life* depends on it.'

'Yes, my lord.'

'How well do you know Simeon de Beverley?'

'By reputation only,' Paul lied, relieved that there were none present who might say otherwise. 'I come from a small village south of Beverley, and I am only lately come to this place.'

Hector nodded, satisfied by the reply, then paced the line of clerks, his manner threatening. 'Be warned, each one of you. No clerk of mine will visit St Peter's or speak with anyone who comes from there. The work you do for me is confidential. It must be accurate to the letter and none must know of it beyond this house. Is that clearly understood?' Five heads bobbed in unison and five voices answered, 'Yes sir,' taking their cue from Paul as to how to address this simple curate who claimed to be a nobleman.

He dismissed the rest but held Paul back with a signal. 'You have an honest face and recommendations from your provost. Are you prepared to take on extra work?'

'I am grateful for all work, sir.'

'Good, good. When the clerks are done I intend to remove certain items from their completed lists, items that are mine by right. Do you understand?'

'Yes, sir,' Paul nodded. This surreptitious doctoring of accounts to filter profits into undeserving pockets had been the very cause of his distress five years before. The clerk obeys the instructions of his master and produces a record, in his own hand, that veils the master's guilt. He kept the bitterness from his voice and added, 'I understand.'

'I will expect you to copy out the final sheets, excluding items I will underscore, and allow no sign that anything has been omitted. Is that clear?'

'It is, sir.'

'All this you will do in strictest secrecy.'

'I will, sir.'

'You will be well rewarded for your efforts, and for your silence.'

'Thank you, sir.' Paul allowed himself to return the curate's smile, certain now beyond all doubt that this flint-eyed man, despite his reputation for piety, was every inch Cyrus de Figham's brother.

Hector dismissed him with an elegant flourish of his fingers, then sprawled back in his chair and called for wine. As he drank from his brother's cellar, not the plain red rough wine available to a curate but the rich full-blooded stuff specially imported for the tables of the Church elite, he blessed the day young Fergus de Burton had come riding into his life. He had thought his ambitions exhausted until they'd met. He had come to believe that his choices in life were strictly and narrowly limited by his office. He had even believed that too many disappointments had dulled his hopes for a better and richer future. Fergus de Burton's persuasive tongue had changed all that. If but a half of that young man's plans came to fruition, the public recognition of the Archbishop of York himself might soon be offered to Father Hector, the new master of Figham House.

Later, in the yard, he spoke to the man who kept his brother's dogs, a sturdy, ugly brute who wore a leather skullcap to conceal the fact that his ears were clipped to mark him as a thief. Two snarling mastiffs, branded on their shoulders with de Figham's mark, strained against his grip and bared their teeth, bristling as Hector approached. The man who held them back had lived in the stable for the last eight weeks. With his band of rogues and their women, he had guarded the property personally by day and released the dogs to roam the grounds at night, and his efforts had helped keep looters from the house.

'You are Bruno, are you not?'

'Aye, the canon's man.'

'Your canon is dead.'

'Some say so,' Bruno shrugged. 'Some say he lives.'

Hector indicated the snarling dogs. 'My brother is accused of burning that same brand of ownership into the breast of a woman from St Anne's convent. Is it true?'

'Some say he did, some say he didn't.' Bruno shrugged again. His wide, strong shoulders were covered by a cat-skin wrap tied at the front with thongs pushed through ragged holes. It stank as only poorly treated animal skin can stink.

'I am told she hanged herself when he was done with her.'

'Some say she did, some say—'

'A straight answer, if you please,' Hector snapped. 'I hear enough rumours on the streets. I need no more from you.'

'I don't know nothing about it,' Bruno answered with a sullen shake of his head. Though uneducated and untrained in anything beyond his own survival, he knew that a show of

145

loyalty towards one master was likely to gain him employment with the next.

'Who has paid you for your services all these weeks? Who provides your meat and ale?'

'The archbishop's man, Fergus de Burton.'

'Ah, of course.' Hector smiled. 'What other would have such foresight?' As he spoke, one mastiff rose up on its chain and snapped its teeth, encouraging the other to follow suit. 'Get these animals from my sight. That brand offends me. And get rid of that stinking cat skin.'

'Nay, I'll freeze without it.'

'Then you must have a better one, and decent boots for your feet. You have served me well, Bruno.'

'Me?' the man asked stupidly. 'I don't know who I serve. Father Cyrus, Master Fergus . . .'

'Hector of Lincoln. You serve *me* now.'

'You'll be the new master, then?'

'I am.'

'And a gentleman, like your brother, Father Cyrus.'

'I am indeed a man of means,' the curate boasted, and felt a flush of satisfaction at the ease with which he had assumed his brother's long-envied status.

'You'll be needing a night guard, then, someone to tend the yard and keep the dogs and feed the horses?'

'Indeed I will.'

'Father Cyrus was always generous,' Bruno lied.

'I doubt that,' Hector answered, having studied his brother's meticulously kept accounts. One mark each quarter was all the man had received, a sum so meagre as to encourage him to pilfer in order to meet his basic needs. 'You will receive one mark a month, a meal every day and a flagon of ale on Sundays. Take it or leave it.'

'I'll take it,' Bruno said at once, gasping in surprise.

'You will be expected to work for it,' Hector warned.

'I will. Day and night, as God is my judge.'

'And as God is *my* judge, I will have you hanged if you ever steal so much as a crust of bread from me. Now get these ugly brutes out of my sight and keep them tethered.'

146

As the curate strode back to the house, Bruno showed his discoloured teeth in a grin of satisfaction. Between Fergus de Burton and this untried brother of his master, his fortunes were increasing by the day. It remained to be seen how tightly his new employer ran his household and how easily Bruno could gain a little here, a little there, according to the depth of his pockets and the quickness of his fingers.

At the prebendal house in Minster Moorgate, Fergus de Burton insisted that the mountainous canon be roused from his bed by his reluctant servants. Two common men were ushered into the yard and ordered to wait there on the canon's pleasure, one leading a sullen young woman by the arm, the other with a wide-eyed girl, little more than a child, in reluctant tow. Chad sucked air through his teeth at the sight of them, for he knew that Wulfric de Morthlund purchased women for but one purpose. These times of want were much to the canon's liking. He had a taste for a certain delicacy that hardship made more accessible to him. Poor men brought their wives and daughters, their servants and sisters to him, and then left his house with rich food in their bellies and loaves in their pockets, so long as the woman had ample milk to suckle. That babes were left to starve by such transactions was a blight on no man's conscience, since hungry men must eat and the canon was generous to the poor, as his Office demanded.

De Morthlund was in the habit of sending his priest to the early services in his stead, being content to pay the daily fine of five pennies to the Church for his absences. He was not content to have his sleep disturbed, so the arrival of visitors at dawn's first light displeased him. He met de Burton in his night robe, a heavy cloak around his shoulders and a glowering expression on his face.

'Damn you, Fergus! How dare you drag me from my bed at this ungodly hour?'

'Needs must,' Fergus replied. 'Cyrus de Figham is on his way here.'

'Tell me something I do not already know, de Burton.'

'You know of it?' Fergus feigned surprise with expertise, having guessed that this obese canon would be the first to know of Cyrus de Figham's plans. 'Forgive me, then, for my untimely visit. Like you, I had thought him dead. I came directly to warn you when I heard the news . . . and to bring these papers from my Lord Archbishop.'

'Papers? More papers? What the devil do you give me this time, de Burton?'

'You'll recall, my lord, that the Bishop of Lincoln bound you to the protection of Figham House, its contents and environs when Father Cyrus vanished?'

'I recall it well enough,' the fat man glowered. 'That cunning devil had me as good as hamstrung.'

'Indeed. And now the elder brother, Hector, is here to claim the property for himself and Cyrus is on his way to stay his hand. As custodian, Father Wulfric, you have been placed like a bone between two fighting dogs. These papers, signed by Geoffrey and legally binding, relieve you of all involvement in the issue.'

'They do? Let me see them.'

As the fat man snatched the papers and held them close to the candle with his eyes narrowed in concentration, Chad sucked in his breath and wondered how his young master would explain away the date so clearly written on each sheet. The papers had been obtained two months ago, within days of Fergus's clever drawing-up of the document in Hector's favour. His had been the hand that bound de Morthlund to the protection of Figham House, his the ploy that kept those fleshy fingers from picking over the Figham assets. Chad knew, as Fergus surely did, that one hint of this might see the offending hand removed from its owner's wrist.

As if he had read the soldier's mind, the young man drew the canon's attention directly to the date. 'You will note that I have taken the precaution of having the sheet predated,' he told the canon. 'It occurred to me that your unfortunate position in this affair has left you vulnerable to false accusation. Should Hector pocket so much as a ring

148

or a silver candlestick, and should Cyrus suspect him of it, both men might point the finger at you and swear that their custodian had been dishonest.'

'Damn it,' Wulfric bellowed. 'I took not one single mark for my troubles.'

'When the locusts settle, some might claim otherwise.'

'I've had not so much as a barrel of wine or a pretty trinket.'

Fergus smiled, knowing his own efforts had ensured that it was so. 'You will find the papers quite clear on the matter. I judged it vital for your protection,' Fergus lied convincingly, 'though Geoffrey required some persuasion on the point. I think you will find the documents very much to your advantage, Father Wulfric.'

The fat man bent his head over the papers, his moist lips moving as he read the words. 'By God, you are as good as your word,' he said at last. 'By this I am relieved of all responsibility, and have been so for many weeks. Let them quarrel over the spoils as fiercely as they will, no hint of dishonesty can be levelled at *this* house.'

'Indeed not, my friend. It was a small precaution, but a necessary one.'

'You are a cunning young whelp, de Burton.'

'I aim to please,' Fergus smiled.

Chad set his face and stared at the wall, impressed by his master's slyness but wary of it. He admired no man who deliberately plunged his hand into a hive of bees, even when that hand was withdrawn unscathed. Clever but untrained, this brash, self-confident upstart relied too much on charm and too little on experience, and risked all on his juggling of the two.

Wulfric de Morthlund slapped the papers with the backs of his fingers. 'Hector of Lincoln will be informed of this today, this very morning.'

'Be sure he puts his official mark to it,' Fergus insisted. 'As archbishop, Geoffrey's seal overrides that of the Bishop of Lincoln, but Hector's signature and your own must be added to make the transfer legally binding. I intend to leave

149

you with no cause, my Lord Canon, to question my integrity or my knowledge of our law at some later date.'

Wulfric stood back to survey the young man with open admiration, noting the handsome, animated face and the short, thick hair curling softly around his ears. 'The eyes and the grin of an imp,' he said, licking his lips. Then he looked pointedly at the girdle encircling the slender hips. 'A gift from Geoffrey Plantagenet?' he inquired. 'For services rendered?'

'This was my payment for representing York during the Beverley riots,' Fergus told him. 'Is it not a splendid thing?'

'I own a better one,' Wulfric told him.

'I do not doubt that for a moment,' Fergus smiled.

'I own one fashioned from purest gold and set with ruby, sapphire and opal. A magnificent girdle it is, brought all the way from the master craftsmen of Egypt. It would sit well on you, Fergus, if you would have it.'

'As a fee for drawing up the papers?' Fergus asked.

'Aside from your fee.' The fat man licked his lips again. His eyes had softened and his gaze was intense. 'We might call it a simple gift *for services rendered.*'

The young man's smile did not falter for an instant, though he held the other's knowing stare as he replied. 'My lord canon, I regret I am not free to barter for your gifts, however generous.'

'Not free?' Wulfric pouted. 'Come now, young Fergus, a man of your pretty features and undoubted talents could do much better than labour for his keep for the likes of Geoffrey Plantagenet.' Wulfric cocked his head and his smile became a leer. 'Or does our unmarried archbishop keep you bound to him by other incentives, eh?'

'Our arrangement, formal as it is, suits my requirements,' Fergus told him carefully. Acutely aware of the essence of the conversation, and cautious of the delicate nature of it, he added with grace and the friendliest of smiles. 'I must confess that my natural inclinations in certain areas are, shall we say, somewhat limited, my lord.'

'I see. You disappoint me, sir.'

150

'Then I apologise for that,' Fergus said with a bow. 'And you may rest assured, my Lord Canon, that I decline your generous gift without offence.'

'Then hold the matter in abeyance. Think on it.'

'Indeed I will.'

The fat man suddenly grinned and massaged the great mound of his belly with both hands. 'I regret your limitations, Fergus de Burton, and yet I have a mind to reward you handsomely in this matter of the Figham property.'

'I had rather hoped you might.' The young man grinned in return.

They left the house with Wulfric's laughter bellowing in their ears and yet another purse of gold attached to Fergus's jewel-encrusted belt. As they mounted their horses in the yard, the poor men and their women were ushered into the house, and they heard the canon call from across the hall, 'Have them wait here. Bring me the young one first.'

'Animal!' Chad cleared his throat and spat on the ground. 'He preys on every form of life.'

'Aye, and survival is ugly and unscrupulous,' Fergus reminded him. 'Hungry men will sell whatever commodity they possess to fill their bellies, and their women have no choice but to comply. You can pity the helpless babes whose milk he suckles, but you cannot deny that survival sets up its own stall in the marketplace. Canon Wulfric is merely a buyer who offends no law in the purchase, and they offend no scripture in the trade.'

'It offends *me*,' Chad retorted.

'Aye, and it sickens me,' Fergus admitted. 'Mount up. Let us be away from here.'

They turned their horses for the gates, Chad glowering and tight lipped. 'You damn near came unstuck in there, Fergus. That spoiler of boys has taken a fancy to you.'

'And he may have me, body and soul,' Fergus quipped, 'on the day hell freezes over.'

'He'll not rest on his disappointment,' Chad warned. 'Damn it, Fergus, you had him convinced that time and circumstance will bring you around to his persuasion. He'll

151

trap you, if he can. He'll take by force what you refuse to give up willingly.'

'And I will kill him if he ever tries to lay his vile paws on me.' For a brief moment the twinkling eyes were hard, the young face grim, then Fergus laughed aloud and patted the purses at his belt. 'Relax, Chad. My honour remains intact and my coffers are swelling.'

'Aye, and the soup's thickening. Take care lest you choke on your own brew, Fergus.'

'Shame on you Chad, for your doubts. I have merely added the water to the pot, lit the kindling and thrown in a handful of spice. The proof of the brew will be in its meat and that, my friend, will be cut from the hide of Geoffrey Plantagenet.'

'Have a care, lad. You hang between an infamous canon and a villainous archbishop. One slip and you're undone.'

'Aye, but by the gods I'll give those two a fine run for their money.' Fergus chuckled and scratched at the stubble on his chin. 'Father Cuthbert has provided the first step in my ascent. I am on my way to higher things, Chad. Nothing, and no one, will stop me now.'

As if by way of an omen, a man in a monk's robe strode into their path as they left the gates and turned their mounts into the street. His sudden appearance startled Fergus's mount and caught its rider off his guard. The monk fearlessly stood his ground as the whinnying horse reared up before him, then stepped aside and bowed his head as he signalled them to pass.

'Have a care, monk,' Fergus warned. 'Have you no ears? Did you not hear the clatter of our hooves?'

The man raised his head to survey the riders with an untroubled expression, then turned without comment and continued on his way towards the gates of the Moorgate house.

'Ill-mannered fool,' Fergus muttered. 'The horse might have killed him with a single kick. What idiot walks like a blind man into the path of mounted men then stands his ground while hooves fly past his head?'

'Perhaps his prayers distracted him,' Chad suggested.

152

'Aye and sooner or later that careless monk will pray himself into the grave. Come, Chad, we have a lengthy journey ahead of us.'

Chad's face was dark, but Fergus, the incident with the monk quickly forgotten, was grinning broadly as he signalled to his waiting men, drew up his travelling hood and heeled his mount towards the York road.

Wulfric de Morthlund had sent urgent word that he would arrive at Figham House at nine o'clock. He came, conspicuously attended, at noon, borne in a heavy litter to spare the horses. From an upper window, Hector marked his progress along Flemingate and past the port to the twisted lane serving Figham Pasture. He could have taken the faster, more direct route over the common land, but then his coming might have gone unnoticed. This canon demanded a welcome on every journey. He travelled in brazen style, his priest scattering coins and bread to the poor so that the Canon of St Matthew's might be blessed a thousandfold for his generosity. That the coins were small and thin, and often clipped of all their value, and that the bread was stale and of suspect quality, was of no consequence to the destitute who scrabbled for a portion. He gave, therefore he was a generous man. They received, and so they took their pittance and gladly blessed his name.

After the Beverley riots and the supposed killing of Cyrus de Figham, Wulfric de Morthlund had presented the major threat to Hector's claim on the Figham house. That ostentatious canon might well have marched upon the house and stripped it bare, or else employed a band of hired looters and then denied all knowledge of the deed. He might simply have admitted himself by force as its protector and, at his leisure, creamed off the best of it. Fergus de Burton had prevented that. He had persuaded Hector to forestall the man by serving official papers making Wulfric de Morthlund solely responsible for the safety of the Figham property. As full custodian, he was answerable to the Bishop of Lincoln for any losses and yet denied right of entry to the house and its well-stocked barn. All hopes of an easy profit had faded, and Wulfric had been forced to stand aside without benefit or reward. Watching the slow procession approach the house, Hector guessed that here was a man to be entertained with caution. The Canon of St Matthew's would bear a grudge against his host, and must never suspect that Fergus, for his loyalty, would pocket the handsome bonus that de Morthlund might have taken for himself.

Wulfric de Morthlund stepped from his litter in royal style and, leaving his sweating bearers in the yard, swept into the house with his priest and his clerks in attendance. He halted in mid-stride as Hector entered the hall to greet him.

'By the Devil! You are your brother's image, sir.'

Hector smiled politely but did not offer his hand. This leering, obese canon and his catamite priest offended him to the core. The lust for women he could understand, distasteful as it was in learned men who wore the cloth, but the vile, unnatural lust of one man for another was beyond his comprehension.

The best of Cyrus de Figham's wines was brought to the table with platters of cold meat and sugared fruits. Fresh logs were tossed into the grate, the servants dismissed and the leathers hung across the door. As the curate and his guests lowered their voices in earnest conversation, Paul set down his writing tools, tiptoed through a darkened room and bent his head to eavesdrop at the door.

While Hector entertained his guests and the clerk from St Peter's listened at the door, a small intruder slipped into the house. In the tiny chapel towards the rear of the house, a boy in a light-grey robe appeared through a hole once used to draw water from the stream below to feed the piscina. He moved directly to the modest altar stone and lifted the hidden pouch. He tipped out the gems, weighed them in his hands and noted the richness and depth of colour of each in turn.

'To the glory of St John of Beverley,' he whispered. 'The saint's own property.'

154

Only when he was satisfied that he had committed the finer details of each stone to memory did he return them, and their pouch, to the altar dust. After that he signed the cross before the altar, then gathered his robe around his knees and slowly lowered himself back through the hole into the ground. He emerged again from the mouth of a well some distance from the house and made his way to a house in Keldgate, close to the watercourse.

'Well lad? Did you see them?'

'I did, and they are indeed St John's stones, as I suspected.'

'God be praised.'

Stephen Goldsmith, canon and craftsman, had been watching anxiously from the door of his gloomy workshop. Now he placed his palm on the boy's head in blessing and said, 'Well done. Now come inside and we'll begin at once.'

His colours and his moulds were all prepared, his dishes of ground glass set about his desk, his tools laid out. This goldsmith was the craftsman who had produced a perfect replica of St John's shrine, the man who had fashioned, in painted metal and coloured paste, the substitute casket before which pilgrims worshipped in their unsuspecting droves. Until the saint was safe and the shrine secured against all harm, St John of Beverley rested in the bowels of the earth while men and woman knelt before a clever representation of his casket.

'Is Simeon well?'

'He is strong,' Peter replied.

'There is a rumour that the dark priest lives.'

Peter's eyes were clear and very blue in the light from the burner. 'He lives,' he answered softly.

'Will he return?'

'He must. Like us, he is bound to Beverley with ties he cannot sever.'

'And yet he hates this town,' Stephen sighed. 'He hates it with a passion.'

'No matter. Hatred and love are equal forces,' Peter reminded him.

Grinding a pestle in a mortar, Stephen Goldsmith contemplated his own part in the intrigues of the town. He owned the land on which St Peter's enclosure stood, and he had sworn to gift it to humble monks rather than yield to pressure to sell his portion to the Church. Should it fall to the Church, his land would become a prized piece in the power games played out between Beverley's canons and York's archbishop. Of the many victims left to fall or suffer in those games, Simeon de Beverley would be foremost. While Stephen Goldsmith lived, St Peter's would house only honest, dedicated priests, and when he died the good monks would have control.

The first of fourteen substitute gems was ready within the hour. Stephen passed it, still warm, into Peter's waiting hands.

'It is exquisite.' Peter smiled, holding the mock ruby so that light from the burner played across its glowing blood-red surface. 'A perfect copy. You are a master craftsman, Stephen Goldsmith, and an honourable man. You choose to toil for St John while your skills could make you rich beyond men's dreams.'

Stephen smiled and touched the burnished silver crucifix hanging at his belt. 'Aye, lad, so the Devil is constantly reminding me.'

CHAPTER ELEVEN

At the house on Figham Pasture the talk had progressed to crucial matters. Wulfric de Morthlund stretched his feet out towards the hearth and balanced a goblet of wine on the rise of his belly. By degrees he had gained the measure of Hector of Lincoln. He found him pious yet also covetous and bitterly resentful of his younger brother's high position. These three faults would help him manipulate this newcomer, this would-be claimant of Cyrus de Figham's fortunes. An elder son usurped of his inheritance by a sibling provided a situation to be exploited, and exploit this man he would, for despite being garbed from head to toe in borrowed finery, Hector was too small a man to walk with any stature in his brother's boots.

'I am not given to bandying words wrapped up in niceties,' Wulfric told him after a lengthy, thought-filled silence. 'You and I are men of the world and servants of the Church, and as such our aims lie parallel. Let me speak frankly, Hector. I believe your brother is still alive. If so, he presents a danger to us all.'

Hector nodded, loathing the implication that he and de Morthlund were of a kind, yet eager to make this powerful man his ally. 'Alas, my brother, Cyrus, has sinned against his Church and his fellow man.' He spread his hands to indicate

157

that matters had run far beyond his control. 'I had no idea that things had come to this. His behaviour has left me deeply shocked.'

'So, will you simply sit back and wait for him to make what move he will, whether it be to your advantage or your detriment? He is your brother, Hector. Honest men will look to you and ask why he was not restrained before his hands were stained with the blood of innocent men and women.'

'I know that,' Hector admitted, 'but what can I do? I cannot alter the sorry fact that he's my kinsman. Perhaps you, Canon, can suggest an acceptable course of action?'

Wulfric smiled and rubbed his belly with his palm. Hector's answer was predictable. He had judged the curate correctly as one more likely to follow than to lead, and here he was asking Wulfric to show the way through his predicament. The fat man took a direct approach and chose his words for their bluntness.

'If your brother returns to Beverley he will be charged with murder, with inciting the town to riot, with bearing false witness against a fellow canon, with striking down a bell-ringer and with wounding the monk from Flanders.'

'And with sacrilege, theft and rape, if even half the things I hear can be substantiated,' Hector added with a shudder of revulsion.

'Serious indeed,' Wulfric stressed. 'But if they find him not guilty, or if the accusations are unproven, he will resume his position here and profit handsomely from his crimes.'

Hector sucked air through his teeth and shook his head emphatically. 'No Christian worth his salt could possibly allow that.'

'Indeed not. Such a thing would strike at the very core of Christian principles. You must remember that any who disagree with such a verdict will vent their discontent on you, since once exonerated he will be unreachable.'

'God forbid that I, a good, God-fearing Christian man, should become the scapegoat for a criminal who, by an accident of birth, happens to be my brother.'

Wulfric licked his lips, feeling much like a hunter sighting his prey. 'If, however, the verdict goes against him, his assets might well be confiscated by the Church. In either case, you stand to lose your entitlement.'

'Do you believe I have a valid claim, then?' Hector asked hopefully, and Wulfric knew this curate would not prove difficult to manipulate.

'Of course you have a claim. My dear man, here we have two brothers, one a pillar of virtue, the other a perpetual offender, and but one high position to be allocated. Stand back and answer honestly: which of these brothers would *you*, as a righteous man, consider more worthy of favour?'

Hector shifted in his seat. 'Your words remind me that my duty to the Church outweighs my loyalty to my brother.'

'Indeed it does. Regrettably, he has passed beyond the pale. He has abused his position at every turn, and the Church will expect you to act conspicuously in bringing him to heel. Fail to comply, on whatever well-intentioned grounds, and they will see to it that you follow him to hell.'

'I have no choice then?' Hector asked. 'Are my hands so tightly bound that even Cyrus, if he lives, will understand that I am helpless in the matter?'

'Without a doubt,' Wulfric assured him. 'You are left without choice, Hector. You are subject to the will of the Church and, as you say, quite blameless in the matter.'

'It seems I am in a terrible dilemma.'

'Absolutely. By doing nothing, or by waiting to answer only when required to do so in your own defence, you risk aligning yourself so closely with Cyrus as to be judged his equal in the felony. You must be seen to act at once in the interests of the Church, no matter if it proves injurious to your brother,' Wulfric insisted, pressing his advantage. 'Remember, too, that Cyrus can neither enter heaven nor receive pardon for his sins whilst still encumbered by the burden of worldly riches. Relieve him of them and so retrieve his immortal soul from the Devil's clutches.'

'Ah, yes. It is clearly my duty, as a priest and as his kinsman, to relieve him of this soul-destroying impediment.' Though his eyes were bright and eager, Hector was still reluctant to take the final plunge until he knew for certain that Wulfric would be there to keep him afloat if he should flounder. He pursed his lips and sat for a while in contemplative silence. 'As you know, Canon Wulfric,' he ventured at last, 'a man might rise or fall on the opinions of his peers. Too many will believe I have no right to enjoy my brother's comforts while he pays a heavy price for acquiring them. The Church itself will expect to strip him, and therefore me, of every stick and sack contained in Figham House.'

'Not while I assert otherwise,' Wulfric assured him.

'Then I can count on you to champion my cause?'

'You can indeed.'

'At every step?' Hector pressed. 'As far as the legate's court?'

'Absolutely, my dear Hector. Absolutely.'

Hector sat back in his chair, well satisfied. 'Then between us, sir, I believe we can shape this situation to our mutual advantage.'

Wulfric de Morthlund swallowed his wine and called for his glass to be refilled. 'To our mutual advantage . . . *Hector de Figham*!'

The curate puffed out his chest like a prize cock. 'The name has a handsome ring to it. Hector de Figham. Oh yes, I confess I like the sound of that.'

With a slick smile, Wulfric said, 'I thought you might.'

Seated between them, Daniel Hawk was impressed by the sly performance of both men. The curate was garbed in his brother's clothes, entertaining this powerful canon in his brother's house. He had made no secret of the fact that he was prepared to take the helm and leave Cyrus de Figham cast adrift in troubled waters, but he would not be seen to snatch and grab at that which he most coveted. Instead he would become the innocent recipient, the one who gained by simply doing his duty as a Christian. Wulfric de Morthlund had read him with an expert's eye. The game was set, the pieces in position and the players keen to play their chosen parts. All that remained was for one of them to set the game in motion.

It was Wulfric who made that opening move. Breaking into the thoughtful silence, he voiced the first stages of his plan. 'On your behalf, Hector, though not in your name, I have already approached our provost, Jacob de Wold,' he said, content to have reached the crux of the debate. 'Several others of important standing have been persuaded to do the same. Your brother is thought to be dead, and the Church should have first claim on his property. Jacob, of course, is inclined to trust to Fate, taking the line of least resistance. He would prefer to leave this matter for the papal legate to decide, but now that I've instigated an inquiry, de Wold is required by law to act at once on our formal charges. Official action can no longer be avoided, either on legal or on moral grounds, but the possible confiscation of all this . . .' He raised his fat fingers to indicate his sumptuous surroundings. 'Such a tragedy must be avoided at all costs.'

'Perhaps we should look to enjoy our rewards in heaven,' Hector said, his words tinged with humility even while the glint of greed shone in his eyes.

'What comes to you or to me comes to the Church by a different route,' Wulfric said persuasively. 'We are merely agents of a much higher authority. Besides, our archbishop will press his claim and simply transfer all this to his own pocket unless we prevent it.'

'Well, if that is so, we are *obliged* to protect it, even from the archbishop, in the interests of the Church,' Hector smiled.

'Indeed we are, sir. Indeed we are.'

Daniel Hawk rose inconspicuously to replenish their glasses and draw the platter of honeyed fruits a little closer to his master's elbow. His handsome face betrayed no hint of his thoughts as he observed the two. The game was going well. In the name of honour and for the Church's sake, they would destroy a man, claim his considerable assets and divide the spoils between them. This was the natural way of things. If a poor man walked on the sharp rim of his own folly, none cared whether he slipped or regained his feet. If a rich man trod the same precarious path, then someone, somewhere, would make it his business to nudge him over the edge.

'I want St Martin's for my own priest,' Wulfric announced into the silence, and Daniel was shocked by this unexpected turn of events. He was a priest without ambition and a catamite without status or possessions. That Wulfric, always jealous of his own position and reluctant to apportion power in any measure, should want his own priest raised to the status of canon was a move he had not for one moment anticipated.

Hector shot the young priest an unguarded look of distaste. 'I had thought to take it for myself,' he said sullenly. 'After all, if I am to assume my brother's status . . .'

'Come now. Why be so modest in your ambition,' Wulfric gushed in sugared tones. 'St Martin's is a paltry office for a man such as yourself. I believe you worthy of a far higher position than mere canon of some humble little church.'

'A higher position? What exactly do you have in mind?'

Wulfric reached for a piece of fruit and chewed upon it thoughtfully, then licked the juices from his lips and answered with a flourish of his fingers, 'Provost.'

'What? You mock me, sir. Beverley already has a provost.'

'Jacob de Wold is provost here in name only,' Wulfric remarked. 'It suits our archbishop to have the position filled by a pliable man who will keep our canons orderly and undemanding. So, while Jacob keeps the peace, Geoffrey keeps the office firmly in his own control. When it suits his whim to have it otherwise, Jacob de Wold will be removed and another installed in his place.'

'As simple as that?'

'As simple as that,' Wulfric confirmed. 'And besides, Jacob stands on his feet with the aid of leather and metal braces, and bears his almost constant pain with the help of poppy essence. He was injured in the Great Fire two years ago. He is crippled, tired and rapidly becoming addled in his thoughts. It would take little to persuade him to resign in favour of a better man.'

'But the office is not secure,' Hector complained, and Wulfric took his cue without hesitation.

'Geoffrey Plantagenet can be bought. The return of his stolen wine from your brother's barn would sweeten his

162

temper. A few church artefacts, some holy relics, some gold and silver . . .' He raised his brows. 'Cyrus has boasted of his many acquisitions.'

Hector's gaze went to the roof, a careless signal that de Morthlund was quick to note. The curate was thinking of the caskets safely hidden in that childhood hide hole and the pouch of gems now in his own possession. If Geoffrey could be bought so cheaply and the enviable office of Beverley's provost bartered for a handful of trinkets, then Hector's future was virtually assured. He could never hope for advancement in Lincoln, nor would he be allowed to perform well if such were offered. Too many people knew him there as yielding and ineffectual and so would not respect him as they should were he to be raised above them. Here in Beverley he could set his sights much higher and, on the strength of his brother's reputation, command as much esteem as Figham House and the provost's seat could offer.

Wulfric de Morthlund saw his aims achieved as he watched the other's thoughts pass in transparent succession over his face. By the time this clumsy curate learned how to hide his thoughts and his weaknesses, he would be so heavily in the canon's debt, and in his confidence, that Wulfric would be the true power behind the provost's seat. It would suit his purpose perfectly to burden this man with all the responsibilities of Office, the paperwork and court proceedings, the tedious services, solving of petty squabbles and endless duties. It would suit him, too, to have control of the provost's strings and thus manipulate the favours of Geoffrey Plantagenet.

'*Check*,' Daniel mouthed, seeing the game well mastered, and his master shook his head and mouthed instead, '*Checkmate.*'

At last Hector of Lincoln rose to his feet and nodded his head in agreement. 'How will I set these wheels in motion?'

'You will do nothing,' Wulfric told him firmly. 'You must not be seen to angle for Geoffrey's good auspices, nor can he afford to be accused of the sin of simony by placing you in Office for a fee. Do not forget, my friend, that the

163

selling of sacred items and preferment is strictly against our holy law.'

'Then how . . .?'

'Since I am not without influence both in Beverley and in York, let me act as intermediary on your behalf.' De Morthland heaved himself to his feet with Daniel's assistance. 'Your *sole* intermediary,' he stressed. 'I will require details of your intended offer for the provost's seat, along with papers bearing your signature and seal describing all your brother's crimes . . . *in their entirety*. Any witnesses you require will be easily obtained.'

'Obtained?'

'Bought, bribed, persuaded. Use what word you will.'

'But that is dishonest.'

'Dishonest?' Wulfric echoed. 'My dear Hector, are you questioning my integrity?'

'Far from it,' Hector protested. 'I merely state the obvious, that a man might say anything, true or false, to oblige the one who offers some incentive for his testimony.'

Wulfric shrugged his enormous shoulders. 'And I say a Christian man can be persuaded to speak as a witness if he believes that what he says is true and that the man for whom he speaks is scrupulously honest.'

'A fine line, Father Wulfric, on which to balance my career.'

'The status of all great men, myself included, is first achieved and then maintained on such fine lines,' Wulfric reminded him. 'Consider my suggestions. Decide the nature and value of your bribe and tomorrow, after vespers, we'll speak again. In the meantime, I have some papers for you to sign, and I suggest you put your clerks to work at once. Geoffrey will do nothing until he sees that list of charges against your brother. He needs a strong case to set before the legate, plus a handsome but discrete reward for his efforts. Unless Cyrus de Figham is relieved of his assets and so prevented from buying vindication for his crimes, the archbishop will do no more than laugh in our faces.'

* * *

Paul was once more stooped over his desk when Father Hector entered the room some time later with a flush of excitement on his cheeks. He handed over several sheets of paper bearing the many seals of Beverley and her canons and bade the clerk trim his candle and his quill.

'Write thus, in the appropriate sections,' he instructed. 'I, Hector de Figham, Curate of St Mark's, Lincoln, do charge my kinsman, Cyrus de Figham of Beverley, with the following crimes against our holy Church . . .'

While Hector still paced the room, firing one statement after another at his scribbling clerk, his visitors had reached the port on the long, slow journey home to Minster Moorgate. Snow was falling steadily, creating a curtain that concealed their passing, so that the canon who had travelled to Figham Pasture in the manner of a prince was rendered anonymous on his homeward journey. The horses of the guard were so hard-pressed to keep their footing that their riders were compelled to dismount and lead them by the rein. The bearers stumbled and skidded, causing the litter to lurch precariously.

'Damn you! Keep your feet!' de Morthlund thundered from inside. 'I do not pay you curs to throw me about like so much cargo on a ship.'

A half-mile further along the road the bearers were exhausted. When the bar of the East Gate loomed in ghostly silhouette through the snow, Daniel persuaded his master to travel the rest of the way on foot, lest the weary litter bearers let him fall. The fat man did so grudgingly, then found the walk quite pleasant compared to the uncertain movements of the litter. He was aware that his crimson cloak with its yellow hood and inner panels, his green and purple robe and his triple-banded girdle were all set in colourful contrast against the stark white of the snow. Men would look on his colourful figure in awe. This pleased his vanity and made him amiable.

'My lord, will you really make Hector provost as you offered?' Daniel asked.

'Do you doubt my power to do so, Little Hawk?'

165

'By no means,' Daniel answered truthfully. 'I merely wonder how the matter will stand once Hector has given over the payment intended for Geoffrey Plantagenet.'

'My pretty priest, what *can* you be suggesting?' Wulfric grinned.

The young man shrugged and showed his teeth in a cynical, only half-amused smile. 'Many shipments of goods to York are intercepted en route by robbers. If these artefacts and relics really do exist, will you surrender them to York just to set that pale reflection of Cyrus de Figham in the provost's seat?'

'Speak out, Daniel. Feel free to speak your mind.'

Wulfric's easy humour gave Daniel courage. 'I think you will arrange to have the shipment intercepted, my Lord Canon. Hector can hardly hold you to your promise if the bribe intended for Geoffrey Plantagenet falls into other hands.'

Wulfric roared with laughter and clasped his massive arm about Daniel's shoulders. 'You judge me well, my boy, and yet that "pale reflection", as you so aptly describe him, is the very key by which the doors of York will be unlocked to me. I grow weary of being cock bird in this back yard men call *Beaver Lake*. I want more status, Daniel, *more power*. With you as Canon of St Matthew's, Hector as our official provost and Cyrus de Figham cleverly disposed of, I shall have it.'

'My lord, I bow to your superior hand in dealing with this delicate situation.' Daniel smiled, using flattery to draw out his master's plans. 'You use men with admirable skill. You guess their hearts and—'

'And recognise their weaknesses,' Wulfric told him, then glanced back at the Figham house, now but a dark spot in the snowy landscape. 'Would you say he is as handsome as his brother Cyrus?'

The question alerted Daniel to Wulfric's darker schemes. Here was his master's real weakness, that of the flesh, clearly revealed. In the past he had goaded Cyrus de Figham to the point of rage by his subtle advances and vulgar innuendo. If he sought to beguile this Hector as compensation for his failure with Cyrus, he declared a weakness of judgement equal to any he despised in other men.

'Handsome enough,' he answered cautiously.

'And perhaps a trifle more amenable than his brother?' Wulfric probed. 'Less rigid, do you not think? Perhaps more susceptible to persuasion?'

'On the contrary, my lord, I believe he will prove even less willing than his brother in such matters.'

'Every man has his price, dear heart.'

Daniel, who had noted Hector's barely concealed distaste for the canon and his priest, doubted that the curate would ever lower himself to consider a price.

'I think this curate is unbendable, my lord,' he offered.

'Why so? He has ambition. There is much he covets that I can help him gain.' De Morthlund hugged his belly with both hands. 'Cyrus was a fool to hold off from me as he did. He might have had my patronage now, when his back is against the wall, had he proved less singular in his preferences. Let us hope this handsome brother of his proves more obliging when he sees the office of provost within his grasp.'

They had reached the bar and the south wall of St Peter's enclosure. From the tower of the little church came the slow, sad tolling of the passing-bell. Smoke from an open fire within the grounds was billowing in fitful strands into the snow-filled sky.

'And what of Simeon de Beverley, my lord?'

'Ah, what indeed?' de Morthlund asked. 'That, my Little Hawk, will depend entirely on how well our young friend Fergus presents our case to our archbishop.'

The smoke observed by Wulfric and his priest rose from a large fire in which Simeon and Osric were burning the shrouded body of a man. The corpse was wrapped in layers of sacking and tightly bound with ropes, doused in lamp oil and packed all about with logs and branches. A blanket, a mattress and a bundle of clothes were laid across it, along with a pair of boots and a walking staff. Everything the man had owned in life had been given back to him in death.

Simeon was deeply troubled by this pagan-like dispatching

of a man. 'It is unchristian,' he said, and added with a shake of his fair head, 'barbaric.'

'So, too, is the giving of poison to our worshippers,' Osric grunted, tossing a dry branch on the fire.

'I wonder if God will receive him?'

'If not, then Satan will have his place prepared.'

'But he repented of his sins. He made full confession,' Simeon said.

'Aye, he babbled before he died, as many do.'

'Was he absolved?'

Osric shook his head and brushed particles of tree bark from his beard. 'There was no time for that. Our first concern was for those who were about to drink the poison. While we were in the church Death came and took him, sins and all.'

Simeon lowered the branch he had intended for the flames. 'No name, no full confession, no absolution. He died unshriven, Osric.'

'If God wants him, God will take him,' Osric growled. 'Our rites and rituals will not alter that. For my part, I am satisfied to have this putrid body safely consigned to the flames. Any precaution we can take to prevent this pestilence spreading through the town is worth more to me than the soul of one murderous stranger.'

'Elvira and Edwin nursed him,' Simeon said. 'And all those others . . . Will this burning protect them from infection?'

'Who knows?' Osric asked with a shrug. 'Who knows how any sickness is carried from one place to another? As a soldier I saw first-hand every manner of sweat and deadly flux, and all I know with any certainty is that the sick will somehow infect the healthy who tend them, and the dead will infect the living who touch their flesh. Allow no vigils, burn the corpse, and corruption of the living might be avoided.'

'Then all your remedies and cures amount to nothing?'

Osric compressed his lips in careful thought. His craggy face was smeared with wood smoke, his dark eyes narrowed against its sting. 'What more can any of us do, Simeon?'

'We can pray,' the priest replied, his sigh resigned.

168

'Aye, we can, for all the good it does.'

Just then the bell priest of St Peter's, having rested for a measured interval, resumed his steady tolling of the passing-bell. Watching the flames, Simeon lowered himself to the ground and clasped his hands. Osric looked on grim-faced, offended to see his friend on his knees after coming so close to offering deadly poison to his flock in the communion wine.

'How can you pray for this wretch?' he demanded.

'I must. We must all believe that every soul is capable of redemption,' Simeon reminded him. 'If not, what will become of hope?'

Osric sighed and wiped his sleeve across his brow. 'You cannot help him, Simeon. Your powers as a priest cannot exceed the limitations of your office. His absolution is beyond you.'

'I know that,' Simeon told him. 'Only a bishop can absolve him, but I can forgive him. That much I can, and must, do for the poor wretch.'

Osric turned and walked away, exasperated by his friend's reasoning. Simeon had the Devil's own temper and yet the disposition of a saint. He could fight like an enraged warrior when his blood was hot and be maddeningly inoffensive when it cooled. For Osric, who had been blessed with a brusque but consistent disposition, the duality of Simeon's nature was a constant source of aggravation. As he strode away he pushed aside his suspicions that the wretched man for whom his friend was praying had died not of the pestilence but of a broken neck.

Near the scriptorium Osric saw a familiar figure approaching, a young clerk burdened by a stack of books and a tray of inks and pens. His hood was thrown back and his progress was erratic. Osric slowed to watch the clerk, his practised eye detecting that much seemed to be amiss. The clerk's boots were good and the pathway had been cleared, so that he trod where no dangerous ice had formed, nor did he seem overburdened for a man of his size and substance, and yet he swayed and staggered as if the strength ebbed from his limbs with every stride.

'Andrew? What ails you?'

As Osric hurried forward, the young man fell to his knees amid scattered inks and books. His face was flushed and running with perspiration and, as he lifted his hands to the infirmarian, livid blotches could be seen raised on his forearms.

Osric's urgent whistle brought Simeon to his feet and had him running across the grass, his prayers abandoned. He reached the pathway as the stricken man emptied the contents of his belly over the ground. Osric's face told him the worst before the words were even spoken. 'God help us, Simeon. I think he has the pestilence.'

CHAPTER TWELVE

That same afternoon, two clerks and a woodsman collapsed at their work and were found to be infected. Gripped by a fever, chills and sweats, they vomited whatever passed their lips or else emptied their bowels in agonising spasms. Like the first clerk to be infected, the woodsman developed sores on his skin, large blisters that ran with liquid when punctured. Well-meaning surgeons practising rudimentary medical skills lanced these sores and, with their unwashed instruments, introduced additional infections to the wounds. Those who survived the feverish flux were likely to die of blood poisoning. In a town where virtually every household was alive with vermin, it was the surgeons who became the primary means of spreading infection.

Osric ordered all four of his patients confined to a hut beside the infirmary. Here herbs were stored in sacks and bunches alongside bottles of extracts, jars of ointments, powders and infusions. A circular fireplace was dug in the ground at the centre of the hut, with a ring of stones to control the flames and keep the logs confined. Small slits were made in the roof above to draw away the smoke. Over the fire was a metal bracket on which were hung great pots whose simmering contents filled the hut with the scent of peppermint, motherwort and foxglove. The sick were tended by three Little Sisters of Mercy, who had strict instructions to keep themselves apart from other people. Osric had them take the same medicines as their patients, a half-dose for the healthy, a full measure for the sick. They were given aprons on entering the hut, and made to wash their hands in the trough outside each time they left. He was determined to employ every cure and remedy known to him to prevent the infection spreading.

The monk they knew as David came and went in silent but dedicated toil. He gathered wood, tended fires, drew and carried water, and several times a day brought captured birds and even rabbits for the cooking pots. Edwin had named him Crow Man for his skills in catching the birds without a net, and many had noted his habit of staring for long minutes at his food before passing it, untouched, to someone else.

Osric was at the water trough, oiling and salting his hands, when Antony found him. The monk had come from the house in Keldgate, which he held at the convenience of Wulfric de Morthlund, a once-fine manor house where the sick and homeless now claimed every inch of space. He had seen first-hand how this harsh winter, coming hard on the heels of a scorching summer, had caused the flour and rye to spoil in the sack. The hungry ate what they could get, while the merchants cared nothing for the quality of their goods, and so tainted stock went with good and poisoned bread was common fare for the poor.

'Can we assume that what we have here is an epidemic of ergot poisoning?' he asked the infirmarian. 'It seems likely, since many unscrupulous bakers are selling bread unfit for pigs to eat.'

'If a man is poisoned by ergot, we will live, so long as we refuse to share his bread,' Osric answered grimly. 'If he has the pestilence or famine fever, we too will die of it. That is all we know.'

'Small comfort,' Antony told him.

'Aye, but all we have,' the old soldier replied.

*　　*　　*

A young woman arrived at St Peter's begging shelter for herself and her sickly infant. Her husband had sickened and died during the night and his neighbours, fearing disease, had driven the woman out and torched the house. The child she clutched to her breast was already dead, and the mother followed soon after her arrival. Osric brought news of her to Simeon while the priest was working in the scriptorium with his father and Elvira.

'She comes from the tanning houses by Keldgate Bar. Two days ago her husband found a body floating in the town ditch. He dragged it out and stripped it naked and, when the clothes were dry, wore them himself.'

'Was that the source?'

'Undoubtedly.'

'And the body?'

Osric shrugged. 'The body was not his concern, so he threw it back in the ditch.'

Simeon's gaze was troubled. 'That ditch surrounds the town and feeds most of its lesser waterways. It collects our filth, our defecations, our animal dung and the waste from our daily labours. Where a woman has no other source, she draws its water for her cooking pots, and where a man thirsts, he will not hesitate to drink from it.'

'Aye, and to save the priest's fee he is content to dispose of his dead there,' Osric nodded. 'Thank God our own springs are fresh and our wells untainted.'

'Drinking water,' Simeon said, frowning. 'We priests ensure ourselves a fresh supply because we prefer the taste and because we need to protect ourselves from drought. Think, Osric, how rarely our walled enclosures are affected by these plagues, except where the sick have brought it to our gates.'

'True enough,' Osric shrugged. 'The poor share their beds with vermin and their clothes with fleas and bugs, and the food they eat is often putrid. They breed disease and we take it from them when we allow our paths to cross with theirs. Is it not part of our Christian teaching, my friend, that the further a man can get from the common people, the closer he might stand to the shadow of God?'

Simeon's smile was without humour. 'I think that teaching refers to the separation of his soul from worldly matters.'

'It was written down by mortal men who knew the perils of mortal sickness. In times like these, when all men are at risk, our priests are swift to apply a more literal interpretation.'

'Fear makes cowards of them,' Simeon said. 'The poor are with us always, Osric, and they seem to carry our downfall in their pockets.'

'Aye, so any man of substance strives to avoid them.'

'And that is precisely why Christ charged us to help them,' Simeon said firmly.

'And precisely why we now have the pestilence within our walls,' Osric countered. 'Had you not been in such haste to offer mercy to a stranger, he would have taken his share of the plague elsewhere.'

There was neither hurt not censure in Simeon's eyes as he searched his friend's face for the full meaning behind his words. 'Was I in error then?' he asked. 'Should I, like so many others who take the cloth, turn a deaf ear to others' cries because I fear to share their distress?'

Osric shrugged again and shook his head. 'I too have tended the sick and dying because my conscience dictated that I must, but I question our wisdom and our *right* to intervene in matters of life and death where such things do not concern us.'

'But they *must* concern us,' Simeon protested. 'To serve God we must serve all men.'

'Aye, and we are meant to accept His will in all things. So here we are, Simeon the priest and Osric the infirmarian. God says a man must die and we fight to save him. God sends a pestilence and we do our best to rid ourselves of it. How then can we know God's will from our own? How can we decide what to refuse and what to accept?'

'We must let our hearts decide.'

Here Osric offered his friend a wry smile that said their argument, as always, had come full circle. 'Simeon, your heart was settled years ago on Elvira, and yet you hold her off and keep your vow of celibacy because you believe the sacrifice

174

to be God's will.' He rose to his feet and gripped Simeon by the shoulder. 'Do not speak to me of *heart*, Simeon, while your own is so divided.'

Simeon watched him walk away. 'Osric?'

The infirmarian turned before he reached the door. He saw that Elvira had moved to stand beside Simeon's stool, her hair aglow in the torch light and her pale hand on his shoulder. She was as dark as night, as slight and delicately shaped as an angel carved in smoothest alabaster. He was as fair as day and as fine a man as God had ever fashioned or as fools had ever worshipped as a saint. They were so perfect in their pairing that Osric felt the old anger stir inside him, that familiar, quiet rage against the wasting of two young lives for the sake of a small and ill-judged vow.

'Marry her,' he snapped, speaking his mind.

'You know that is impossible.'

'Then do not preach to others that truth lies in the heart.'

'Perhaps we are meant to find our own truths, Osric.'

'Aye,' the infirmarian growled. 'And mine tells me to bar our gates and leave the poor to accept the will of God.'

Rufus de Malham dropped the bar across the scriptorium door and leaned against it, his arms folded across his chest and his eyes fixed on his son. 'Your friend is right on both counts, Simeon. You should marry Elvira and leave the priesthood. Bar the gates and save your own from harm. Listen to Osric.'

'I listen first to God,' Simeon told him softly.

Leaving his son to continue his work, Rufus drew Elvira aside and asked her, in the privacy of his own corner of the room, 'The truth, child. Would you marry him if the choice were yours to make?'

'I would,' she said.

'And would you leave this place?'

'With Simeon, yes.'

Rufus nodded, satisfied. 'Then my son must be persuaded, for all your sakes.'

Elvira offered her sad little smile and shook her lovely

head. 'Only dreams, Rufus,' she told him. 'His place is here, in Beverley. And what of Peter? You know how he came here, naked and newly born. You know of the hooded rider and the warhorse with the tempest at its heels. You can see for yourself how he grows, strange and wise beyond his years and ever more aware of his destiny. No power on earth will take him from Beverley, Rufus, and neither I nor Simeon would ever leave without him.'

Rufus raked his fingers through his hair in the same way that his son, despite his shaven crown, still did in moments of distraction. 'One town is little different from another.'

Elvira placed her hands over his and looked deeply into his eyes, willing him to understand the unseen forces present in their lives.

'Rufus, he is the Keeper at the Shrine. Simeon knew that when he first spoke his name in baptism. I knew it when I first suckled him at my breast. We are his godparents and he is our borrowed son. We will not be divided, and we cannot alter Peter's destiny.'

'What destiny?' Rufus demanded. 'How can you even begin to assume that Peter has some special life to live, some destiny, as you call it, to fulfil?'

'Your son's faith teaches that all life has a special and very particular purpose,' Elvira reminded him.

'Aye, and he believes it, but do you? Most men and women, aye and children too, live wretched little lives that end in suffering and death. All they have is the vague hope of a kinder afterlife to come. Is that what you call destiny, Elvira? Do their lives, too, have purpose?'

Elvira thought of the gentle Alice, shamed by de Figham's cruel branding iron and driven to suicide by his brutality. She thought of her child's brief struggle to survive, of good men lost and wicked men spared, and it seemed to her that Simeon's Christian teachings were deeply flawed. Then she recalled the hooded figure who had brought Peter into their lives, and the way good men were moved to risk their own lives so that Peter should survive.

'I believe it,' she told Rufus at last. 'For some, at least, the

176

way is preordained. Peter's destiny is here in Beverley, Rufus, and we deny that, or seek to change it, at our peril.'

'Dear God, what you say chills my blood,' Rufus told her with a shudder, and Elvira, smiling again, made the soft confession, 'It chills mine, too.'

The bodies of the woman and child from the tanning house were burned in the grounds the following day. After that, as the Sabbath dawned, two more were consigned to the flames. Those men of Beverley professing medical skills were called to a gathering in the Minster, their numbers swelled by hard-working monks, spinsters and many clerks of the lower orders, and several vicars of lesser churches who feared for the safety of their flock and were either unable or unwilling to shirk their duties. Methods of avoiding and treating the sickness were discussed at length, some based on foolish superstition, some on dangerous or barbaric practices. They looked to Simeon to decide the better course of action for them all, since this quiet man had the power to move men's souls.

'I have obtained permission to use the land outside our five town bars as burial grounds,' he announced, when other plans had been decided. 'The corpses must be collected up and carted there to be buried where they might cause least harm to the living.'

A vicar from nearby Swinemore protested most vigorously at this. 'How can you ask us to sanction such a sacrilegious act?' he demanded hotly. 'Are we to preach from our pulpits that the dead must be abandoned to unconsecrated ground? Are we to dictate that they be laid with thieves and murderers in the pits where we dispose of our stinking waste?'

'The pits will be blessed and prayers offered,' Simeon assured them all. 'It is the best we can do for the poor wretches, and the only way we can hope to contain the sickness. No vigils must be allowed and no anointing of the dead. Every death must be reported without delay and the corpse left untouched until it can be taken by hired carters to one of the pits.'

177

'I refuse to do it,' the vicar told him. 'I will not tell those who look to me for help that God is prepared to rummage amongst hungry rats and fetid waste for the souls of their dead.'

'Then let them bring their dead to you,' Simeon suggested. 'Bury them in the yard of your own church.'

'Impossible. My yard is small and already its corpses are lying three or four deep.'

'Then swallow your indignation and recommend the pits,' Simeon told him firmly. He turned to address the others, who either crouched or stood in a circle around him. 'The same thing applies to anyone here. Abhor the pits if you must, but do not forbid them unless you can accommodate the dead yourself or are content to have rotting corpses dumped in your streets and in your water supplies. Think to the ends served by these regrettable means. A large-scale epidemic could bring about the end of Beverley and the fall of all our churches. Swallow your pride and your Christian principles and trust that God will take good souls regardless of where they are lain to rest. The plague pits are a necessary evil. Better that small indignity for the dead than the total devastation of Beverley's people.'

They came out from the meeting little wiser than they had gone in, each comforted only by the knowledge that he was not alone in choosing to make a stand, however feeble, against their common enemy.

Two very dissimilar men arrived at their destinations on the morning following that second Sabbath in January. One travelled by road to York, having made a journey of thirty hazardous miles on horseback. The other came by river to Beverley. Divided by distance and unaware of each other, they shared a like purpose and were driven by like ambitions and, by their initiation of certain events, each would play a vital part in the writing of another page in Beverley's troubled history.

The weather had eased its stranglehold without bringing the thaw that would give rise to dangerous flooding. The sky was a clear and cloudless blue. Bright sunlight burnished

178

the snow-covered ground and lit the waterways. A black-eyed priest surveyed the town of Beverley as he approached, and in his soul he wanted to burn it to the ground. Thirty miles away, a weary young man encountered the sunlit walls of ancient York, and for him journey's end was a blessed relief. They arrived at nine o'clock on the fourteenth day of January, St Hilda's feast day. By tradition it was the coldest day of the year, bringing hope that winter had already done its worst.

Fergus de Burton and his exhausted band of soldiers rode through the gates of York and were escorted directly to the bishop's palace, there to be given hot baths and fresh clothes, good wine and the best of meat. The soldiers were then dispatched to more modest quarters while Fergus, as the archbishop's special envoy, was installed in magnificent rooms in the palace's west wing. A suit of clothes was laid out on the bed, and by the rich silks and quilted patterns Fergus saw how well his fortunes lay. He fingered the pelts stitched into a cloak of heavy crimson cloth, and he knew that the archbishop would dance to his tune. Rare beaver, available only to the noblest and wealthiest of men, had been selected by Geoffrey to grace the shoulders of his favoured friend, and all who saw it would know at a glance that Fergus de Burton was held in high esteem.

In his private rooms, Geoffrey Plantagenet paced the floor in a rapid figure of eight, his footsteps ringing on the boards and his brows drawn down in a scowl. He was a big man with thick dark hair and powerful limbs. From time to time he stroked his chin or tugged at his cheeks as if his beard still grew there. His thoughts displayed themselves in passing shadows on his face, and his volatile temper gave him a restless, agitated manner which set his feet to constant pacing.

'Where is he? Why isn't he here?'

Along with a dozen clerks and church officials, Geoffrey's deacon and his treasurer were present in the room. Neither had cause to welcome the return of Fergus de Burton. His influence on Geoffrey stirred up jealousies and fears amongst their number. He had the archbishop's respect where they did not, and his presence here upset the delicate balance that they struggled to maintain. The treasurer bore a grudge against de Burton, for he suspected that Geoffrey's present tightening of the purse was at de Burton's instigation. The deacon, Father Bruce, already resented the archbishop's lack of sincere commitment to his office, and he sought to discredit Geoffrey by any means. There were men in high authority who begrudged the king's brother his high position at York. Father Bruce burned to have his suspicions reach their ears and this swift, unorthodox friendship branded as an unholy alliance.

'Where is de Burton?' Geoffrey demanded.

'I am assured he will be here presently, sire,' the treasurer said, pushing his hands into his sleeves and lowering his head.

Knowing the unstable nature of Geoffrey's temper, Father Bruce was disinclined to be generous on Fergus de Burton's behalf. He cleared his throat and offered, with a touch of malice, 'I confess I barely understand what would prompt him to disregard your summons, my Lord Archbishop. But then, he is a man who likes his comforts. He has travelled a great distance in somewhat unfavourable weather. Perhaps he is sleeping.'

'Sleeping?' Geoffrey bellowed, halting to glower at the deacon. 'With whose consent? I gave him no leave to rest while I click my heels on his account. I want him here. *Now!*'

'Then by your leave I will go immediately to rouse him from his bed, my Lord Archbishop,' Father Bruce offered, smiling to himself as he bowed from the room.

Geoffrey Plantagenet was dressed in gold and green, with the decorations of his holy office emblazoned across his chest. Across his shoulders hung his bishop's cloak, fur trimmed and heavily embroidered. His high leather boots were designed for riding and totally ill suited to the finery of his robes, but his personal comfort outweighed his respect for protocol. He would not wear the elaborate bishop's shoes that pinched his toes and irritated his skin with their fancy stitching. But for his robes no man would guess his occupation as anything other than that of a military leader. His movements were

180

belligerent, his speech coarse and his manner brusque. He lacked refinement as surely as he lacked humility. If those who served him had hoped to see the soldier refashioned by the high demands of his office, then time had proved their hopes to be unfounded. Geoffrey was a soldier through and through, as roughly hewn as any who ever drew a sword.

While the treasurer stood with clasped hands and lowered head, Geoffrey voiced his complaints so loudly that they carried to the corridors beyond.

'Damn the brat,' he said. 'How dare he sleep? How dare he keep me waiting on his convenience?'

'My lord, this is unfortunate . . .'

Just then the door swung open and a smiling Fergus de Burton appeared with a disgruntled and disappointed Father Bruce at his elbow. 'Be assured that I have washed and dressed in all haste, my lord,' he announced. 'None but a magician could have reached here ahead of me.'

'Not sleeping, then? Not resting after your journey.' Geoffrey demanded testily.

'Indeed no, my lord.'

Fergus de Burton strode across the room and dropped to one knee in a deep bow, too ingenious to neglect, while others were present, the lofty position of his friend and benefactor. Geoffrey stepped forward to hug him in a welcoming embrace, then slapped his shoulders and bellowed into his face.

'Damn it, Fergus. I was beginning to think you were lost on the marshes. Three weeks without word, and the weather still set against you . . .'

'My lord, I sent word by special messenger over a week ago.'

'No word from you has reached me here,' Geoffrey assured him.

Fergus glanced at the deacon and the treasurer and wondered which of them had dared to intercept his message. For the moment he chose to let the question rest in favour of the more pressing issue of Cyrus de Figham's return to Beverley.

181

'I come directly from Beverley, my Lord Archbishop, and—'

'And damn good it is to have you back,' Geoffrey boomed, slapping Fergus's shoulder once again. 'Let me tell you, lad, these pious priests and cringing clerks are driving me to distraction. I've done nothing but hear petitions and set my seal on documents for weeks. What work is that for a real man, eh?'

'You are bored, my Lord Archbishop,' Fergus told him.

'To the eye teeth,' Geoffrey spat. 'I belong on a horse, not in this gilded cage dressed up in robes far better suited to a woman.'

'Geoffrey, you are as fine as any monarch in those robes.'

'Aye, fine and useless,' Geoffrey complained. 'This easy living does not suit me, Fergus. It gelds a man to live like this, dulled by the bland routine of ecclesiastical life. I should please my pope and my brother the king by resigning, as I did from Lincoln.'

Fergus shook his head. 'No, my lord. Impress them, amaze them, dazzle them with your excellence, but do not seek to *please* them. Leave that to lesser men who do not share your gift for greatness.'

Ever susceptible to flattery, Geoffrey squared his shoulders and grinned to hear such words. 'By God, you cheer me, Fergus.' He clapped his hands and yelled for wine and fresh logs for the fire, then dismissed the others from the room and drew two chairs close to the hearth. The wine was set out between them. He surveyed the handsome Fergus with approval. 'Are the new clothes to your taste?'

'They are indeed.'

'Then I must be thankful that you find my gift acceptable.' Geoffrey's eyes danced with mockery, though his amusement merely masked the dangerous undercurrents responsible for his rapid changes in mood. 'I have not forgotten that I offered to make you my chancellor and you refused the honour.'

'My lord, the last thing you need is yet another fawning servant in a pretty gown,' Fergus reminded him. 'This splendid suit of clothes is much more to my liking, and to your advantage.'

'Aye, true enough, and I must confess the fit could hardly be a better one.'

'It is excellent, sire, and greatly appreciated. My compliments to your tailor and my gratitude to you.' The blue eyes lost their twinkle as, aware that Geoffrey was first and foremost a man of action, he came directly to the point and added bluntly, 'Cyrus de Figham is still alive.'

'Damn it!' Geoffrey hissed. 'I'd hoped him dead. This news is unwelcome, Fergus. He was to be the scapegoat for the Beverley riots so that I might avoid unseemly squabbles before the legate's court. While he lives, his voice will be heard and his case defended. Let the full truth be told and my enemies will say I turned a blind eye to the intrigues of those Beverley canons. Damn it, I might even be accused of accepting bribes for my inaction. My plans are ruined. This is most inconvenient.'

'Not ruined, my lord, merely altered, and with cautious planning altered for the better.'

Geoffrey narrowed his eyes and asked, 'How so?'

'I believe the time is ripe for you to take control of Beverley,' Fergus told him. 'Believe me, I have wasted no moment of my time in these past weeks. I have been your eyes and ears, as I swore to be, and now I see a way for you to settle things with Rome and with your brother.'

Geoffrey shifted in his chair and scowled at the wine in his glass. 'I have enemies at every turn,' he grumbled. 'They whisper behind my back and plot to have me robbed of my position. They hate me. Perhaps you're right. Perhaps the time has come to make peace with Rome and—'

'God forbid that you reduce yourself to that,' Fergus declared, then hastily apologised, certain that his words had struck the right cord with this power-hungry man. 'Forgive me, sire, I had no right to speak my mind so bluntly.'

Predictably, Geoffrey snapped at the bait and probed for more. 'You may speak freely, Fergus. You know how the land lies in Beverley and you understand the slippery ways of its canons. The papal legate will arrive there soon and I'll be expected to defend my position to Rome's satisfaction or else travel back with the legate to plead my case like a common criminal. They'll humble me if they can. They'll bring me before His Holiness and rub their hands in glee to see me on my knees, reduced to pleading for his indulgence.'

'If that were to happen, King Richard might consider it expedient to speak against you, sire. His love of a brother, a mere half-brother at that, will be fair exchange for the favours of a pope.'

'Aye, no brother can hope for even half the love Coeur de Lion has for Rome. Damn it, I'd rather resign my Office right here and now than allow my enemies, or my brother, the satisfaction of relieving me of it.'

'You are a soldier,' Fergus reminded him. 'Tactics have always been your speciality. Use them in this, and you will not only win the day but advance yourself in the process.'

Geoffrey laughed bitterly. 'Advance myself? Ye gods, I'll be content merely to keep myself in office.'

'Tactics,' Fergus repeated, touching his forefinger to the side of his nose. He pulled a letter from his coat and handed it to the glowering archbishop. 'Here, read this.'

Geoffrey read the letter penned in Cuthbert's spidery hand, then tossed it on the table. 'The Canon of St Peter's is prepared to resign in favour of his priest. So what? Simeon is already canon there in all but official sanction.'

'Give him the Office and the power. He will need it.'

The keen, small eyes were narrowed in suspicion. 'I'm not in the habit of handing out such power on a whim.'

'And wisely so, but consider this truth for a moment. Give power and prestige to an ambitious man and you offer him the means to set himself up in opposition to yourself. Give it to a *good* man and you create a useful tool.'

'That's a fine maxim. Who coined it?'

'I believe you did, my lord,' Fergus lied.

'I did? But of course.' Geoffrey smiled and examined the large ring on his finger. 'I shall have my clerks commit it to paper. Men should read and remember such gems of inspiration.'

'Yes, my lord. May I continue?'

'Please do,' Geoffrey said with a flourish of his hand.

'It is clear that the balance of power in Beverley is unsettled. Restore it, stabilise it to your own advantage and show Rome that you are truly at the helm.'

'No easy task,' Geoffrey grumbled.

'I have seen how it can be done.'

'By God, Fergus, if I ruled Beverley, as I'm entitled to do as its overlord, the relics of St John would rest here in York, where he was bishop for half his lifetime.'

'Aye, and if that were possible both Rome and York would heartily applaud you. You would have no quarrel with your brother if you could so enrich your office, sire, and none with Rome, I'll wager.'

'You're right. I need those relics, Fergus. I must have leverage, something with which to impress my pope and my king.'

'What you need most of all, my lord, is a challenge, a personal battle to bring your idling talents to the fore again, where they can best serve your needs. You are wasted here, with nothing to do but defend yourself against petty plots and spiteful enemies.' He glanced towards the door through which so many resentful dignitaries had filed, dismissed from Geoffrey's presence in Fergus's favour. 'My letter of a week ago was clearly intercepted by a member of your household. It matters little, since I wrote nothing that might be open to misinterpretation, but I wonder, sire, which of your servants dared commit so arrogant a trespass, and to what end?'

'Can you be sure the letter reached the palace?'

'Quite sure.'

'Then I'll find the culprit and have him chastised. I'll do more than that. I'll have him disgraced and dismissed from the palace.'

Fergus shook his head. 'Too hasty, sire. I would rather have him known to us and a way devised to avoid his prying eyes. Forewarned is forearmed. I believe I can identify the

185

culprit, whose motive is more likely to be vindictive than political.'

'Bruce?'

'Perhaps, or else Wilfred, your disgruntled treasurer.'

'Aye.' Geoffrey grinned. 'Your timely observations put an end to his practice of dipping into my coffers. He'll not love you for that.'

Fergus sat forward in his seat, his expression grave. 'A moment ago you suggested you resign your office.'

'Aye, it might well prove expedient to give up my seat before the pope and King Richard conspire to relieve me of it.'

'And where will you go from there?' Fergus demanded. 'What following will you have once you set aside the greatness York can offer? I see before me a great man cruelly shackled, a man of courage forced into a role that is unworthy of his great talents. May I say more?'

'Go on. Your passion intrigues me.'

'I suggest you set yourself on the opposite course and take them completely off guard. Lead them by the nose before they can do as much to you.'

'What opposite course?'

'Take holy orders.'

'What?' Geoffrey leaped from his chair and slapped the chimney stone with his palm. 'I, the son of one king and half-brother to another? I, Geoffrey Plantagenet, a soldier all my life, *become a priest*? Never!'

Fergus sat back and sipped his wine, unabashed by Geoffrey's sudden burst of indignation. 'Geoffrey, you are neatly hung between the conceits of our pope and the capriciousness of our king. If the throne of York were truly yours, neither would attempt to shift you from it.'

'And for that I must become a priest, dressed up in fancy robes and false piety?'

'Forgive me, my lord,' Fergus smiled, eyeing the splendour of Geoffrey's robes, 'but is that not the measure of your present predicament?'

'I will not do it. I'm a soldier, not a priest.'

'Geoffrey Plantagenet will never be less than Geoffrey

Plantagenet,' Fergus reminded him. 'Only the power will shift, and I believe it will sit admirably well on your shoulders.'

'By God, Fergus de Burton. You know how best to scratch across my grain, but your arrogance lifts my flagging spirits.'

'I would rather lift your purse, my lord.'

'Aye, you clever whelp, I don't doubt you would, and for your impudence I might be tempted to lift your head.'

'You might, but not until you hear my plan to set you amongst the most powerful men in England, eh, my lord?'

Geoffrey smiled, though his forehead was creased with doubt. 'A shift of power, you say?'

'And you, my lord, will hold the balance firmly in your grip. Let your enemies whisper that you profane the Sabbath with your hunt. Let them mutter that you befriend a Jew . . .'

'Do they say that? God's teeth, is that how they whisper and sneer behind my back?'

'Your enemies will employ any means by which to harm your reputation, but their efforts can easily be neutralised once the balance is shifted in your favour.'

'How will we do it?'

Fergus set down his glass, extended his fingers and marked them off one by one. 'Trap Cyrus de Figham in the web of his own lies and show Rome that you are swift to punish those who dare transgress against the Church. Make Daniel Hawk Canon of St Martin's in de Figham's place—'

'The Hawk?' Geoffrey demanded. 'Am I to favour that miserable catamite above more worthy men? Never! He'll have no gift from me to help increase his master's influence and—'

'He is Simeon's man,' Fergus cut in.

'What? Since when?'

'Since he began to fear for his immortal soul. He will shy from open defiance of his master, but whatever plots are hatched by de Morthlund and his supporters, you can be sure that Simeon will hear of them in due course.'

'So, does the fat man's catamite set his pretty gaze elsewhere?'

'No, sire. Be in no error on that score. The Hawk has but one master and Simeon de Beverley is beyond such inclinations. Were he not sworn to celibacy, he would be husband to a woman, not to a man.'

'And yet you say this Daniel Hawk is his man?'

'In loyalty, sir, nothing more. I urge you to make him Canon of St Martin's. Give him a living, a church and decent status of his own, and he will cease to be so dependent on Wulfric de Morthlund.' He continued counting on his fingers. 'At the same time, make Simeon de Beverley Canon of St Peter's so that he has an official voice, and he will help keep the other canons in their places. He will also force the issue of restoring the Minster church to its former glory and gladly allow full credit to you for the restoration. If you then make Cyrus's brother, Hector of Lincoln, Provost of Beverley in Jacob's place, he will report every misdemeanour amongst the canons directly to you.'

'What, *full* provost?'

Fergus nodded. 'Nothing less will bind the man effectively. I know him. He'll not fare well as a mere figurehead without true power, as Jacob de Wold has for eight long years. Give him but half an office and stronger men will pull his strings. Give him full power and I believe he will serve you well.'

'Aye, he might, until he finds a more practical use for his position and begins to plot against me from the very seat in which I've had him installed.'

Here Fergus offered a crooked smile. 'My lord, have you forgotten the barrels of wine in the Figham cellar, the barrels that bear your seal and can be verified as stolen when your shipment was attacked by robbers on the road from Beverley?'

Geoffrey chuckled and slapped his thigh. 'By God, I *had* forgotten. That was a handsome plan of yours, young Fergus.'

'It was *your* plan, my lord, if I recall correctly,' Fergus corrected, and then sat back while Geoffrey preened like a cock bird on the falsehood.

'And if *I* recall correctly, it was you who "chanced" to slip de Figham the details of my shipment and its movements. You encouraged him to rob it at his leisure and then agreed to divide the spoils between you. Those barrels provided a means of possible leverage at the time, but now . . .?'

'Now that same leverage has increased twofold,' Fergus assured him. 'Cyrus was the original thief but Hector, by ignoring those conspicuous seals of York, is guilty of theft and plunder by default. Fourteen barrels were lost in all, my Lord Archbishop—'

'Aye, seven of which are resting in your own cellar,' Geoffrey cut in.

'That much will never be proved, my lord,' Fergus told him with confidence. 'However, you could safely claim that *all* the barrels were sold off to profit the brothers and that they have conspired together to deprive you of rightful ownership or of suitable compensation for your loss.'

'By God, I like it,' Geoffrey said, scratching his chin. 'And what else must be done?'

'You must declare your intentions by lodging an official claim to the Figham estate, as is your right. At the same time, let it be known that you will agree to a private settlement, were such to be offered, to avoid a public squabble over property not legally owned by the Church. Give these canons a show of real strength, my lord, and they will gladly pay you off by private arrangement. King Richard would be most impressed to receive a gift from you to assist the progress of his holy crusades.' Here Fergus dropped his hands and offered Geoffrey his most dazzling smile. 'Well, my friend, idling Archbishop of York, frustrated soldier in a clergyman's gown, what do you say? Is all that challenge enough for a man of your mettle?'

For a moment Geoffrey stared at his visitor with a grim expression masking his inner doubts. Then he began to roar with laughter, slapped his thigh and strode to the door. He flung it wide so that his yelled commands might echo along the corridors outside, and several men dashed away to bring the fresh wine their archbishop was demanding. Geoffrey seated himself by the fire, propped his feet on a cushioned stool and surveyed Fergus de Burton from beneath his furrowed brows. 'I will hear it all,' he said at last. 'Every detail of it, right from the beginning.'

'So you shall,' de Burton told him. 'But first you must consider your precarious position as mere archbishop elect. You cannot fight such a battle as this on a lame horse. If you could be properly mounted and armed, victory would be assured.'

'Do you see my position here as a *lame horse*?' Geoffrey asked.

'I do indeed, as a poor, inferior mount unfit to serve the soldier Geoffrey Plantagenet once was,' Fergus nodded. 'On the other hand, if you were ordained and fully consecrated, your pope and your monarch would become your strongest allies. If you were officially enthroned, you would cease to be vulnerable to those who plot to relieve you of your office. Think of it, Geoffrey. No more trivial and frustrating restrictions. No more begging leave of Rome or the Coeur de Lion whenever you have a mind to *act* instead of idling. Your power would be virtually limitless, and it's all right there within your grasp. Your future success rests firmly on your enthronement as the absolute and indisputable Archbishop of York.'

'By God, Fergus, you almost have me persuaded.'

'Then I propose we drink a toast to power,' Fergus offered, raising his glass. 'And to all those enemies soon to be astounded and outwitted by the clever fighting tactics of Geoffrey Plantagenet.'

'I'll gladly drink a soldier's measure to that. It was a favourable wind that blew you into my life, Fergus de Burton. You speak my mind most eloquently.'

'I serve a great man and so speak as I find,' Fergus told him guilefully.

'Then let's proceed with our plan—'

'*Your* plan, my Lord Archbishop,' Fergus cut in, bowing his head.

'Indeed. I won't deny that similar thoughts have been playing through my mind for many weeks. It was simply a matter of time before they settled into a workable plan of action. Can we do it, Fergus?'

'I am wagering my career on it.'

'Well, then, I'll wager that by the time we've sunk another bottle of wine, I'll have Rome, the king, my enemies *and* the Beverley canons safely in my pocket.'

The young man grinned, blessing the day he found in himself the natural skills to manipulate such men as this mercurial archbishop. In his mind's eye he saw another foundation stone set in the fertile ground at Ravensthorpe, where he would make himself lord of the manor and set up a splendid shrine to his own St Fergus. Raising his glass, he grinned and said, 'Of course, my lord.'

CHAPTER THIRTEEN

On that clear and sunny morning of St Hilda's feast day, a man cast in a very different mould arrived in Beverley. He wore a hooded cloak of wool, a shabby garment hiding grander clothes and fine leather boots. The river-going craft that carried him into the port was crammed with cargo, bundles of faggots and sacks of vegetables barely fit for pigs to eat. Amongst the bags and baskets, men, women and children stood or crouched like wary sentries over their precious goods. Many were bringing the last of their winter stores to trade in Beverley, and every damaged pot, every scrap of food or makeshift utensil might mark the line between a family's ruin and its survival into the warmer, kinder season.

Cyrus de Figham set his gaze on the Minster church, a half-mile beyond the port. His face was grim beneath the folds of his hood, his dark eyes narrowed, his forehead beaded with perspiration. Close by the port stood the home church of St Nicholas and, as his gaze went to it, de Figham's fingers sought the priest's knife hanging at his girdle.

'Thorald!'

He hissed the despised name, cleared his throat and spat into the water. That priest's knife had left a hole in his back and a dull ache in his ribs where the blade had chipped two bones on entry. Thorald had made his first error when he had aimed it at de Figham and his second when he had failed to ensure that his quarry was truly dead. He would pay a high price for those mistakes, for Cyrus de Figham never forgot a wrong inflicted on him. Soon that arrogant priest of the home church would see his hasty actions come full circle and feel the sting of his own blade in his flesh.

'I will have my revenge,' de Figham muttered. 'I will have it, Thorald, on you and on the priest you serve.'

A narrow path ran along the waterside, its length and breadth crowded with beggars, would-be traders, thieves and those simply hoping to earn a crust of bread by lending a hand with the loading and unloading. A young priest with a glossy brown beard threaded his way among them, hiding his own face whilst struggling to identify the passenger in the hood on the boat. He knew that sharply aristocratic profile, the dark eyes and the black hair curling out from the lifted hood, and he knew the elegant hands that gripped the shoulders of a child pulled close to his legs.

'Cyrus de Figham!'

Father Richard shoved and elbowed his way into the crowded port. Hearing that the dark priest was still alive had caused him such anguish that his sleep had been disturbed and his appetite diminished. Seeing him here, arriving in Beverley as any innocent traveller might, cut Richard so deeply that he felt his hatred rise up as bile in his throat. Ten years had passed since that evil hand had struck old Father Bernard from behind, ten years since Richard had urinated in the dark and then discovered that by his natural act he had defiled the body of his beloved canon. The guilt of that, underscored by a sense of outrage that Father Bernard's murderer had still not been brought to account, was a festering sore that would not heal. Cyrus de Figham cast his shadow across the lives of every man and woman at St Peter's, as ominous and injurious as the shadow of Old Lucifer himself. It hung between Simeon and his destiny. It was the darkness endangering Peter's future, and now, insidious as the pestilence itself, that shadow was reaching out again for Beverley. Watching that tall shape swathed in a pilgrim's cloak, Father Richard knew his soul was threatened so long as Cyrus de Figham breathed the same air. He was a priest who loved his fellow man, but first of all he was a man who hated his enemy with a burning and unpalatable passion.

The woman slumped behind de Figham was young and pretty, though her clothes were stained with grime and sweat and her hair was unbraided. From time to time the small captive turned her head and the woman moved as if to offer her child some reassurance. Even from the distant bank, Richard was able to judge the situation at a glance. De Figham had the child, and so the woman, like a hound too fearful to run from a cruel master, stayed close to him and offered no resistance.

When the boat was safely moored, de Figham pushed his way to the side and jumped ashore. He was sweating despite the cold, and his stomach heaved at the indignity of having to share the journey with those he considered no better than animals. As he hurried from the stinking boat, he cursed the labourers and the beggars alike, dragging the child while the mother gathered up his bundle and followed after him. By showing a few coins he persuaded the driver of a sled to drag two passengers from their places and dump their goods in the snow. He claimed the vacant places for himself and the child, then allowed the woman to clamber on the rear of the sled with the sacks of cabbages and flour.

Striding towards the port along the little home church lane, Thorald was met by Father Richard coming towards him at a run.

'He's here,' the young man panted. 'Cyrus de Figham! He's here!'

'God damn him,' Thorald spat. 'He had the Devil's own protection if that dagger of mine fell so far short of its mark. Does he have the woman and child with him?'

Richard nodded, pointing out the sled beyond the crowd.

194

Thorald squinted at the port. He was already moving forward at a faster pace as he picked out familiar faces in the crowd. 'There's Father Patrick, standing beside the wooden hoist, and over there his brother helps with the unloading. Bring them, Richard, and any others we know. If we can overturn the sled—'

'What? Are you mad? Cyrus de Figham will have you arrested on sight for attempted murder.' Richard was running to keep pace with the bigger man. 'All Beverley knows you stabbed him in the back, Thorald. They will declare him blessed by heaven to have survived. On the word of a canon seemingly returned from the dead, they will stone you before you can utter a single word in your defence.'

'He will not see me,' Thorald vowed, dragging up his hood and stooping low to conceal his distinctive size. At the cargo hoist he dropped to his knees to snatch up what stones he could find, and even before Richard had gathered the other men together Thorald was aiming missiles at the driver of the sled. The stocky man between the traces roared with indignation as a large rock struck his arm. He aimed a blow at the woman who had lost her place to de Figham, earning for himself a punch from the husband whose goods had been so unceremoniously dumped from the sled. In the ensuing scuffle, Thorald shoved the crowd from behind so that a press of bodies met the side of the sled. Father Patrick and his brother followed Thorald's example, urging the crowd by word and gesture towards the water's edge. With every surge, the overladen sled tipped and rocked on its narrow runners. Men shouted and women screamed as bags and bundles fell to the ground. Scattered goods were instantly seized by opportunist thieves who made off into the crowd, provoking fresh skirmishes at every turn. A ragamuffin boy with long black hair moved like an eel through the confusion, dipping his fingers wherever he could reach, snipping with his scrap of blade at purse strings, pockets and brooch clips. In the midst of the chaos, Cyrus de Figham drew his sword for his own protection. The woman travelling with him reached for her child and attempted to make good her escape, only to shriek in pain as de Figham's fist closed around her hair and a savage tug almost pulled her off her feet.

The frightened little girl was grabbed while the woman was off guard and de Figham was distracted by his concerns for his own safety. Unseen hands took hold of her and slipped her swiftly into the crowd, which opened and closed and swallowed her into its midst. By the time the port wardens and labourers could bring the furore under control, several people were lying injured and many more were struggling for their lives in the freezing waters of the beck. The sled was all but stripped of its load and the little girl was lost without a trace.

Held by the hair, Martha was pulled towards the righted sled by de Figham. She saw no face she recognised but heard the words distinctly as someone brushed against her and spoke sharply into her ear: 'Have courage, Martha. Your child is in safe hands.'

As the sled made haste from the port, the black-haired boy stared after it with hatred blazing in his eyes. He knew that priest. While he, the unloved son of a miserable fishmonger, was condemned to live by thievery and stealth, that priest enjoyed the status of a prince. While the boy risked being hanged or maimed for every meal he ate and every coin he handled, that priest knew every comfort life could offer. The pickpocket wore rags and slept with vermin, a beggar amongst beggars, a thief amongst thieves, while Cyrus de Figham wallowed in luxury, defiant of his obligations.

The boy stared down at the ruby brooch lying in his palm, severed by his blade from de Figham's under robe. He was ten years old and already a master in the delicate art of survival, and his burning hatred for Cyrus de Figham was as vital to his existence as drawing breath.

The road to Figham House was packed with ice beneath a covering of recently fallen snow. The man dragging the sled stumbled between the wooden traces, while those behind, bending their backs to shift the weight along, spent the better part of the journey on their knees. In the slithering, unstable conveyance, Cyrus de Figham seethed with fury. The woman crouching at his side had become repugnant in her terrified compliance. He had wanted the child, Alice. A man played God when he claimed a child. Women were chattels designed by nature to absorb the abuses of a master, but a child was tender, delicate flesh, and the man who used her made himself the ultimate conqueror. De Figham had denied himself, had resisted almost unbearable temptation, waiting to reach the house where he could take her in comfort and at his leisure. Now the rewards of his abstinence were gone, snatched away by some grubby little port thief unable to appreciate the value of his haul. The loss of Alice vexed him beyond endurance. That thief deserved to be publicly castrated for daring to touch what rightfully belonged to him.

'*You* will pay for this,' he told the woman. 'She was mine, *mine*! God damn this town and everybody in it. Can a man not keep his own without some thief stealing it away? I am not yet inside the gates of Beverley and I am robbed of my ruby brooch, my purse and my enjoyment of the girl. Damn it to hell. Damn this town to hell!'

He climbed from the sled when it was still some distance from the house, paid the drivers grudgingly and strode towards the high wooden gates, still holding the shivering Martha by the hair. His whistle brought the dog handler to the gates with the hounds at his heels, and de Figham vented his rage by lashing out at the nearest animal with his boot. It yelped as the leather struck its ribs and ran, dragging the other dog after it as it fled.

'Welcome home, Father Canon.' Bruno showed his rotten teeth in a grin. His manner was easy, but his eyes were wary.

'Who burns my lamps?' de Figham demanded, seeing the lighted windows. 'Who dares to enjoy the comforts of my house?'

'Your brother, sir.'

'My brother? That snivelling priest from Lincoln? What in God's name is he doing in *my house*?'

'Making free with your hospitality, Father Canon.' Bruno knew this priest for his jealousies and his tight grip on his purse, and he sought de Figham's favour by pointing directly to his brother's faults. If it came to a battle between the two, Cyrus would oust the trespasser without so much as a twinge of conscience for their kinship. Bruno had already seen this dark priest's rage at its worst and would rather do battle with demons from hell than be caught downwind of it.

Cyrus de Figham's face had grown still and tight. 'Does Hector of Lincoln dare to entertain at my expense?'

'He does, Father Canon. He's feasted the Canon of St Matthew's and several others at your table. He serves a fine boar and pours a splendid wine, so I believe.'

De Figham's face had tightened and his eyes were black with anger. 'How dare he? How dare that pious fool make ready with my stores and my wine in the comfort of my own house?'

Bruno stepped back, cautious of the priest's explosive temper. He could have kept to a safe path and held his tongue, but de Figham's sudden return indicated a swift turn of allegiance if he was to gain from it. He saw that the man was shivering, though his face was wet with sweat, and he guessed that his infamous fury was about to be unleashed.

'Sir, he's taken one liberty after another. He's filled the house with clerks to list all your possessions. He's signed papers for the legate's court. He thought you dead and so he spoke against you freely.'

'To whom?'

Bruno shrugged. 'The pope's agent is expected from Rome. The provost has gathered papers and had copies carried to York. Men fight amongst themselves for what's rightfully yours, my lord. I've kept guard here for all these weeks, day and night, with never an hour's rest, but now your brother's here and—'

'Who has kept you here?'

'I stayed for loyalty, Father Canon,' Bruno said, offering up his palms in supplication.

'Liar!' de Figham spat. 'Who paid for your ale and meat?'

'Fergus de Burton,' the man admitted grudgingly.

'Ah, the archbishop's eyes and ears.' De Figham brought his sleeve to his face as a fit of coughing left him sweating and short of breath. 'And why should Fergus de Burton concern himself with the protection of my property?'

'Don't know,' Bruno said sullenly, then brightened as an idea came to him. 'He didn't pay me well, that much I do know. It was a meagre sum, barely enough to keep body and soul together, a pittance for the work I've had to do.'

De Figham dipped into his purse and pressed a coin into the dog handler's dirty hand. He had no doubt that Bruno had made a handsome profit from the deal, but he knew enough about dishonesty to pay for it when he could, and a coin in the villain's pocket pulled the strings of the villain's skills.

'That hood is new,' he observed with sudden suspicion. 'Where is your cat skin?'

'Father Hector disliked its stink. I sold it to a waterman for a penny.'

De Figham's eyes were glinting black slits. 'No penny bought so fine a hood. Nor did it pay for those boots you wear.'

'No, sir. Father Hector was generous. He sought to bribe me with gifts.'

'Aye, he is generous with *my* purse,' de Figham growled. He grabbed the startled Bruno by the folds of his new hood and pulled him closer. 'Bribe or no bribe, do not forget that I am still master here. If it should slip your mind I will not hesitate to use my branding iron to remind you of the fact. Is Hector guarded?'

'No, sir. Only the servants and a clerk are with him.'

'Good. Unlock the gate and keep those dogs quiet, and make sure you come at once if you hear me call. I intend to catch this uninvited guest off his guard and show him who is *truly* master here.'

Bruno watched the priest stride towards the house, allowing a safe distance to extend between them before adding the final barb to his report.

'My Lord Canon, your brother styles himself Hector de Figham.'

The tall priest stopped, his body suddenly rigid and his fists clenched at his sides. His head turned slowly and he glared at the dog handler. A pulse throbbed in his cheek as he said coldly, 'I am de Figham. I own this land and everything on it, every blade of grass and drop of water. *I* am de Figham.'

'The whole town knows that,' Bruno said.

'Damn him . . .' De Figham was overcome by another bout of violent coughing. He spat a dark mess into the snow and watched it seep away. The spasm left him exhausted and clutching at his belly.

'Father Canon . . .' Bruno stepped forward, checked himself and instinctively drew back. 'Are you ill?'

'Ill?' the priest demanded, rounding on the dog handler in fury. 'Of course I am, you idiot. I was pierced by a murderer's knife and left for dead. I have survived on monk's fare for two months and swallowed wine not fit for pickling fruit. Their rancid bread and salt meat have left my belly raw. What decent man would not be sick to his stomach from such as I have been forced to endure?'

At the door of the house he leaned against the lintel and lowered his head onto his forearm. His stomach heaved. The stench of the boat was still in his nostrils. He stooped and rubbed both legs where the heavy curb brace had taken its toll, then came erect as the sound of music drifted in gentle tones from beyond the door. A lute was playing somewhere in the house. The sound incensed him. Taking Martha by the hair, he unlocked the door of his house and stepped inside.

In the sumptuous lower room of Figham House, Hector sprawled in a carved oak chair with his boots unlaced and his feet propped on the hearth. Here in this house he was warm, well fed and perfectly content. This man of humble lifestyle and few expectations had been lifted from obscurity and plunged into a world of luxurious idleness. He found himself holding the cards that others hoped to deal, standing between great men and their ambitions. The likes of Wulfric de Morthlund sought his favours, while Beverley's provost, the highest authority in the town, saw his own position threatened by the unassuming, softly spoken priest from across the Humber. These days of opulence had given him an appetite for something more than a life of piety and repetitious ritual. He had tasted power and found it to his liking. He had basked in the respect of those who, only a few short weeks ago, had considered him inferior. His new status provided a heady brew far more intoxicating than the excellent wine from his brother's well-stocked cellars. His stolen inheritance was restored to him a thousandfold. His eyes were closed and he was dozing peacefully when the door of the room burst open and a loud voice brought him instantly to his feet.

'Usurper! I will have your miserable head for this!'

For a moment Hector was convinced that he was dreaming. Then he saw the sword in his brother's hand and the murderous glint in his eye, and he knew that his dreams of a better life were about to come to an end.

In the brittle silence that followed the sudden crashing open of the door, the brothers stared at each other in equal horror. Hector saw the fury and indignation set to erupt in this isolated and virtually unguarded house. Cyrus saw the rings and jewelled girdle, the wolf-skin coat and linen breeches, the crisp white shirt and high leather riding boots that came from his own robe chests. He saw the wine in crystal glasses, the rich food on the table and the silk-clad musicians standing with instruments poised and mouths agape. He was angered to his soul.

'Thief!' he hissed. 'Plunderer!'

'All this is rightfully mine,' Hector protested, finding his voice at last. 'You are the thief, Cyrus. You stole it first from me.'

'My wolf-skin coat ... my boots ...' Choking on his indignation, Cyrus raised his sword and strode into the room, his menacing movements driving Hector back until the great oak table was between them. With a roar he threw himself forward and swung his weapon in a wide arc. The blade missed Hector's head by inches before embedding itself in the hind of beef in the centre of the table.

'Murder! Murder!' Hector leaped sideways and back, still

201

keeping the table between them. 'The mark of Cain be on you, Cyrus, if you strike your brother down.'

The next swing of the sword lashed a tear in the sleeve of Hector's borrowed shirt and drew a terrified scream from him as Cyrus, swept off balance, sprawled across the table, scattering food and dishes everywhere. The musicians fled, elbowing Bruno and Martha aside in their haste to escape the mayhem. Hector saw his chance and lunged for the door, only to find his feet hampered by the loosened laces of the boots he wore. He tripped and fell against a chair, which overturned beneath his weight and sent him sprawling in a corner. He attempted to flee on hands and knees then turned to find his brother lurching after him with his sword raised above his head.

'My house, my clothes, my name!' de Figham screamed. His face was flushed, his hair plastered in damp black strands to his perspiring head and neck. Not merely rage but madness glinted in his eyes as he loomed over his brother. Spittle dribbled between his teeth and sprayed in droplets as he spat words at the fallen man. 'You stole it all! This time I will kill you . . . I—'

'Spare me!' Hector pleaded. 'I will do anything you say! In God's holy name, *spare me!*'

'Take your snivelling pleas to the . . . to the . . . to . . .'

While Hector cringed against the wall, sobbing in terror and begging for his life, de Figham slowly lowered his sword as his senses began to swim and his vision clouded. All strength suddenly rushed from his limbs. He was trembling and his breathing was fast and shallow. The sword slid from his fingers and clattered to the floor and, with a shudder and an agonised groan, its owner toppled after it.

Hector shrieked again as the body of his brother fell across him. He struggled to free himself of the leaden weight, then scrambled to his feet and made frantic attempts to regain his lost composure. He saw the woman and the dog handler at the door and a startled clerk hovering behind them in the corridor. He hastened to bring them all to his support.

'You saw it. He tried to kill me. He saw I was unarmed and unable to defend myself, yet he attacked me with his sword. He tried to murder me.'

Bruno shrugged his shoulders, then moved into the room to make a brief inspection of the fallen man. Seeing that inert form with its florid face and spittle-stained mouth, he realised that his fortunes had taken yet another swing. Hector's was now the stronger case. He held the purse and would be master here.

'I saw it,' he agreed at last. 'He tried to kill you.'

'He is insane.'

'No, sir, I think he's sick . . .'

'You are my witness,' Hector insisted. 'When you tell the court of the papal legate of these events, this madman will be convicted on your evidence.'

Bruno backed away at Hector's words, appalled by the prospect of being publicly identified as Cyrus de Figham's accuser. 'What, speak out against Father Cyrus? Look him in the eye and bear witness in open court against *him*?' He shook his head and took another few steps towards the door. 'Not me, Father Hector.'

'You will do it!' Hector shouted in his face, displaying a measure of his brother's fury. 'The law requires it.'

'No, sir, not me.'

'Then you will hang with him!' Hector screamed. 'I will have you arrested as his accomplice to murder. I will swear you were a party to his actions. You may either accuse him or else stand accused *with* him. I will see to it.'

'Accused with him?' Bruno gasped. 'Me? But my lord, I had no part in this attack.'

'So help me God, I will swear that you did.' He turned to the others. 'You, clerk, will describe what happened here, on paper and in close detail. And you, woman—'

'I am his prisoner,' Martha muttered, still staring at the fallen man. 'He took me by force and he—'

'Vow to speak out,' Hector told her. 'Swear now, before this clerk, that you will tell the truth at the appropriate time. Swear it and you are free to go.'

'Free?' She stared at Hector and saw him nod his head, then turned to the clerk and hurriedly agreed. 'Master clerk, I swear to speak if I'm called. I saw him attack this man without cause or provocation. I will bear witness.'

Martha was led by the young clerk to the corridor beyond the room. She moved towards the main door of the house, uncertain and exhausted by the events of the last few days.

'Am I really free to go?' she asked the clerk.

'You are. Go quickly to St Peter's. God protect you.'

She looked back only once, to see the curate and the servant, Bruno, hoisting the stricken man between them. Then she stepped into the icy brightness beyond the door and wept with relief.

Inside the house, Bruno panted and sweated with the strain of bearing the better part of Cyrus de Figham's weight. 'My lord, his clothes are drenched. He has the sweats.'

'And little wonder, when he's possessed by such devilish rages. Do not stand there with your mouth agape, clerk. Bring a light. These steps are treacherous in the dark.'

They dragged the prostrate man to the foot of the stair, where rats ran in the dark and the walls were thick with stone mould. Here and there the walls were lined with a covering of ice where damp on the surface of the stones had frozen in the wind from unglazed windows. Four cells were built beneath the barn, with small barred apertures set into their doors and a simple crucifix hung below their window slits. Here sinners were left to reflect upon the folly of their ways and the promised joys of heaven, to repent of their sins and, in many cases, to prepare themselves for an imminent journey to the afterlife.

Hector paused at one such door, his features tight as he recalled past horrors inflicted upon him at the malicious instigation of his brother. In this particular cell he had languished, cold and terrified of the dark, when Cyrus had carried false tales of him to their father and then stood by in silence while Hector bore the blame for his crimes. It seemed appropriate now that the evildoer of their childhood should receive a taste of the fare he had so often forced upon his brother.

'My lord, he's barely breathing,' Bruno observed.

'Leave off your bleating,' Hector snapped.

Paul held a torch aloft and, by its flickering, eerie light, guided them into the tiny room. The walls were slimy with mould and when their feet disturbed the ancient straw covering the floor, it gave off a stench that was sickening.

Cyrus de Figham began to regain his senses as his body made contact with the cold ground and his throat was filled with the fetid stink of the cell. Confused and giddy, he struggled vainly to gain his feet, grasping at every limb or fold of coat within his reach. His fingers were too weak to grip, his legs too shaky to bear his weight, so that he groped and floundered like a drowning man. He crawled after the figures that moved like phantoms in the torch light and managed to reach the door just as it swung shut with a clang. A key turned in the lock. Footsteps sounded on the stones outside, and then the light was gone and all was hushed.

'No . . . *no!*'

With an effort born of outrage he dragged himself up and pressed his face to the small barred opening in the door. Now the full reality of his situation descended on him with brutal clarity. He was trapped in the dark, imprisoned like an animal or a criminal in a cage. His was confined in his own dark cellar where only the rats would find him and no living man would ever hear his screams.

That afternoon urgent messages were sent to the Provost of Beverley and to the Canon of St Matthew's, Wulfric de Morthlund. A rider left for York with letters for the archbishop and for Fergus de Burton. This horseman carried his payment in advance, lest he fail to reach his destination due to the dangerously uncertain weather. Just a half-mile from Figham Pasture he turned his horse aside and made for home, where he burned the letters beneath the cooking pot. No man in his senses would make such a journey with nothing to gain from his efforts. Hector was either a fool to pay his rider in advance, or else a clever man who did not intend his messages to reach their destinations.

CHAPTER FOURTEEN

At his house in Minster Moorgate, Wulfric de Morthlund threw back his priestly robe and bellowed into the face of his physician, Job, 'What the hell do you mean, *he's dying?*'

'He bleeds from his insides, my lord.'

Wulfric de Morthlund surveyed the elderly physician with contempt. What he saw was a stooped, sparsely bearded individual with tired eyes and an air of detachment unsuited to the august company he was called upon to serve. 'I pay you well enough, so earn your purse. You are a physician, or so you claim, and your skills, such as they be, do not come cheaply.'

'No physician is infallible,' the man replied wearily.

'You will cure the brat of his inconvenient bleeding.'

'I cannot do that, my lord.' Job raised his hands in a hopeless gesture. 'The injuries are too deep. The boy will not survive.'

'You stand before me with your expensive potions and instruments of healing,' de Morthlund bellowed, 'and you dare to tell me that *he will not survive?* Damn it! I want him cured!' The Canon of St Matthew's began to pace the room in agitation. The flesh around his neck and chin had flushed to crimson. He would not surrender his pleasures on the word of some ageing physician, however skilled he professed to be.

'Such injuries are impossible to remedy,' Job told him, 'and in one so small, the infection will spread rapidly.'

'What infection?' De Morthlund halted. He placed his fists on his hips and drew himself up to his full height, his face creased with distrust.

'Father Canon, Tobias has a raging fever. He sweats. He vomits. His bowels are bleeding. Many such cases have already been reported in the town and . . .'

Wulfric's fleshy face took on a look of horror. 'Ye gods. Is it the pestilence?'

The physician shrugged and de Morthlund, his face suddenly robbed of its florid aspect, drew his robe across his belly as if to close himself off from the dreaded word.

'I cannot say for certain . . .'

'But you suspect?'

'Alas, Father Canon, I do.'

'Dear God in Heaven!' The fat man moved backwards until a chair prevented his retreat, then lowered his body into the seat.

'If, by some miracle, he should survive the injuries to—'

'Who cares a damn if he survives?' de Morthlund suddenly exploded. He sprang from the chair, his rolls of fat aquiver. 'If that cur has brought the pestilence here, to my own house . . . Get him out. Have him removed at once.'

'Removed to where?' Job asked, his tired face creased with concern. 'Who will give him shelter in his condition?'

'Not I,' de Morthlund spat. 'He will not find shelter in *this* house while he harbours the plague. Get him out. Let him spew and flux beyond the reach of decent, God-fearing men. Let him lie in the street whence he came, since he proves himself fit for nothing better.'

Father Daniel had been standing in a corner, praying silently for the soul of the child while his master sought only to rid himself of the burden of his sick body. Now he placed himself between the fuming canon and the physician, lowered his voice and offered words of caution.

'My lord, if the provost should hear of this . . .'

'You can be sure Jacob de Wold will hear of it from my own lips,' Wulfric bellowed in reply. 'Cyrus de Figham has placed a deadly poison in our midst. He sent that infected wretch to me. I intend to make him pay for this. I intend to lay every charge on his head from sacrilege to murder. I will see him in his grave for this . . .' De Morthlund choked and spluttered his indignation. 'I will have him excommunicated . . . outlawed . . . I will—'

'My lord, you are distraught.' Daniel took his master by the elbows and attempted to reseat him in the chair. 'Job, attend your canon.'

As the elderly man stepped forward to lend assistance, de Morthlund shoved him roughly aside and shook his clenched fist in his face. 'Get away from me, fondler of vile and unclean things,' he shrieked. 'Do not touch me. Here, take your purse and go from this house. I will not suffer the company of one who tends the pestilence, who dips his fingers in the leper's flux and sniffs his vomit to determine what lies inside. Get out of my house and out of my sight!'

The physician left in haste by the front door as servants rushed to do their master's bidding at the rear. Tobias was lifted from his bed and carried into the street. They left him lying in the snow, a small dark bundle wrapped in a blanket, and hurried back to the house to pray that the pestilence was gone with him.

A man in a pilgrim's robe and woollen hood witnessed the expulsion of the boy from the canon's property. Brother David watched de Morthlund's house whenever he could find no other task to fill his empty hours.

'Tobias,' he said. 'Do you know me, child? I am Brother David from the abbey where you stayed with your master and mistress. God bless you, Tobias.'

The boy's eyes flickered open. 'The canon . . .'

David shook him gently, then withdrew his hand in haste as vomit oozed from Tobias's mouth. 'All right, you poor child, I will take you back to St Peter's.'

'The canon ... Oh please, make him stop ... Help me ...'

'Hush, lad, I am here to help you.'

At the house, Daniel Hawk rubbed his palm across the glass and pressed his face close to the window.

'What is it, Daniel? What do you see out there?'

Wulfric still marked the length and breadth of the room with his agitated pacing. He had ordered the blood-stained mattress removed from the bed where Tobias had slept, his bowl and platter broken, his linens burned, and now he fretted that even these precautions would prove useless against the plague.

'It is the monk again,' Daniel told him. 'The one who has taken to lurking just beyond the house. He is kneeling over Tobias, praying, I think.'

'Or questioning the brat. Move aside. Let me see.' The canon peered out, then called for his cloak and marched from the house, with Daniel following close behind, to confront the man.

'You there! What are you doing at my gate?'

'Giving aid to a sick child,' was the monk's prompt reply.

'By whose leave? This is the house of Wulfric de Morthlund, Canon of St Martin. I have seen you out here before, hiding in the shadows with the thieves and vagabonds. You have no right to interfere here. Be off with you.'

David rose to his feet and surveyed the fat man with a matter-of-fact stare. 'I am well within my rights as a citizen of this town.'

'The devil you are. No man has rights on *my* property.'

'But I trespass on no man's private land.'

'You trespass on *my* land,' Wulfric told him. 'I own this house and all its grounds.'

The monk spread his hands to indicate the spot on which he stood. 'But you do not own the street.'

'By the gods, are you aware that I could have you flogged

210

for your impertinence? I could have your tongue clipped and your—'

'On what grounds would you dare inflict such punishment on a blameless man?'

'On the grounds that you are an ill-mannered monk and surly in your speech,' the fat man growled.

'Sir, I am David, of the brotherhood serving St Dominic the Mailed. Your provost found no fault in me, so why should you?'

De Morthlund's head moved in a birdlike gesture of inquiry. 'St Dominic the Mailed, you say? Then you must know of Cyrus de Figham, who was carried there some weeks ago by misguided fools who sought to save his life?'

'I know of him.' The monk nodded grimly.

'Good, then you must tell me everything,' Wulfric said and, with a flourish of his cloak, turned towards the house. 'Come inside. You shall have bread and wine while I hear your story.'

'No. This child has pressing need of my assistance.'

Wulfric had taken several steps towards the door of the house, expecting the monk to follow him. He rounded on him now, his eyes blazing. 'No man says no to *me*! Are you aware whose hospitality you are refusing? I am Wulfric de Morthlund, the most powerful man in Beverley, a man to be respected, to be feared . . .'

'I fear no man,' the monk said quietly, interrupting Wulfric's flush of self-praise.

'Then you are a fool. Any who fears God Almighty must also fear His privileged elite.'

David held the man's gaze and said again, 'I fear no man, whatever privileges he claims.' He stooped to lift the child and received a bellow from the canon.

'Stop that! Set him down at once!'

'I will not.'

Wulfric would have raised his sword, but Father Daniel stayed his hand. 'Think before you act in haste, my lord. If the child is taken to another place, your duty towards him is totally discharged and any event that follows will not—'

'What duty?' Wulfric demanded. 'The brat is sick. Am I to be held responsible for *that*?'

'My lord, his injuries . . . Have you forgotten that he bleeds internally?'

'Well perhaps, on second thoughts, this monk does me a service. I am well rid of Cyrus de Figham's little *gift*.'

'You are, my lord.'

As the sword was lowered back into its sheath, the monk made as if to walk away with his burden. Wulfric de Morthlund, however, was reluctant to relinquish his authority without due protest.

'Very well, monk. You have my leave to take the boy.'

David halted and turned his head to fix de Morthlund with his placid stare. 'I require no leave, since we have already established that you do not own the street into which your servants have expelled him.'

'Damn your insolence. You will address me as Father Canon.'

'I will not address you at all, since I have pressing work to do.'

Only Daniel's grip on his arm restrained de Morthlund. 'Let me remind you that the child is my property,' he blustered. 'I have the right to keep him if I so choose.'

'Then keep him,' David suddenly declared, moving forward with Tobias held out before him. 'Take him. I give him back to you with my blessing.' As Wulfric de Morthlund stepped back several paces and raised his sleeve to cover his mouth and nostrils, David strode after him, persistent in his offer. 'Let me carry your property back inside, where you can tend his hurts and give him your protection. Here, take him. *Take him!*'

'No! Get back! Get back!' The fat man cried the words in a shrill voice, wafting his hands before him. 'Get that tainted wretch away from me. Take him, and be gone from here, and may his sickness corrupt you for your arrogance.' Shaking with anger, he watched the monk retreat, and then called after him, 'Take the brat to St Peter's enclosure, to Simeon de Beverley. Let *him* receive the worthless baggage with compassion. He will not find his life so charmed when there is a pestilence within his walls.'

Dismayed, Daniel Hawk caught his master by the sleeve. 'My lord, if this monk has the provost's ear, a bad report of you might reach Hall Garth. At least pay him for his trouble, as is his due, so that none can say he was dutiful in God's name while you were not.'

'I am *damned* if I will.'

'My lord, it is the custom and the law. Two marks should be enough to demonstrate your goodwill.'

'*One* mark,' Wulfric conceded, 'though it galls me to pay so much as a clipped penny for the wretch. Here, take it, and warn that monk I will not forget this day, that I will not forget this David of St Dominic's.'

Daniel hurried into the street and pressed the coin into the monk's hand with a whisper. 'Warn Simeon that the boy might be infected with a pestilence. He has the flux and the sweats, and he bleeds from a particular injury.'

'Particular?' the monk inquired.

'An internal wound. Simeon will understand.'

Daniel did not see the monk meet with another man at the farthest corner of the street and, after a brief exchange, continue on his way with a lighter step. The other was Job, physician to Wulfric de Morthlund, and his whispered words to David gave him hope that Tobias would survive.

Inside the house Wulfric de Morthlund seethed and blustered in his chagrin. Two runners were sent in urgent haste to fetch his physician back, while the obese canon took to his bed complaining of a sore head and stomach cramps.

'Oh God, my belly heaves like a thing alive. Help me to my couch. I think I'm dying.'

His groans and protestations of impending death echoed through the house. Ensconced on his splendid couch, he demanded wine and sugared dates to ease his torment, and while he stuffed himself with these, his cries became the louder.

'Flatulence, brought on by chronic constipation,' the

physician concluded after a cursory examination of Wulfric's distended belly. He drew Daniel to the corridor and spoke in lowered tones. 'Too much rich food and too many rich imaginings are all that ail your master. Give him an infusion of blackthorn every hour. It is a powerful purgative that will cause him griping pains and heavy sweating, and eventually it will force his belly to expel the blockage.'

'Only common constipation? He'll not thank you for so violent a cure for such an inglorious ailment,' Daniel warned.

'Then keep him in ignorance,' Job smiled. 'Let him remain convinced that he has been visited by the pestilence. He'll consider himself blessed by God when he recovers.'

'You have my thanks,' Daniel told him. 'I pray that poor Tobias has not left the plague with us.'

The elderly man drew Daniel towards the door of the house and waited for the torch bearer to move away before explaining. 'The boy's injuries are serious but accessible to a man of Osric's skill. With care he will survive them, just as surely as he will recover from the dose of blackthorn I persuaded him to take.'

'What? You gave the boy essence of blackthorn to induce a flux?'

'I did,' Job smiled, 'on excellent advice. How else was I to get him out?'

Daniel grasped him by the hand. 'Bless you a thousand times for doing this.'

'You may bless the simple blackthorn, and the monk who bade me use it,' Job said gravely. 'If you have need to thank me, just take care your master never learns the truth.'

Simeon and Elvira sat beside the bed until the boy began to show awareness of his surroundings.

'So, Tobias, you are returned to us at last. Drink this. It will help you recover from your sickness.'

The boy opened his eyes to find Simeon bending over his bed and several familiar faces hovering over him. Here was Edwin and the beautiful lady, Elvira, and the big, stern man with the long moustaches who was Simeon's father. Here too were those other priests who had been kind to him, the fierce Thorald and the bearded Richard, and with them the monk whose sandals left his toes exposed to the cold. Osric had bathed his torn flesh with herb-scented water and smoothed on a cool, thick ointment to ease the fiery pains that stabbed like so many sharpened blades inside him. He was amongst friends, that much he knew, and the terrifying fat man had gone away.

'He beat me,' Tobias complained. 'I delivered the message as the dark priest said, but the big man beat me and made me bleed.'

'He was wrong to hurt you, Tobias,' Simeon told him. 'But you are safe now with us. Father Wulfric will never beat you again so long as you stay within these walls. We will protect you.'

'Father Simeon, my mistress ... Alice ... They mustn't go to that house. He'll hurt them ...'

'Rest easy, boy. Your mistress and her daughter are here with us.'

'Here? Safe?'

'Yes, Tobias, and you will see them again very soon.'

With a sigh Tobias closed his eyes. Large tears rolled out from between his lashes and left a glistening track on his skin before vanishing into his hair. When he opened his eyes again there was bewilderment as well as pain in their dark centres.

'Why did he hurt me, Father Simeon? Why was I punished? What did I do wrong?'

'You did nothing wrong, Tobias. Alas, in this world there are wicked men who will harm us without cause. We can only beware of them and trust that God in His mercy will protect us from them.'

Simeon heard Elvira's sharp intake of breath and felt the sudden tension in her body. As he looked up, her glance told him what her silence left unsaid, that he was wrong to teach the boy to trust when already he had trusted and suffered injury at the hands of a

215

monster. She withdrew her hand when he reached for it.

By the door, Martha sat with her sleeping child clutched to her breast and her eyes constantly alert for any movement. The marks of Cyrus de Figham's lust stood out in livid bruises and scratches on her face, neck and forearms. Elvira knew, as any woman must, that the deeper wounds were impossible to see, and that their healing, if they healed at all, was likely to leave much hidden scarring.

Simeon drew Osric from the bedside and spoke to him in a whisper. 'Tobias seems confused. He believes he has been beaten.'

'Then we may thank God for that small mercy,' Osric growled.

'Will he heal?'

'It is too early to say.' Osric shrugged his leather-clad shoulders, uncertain of his own skills in the presence of such injuries. 'There are many lacerations, some very deep. If I can keep the passage open until they heal, and if the wounds do not become infected . . .' He shook his head. 'He is such a small boy, and the flux brought on by the blackthorn might have saved his life today only to kill him at a later date. He is such a *small* boy.'

'And not the first to be so used by Wulfric de Morthlund,' Simeon hissed. 'First Stephen, then James and now Tobias, and who knows how many more beyond our reckoning? This time he must be made to pay for the harm he has inflicted.'

'How?' Osric demanded. 'With a purse of gold to the Church, a paltry fine that will make no impression on his coffers?'

'The Church has the power to give ten years' penance for the sin of homosexuality,' Simeon reminded him.

'Aye, but our Church is lenient on matters of such delicacy. No record exists of any such punishment ever being imposed on one of its own.'

'Then the law is ignored.'

'Aye,' Osric said wearily. 'There are none so blind, my

216

friend, as those who consider it more expedient not to see.'

Rufus joined them, his face dark with hostility and his manner belligerent. 'Perhaps the Church believes that no such crimes are ever committed by its privileged servants.'

'But we *know* they are, and frequently.' Simeon glanced at Tobias and shook his head. 'And often with the most devastating consequences.'

'And just who is to prevent them if the Church will not?'

'*I* will,' Simeon said through his teeth. 'I will have him charged and brought before the court. I'll demand an inquisition and—'

'There will be no charges. Damn your naivety.' Rufus was so angry that he almost spat the words. The sight of Tobias's injuries, and the knowledge of how they were inflicted, sickened him. 'De Morthlund cannot be touched. As far as the law and the Church are concerned, no crime has been committed.'

Simeon stared at his father in disbelief. 'How can you say that? Father, that eight-year-old boy has been ripped open by—'

'Prove it!'

Simeon drew back, his eyes narrowed. 'So, you choose to play devil's advocate on his behalf?'

'Damn it, Simeon, your Church will do no less. Have him charged and you will stand alone. Not a single man who knows of his crimes will dare point a finger at him, lest the shadow of it falls on himself or on those he fears to offend.' Rufus raked his fingers through his hair. 'Ten years ago, when Peter was first brought to Beverley, a boy hanged himself after being horribly violated inside the Minster itself.'

'His name was Stephen,' Osric growled.

Rufus ignored the interruption and continued to glower at his son, whose own anger simmered behind the set of his features. 'The altar was reconsecrated and the boy laid to rest as a suicide. You had your proof then, ten years ago, so what was it, Simeon, that stayed your hand on that occasion? Why did the beast go unchastised and free to mutilate another innocent child?'

'The holy seal of confession,' Simeon hissed. 'You know it well enough, Rufus de Malham. I was tricked into hearing de Morthlund's confession.'

'Another innocent defiled, and what, in God's name, changes?' Rufus demanded 'The deed was done behind closed doors, and Tobias is too innocent to understand what has happened to him. Where is your witness to these charges? Where is your proof? Put an end to this futile talk of bringing Wulfric de Morthlund to book. It will never happen.'

'Then I will speak to Geoffrey Plantagenet, man to man.'

'Oh yes? And will you hand *him* the role of devil's advocate? You clutch at straws if you hope to succeed with any appeal to Geoffrey. He is too busy keeping peace with Rome and England's king to risk soiling his hands on such trivial matters as we have here. He will gladly furnish Wulfric de Morthlund with a dozen Beverley boys if doing so will keep his own nest unsoiled.'

'An arrogant argument, sir, for one so lately come among us,' Simeon bristled, matching his father's barely contained fury. 'While you carry so high an opinion of your own judgement, and while you clearly have but scant regard for mine, perhaps you'll be good enough to tell us all what *is* to be done about de Morthlund.'

'Do exactly what you pious men of St Peter's have done in the past. Lick your own wounds, do what you can for the boy, and then sit back in your piety and your impotence and do what you apparently do best – *nothing*!' Rufus all but snarled the word.

'By heaven, sir, if you were not my father . . .'

Seeing that the quarrel had reached its peak, Osric and Antony stepped between the two while father and son glared fiercely into each other's eyes. Both men were stiff with tension, their fists clenched and their eyes blazing. Elvira rose from her stool and stared from one tense profile to the other.

'Would you settle this with your fists?' she demanded, her own anger smouldering in her eyes and giving an edge of bitterness to her voice. 'Or perhaps you both prefer to draw your swords and settle it with steel while that beast de Morthlund casts around for a child to replace Tobias? And tell me this, father and son, while you quarrel amongst yourselves, who will play devil's advocate if that animal ever lays his hands on *Peter*?'

'Believe me, I would dispatch him to Satan's realms with my bare hands,' Simeon told her.

'Yes, Simeon, I do not doubt you would.' Elvira touched his arm and her gaze grew tender. 'But ask yourself this, my love. Will it take the rape of our own precious Peter to stop this vile debaucher of small boys?'

'You see? Even your wife fights in my corner,' Rufus boasted.

Elvira's eyes flashed anger. 'I do not, sir. I merely point out that while father and son disagree like quarrelsome children, Tobias and others like him remain unprotected. Stop fighting amongst yourselves and find a way, lest some mother take a knife to Minster Moorgate and do what her menfolk have failed to do.'

Her words were shocking in their quiet certainty, and both Rufus and Simeon were humbled by the courage that had shaped them. Simeon offered his hand and Rufus took it, though the truce their handshake signified was as thin and vulnerable as the shell that held their tempers in control.

It was Peter who offered the solution to their problem. He was sitting beside the bed where Tobias lay, helping Osric shape the linen plugs that would prevent the boy's lacerated body from sealing over as it healed. His eyes were still downturned as he suggested, 'Father, you must allow Cyrus de Figham to assist you in bringing de Morthlund before the courts.'

'De Figham? How?'

219

'By telling him the truth,' Peter offered, 'that Wulfric de Morthlund will be persuaded to speak against him at his trial.'

'We do not know that he will,' Simeon told him.

'Oh yes, he will certainly speak, since he will not forgive Father Cyrus for sending a sick boy to his house. Father Cyrus will then retaliate by accusing Father Wulfric of homosexual practices. Hector of Lincoln will voice his loathing, and so others will be courageous enough to follow his example. Thus Father Wulfric will find himself beset by enemies within the Church. Your charges will be corroborated by many, and the papal legate will be obliged to act strictly according to the law.'

'By heaven, you are right, boy.'

Rufus was astounded by Peter's calm direction of one man against another and by Simeon's admiration of this deceitful little plan. 'Do you teach your son to scheme and manipulate, to be as cunning as the priests he serves?' he demanded of Simeon.

'I teach my *foster* son to know his world and those who wield power within it,' Simeon countered. 'All priests are men, and all men have their failings and their vices. How else will he survive to do God's work when he is ordained and . . .'

Rufus stepped back, aghast at his son's words. He seemed incensed, but the anticipated explosion of temper was not forthcoming. Instead he stared at Simeon in disbelief and asked in frosty tones, 'Do you intend to make a priest of Peter?'

'Such is his calling.' Simeon nodded.

'His *calling*? What does a ten-year-old boy know of such things? He will not be sacrificed to the priesthood while I live.'

'I am his guardian, Rufus. I must respect his persuasion to the priesthood.'

'Then know that I oppose you, sir. You will make that boy a priest over my dead body.'

'So be it,' Simeon said coldly. 'His way is chosen.'

'He is a *child*!'

'He knows his own heart.'

'Then I will be the one to change it,' Rufus hissed, 'and amen to *that*, Simeon de Beverley.'

CHAPTER FIFTEEN

Dawn saw carters out in the streets collecting corpses, and priests wearing face cloths conducting special services at the pits beyond the town bars. The wealthy merchant who had travelled to Beverley with Rufus placed two of his servants amongst the dead, then took his offering, and his deaf-mute daughter, to the holy shrine of St John, where he spent long hours on his knees, praying for a miracle.

After the midday offices, the alms bell was rung for half an hour, calling the hungry to the Minster churchyard, where bread was to be distributed to the needy. Yesterday's brilliant sunlight had returned in equal measure with the dawn, but by noon a freezing fog had fallen on the town. It blurred the edges of sound and vision and crept like a silent thing into every gap and crevice. It slithered under doors and stole beneath warm cloaks and hoods, fondling and caressing with an icy touch. Dark figures bent their heads before it as they hurried to the Minster yard, where their benefactors stood guard beside a score of laden baskets. All about were crowds of ghostly figures waiting in the fog, hundreds of hungry people clamouring for bread.

Groups of priests patrolled the crowds to ensure that none took an extra share by force. They were there to protect the alms givers from the mob and to prevent opportunists stockpiling extra portions to sell in the streets. At the closing of the alms prayers the crowd surged forward, every man and woman clamouring for his or her entitlement, and every child in peril of being trampled in the crush. Within minutes the baskets were empty and the alms bell silenced. Those priests and clerks who had kept order now turned their efforts to driving the townspeople from the church grounds. Not a single belly had been adequately filled, and yet no nostril had failed to detect the scent of meat and soup clinging to the fog as servants prepared a midday meal for the priests.

'It is too little. However deep the baskets, however many the loaves, there will never be enough to feed the hungry.'

Jacob de Wold, Lord Provost of Beverley, stood with his lifelong friend, Stephen Goldsmith, at the Minster door. The provost's bald head was uncovered and he was splinted from neck to heel in iron and leather because his bones could not support his weight. The heat of an inferno had exploded in his face two years before, lifting him into the air with the force of its blast. It had broken his bones and burned his skin, and the brave priest who had flung him over his shoulders and borne him from the fire's midst had innocently added further injuries. Strapped to a wooden beam and splinted for many months, Jacob had lived but never fully recovered. He was in constant pain with or without the heavy brace that kept his spine erect and his legs from collapsing under him. But for the ever-increasing doses of poppy essence provided by the infirmarian at St Peter's, he could not hope to endure the agony that was his daily fare.

Stephen surveyed the crowds and answered, 'The poor are with us always, but the bread is limited.'

Jacob sighed. 'And yet the priests who give so little have meat and bread beyond their needs.'

Stephen glanced sideways at the pain-creased features of his provost. 'My friend, the Devil thrives where there is want. If the priests who serve the poor are allowed to go hungry, Satan will triumph by way of their empty bellies. So long as they have food surplus to their needs, that surplus will fill our baskets and the poor will benefit.'

They watched the last stragglers herded from the church-yard while the priests gathered up their empty baskets and hurried to take their places at the tables.

'I fear the curate from Lincoln will have my seat here,' Jacob said, raising a tiny bottle to his lips and swaying like a bough in the wind as the thick, sweet essence of poppy found its mark. 'Daniel Hawk will be Canon of St Martin's and Simeon Canon of St Peter's.'

'Times are changing, Jacob. All the signs tell us that St John of Beverley stirs in his sleep.'

'Is it time for me to stand down, Stephen?'

The goldsmith smiled and gripped his friend by the elbow. 'Why end the game before it is even begun?' he asked. 'Let them shift you if they can, Jacob, but do not give up your seat. You have done your best for Beverley and St John these last seven years and more, without benefit of official recognition from our archbishop. The seat will not be readily bartered if Geoffrey must replace an untroublesome diplomat such as yourself with an unknown quantity spawned in the same nest as Cyrus de Figham.'

'I fear these changes,' Jacob confessed, 'and yet each day reminds me that I am weary, Stephen, of life, of pain, of the burden of my Office . . .'

The goldsmith's fiery brows met across the bridge of his nose in a sudden frown and, hidden within his bushy red beard, his lips became compressed. 'I have already spoken to Osric,' he reminded the provost. 'He sympathises, Jacob, but he will not be persuaded to increase your supply of the extract. You must bear the burden, as you have borne it for the last two years.'

'I too have spoken to Osric,' Jacob told him with a sigh. 'He insists that my long dependency on his poppy extract has reached the limits of my body's endurance. Any more and the stupors I already suffer will become the norm. My lucid periods will cease and I will slip into a living death, where I will be aware of nothing and care the less for my

224

predicament.' He turned to Stephen Goldsmith and held his gaze. 'It is a tempting thought, such a sweet and blessed relief. Stephen, my dear and loyal friend, if I could just obtain a little more of the extract . . . If it could be bought elsewhere, so that Osric cannot intervene . . .'

'No, Jacob. Be guided by Osric, who loves you as a friend but also knows your limitations. What you ask is too dangerous. You are divided from the world by your suffering and I pity you for that, but would you be so divided from God? Would you addle your mind so that communion with the Lord is denied you?'

'But if the poppy had a measure of rue and hemlock added,' Jacob suggested, 'my passing would be eased and God would receive me in His mercy.'

'But they are deadly poisons, Jacob. What you suggest would be—'

'A gift, my friend. It would be a gift. You could do it, Stephen. You could help me into that blessed state and from there to the afterlife.'

'God forbid!' Stephen exclaimed. 'How can you even consider such a thing?'

'Stephen, my life has run its course. Allow me to go to my God with dignity. Help me. Be merciful.'

'I cannot. I *will* not,' the goldsmith insisted, shocked and dismayed that his friend's distress had come to this. 'It is not for us to relinquish the gift of life before our allotted time. Such talk is forbidden, even between friends.'

'And yet I would bless the friend whose true compassion secured my release,' Jacob persisted. 'God would not frown on one who offered such mercy to a friend in his hour of need.'

'Jacob, do you realise what you ask of me?'

The provost touched his finger to his lips and winced with the effort of lifting his arm even that small distance. 'Say nothing, Stephen. Think on it, but say nothing. You know my heart as you know my pain, so I will press you no further. Come, help me inside. We privileged members of the Church must keep our bellies filled to the brim

225

lest the Devil be drawn from his lair by the scent of our hunger.'

The quarrel between Simeon and his father still smouldered behind the high walls of St Peter's. Paul, the clerk who had found so many years of honest sanctuary and friendship there, had come to them in haste from the great house on the Figham Pasture, and what he had to tell them quickly stirred the simmering conflict into flame.

Rufus de Malham was not the only man shocked by Simeon's response, but he was the first to speak out, in a thundering voice that caused young Edwin and his sister to jump like startled rabbits at the corner desk they shared.

'What? *Do* something? Do I hear a son of mine bleating that something must be done to ease the hardship of his enemy?'

Simeon's voice was calm despite the hardness of his gaze. He swept off his cloak and dropped it across a stool, then squared his shoulders as he faced his father.

'Sir, what you hear are the words of a priest who knows the Scriptures and intends to act on what is written there.'

'Damn it, Simeon, that devil has tested every man here beyond all reasonable endurance. He is evil. He is a murderer and a defiler of innocent women.'

'And he is dying,' Simeon answered softly. 'He is sick, thirsty, exposed to the cold and deprived of all assistance.'

'Then he is brought to book at last,' Rufus countered. 'This is not your responsibility, Simeon. You were not to know that Hector would throw him into a cell and leave him to rot.'

'No, Rufus, but I know it now.'

'Then call it God's will and have done with all this talk of easing his predicament.'

Richard, who burned with hatred for de Figham, tempered his feelings as a man with his integrity as a priest. 'God could have kept us in ignorance of de Figham's fate,' he reasoned. 'Why then has He included

226

us in this? Why has He brought this news here, to St Peter's?'

'God did not bring it here,' Rufus protested, glaring as he pointed an accusing finger at Paul. '*He* did, and by heaven I, for one, could find a better use for his tongue.'

Elvira drew up extra stools around the covered well, setting out their places as if at a huge debating table. Brother David, who had watched and listened to the talk passively, assisted her.

'While you bicker amongst yourselves you place a weapon in his hands,' Elvira said. 'Sit down together and find a better way.'

She watched them take their places and shuddered as she remembered how Cyrus de Figham, by treachery, had once invaded this peaceful sanctuary. She would have killed him then, had she been stronger. She would have plunged her concealed knife into his black heart and gladly watched him die. It shamed her still that strangers had bared her breasts as they had dragged her, kicking and screaming, from her objective, that they had spat on her and called her a witch, then tortured her in a filthy cell in the name of Christian atonement. And now Simeon, the very best of men, was torn between his hatred and his vows, and when the talk was done she knew that he, who had most cause to want de Figham dead, would be instrumental in keeping him alive.

Harsh words flew back and forth across the table. Tempers flared and were subdued, and flared again. Then Peter, who had listened from a quiet corner, solemn and withdrawn, stepped forward to place his hand on Simeon's shoulder. All argument seemed exhausted now that each had had his say, and only Peter was left to offer an opinion.

'"If thine enemy hunger, feed him. If he thirst, give him drink."' He quoted softly and precisely the words of St Paul. '"And in so doing, heap coals of fire upon his head."'

'St Paul was a saint,' Thorald countered. 'We are men.'

'What do those words mean?' Rufus demanded. 'Are we to feed him tainted food and lace his drink with poison?

How are we to administer these "coals of fire" if not by leaving de Figham to his fate?'

Peter spoke with quiet assurance that marked him out as wise beyond his years. 'We are taught that by offering succour to the one we hate, we bring the weight of his own sins down on his head. We show him mercy so that he is burned by guilt and scorched by his soul's desire to make amends.'

'Platitudes!' Rufus brought his fist down on the table with a crash. 'De Figham has no conscience. He will bite any hand that feeds him and then laugh in your face as he strikes you down.'

Peter's gaze was steady as he replied, 'St Paul preached, "Be not overcome of evil, but overcome evil with good."'

'And I say that any good you do de Figham now will be returned twofold in evil.'

'He is brought to his lowest ebb,' Peter reminded them all. 'He faces certain death unless he can be helped to bear his imprisonment, and if he dies before his trial, his evil will live on. Only when Cyrus de Figham is charged and found guilty under God's law will we all be free of his influence. Until then we, as Christian men, must help preserve his life and, God willing, his soul.'

'Peter is right,' Richard agreed with some reluctance, rising to his feet so that all could see that he, the most unlikely one among them, could be merciful. 'We need the trial, therefore we must do our best to keep him alive. And remember this, by our good example de Figham might yet repent and make his peace with God. It is clearly our duty, as priests and as true Christians, to show him the way so that he might follow it and find his place at last with God.'

'I would rather disregard the Almighty's wrath and direct de Figham straight to hell,' Rufus declared. 'Osric, what do you say? Are we all to be instructed in this matter by a ten-year-old child? That priest has been a thorn in your side for more than a decade. What would *you* have us do with him?'

'I would gladly leave him to rot,' Osric declared with

passion, 'but not at the expense of our own souls. We need to see him tried and, loathe him or not, we have a clear duty to see that he survives his stay in that prison cell.'

Scowling, Rufus turned to the big priest of St Nicholas. 'And you, Thorald, having once already sought to kill this Cyrus de Figham, what is *your* verdict?'

Above his hunched, bull-like shoulders, Thorald nodded reluctantly. 'I agree with Peter. We are men of conscience, Rufus. We cannot hear the truth and close our ears to it. We must help de Figham.'

'I too would rather see him dead,' Elvira said. 'When he was here I wanted to kill him myself, and after the carting I gave thanks for the strength of Thorald's throwing arm, but now . . .?' She moved to stand by Simeon's stool, her arm against his shoulder. 'I think our first duty is to all those who have fallen prey to his many evils. We must bring him before the legate's court and see that he is justly punished for his crimes. After that his soul must be his own concern.'

Simeon nodded his agreement. 'Jacob will have the charges drawn up at once, so that under no circumstances will Cyrus de Figham be released. I will go myself to Figham House and inform the curate that his brother's predicament is known to us. Hector will then be obliged to keep de Figham alive until the papal legate arrives and the trial can begin. Do not glower so, Rufus. I will simply remind his gaoler of certain obligations set by the Mother Church. If we do the honest and charitable thing today, all else will surely proceed as it should. If any hand is bitten, it will be Hector's, though I doubt he will place himself close enough to that cell to risk the backlash of his brother's fury.'

'You will be feeding a caged jackal and trusting it not to bite,' Rufus insisted. 'But it *will* bite, Simeon, for such is the nature of the beast.'

'Cyrus de Figham will stand trial,' Simeon repeated. 'We, who have so many grievances against him, will see to it.'

Rufus looked at the men around the table, scrutinising their faces for something he, with all his knowledge of de Figham's mischief, could understand. Then he snatched up his warm cloak and strode, grim faced, from the scriptorium.

It was decided that Osric and Thorald would accompany Simeon, first to the provost's quarters and then to Figham House. They reached the house within the hour, assured that the provost's clerks would draw up the necessary papers without delay. Hector received them in the most splendid room in the house, where a fire roared in the grate and the long oak table was set with platters of sugared fruits and marzipans. Two servants hovered by the door. Paul, who had returned directly from St Peter's and slipped in through the kitchens to resume his duties, stood at a corner desk, ready to commit the essence of this meeting to paper.

Hector undoubtedly had de Figham's stamp. He was as tall as his brother and similar in build, handsome and very dark, with hair that glistened in the light and eyes that shone now black, now grey. His movements were just as elegantly expressive, his voice as deep, his manner equally superior. Another season in this place, a little more interaction with the warring canons of Beverley, and the curate from Lincoln would be no more and this new de Figham would be indistinguishable from his brother, Cyrus.

'So, you come to tell me how I am to behave in my own house?' he demanded of Simeon. He was guarded and clearly displeased by what he saw as an intrusion on his privacy.

'Our records show that this mansion belongs to the Canon of St Martin's, Cyrus de Figham,' Simeon reminded him. 'Until any counterclaim is legally proved, the Church is bound to protect the interests, and the person, of the canon.'

'I offend no law, sir,' Hector informed him coldly. 'Nor does my conduct here impeach the rules of our Church.'

'I do not claim that it does,' Simeon replied. 'I am simply here to inform you of the charges being prepared against your brother and to remind you of your duty to protect the prisoner in readiness for his trial.'

'Duty?' Hector queried. 'He tried to kill me. Right here in this room, while I was unarmed and unprepared. I have witnesses to the deed. The man is raving mad. He should be slaughtered like the animal he has become.'

'But first he will be tried for his crimes,' Simeon insisted, and watched Hector's grey eyes harden as the curate studied his face.

'You can be sure I am aware of my duty and will perform it to the best of my ability.'

'I had hoped for nothing less, and yet I understand that you deny your prisoner his basic needs.'

The eyes narrowed and seemed to shift their colour from steely-grey to black. 'Do you indeed? For your information, my prisoner is burning with sweats and has the flux. Let him trust to the grace of God for his survival. I will not have those who tend him take his sickness to themselves and then distribute it throughout my household.'

'Nevertheless, he must be fed and properly nursed.'

'Nursed? By whom? Who is to nurse him while everyone lives in fear of the pestilence?'

Simeon glanced at Osric and received a grim nod of consent. 'My own infirmarian is prepared to remain here and—'

'No.' Hector raised his palms and shook his head as if the very idea of entertaining Osric in his house was distasteful. 'Such measures will not be necessary. No doubt there is a surgeon in this fear-infested town who is willing to brave the flux for a weighty purse.' He turned to the hovering servants and barked, 'See that the prisoner is given food and water at four-hourly intervals. And now, Simeon de Beverley, you may inform the lord provost that all is well here. A rider is on his way to York to beg the archbishop's instructions while we await the arrival of the papal legate. If the pestilence does not take him, my brother will survive to be convicted of his crimes.'

While Simeon stood in silence, flanked by Osric and Thorald, the curate came closer to study the handsome face with its circlet of blond hair and piercing blue eyes.

'Your concern for my brother's welfare intrigues me,' he said at last. 'I find it strange that you, of all people, should have even a passing interest in his comfort.'

'I am a priest. All men are my concern.'

'Even Cyrus de Figham?'

Simeon turned his head and looked squarely into the other's eyes, his gaze so searching that the other, discomforted, avoided it. 'Cyrus de Figham will stand trial before the papal legate, the archbishop and his peers,' he told the curate. 'Allow nothing to prevent that, sir.'

'Nothing but the pestilence,' Hector shrugged. 'I will not shirk from the fullness of my duties. He will be properly fed and given water, you have my solemn word on that. Tell me, is the woman, Martha, with you?'

'She is,' Simeon nodded, 'and happily reunited with her child.'

'Ah, just as I thought,' Hector nodded. 'I should have known she would repay my kindness by speaking of this beyond my doors. What woman can be trusted with discretion, eh?'

Simeon ignored the harsh words and, since Martha was safe inside his own walls, allowed Hector's assumption to go uncorrected. Having said all he had come to say, he bowed respectfully to the curate and prepared to leave.

From his corner desk, young Paul mouthed his thanks and went about his work as if the three visitors to Figham House were strangers to him. At the door Thorald touched Simeon's arm and hissed, 'Look. There in the shadows. It's Peter.'

As Simeon turned his head a small grey shadow slipped between the hangings at the far end of the hall. For an instant, as he passed beneath a torch, light played across the fine blond hair and over the delicate face. Not until they were safely outside did Simeon ask in a whisper, 'Does anyone know why he is here?'

The others shook their heads, then raised their hoods and began to tramp from the house, each allowing no sign that anything they had seen there had disturbed them.

* * *

232

When Peter met them later in the scriptorium, his face was flushed from running through the snow and his blue eyes danced with secret pleasure.

'What were you doing at Figham House?' Simeon demanded.

'I was trading,' the boy said simply.

'You were lurking in the shadows, boy. What was your purpose there?'

'I was trading, Father,' Peter repeated, pulling a leather pouch from beneath his tunic. 'Fourteen of Stephen Goldsmith's very best forgeries . . . for these.'

As the stones tipped onto the table and their colours caught the light in twinkling lustre, all present drew gasps of astonishment.

'St John's?' Simeon asked, then held a ruby to the light before squeezing it in his palm. 'By heaven, they *are* the missing stones from St John's shrine. Look here, everyone! Peter has found the stones and brought them back to us.'

Merriment exploded in the room like firecrackers, and all the tension of recent hours was forgotten as the stones were examined, passed from hand to hand as if they were as delicate as freshly laid eggs.

Their talk gradually turned to the chequered history of St John's shrine, to tales of pilgrimage and plunder, of miraculous healings and princely endowments. Many recalled the young man caught looting the shrine ten years before, when the freak storm that brought Peter to Beverley had all but destroyed the Minister. His accuser had been Cyrus de Figham, his cruel gaoler Wulfric de Morthlund, his executioner the mob. He had died protesting his innocence, despite the inducement of a savage beating, strung up by a frenzied crowd before his statement could be taken and appraised. He admitted prising four gems from the holy shrine and dropping them at the feet of the priest who disturbed his sacrilege, but fourteen stones were lost and never found. Many thought the two canons had colluded in the outrage. St John's priceless gems attracted glory and infamy in equal measure. Not until they were returned to the underground cavern where his relics were safely hidden would the saint be free of the evils men were wont to do in his name.

Amid this talk, young Peter slipped away. At Figham House he too had heard the curate instruct his servants to feed his prisoner. He had also stayed behind to see Hector dash the prepared platter to the ground and swear to sever any hand that dared offer assistance to his brother. The curate was not an honourable man. Despite swearing to the contrary, he planned to starve his brother to death and claim pestilence as the cause.

The bottles Peter carried were slender enough to slip through the narrow window slit. He lowered them into the dark hole that was Cyrus de Figham's cell on a length of twine attached to their necks. When the twine began to yank against his fingers, he knew the bottles had reached the imprisoned man.

'Are you able to draw the corks?' He heard a scuffling in the straw and peered into the darkness, seeing nothing. 'Father Canon, are you able to draw the corks?'

'Who are you?' The voice was weak but contained aggressive undertones.

'You know me,' Peter said through the slit. 'I am Peter.'

'*Simeon's* Peter?'

'I am he.'

'Why in heaven's name does he send his brat to me? By the Devil, if he intends to poison me—'

'I am here to help you,' Peter told him. 'Here is medicine and fresh water, mutton broth and good bread from the morning ovens.'

'Why?' A fit of coughing stilled de Figham's words, but when the spasm was over he demanded, in a weaker voice, 'Devil take you, tell me why.'

'Because God wills it,' Peter said. 'And because our faith demands it.'

'This is trickery ... poison ... a ploy to kill me ...'

'Look for me twice each day, at the first and last Angelus.'

De Figham heard something fall from the window and called out several times to no avail. The boy was gone. He groped in the straw until he found the blanket Peter had fed through the narrow window and the portions of bread lying scattered beneath the cloth. Wrapped up against the chill, sipping mutton broth from a bottle and with the bread held against his body to keep it from hungry rats, Cyrus de Figham shivered and coughed and felt no gratitude.

'Damn you, Simeon,' he said aloud. 'Even now you seek to place me in your debt, but I will not be beholden to you or your snivelling brat. I will eat your food and drink your water, and I will curse you, Simeon de Beverley, with my last breath.'

CHAPTER SIXTEEN

In York the bishop's palace was buzzing with speculation. Rumours flew this way and that, embellished by the fears or aspirations of every man who heard them, then modified to each individual's design before flying on to other ears. They said that Fergus de Burton came directly from the king, from the papal legate, from the pope himself. Speculation was fed by Geoffrey's lack of popularity. Hugh du Puiset, Bishop of Lincoln, wanted the bishopric of York for his nephew, Bourchard. The powerful Hubert Walter wanted the see of York for himself. Both had petitioned Rome for Geoffrey's removal on the grounds of his illegitimacy and his refusal to be ordained, and claimed that their exclusion from his election rendered his bishopric invalid. Prince John supported both claims, since it suited him to keep his brothers divided, the better to strengthen his own claims to the throne of England.

So the rumours were, in turn, that de Burton brought honours, threats, disgrace to pile upon this unloved royal bastard. According to the nature of the teller, he brought good news or ill, grief or honour, demerit or advancement. One thing remained inarguable: Fergus de Burton, upstart and opportunist, was wafting the winds of change through the corridors of York, winds that could blow any one of them into a higher position or out into the streets.

Geoffrey's excitement was raised to fever pitch. He gathered about him hordes of scribbling clerks and bewildered advisors, filling the hall with the babble of voices and charging it with the atmosphere of a madhouse. At last he had glimpsed the way ahead and the making of his career, and he was impatient to begin his headlong battle charge. His advisors were cautious on his behalf and deeply concerned on their own, but Geoffrey would brook no reining in of his elation. He accused those who opposed him of serving the interests of his enemies, and suspected those who supported him of either seeking their own advancement or of pushing him into hasty acts in the hope of seeing him fall from grace and power.

That crisp, bright January afternoon saw tempers frayed and men put in fear of their lives, for none was in any doubt that Geoffrey Plantagenet was girding himself for war. The papal legate, one Roberto Madriosi, Bishop of Florence, had arrived from Rome and installed himself at Canterbury. He was to preside over the ecclesiastical courts there and, when the weather changed for the better, make his way by road to York and Beverley. It was rumoured that Coeur de Lion was to slip quietly into England to join the legate at Canterbury, and Geoffrey intended to greet his brother personally in the splendour of Canterbury Cathedral.

'By the gods!' Geoffrey declared in loudest tones. 'By the time this Italian bishop gets here, his business concerning the Beverley riots will be nothing more than a mere formality. Every detail must be put before him on paper: the iniquities of Cyrus de Figham, the prolonged absence of half the canons of Beverley, the lifting up and pulling down of certain individuals there, and the pressing matter of Beverley's holy relics.' He rounded on Fergus with a glowering expression. 'Are you certain of your facts?'

'Quite certain, my lord.'

'Then inform these doubting clerks. I want the truth recorded.'

237

Fergus cleared his throat and addressed the room. 'It is a matter of Church record that four hundred years ago York's then archbishop, the blessed John, found a parish church at Beverley dedicated to St John the Evangelist. He transformed it into a monastery and staffed it with monks. He had the misfortune to die whilst away from home. Had he died at York instead of at Beverley, his relics would lie here in York, where he served as archbishop for over thirty years.'

'You see?' Geoffrey demanded of them all. 'You see the truth in my claim that Beverley enjoys its hordes of pilgrims under false pretences? These relics are rightfully ours and must be returned at once.'

'But my Lord Archbishop,' the deacon dared to protest, appalled by this idea that a buried saint should be uprooted and replanted like a common garden flower, 'St John *chose* Beverley as his final resting place. Had it not been so, his bones would now rest at Harpham, where he was born.'

'He was York's archbishop for thirty-six years. We have first claim on him.'

'Sire, the saint's wishes were clearly expressed while he still lived. He chose to be buried in St Peter's church and was translated to the Minster church following his canonisation. His Holiness the Pope will never sanction the taking away of a saint against his own recorded wishes.'

'Then I'll not appeal to Pope Clement,' Geoffrey snapped. 'I'll persuade Beverley to give up the relics.'

'You cannot, my lord. The argument remains the same whether argued in Rome or England, and those Beverley canons—'

'Cannot?' Geoffrey thundered. 'Geoffrey Plantagenet, the son and the brother of monarchs, *cannot*?'

Father Bruce clasped his hands together in entreaty. 'Your Grace, no bishop in the whole of England would support you.'

'Then let them *all* stand against me,' Geoffrey declared, and began to strut about the hall, flushed and puffed up with his vision of future greatness. 'We'll see who wields the greatest power once my office is secured and my king appeased. Beverley is mine. I am its rightful overlord and that miserable little town is answerable to *me*. The land on which that Minster stands is mine, along with half the acreage and woodland in the town. Its tolls on water-borne craft, on incoming traders and pilgrims belong to *me*, and I'll have my due, *to the penny*, if I have to choke those troublesome canons in the process. Aye, and I'll have St John. He belongs in York and, by all that's holy, York shall have him!'

Geoffrey bellowed at his ministers, taunted his advisors and struck terror into the hearts of his humble clerks. He threatened and ridiculed, boasted of his royal courage and mocked the uncertainties of lesser men. In the end, intoxicated by the promise of glory, he argued himself into taking holy orders without delay.

From his seat on the right of Geoffrey's throne, the archbishop's envoy, Fergus de Burton, was by now a mere spectator. He had demonstrated to this fine-robed gathering of ecclesiastical dignitaries that there were easier ways to shift a stubborn and dangerous bull than by trying to shove their weight against its flanks. A timely prick was all it took, and the owner of the pin could then observe, from a safe and diplomatic distance, the raging bull borne along by its own momentum.

Geoffrey was still strutting and bellowing orders when, much later, Fergus slipped from the palace and made his way to Copper Gate. At a plain stone house he left his horse with Chad, rapped on the door and stooped as he went inside.

'Is it done?' his host asked. 'The word is out that Geoffrey Plantagenet is to be ordained and fully consecrated as York's archbishop.'

'Aye, it is done, save for the customary display of pomp and ceremony. He kept a score of clerks at work until the first Angelus. His plans are watertight.'

'*Your* plans, I think, Fergus de Burton. So, you are to succeed where two kings and three popes have failed, and by wizardry you will make a priest of Geoffrey.'

'As I vowed to do, and it was achieved by clever strategy,

not wizardry, my friend.' Fergus bowed, and when he raised his head his eyes danced with merriment and his grin spread from ear to ear. He stepped forward to clasp his host in a strong embrace, slapping the hard muscles of his shoulders. Then he stood back and, bowing again with solemnity and respect, clasped his palms and said, '*Shalom*, Rabbi.'

'*Shalom*, my slippery friend.'

The Jew's house stood amongst the workshops and furnaces of the whitesmiths. It was built of stone, as all Jews' houses must be so there is no thatch that Christian mobs might torch or timbers against which they might turn their axes. Rabbi Aaron was a man of princely stature and striking appearance, with hooded black eyes above a long, wide nose, and hair that hung in glossy raven coils about his face and shoulders. His palms were deeply etched with lines that might have been scratched there with a pen and stained with darkest ink. This calm, strong Ethiopian was the figurehead of York's Jews, a teacher who led his people with skill through the troubled waters of their Christian town. He was also the wealthiest Jew in England, so many believed, and most certainly the richest Jew in York.

'My humble abode welcomes you,' he said.

The house was indeed humble, a simple dwelling of two rooms, one above the other, with a central pillar against which a wooden stair was set. His hearth and his table were modest, his comforts few, and any who sought to loot this place went away with little more than a few pots and pans and their disappointment. His father had been slain in the last spate of serious rioting against the Jews, and Aaron, though he might one day lose his life to Christian hatred, would never forfeit his wealth to a Christian king, as was the law.

'I see you have brought more gifts for me to hold in custody on your behalf,' he said, inspecting his visitor's baggage. 'What, yet another decorated saddle? And is this not the seventh purse to be deposited?'

'The *eighth*,' Fergus corrected. 'I too keep careful tally, Rabbi.'

'As well you might,' Aaron told him, wagging a long, slim

finger in the air. 'I have heard it said that Jews cannot be trusted. Do you travel alone through these dangerous streets?'

'I am not so reckless,' Fergus told him with a shake of his head. 'Chad and two others are posted nearby for my protection, should it be required.'

'No Jew will attack you, not even one with an empty belly.'

'I know that, Aaron.'

'So, first to business, then we can talk. A moment's privacy, if you please.'

Fergus chuckled as he turned his face to the wall. This ritual was performed at every meeting, and when he turned around again the ledger of accounts was on the table. He had detected no sound that might give away its hiding place, no lifting of board or sliding of stone, no telltale shadow on the wall, and yet the great book was there, wrapped in its cloth, as if conjured by magic. He watched the rabbi carefully examine and value every item, then enter it in his ledger in his clear, precise script. He checked the items for himself, from the first purse of gold and casket of silver plate to the last ornamental sword and decorated saddle.

'How much am I worth?' Fergus asked.

'Twenty thousand pounds, give or take a mark or two.'

'I am a wealthy man.' Fergus grinned. 'Where is it kept?'

'Your money and goods are safe,' Aaron replied. 'More than that I will not tell you.'

'Is that Simeon's name I see on the adjoining page?'

Aaron closed the book with a snap, secured the metal clasp about its pages and touched the side of his nose with his index finger. 'Privacy, if you please, while I replace my ledger.'

With his face to the wall, Fergus watched the shadows play across heavy hangings. 'So, Simeon also takes advantage of your services. He too would sooner trust his riches to a Jew than to his own archbishop.'

'You saw the Ethiopian chalice he brought here some months ago, hoping to persuade me to fund his efforts to rebuild the Minster church. It came to him through Antony of Flanders, but it is a priceless relic from the vessel house of Tirkaha, our one-time king. I intend to offer him a fair price, when he is ready to receive it.'

'I saw several other entries in your ledger,' Fergus pressed.

'Those things were entrusted to me by Canon Cuthbert when he feared for Simeon's life . . . a few Church treasures, nothing more.'

'Church treasures?' Fergus turned around, grave faced and no longer smiling. 'Do you realise what risks you take, Aaron? If you, a rabbi, should be caught in possession of Christian artefacts, every Jew in York will answer for the sacrilege.'

'What else was I to do?' Aaron asked with a shrug. 'The men of St Peter's saved my life and restored me to Geoffrey's favour. Was I to refuse that troubled old man's request when I was about to return to York with an armed escort?'

'*My* armed escort,' Fergus reminded him. 'Hell's teeth, Rabbi Aaron, I have no desire to stand beside you against the might of the Christian Church. Remember that, if you please, when we next have occasion to ride together.'

'I will remember it,' Aaron chuckled.

'Now, where have you hidden my money?'

'Fergus, you are inquisitive to a fault,' Aaron smiled. 'Allow me to offer a piece of advice to one who lives by guile and prospers on other men's secrets. He who spies at another's door should not complain when a finger pokes his eye.'

Fergus roared with laughter and slapped the table heartily. 'Aye, by my sword, I like you well enough, Aaron of Ethiopia,' he declared, then glowered with mock indignation. 'Even so, I can't help noticing that your heathen hospitality leaves a lot to be desired. My throat is parched.'

Over wine and buttered oatcakes they discussed the situation in York and Beverley, and it wasn't until he was ready to leave that Fergus remembered the message he had promised to deliver to the Jew. 'It is time. Those were his exact words. He said you would understand.'

The Jew heaved his broad shoulders and sighed. 'Then I

must leave for Beverley at once. Is there something happening there that you have omitted to mention?'

Fergus nodded. 'Cyrus de Figham has returned.'

The Jew stared long and hard at his guest, then asked, as if the news neither disturbed nor surprised him, 'Is there more?'

'Only that Cuthbert intends to stand down as Canon of St Peter's so that Simeon can have the Office.'

'Ah. He speaks wisely when he says it is time. Very well, I'll leave at dawn.'

'Leave? And who will protect my goods while you're away?'

'I think you may trust in God to perform that chore.'

'I'll do no such thing,' Fergus protested. 'You barely survived your last visit to Beverley. Or have you already forgotten that you were attacked by robbers there and left for dead?'

'I was robbed because the fine horse you gave me was so conspicuous, Fergus. They attacked me because my mount was a prize worth having.'

'Aye, and they beat you to within an inch of your life because your skin's as black as coal. *You* were conspicuous, Aaron, not the horse. How am I to reclaim my money when you're dead?'

Aaron placed his palms together as if in prayer and tapped his lips with his fingers. 'A good question, my friend. How indeed?'

'Damn it, you're holding everything I own. Have I diced with the temper of Geoffrey Plantagenet all these months only to lose my rewards because one stubborn Jew falls prey to robbers on the road?' When Aaron continued to tap his lips in contemplative silence, Fergus grew impatient and demanded, 'Let me deliver the artefacts to Cuthbert.'

'What, and be guilty of transporting Christian artefacts?'

'Do not mock me, sir. I travel with six men-at-arms and—'

'No. I intend to go there myself.'

'In this bad weather and carrying property belonging to

243

the Christian Church? One man against all comers? Have you a death wish, or do you Jews also revere martyrs who toss away their lives for the sheer perversity of it?'

'I will be safe enough if I travel as I always do, as a penniless Moorish monk with nothing worth stealing.'

'That ruse is no guarantee of safety,' Fergus said angrily. 'At this time of year, when men are starving for want of a crust of bread, the meat on your donkey's bones will be enough to tempt every robber from his lair.'

'You underestimate me, Fergus. Besides, I'll have my staff and my hidden dagger to protect me.'

'Paltry defences against robbers who gather in bands. Why must you be so obstinate?'

The Jew spread his hands. 'I am by nature an obstinate man.'

'Think again, Aaron. Do not go to Beverley.'

'I must,' the rabbi told him.

'Then I suspect Elvira is the cause.'

Aaron smiled. 'Perhaps.'

'As I thought. By heaven, should we wonder that popes and bishops regard all women as Satan's tools when a sane man is willing to risk his life for just a glimpse of one, even though he knows he can never possess her?'

'I might have, had I kept her to her bargain.'

'Aye, but you released her from it, knowing she could never love you in return. She offered herself to you in the hope of saving Simeon's life. She loves you well enough as a friend, Aaron, but her love for Simeon will always keep her from you. You did the noble thing when you released her.'

'I did the *necessary* thing, my friend, and every day I have cause to regret it.'

'Then why torture yourself by seeing her again? Leave Elvira to Simeon and give up this plan to travel all the way to Beverley for little purpose.'

'You have not yet loved,' Aaron told him gravely. 'Until you do, until you know how deeply it can wound, you cannot understand why I must go.'

'Then go and be damned, if she means that much to you, but tell me first where you've hidden my fortune, so that I can retrieve it if you come to harm.'

'My secret,' Aaron told him.

'I'll see my money or you'll not leave the city.'

'Would you restrain me, Fergus?'

'I will have you arrested and thrown in a cell if I must, but you will not get through those town gates until I see my money safe.'

Eventually, the rabbi conceded. It was common sense that he and Fergus should travel together.

'Come, secure the door and bring the lamp. You are about to behold a small section of my treasure house.'

Aaron's fingers probed at the stones in the gloomiest corner of the room until those set on cantilevers swung smoothly aside. A stair was set in the outer wall of the house, a set of curved steps in a shaft so narrow that its walls compressed the two men's shoulders. A passageway little wider than the stairwell took them through the inky darkness underground. Other passageways led off, some no more than crawl holes in the earth, others half bricked or fully tiled from the days when York's main waterways had been diverted along this route. They emerged from a crawl hole into an abandoned crypt with walls of solid brick.

'By heaven, what is this place?'

'The original crypt of a church some distance from my house. It was bricked up more than a hundred years ago and covered over, and I doubt any living tongue could tell you of its existence. My father had his architects make use of the old waterways and tunnels when he had the house built more than half a century ago. So you see, my friend, I can protect what I own from looters while in this world and from the hands of that other plunderer, King Richard, Coeur de Lion, in the next. I can also escape my house if I am besieged by your Christian hordes. We Jews are cunning as foxes, are we not?'

'Ingenious.' Fergus grinned.

'And I spoke the truth when I said you could trust to God

245

to keep your property safely hidden. What better place for a Jew to hide his gold than beneath the altar of a Christian church?'

'Which church? In which direction have we travelled?'

'North, south, east and west,' the Rabbi chuckled. 'You will have to dig up every church and chapel in York to find it. A daunting prospect, eh?'

'An impossible task,' Fergus agreed. 'How much of your wealth is here?'

'In this particular place? Only your own and that which is owed to St Peter's Church, plus a small store of coins for emergency use. The rest is distributed throughout this rabbit warren. If I am killed you will find your own and very little else . . . *if* you can calculate how to free the entrance mechanism and *if* you memorised the route we took.'

Fergus looked dismayed. 'I can never hope to do that,' he confessed. 'I lost my bearings on the stair, and after that, with all the twists and turns . . .'

'Do not worry, Fergus. If I am lost while I still hold your goods, let my death be known amongst the Jews and the one man who knows of our arrangement will be honour bound to see that you are repaid in full . . . less the interest owed to me, of course.'

'Of course,' Fergus conceded.

By torch light Fergus confirmed that all his treasures were intact, the jewelled girdles, rings and precious glittering brooches, even the seven barrels of wine belonging to Geoffrey Plantagenet, each now stripped of its distinctive seal and skilfully stamped over with another. On their return journey, Fergus was not convinced that they were taking the same route by which they had come. Whatever the Jew's intention, when they reached the house the young man was none the wiser as to where his wealth was hidden.

Fergus stayed at the palace overnight as Geoffrey's special guest, only managing to grab a few hours' sleep before he met again with Aaron at first light. He had decided that

Aaron should travel as a foreign monk who, being fluent in the Spanish language and versed in law, was to act as interpreter to Bishop Roberto, the papal legate. He instructed the rabbi to hold his tongue if they were stopped and he was questioned on any matter of religion, but Aaron laughingly reminded him that he was not unfamiliar with the Roman Church.

'In fact,' he said, 'I doubt very much that you or Chad, or even your archbishop, are as well versed in your Christian faith as I am.'

'Poke a Jew and shame a Christian,' Fergus quipped.

'So it is said, my friend. Have you considered, Fergus, that when Geoffrey is fully consecrated as archbishop his power and his vanity will know no bounds? Will he be so accommodating to the Jews when he no longer needs to profit from us?'

'He will protect your people, in his fashion,' Fergus assured him. 'Do not forget how often you Jews have been baited and discredited in past attempts to tip Geoffrey from his seat. Once he is safety installed, his enemies will no longer seek to use you against him, and his interests will be best served by keeping peace between Jew and Christian. To that end he will use an army if he must.' He laughed throatily and shook his head. 'What a sight you were when you went to the palace in answer to Geoffrey's summons, Aaron. As black as night and as handsome as the Devil, and as proud as a sultan, too, as I recall. Those priests were quaking in their boots to have a Jew set his feet on their consecrated ground.'

'I have met Geoffrey twice since then,' Aaron told him. 'We discussed a great deal in a short time, mainly on the subjects of Church politics and the wisdom of ancient philosophers. His mind is surprisingly sharp beneath that brash exterior and uncertain temper. I might have liked him, given better circumstances.'

'He still talks about those meetings, Aaron. He is starved of intellectual stimulation. He needs men like you around him if he is ever to be halfway content in holy Office.'

'I think you like him, Fergus.'

'I should, while he makes such a wealthy man of me.'

'And you are laying a hazardous path for Simeon to tread when he is made full canon. You like him too, I believe.'

'I do indeed, though as yet he does not offer me the same challenge, the same excitement that I enjoy in my dealings with our archbishop.'

'He will,' the rabbi chuckled knowingly, 'if you ever make the mistake of crossing him.'

'I doubt if even Simeon de Beverley could aggravate and frustrate as our Plantagenet does. Manipulating Geoffrey is much like trying to train a wild bear to roll over and have its belly fondled.'

'Take care, my friend. You treat with a fickle man in Geoffrey Plantagenet.'

'I have his measure.' Fergus smiled.

'So you insist. Just be sure, for your own sake, that he does not have yours.'

Once again the young man laughed good-naturedly. 'You use my father's exact words, Aaron. Hugh de Burton also believes that I will slip and cut my own throat before I realise my ambitions.'

'I would regret that very much,' Aaron told him, then fell silent as they clattered through the town gate before asking, 'Where next do your ambitions lead you? Will it be Ravensthorpe?'

Fergus shook his head and drew himself up in his jewelled saddle. 'I aim for the core, the very arena of the play,' he said. 'I aim for the heart of the matter, where the eyes of Rome, Canterbury, Durham, Lincoln and York will soon be turned, and where powerful men will soon have their ambitions tweaked and polished. Ravensthorpe can wait a little longer. First I stake my claim at Beverley, Aaron.'

The Jew fell silent, thinking of Elvira and the bargain that would have brought her to York to be his wife. He envied

Fergus, who would obtain at any cost that which he most desired, and Aaron wished, right to his soul, that two months before he had not been too proud, and too compassionate, to do the same.

CHAPTER SEVENTEEN

In Beverley the freezing fog had lost its sting. Instead of biting at the skin it left a layer of dampness everywhere it touched. There was warmth, now, in the vivid winter sunshine, and the trees revealed patches of bare bark as their covering of crisp, white snow began to drip away. Dark areas were visible on the Westwood and the marshes, clear indications that the snow was beginning to melt. Small pools were shedding their covering of ice, and streams were beginning to run more freely. At these first signs that winter would soon release its hold, new dangers threatened Beverley and its occupants. When those acres of snow began to melt and seep down into the town, its ditches would swell, its drains fill, and its subterranean warrens would be susceptible to flooding.

'This rise in temperature is too sudden, Osric.' Simeon observed. 'There'll be flooding if all this snow melts too quickly.'

'Aye, and the warmer air is likely to provoke a sudden upsurge in the flux,' Osric told him with a sigh. 'All life is a constant battle, Simeon. When our prayers are answered, our problems are merely replaced by others. It's wearying.'

'Do not lose heart, my friend. Our lives have purpose.'

Simeon had completed the Morning Offices and was helping Osric pack up the herbs and potions he would

need for his day's work. Many more had succumbed to the
sickness that was striking at random throughout the town,
snatching a family here, a single victim there, a cluster of
unfortunates elsewhere. Many priests and vicars, supported
by clerks from the lower orders, had taken to the streets in
an effort to feed the poor and halt the spread of infection.
Among them were monks from the orders of St Dominic,
St Francis and a handful of lesser-known orders. Many
of these hard-working monks were Beverley men. Others were
foreign pilgrims come to worship at the shrine of St John and
trapped in the town when winter closed in with unexpected
swiftness. Although blessed with little enough for their own
needs, they were, to a man, determined to help those creatures
who had less. Only the Church elite remained aloof. As always
in times of misfortune, Osric constantly grumbled at the lack
of support from those who might give the most, had they been
so disposed.

'They live in ease, they chant their Latin, and they believe
God loves them for it,' Osric said with bitterness in his voice.
'They could do more. They could give more. They could at
least *care.*'

'That is very true, Osric. Whatever arguments they use and
whatever laws they hide behind, these priests and canons are
derelict in their duties and we are left to make up the shortfall
where we can. While they ensure the survival of God's Church
on earth, we must ensure the survival of His people. Will you
return for the Mass to celebrate the baptism of our Lord?'

'Aye, if I can be sure your holy chalice will not contain
a deadly poison. Are our gates to be opened to all
comers?'

Simeon shook his head sadly. 'I have decided against it,
Osric. What right have I to risk the lives of everyone at
St Peter's, when the law does not require me to welcome
strangers to the Mass? No, this time we worship behind
locked gates.'

'A wise decision, Simeon.'

'And a sad one.'

Osric glanced at Brother David, sitting beside Tobias's

bed. 'How do you read his face, Simeon? What do you see in his eyes?'

'I do not know,' Simeon confessed, frowning. 'I know only that something in Brother David is very much askew. He barely eats, he rarely sleeps, and he is inwardly distracted despite his placid and distant manner. He will tell me nothing of how he feels or what bears so heavily on his mind. He refuses to be confessed and attends no services.'

'Does he still grieve for his losses during the great fire?'

'Undoubtedly.'

'Then he is at fault, and gravely so,' Osric growled. 'Two years is more than decent for bearing grief. Life goes on, despite our losses, and to hold the dead so closely to the living is a sin against God's dividing of the two.'

'Perhaps his bereavement left him without purpose,' Simeon answered, touched by the weight that seemed to press on David's shoulders.

'Then let him find another. God in His mercy made the human spirit resilient. Life is a gift, however harsh. This David has no right to give it over to the dead, to hang on to their coat-tails.'

'That is a bitter truth for a troubled man to swallow.'

'But a truth nonetheless. Remind him of it.'

Brother David glanced up as the two men were discussing him. Without changing his untroubled expression, and giving no outward sign of what might be passing through his mind, he rose from his seat and walked slowly to the doorway of the infirmary and stooped as he went through it without a backward glance.

'Cast adrift,' Simeon said, shaking his head.

As Osric left the enclosure he saw Brother David making his way towards the Minster church. Instead of going inside, he continued to Minster Moorgate and there dropped to his knees and crawled into the bushes surrounding Wulfric de Morthlund's house. The infirmarian scowled as he went his own way towards the fish market and the warren of crooked alleyways beyond. Many things were running through his mind as he tramped through puddles of snow turned to filthy

252

sludge by the thaw. He determined to speak to Simeon of his suspicions immediately after Mass. The monk unsettled him. He might be Wulfric de Morthlund's spy despite his rescue of Tobias, and if he came from St Dominic's monastery, as was generally believed, he might also be in the employ of Cyrus de Figham. The monk's behaviour was strange, his habits peculiar, but what disturbed Osric most was the possibility that David was responsible for breaking the neck of a dying man.

'Damn it,' he muttered to himself as he shifted his heavy sack from one shoulder to the other, 'I should have put my fears aside and examined that corpse more closely.'

At the first Angelus of the day, Cyrus de Figham held his cloak beneath the window of his cell and waited for the boy to bring his food. Minutes after the bells finished ringing, two portions of roasted rabbit dropped into the cloth, followed by a bottle of water and a stick of bread. The priest crouched in a corner and ate his fill. He was careful to set the bones aside, for even in that bleak, dark place he had set himself a personal objective.

In the narrow shaft of sunlight invading his cell he could see the rats, black rats with pointed snouts and evil eyes. He had his sights set on the biggest and fiercest amongst them, a beast already emboldened by titbits of meat from the mutton soup and scraps of bread tossed ever closer to de Figham's feet. The rat grew ever more daring in its hunger, drawing closer to the food with every offering. Deprived of human conflict and with no outlet for his rage, Cyrus de Figham filled his wretched hours with the will to triumph over the instincts of that fierce and cunning rodent.

He glanced up as a shadow filled the window slit, cutting off the light.

'Are you there, Father Cyrus?'

'Where else would I be, since the door is firmly bolted from the outside?'

'Shall I drop down my crucifix?'

'What use is that to me? Drop down an axe and I will thank you for it.'

'I will come again at the last Angelus.'

The shadow moved away as Cyrus rose to his feet, still holding his robe in his hands as an apron for his food. 'Get me out of here, boy. Get me out or . . . Boy? Damn you, answer me!'

No sound came from beyond the window slit. Peter had vanished as silently as he had appeared. Cursing under his breath, the priest returned to his crouching position and resumed his patient tempting of the big rat into his corner.

'Come on, my beauty. Here's a juicy rabbit bone. A few days more and I'll have you eating right out of my hand, and then, my fine fellow, we will see how quickly I can crush your ugly skull.'

Outside the cell door, a rush light cast its eerie glow over the stones, and the whisper of soft voices reached his ears. He tossed the bone to the rat and crept to the door, leaning his head as close to the barred aperture as he could get without showing himself. A woman's voice hissed from beyond, using the roughened tones of the lower classes.

'There! Did you hear? He was praying!'

'He was talking to himself,' a man replied. 'He's lost his mind.'

'I tell you, he was *praying*.'

'Aye, we'd all pray if we were in his place. It stinks down here.'

'Everyone knows Father Cyrus has never prayed in his whole life,' the woman insisted, 'except to mouth the words in church when other eyes were on him. It isn't him.'

'Of course it's him, and they'll hang him for his crimes before too long. Let this be an end to your foolishness, woman, and hold up the light, these steps are slippery.'

Cyrus de Figham heard their talk and recognised a straw that might be grasped. He began to pray, loudly and with feeling.

'Dear God have mercy on an innocent man. Deliver me from false accusers . . .'

'There,' the woman hissed. 'He's praying. He says he's innocent.'

'All prisoners say they're innocent,' her companion told her. 'They all swear it until their time comes. He'll change his tune when the papal legate gets here.'

De Figham raised his voice to a wail. 'Send a blessed soul, O Lord, to relieve an innocent man of such injustice.'

'It isn't him, I tell you. It isn't him.'

He heard her protesting whisper as she was ushered up the stair and just before the upper door slammed shut, he placed his mouth close to the bars and yelled, 'I am an innocent man!'

Upstairs the woman struggled against her husband's restraining grip. She was paid to swill the yards and clean out the master's waste pots, and at her hiring she had met the notorious Cyrus de Figham face to face. Now she lifted the curtain at the master's door and peered inside.

'Look for yourself.'

The curate was sprawled in a high-backed chair, a book spread open across his knees and his head hung forward as he dozed by the fire. He was garbed in his brother's finest clothes and high-legged riding boots, and on his finger a blood-red stone shone dully in the firelight.

'That's him,' the woman hissed. '*That's* Cyrus de Figham.'

'Then who— ?'

'The man downstairs must be his brother, Hector, the holy man from Lincoln. Look hard, husband. See the ring and the wolf-skin coat? See the boots? He stuffs himself all day with food and wine, he struts about like a lord and he's got the Devil's own temper. It's him, I tell you, him!'

'God preserve us, wife, I reckon you might be right,' the man replied. He dropped the curtain and drew his wife away. 'Keep silent about this, woman. It's not for the likes of us to interfere in the doings of churchmen. We'll lose our positions here if we dare to speak out, and who'll listen to our complaints, a common ditcher and a yard swiller? Leave well alone.'

'But the holy man is locked in a cell and—'

'He's in the hands of God. Now hold your tongue and get about your work before you are caught slacking and given a taste of the rod.'

Paul appeared in the corridor, noted the lowering of the curtain across the door and fixed the servant with an inquisitive stare.

'What business have you at the master's door?'

'None, sir, that is . . . we were just—'

'Just looking,' the woman hastened to explain. 'Just seeing how like his brother the master is. Might even be taken for him, ain't that the truth, sir?'

'He might, but for his shaven crown.'

'Oh, but any man can take a blade to his head and—' She yelped as a well-placed kick from her husband's boot connected with her ankle.

'A woman's fancy,' the man offered apologetically. 'Pay no heed to my Mary, Master Clerk. I'll take her back to the yard. Mustn't have no dog muck lying around when the master comes out in his fine robes for Mass, eh?'

Shaking his head, Paul watched the pair scuttle away, still muttering to each other in lowered tones. Then he lifted the curtain and stepped into the room, cleared his throat conspicuously and affected ignorance of Hector's sleeping state.

'Forgive this intrusion while you are studying your book, sir. Brother Antony is here from Keldgate on a matter of urgency. He begs a few moments of your time on behalf of the destitute.'

'Brother Antony?'

'The Flanders monk, one of Simeon de Beverley's friends.'

'Ah yes, that swarthy little creature in the tattered robes. Does he speak English? French, perhaps?'

'I believe he speaks any language required of him, sir.'

'*Any* language?'

'Indeed. He has studied and taught at the best schools in

256

Rome and Spain. He was a tutor for many years at the French royal court. He is known throughout Europe as—'

'Enough! Does this monk profess to be a scholar? Does he count himself higher than those he presumes to serve? If so, then he forgets his place.'

'Sir, he is a good man,' Paul hastened to reassure the curate.

'He is a common monk. He wanders from land to land in the name of pilgrimage, but in truth, like the rest of his kind, he is little better than a vagrant.'

Hector closed his book with a snap and tossed it across the table, where it slid against a candlestick so that tallow dripped on its binding. He adjusted his robes, sleeked down his long black hair and positioned himself with one forearm on the mantel stone. 'Perhaps he needs to be reminded of his station. Show him in.'

At Paul's reluctant invitation, Antony strode into the room with his hood thrown back to reveal his lined and weather-tanned features. His sandals slapped a sharp tattoo on the boards. He approached the fireplace, stopped and bowed from the waist.

Hector towered above him but the little monk, though compelled to raise his head in order to meet the other's gaze, gave no hint of being humbled by the stature of his host. Hector tested his nostrils, expecting to find the smell of poverty on the monk's stained and much-repaired habit. He detected only a faint whiff of peppermint, which he guessed was a precaution against the plague.

'Well, monk? What is it? My time is too valuable to be wasted in idle conversation.'

'My lord, I am Antony de Flanders. I run the Keldgate house for destitutes and orphans.'

'You oversee a place of whores and outlaws,' Hector said contemptuously.

'Not so, my lord. Mine is a house of God, where the needy are offered sanctuary and the dying comforted,' Antony corrected.

'That house is the property of the Church.'

257

'It is, my lord. It is the prebendal house of St Martin, of which your brother has been canon for many years. He leased it to Wulfric de Morthlund for a fee and he, in turn, granted me the use of it as an act of charity.'

'Charity?' Hector echoed with a mocking laugh. 'From Wulfric de Morthlund? You speak in contradictions, monk.'

Antony shrugged, noting that Hector had propped his heels up on the hearth in an effort to increase his already considerable height. He felt the tension in the air and saw the antipathy in Hector's eyes. 'To be more accurate, Father Hector, Wulfric offered it to me for services I was then unable to render. Since then he has been loathe to reclaim it, lest his eviction of the two hundred souls who shelter there earn him the censure of the Church.'

'Two hundred souls? All crammed into one house? That is disgusting! Even the rats in our sewers do not live in such conditions.'

'Needs must,' Antony told him with a shrug. 'Shelter, warmth and a daily ration of soup can mark the difference between life and death for those who have nothing.'

Hector scowled down his elegant nose at the monk. He disliked Antony's precise use of language and his total lack of humility. Most of all he disliked the way this small, inferior man professed to be a scholar of renown and met the gaze of better men as if he was their equal.

'Get to the point.'

'I believe you will be canon in your brother's place, or even provost, if rumour can be trusted.'

'So, my fame is spreading, and so it should. I have the recognition of certain powerful men, and at their invitation I will resign my living at Lincoln and reside here in Beverley. If I choose to accept the provost's seat, you may rest assured I will instigate many changes.'

'As I thought,' Antony nodded. 'Father Wulfric's contract on my house expires in a matter of weeks and once a new canon is installed at St Martin's Church, my sanctuary might well be allocated for his use.'

'So? This arrangement you have is against the law. The house will be confiscated as a matter of course.'

'Sir, I had hoped that with your intervention my arrangement would continue.'

Hector narrowed his eyes and lifted one edge of his mouth in a mocking smile. 'The hopes of a common monk are hardly my concern.'

'You have this mansion,' Antony reminded him.

'And I will also have the prebendal house to which I am entitled, should I be offered the canon's seat.'

'Then I beg you to consider the needs of two hundred destitutes, some no more than babes in arms. They must not be turned into the streets and left to starve. We have a duty to—'

'Do not presume to tell me my duty,' Hector warned. 'You were in error to come here seeking favours from me. I have a grave dislike of monks.'

'So I believe, and yet you are, like many others of your kind, content to leave your less agreeable work to us.'

'And rightly so, since you monks are the lowest of all the orders. You do only what becomes your lowly status,' Hector told him.

'We do God's honest work where you priests will not.'

'Damn it, you monks are thieves,' Hector bristled. 'You rob us of our priest's fees by giving blessings and confessions without charge.'

'Jesus Christ made no charge for his compassion, nor did he live in comfort while others starved for want of bread.'

'You live like pigs and you dress like vagabonds.'

The insult had no impact on the monk. 'We choose to live in poverty, as did Christ. Even the most modest of robes would cost three marks in the market place, enough to feed a dozen empty bellies.'

Hector rose up another inch and clenched his fists. 'Do you dare to quarrel with me, monk? Let me warn you that your case is not assisted by impertinence.'

'I ask only that the souls in my care be protected.'

'And I deny your request. I will give you nothing.'

'Two hundred souls, my lord. Their needs must surely outweigh the comforts of a single canon.'

'Nothing,' Hector repeated. He smiled again, and the crooked, almost sensual curve of his mouth belonged to his brother. 'It is quite possible that Daniel Hawk will own the house in the fullness of time. Let *him* bestow favours on your destitute. Go back to Wulfric de Morthlund with your request, or lift up your skirts to tempt his catamite. I will give you nothing, monk. Kindly leave my house.'

As Hector turned his back in dismissal, Antony moved forward as if to challenge him further. The clerk was swift to catch him by the arm and, with a cautionary shake of his head, led him to the door.

'Petition Jacob de Wold,' Paul told the furious monk in a whisper. 'Persuade him to establish your claim to the house before he resigns his seat in favour of Hector. Then speak to Fergus de Burton so that he can urge the archbishop to endorse your claim. Geoffrey's generosity towards your destitute will look well if, as the rumours say, he intends to seek full consecration in his office.'

Antony nodded his head and sucked air deeply into his lungs to steady his temper. 'That curate is insufferable,' he declared. 'I was tempted to strike him down where he stood, for his lack of compassion as much as for his arrogance.'

'He is a poor, disinherited man who lived a humble life until all this,' Paul indicated the lavish interior of the house, 'and the fame of his brother came to him virtually overnight. When such power is dropped into the lap of an untried man, he rarely has the instinct to use it wisely.'

'Beverley does not need another power-hungry priest who hates the common people and those who seek to ease their suffering.'

At a bellow from the other room, Paul hurried Antony to the main door of the house. 'Go now. You will hear from me if I discover anything to your benefit or your detriment.'

'Thank you, Paul. If you had not stayed my hand I might have struck him down and set events in motion that would have my people thrown into the streets.'

260

As the door closed at the monk's back and the clerk hurried through the house in answer to his master's call, the woman who swilled the yard fashioned a cross over her breast and muttered, 'I'm sure of it. It's *him*!'

CHAPTER EIGHTEEN

When Antony arrived at St Peter's later in the day, his mood was still clouded by his confrontation with Hector. As he entered by the Judas gate, the pockmarked clerk, Nicholas Weaver, stepped back to allow him through. As was permitted by his Church, Wulfric de Morthlund had sent his representative to attend Mass in his absence. Weaver was a fawning individual with an oily manner, and Antony was opposed to his presence within the boundary of St Peter's. The canon's representative was here for but one purpose: to carry faults and secrets back to his master.

The scriptorium lay at the northern limits of the enclosure, with woodland behind it and a pond nearby. Its lower storey was to be extended to accommodate Simeon's extensive library and to admit more natural daylight for his growing number of scribes. The plans were drawn up and the foundations laid, but work would not begin in earnest until the better weather. Until then, the stones were kept some distance off, concealed by trees, so that their bulk might not be used to gain access to the scriptorium.

The main building was of stoutest stone, with a slated roof reinforced with metal bars and massive oak beams. Its twin rows of high windows, giving light for the desks and reading tables set below them, were barred with metal rods driven into the stone. The building was impregnable, its thick oak door clad in irons and barred from the inside with an oak beam set in heavy metal housings. At a special signal known to few, a chain could be passed through a small hole in the door to allow the beam to be lifted from the outside. The only other access was by the ancient well in the centre of the room, and this could only be reached by a perilous underground route mapped out by Peter and Simeon.

Antony's rap was answered by the scribe who occupied the desk nearest the door. The monk stepped into a warm room filled with odd lighting and even odder shadows. Its whole length was criss crossed by shafts of light from the windows, and every inch of wall space was claimed by books. The effect was one of immense space and muted colours: the dull greens, russets, purples, browns, blacks and deep, rich blues of lettered spines, the golds and coppers of burnished clasps, the soft creams of parchment and the uncertain white of paper. Added to this was the grey of polished metal candlesticks, the dancing yellow flames of candles and the rows of coloured inks in bottles above each desk. The welcome of Simeon's scriptorium was in its colours and its flickering, misty lighting, in the crackling of its enormous fire and in the uncommon tranquillity of its atmosphere.

Simeon and his father were playing chess at a corner table. Rufus was holding up a pawn depicting a Norman soldier cowering behind his shield and savagely biting its upper rim.

'The sculptor has a keen eye for the absurd,' he grinned. 'These pieces are wonderfully comic. I see your king has Cupid's itch, Simeon, unless he's merely comforting his genitals. My Norman queen has her skirts caught up at the rear to display the plumpest buttocks a man might imagine. Wonderful! Where did the set come from?'

'The sculptor was an itinerant monk unable to pay for his keep,' Simeon told him, still studying the board. 'We cured him of a broken ankle and he left us this to show his gratitude. For one so pious and unworldly, his talent to amuse was quite remarkable.'

263

'Where is he now? I have a mind to seek him out.'

'Dead. He took the plague four years ago and went into voluntary isolation to prevent spreading the disease. His body was discovered many months later in a cave beyond the Westwood.'

'Such a waste,' Rufus muttered, lifting a pawn who cowered behind his shield with a jug of beer raised to his lips. 'I admire his work.' With a grin he moved a bishop across the board. 'And that, Simeon, puts your groin-scratching king in check, I do believe.'

Drawing closer to the game, Antony scanned the board and guessed that Simeon would call checkmate within three moves. 'It warms my heart to see father and son on such amiable terms.' He smiled. 'Oh dear, you are about to lose your bawdy queen, Rufus.'

'Damn. If I knew him less well, I might swear this priest was cheating.'

Simeon glanced up and smiled at Antony. 'Rufus and I have managed to reach agreement on one vital point, at least,' he told him. 'Cyrus de Figham *must* be brought to trial. At the time of the Riots, he made malicious complaints of me to Rome which the papal legate will be obliged to investigate. I want those charges proved to be nothing but wicked invention, and Father Thorald must be exonerated, since half of Beverley thinks him guilty of cold-blooded murder.'

'Aye, and to a man they applaud him for it,' Rufus remarked.

'Once de Figham is brought to open trial, all our major problems will be settled at a stroke,' Simeon continued. 'We will be at liberty to expose the wrongdoings of certain canons and priests, the misuse of Church authority, the dereliction of our absent canons and the corruption at work within our Church.'

Antony nodded gravely, still smarting from his visit to Figham house. 'And this Hector of Lincoln, this puffed up curate who allows his new-found power to addle his senses, will not be free simply to move in and take over where

264

his brother left off. I like it, Simeon. If these pockets of corruption can be purged, there might yet be justice for Beverley, after all.'

'Indeed there will be, once our situation is closely examined by a higher authority, and this papal legate is the highest we could ever hope to obtain. A closer watch will be kept on the exploitation and abuse of holy offices. Our canons and priests will be accountable to Rome, and through them our archbishop will find his own powers restricted. For Beverley's sake, Cyrus de Figham must be properly and publicly tried.'

Elvira handed Antony a jug of beer into which two fresh eggs had been broken. 'I will be content to see him condemned for the murder of dear Alice,' she told them all. 'Her memory is stained with shame because of him. And Richard will only rest easy in his soul when the murderer of Canon Bernard is finally brought to book.'

'Add to all that the slaying of our bell-ringer and the attack on St Dominic's father abbot, and the Devil himself will have to admit we have him.' Antony grinned.

'Checkmate.' Simeon slapped his knees. 'So, we are all in agreement and set to work together towards one just end. If Cyrus de Figham ever performed a single act of goodness, it was in bringing the good men of Beverley to accord.'

'And long may he live to regret it,' Antony offered, raising his jug and drinking deep.

While Simeon made his preparations for Mass, Antony and Rufus walked together through the woods. The rapid thaw had bared the trees and left them standing in pools of exposed earth, their branches dripping. The two men walked to the outer wall and then retraced their steps, their conversation easy.

'Will you stay with us, Rufus?'

The big man stroked his moustaches as he watched the monk's upturned face. 'My plans are not the issue here, my friend. The question is, will he?'

Elvira slipped into Osric's herbery to bring egged beer to David, who was sitting in his customary seat, staring at the ground. She set the jug beside him and moved away, suspecting her presence to be an intrusion on his privacy. By the fence she bent to admire the winter aconite, the beautiful but deadly wolfsbane with its pale yellow flowers and slender, elongated stems. A man with a pockmarked face suddenly stepped from the cover of nearby trees. Startled, she reached for her hood to cover her hair, only to find her wrist caught and held by Nicholas Weaver's restraining hand.

'Don't hide yourself from me, woman.'

'Do not dare to lay your hands on me.' Elvira exclaimed, struggling to free herself.

'Ah, a spirited wench. I like a woman with a bit of fire,' he leered. 'Such beauty was never intended to be left untouched. Hold still, woman.' Twisting her wrist aside, he roughly fondled her breast with his free hand. 'By heaven, you warm my blood.'

'Let me go!'

'Ah, you prefer a rougher touch, I see. Come now, do not play the virgin with me. You are far too luscious to be innocent. No woman with such a face and such a body has a right to be so modest. I intend to take a portion of what these men of St Peter's have from you.'

'Someone help me!' In her distress she saw David on his seat, watching with untroubled eyes as this stranger pawed at her body as if it were his right to handle her thus. 'David . . . for pity's sake help me . . .'

Rufus and Antony came at a sprint when they heard her cries. They saw the skirmish in the garden and the monk who sat close by, heedless of Elvira's predicament. Despite their haste, Simeon appeared from nowhere to reach the herbery ahead of them. As canon elect, he was garbed for Mass in full canon's robes, but the fury on his face and the violence of his attack were those of a man whose woman was in danger. He cleared the fence and, with a roar of rage, threw himself on Nicholas Weaver and grabbed him by the throat. His momentum propelled the man backwards, driving him against the wall of a hut with such force that the timbers shook. Rufus came up behind his son and grabbed his fist as it drew back for a crushing blow.

'Enough! There is no cause to break his jaw.'

'By heaven, I should break his neck for this.'

The clerk was pinned against the wall of the hut, his throat held fast and his toes barely touching the ground. His arms were raised to show that he was unarmed and unwilling to fight, and the look in his eyes was one of purest terror. Spluttering and choking, he stared at the fist that had come so close to smashing into his face, and at the moustached man who held that powerful fist in restraint.

'She's unhurt,' Antony barked, hoping to penetrate Simeon's rage before any real damage could be done.

Elvira had been thrown to the ground by Simeon's bull-like charge. Her clothes were torn and stained and her hair untidy, but apart from that, and the insult thrust so forcibly upon her, she was, as Antony insisted, unhurt. Although she attempted to convey as much to Simeon, his rage would not allow him to release the man, who began to babble frantically in his own defence.

'A mistake ... an honest mistake ...'

'You laid your hands on Elvira,' Simeon snarled, and Nicholas Weaver was left in no doubt that he had insulted the woman this big priest claimed as his own.

'Forgive me ... I meant no harm ... I swear it.'

'Let him go, Simeon,' Rufus hissed in his ear. 'No real harm has been done. Release him.'

By slow degrees Simeon regained his grip on his temper and, assisted by Rufus and Antony, the perspiring Weaver was able to find his feet and move himself out of harm's way. Slowly at first, and clutching his injured throat with both hands, he retreated backwards until he reached the fence, then turned and bolted.

Rufus de Malham was grinning broadly as he watched his son take Elvira in his arms and hold her fast. 'So, these eighteen pious years have not, after all, made a gelding of you, Simeon. Thorald was right, that temper of yours is like a sleeping beast. And when it comes down to what *really*

267

matters,' he glanced at Elvira and nodded his satisfaction, 'I believe your priorities remain intact.'

While Elvira was taken back to the scriptorium to change her torn gown for the Mass, Simeon strode to the bench where David still sat in his infuriating calmness.

'Why in God's name did you not help her?' he inquired of the monk. 'She was attacked right under your nose and you did nothing. What manner of man are you, David?'

The monk looked up as if totally unconcerned. 'It happens.'

'What happens?' Simeon demanded.

'Everything. Life, death, good, evil . . . We can chose to do nothing, or we can stand up and fight like heroes. We place our faith in God and still it happens.'

At these bleak and hopeless words Simeon's anger evaporated. He sat beside the monk, rested his elbows on his knees and turned his head to watch the passive profile.

'Life has a purpose, David. There are times when a man has nothing left but hope. Hold on to it.'

'I have no need of it.'

'David, we *all* have need of it. We must believe that God will never give us more hardship than He made us fit to bear. He created us. He knows our capabilities, our strengths and weaknesses, our limitations. We have no right to set our hearts on proving Him wrong.'

'Is Elvira all right?'

'She was frightened and roughly handled but mercifully unhurt, no thanks to you. You should have helped her.'

As if he had not heard, the monk rose to his feet and began to walk away. 'God help you, Brother David,' Simeon muttered after him.'

The monk from Flanders stepped out of the shadows to place an encouraging hand on Simeon's shoulder. 'He was near St Mary's when the fire spread there two years ago. He saved a number of lives before his own house took the blaze. His entire family was trapped inside, Simeon, and David could do nothing to get them out. He stood in the yard, helpless against the flames, until the last screams died away, and after that we brought him to St Peter's. He lost his wife and three children, his parents and his sister. All he had in the world, everything he loved, was taken from him. His grief still crushes him.'

'What can we do for him, Antony?'

'We can do nothing, my friend. This morbid melancholia will not be cured by any medicines that we know of. The world is too harsh a place for him. He should have remained in isolation, with St Dominic and the monks.'

When the prayer bell had stopped and the Holy Mass was in progress, Nicholas Weaver stood inside the porch, watching the altar from behind a heavy curtain. His throat and his dignity were bruised, but he had seen enough to know that this timely visit to St Peter's would serve him well. Daniel Hawk was here against his master's express orders, not merely as a priest attending the Mass but as a seeker of friendly fellowship amongst the men and women of St Peter's. He could be seen now before the altar, standing beside the woman whose beauty had almost cost Weaver his life. Across the compound in the infirmary building was the soft-eyed boy his master wanted, not riddled with pox as Daniel Hawk had claimed, but hale and hearty and pretty enough for Wulfric de Morthlund's tastes. Weaver had learned that the Hawk was Edwin's confessor, and he guessed that there was more to be known about that secret arrangement. Whether it was innocent or not, Wulfric de Morthlund would reward the loyal clerk who brought the subterfuge to light. All Weaver had to do was tempt Edwin to leave this place without the knowledge of that ferocious blue-eyed canon elect. While Simeon spoke the words of the Mass and his friends hung upon his every word, Nicholas Weaver lowered the curtain, slipped from the church and hurried, smiling, to the infirmary.

Edwin and his sister were stirring herbs into water boiling in pots over the fire. The scents of sage, rosemary and peppermint drifted upward in clouds of aromatic steam that swirled and billowed around the beams. Those others present in the long, shadowed room were either engaged in their duties or gathered in tight little groups reciting the

269

words of the Mass they were unable to attend. A man with a splintered leg lay on a board, his hands clasped and his eyes tightly closed in prayer, while the monks who knelt nearby chanted the Latin words in sweet, melodic phrases. Another monk lay on the floor with his face turned to the wall and his knees drawn up, his body still, his breathing deepened by sleep.

For a few moments Nicholas Weaver watched Edwin as he measured out the herbs. He was tall and slender, with clean brown hair that curled into the nape of his neck, and a face as pretty and soft-eyed as that of his twin sister. Wulfric de Morthlund, now stuffing himself with food and sweets in an effort to ease his terrible stomach cramps, would no doubt recover from his malady at just a sight of this handsome boy. Daniel Hawk would be displaced once Father Wulfric knew of his activities here at St Peter's. Once the fat man had a more immediate interest to distract him, and if the lad proved suitable and willing, Nicholas Weaver would become the favoured clerk and rise up as Daniel Hawk plunged into oblivion. A man need only open his eyes and ears to opportunity and then be prepared to grab what was there to have his status altered at a stroke.

'Edwin, I bring a message from Father Daniel.'

The boy turned around, startled by the sudden appearance of this ugly, pockmarked man with a rasping voice.

'Am I needed at the Mass?'

'No, lad. Father Daniel has been called back to Moorgate, where his master is sick in his bed. He asks that you go there at once, on a matter of pressing urgency.'

'I'm to go to the Moorgate house?' Edwin blinked his eyes in puzzlement. 'But Father Daniel has forbidden me to go there. Only this afternoon he spoke most firmly on that point.'

Nicholas Weaver smiled, and the firelight playing over his face made the damaged skin appear alive. 'Alas, he has grave need of you. The canon is seriously ill and cannot leave his bed, so the way is clear for you to oblige your priest.' He attempted to lower his voice to a coaxing pitch, though the bruising of his throat hampered his efforts. 'No harm will come to you, Edwin, while I'm charged by Father Daniel to protect you. Come, you must make haste.'

While the boy hesitated, his sister leaned against his arm and implored him to be cautious. She did not like this scarred clerk, and she feared for her brother's safety at the house of Wulfric de Morthlund. 'Don't go there, Edwin. Simeon would not allow it.'

'Why am I needed there?' Edwin asked.

Weaver shrugged his shoulders. 'Father Daniel said only that I must deliver the message most urgently. He needs you, Edwin.'

'Then I must go,' Edwin said, unfastening the leather apron that protected his lower body from splashes of boiling water. He took down his hood from its hook and pulled it over his head, then turned to his sister and stilled her whispered protests. 'Tend the pots, Edwinia. Add a ladle of cold water from the bucket if they boil too fiercely, and be sure to keep the fire steady. I'll come back when Father Daniel says I might.'

'Don't go, Edwin—'

'Come quickly,' Weaver cut in. 'Father Daniel hopes to return with you for the sharing of the wine.'

'There, you see?' Edwin smiled to reassure Edwinia. 'An hour, no more, and I'll be back to take the wine.'

Edwinia watched him stride to the door, her eyes wide with dismay. She glanced at the pots, afraid to leave them unattended and yet loathe to allow her brother to leave St Peter's in the company of a stranger.

While she danced from one foot to the other, twisting her apron in her hands and dithering with uncertainty, the still figure of the sleeping monk suddenly sprang to life and Brother David rose to his feet.

'What must I do?' Edwinia implored, but the monk merely showed her his back as he walked to the door. Minutes later, her indecision resolved, Edwinia ran from the infirmary to the church in search of Osric. She found him with Antony, standing with his head bowed in prayer by the church door.

271

As she whispered urgently in his ear, she spotted Daniel Hawk before the altar.

'Look! Father Daniel is *here*!' she exclaimed in alarm. 'The clerk lied. He's taking Edwin to Minster Moorgate!'

Osric and Anthony dashed from the church and, after sending the frightened girl back to her chores in the infirmary, stepped through the Judas gate in time to see the clerk and Edwin passing through the Minster yard. They gave chase without alerting the pair, then caught them up as they reached the forked alleyway leading into Minster Moorgate.

'Edwin, this man speaks falsely. Daniel Hawk is at the Mass.' Osric's gruff voice was sharply edged. 'Step away from him, boy.'

Nicholas Weaver stared back at the flint-eyed infirmarian and, fearing that the former soldier intended to do him some physical harm, held on to Edwin's tunic with both hands. 'You're mistaken, Brother Osric,' he croaked. 'I meant no harm. I'm just a messenger.'

'You are a wicked procurer,' Osric growled, 'a stealer of boys for your master's obscene pleasures.'

Revulsion crept over Edwin as the clerk clawed at his clothes while Osric's accusation rang in the air between them. He wrestled the pockmarked hands away and ran behind Osric. 'He lied. It was a trick to get me out.'

'Aye, lad. You can thank your sister that we got here in time to save you. This clerk is a rogue.'

'I'm just a messenger,' the clerk insisted. He stepped back several paces, then turned to run and found his escape firmly barred by Brother David. 'Get out of my way, you halfwit.' As he attempted to sidestep the obstruction and make a dash for the alleyway beyond, Brother David cut him off and the clerk was forced to turn and face his original pursuers. 'Look, this is all a mistake . . . I meant no harm. I like the boy. I merely—'

A sudden blow from Osric's fist cut off the flow of protestations. With a cry, the clerk sank to the ground, cupping his lower face in hands that came away stained and wet with blood. He had fallen against David's legs and now he leaned against them for support, tasting his own blood from the wide split in his upper lip.

'You struck me,' he said in disbelief, staring at his bloody fingers.

'Aye, and let it suffice to warn you, Nicholas Weaver. If our paths should cross again, for whatever reason, I will not hesitate to break your miserable bones.'

David bent down as if to help the spluttering clerk to his knees, but instead took hold of the man's head with both hands. With a sudden twist, little more than a casual flicking of his wrists, he broke his neck. As David moved away the clerk fell backwards to the ground, his head askew, his eyes wide open.

'He killed him!' Antony said, astonished.

Osric crouched beside the dead man and reached out to close the staring eyes, then turned to watch the monk making his way through the Minster yard. 'The man must be unhinged.'

They had the clerk laid out behind the infirmary when Simeon hurried to join them after Mass. He heard the story without comment, then asked the infirmarian, 'Where is Brother David now?'

'Inside,' Osric told him, jerking his thumb towards the infirmary wall. 'I gave him hemlock and poppy extract with his beer. It was a drastic dose, enough to render him unconscious.'

'Did he say anything? Did he attempt to explain *why* he did this?'

'Simeon, he simply went about his business as if nothing had happened. The killing was as brutal as it was unnecessary, and yet David seems totally unperturbed by what he's done. He exhibits no remorse, no fear of retribution, not the smallest hint that anything is amiss.' Osric wiped his sleeve across his brow and voiced the fears that had been with him since David had first come to St Peter's. 'The man who brought St Bridget's horn was sick with a pestilence, but he didn't die of it, Simeon. His neck was broken.'

273

'What? And you kept that knowledge to yourself?'

'Aye, because I could not be absolutely sure,' Osric explained. 'The head of a corpse often hangs grotesquely when robbed of the muscles needed for its support. I suspected the neck was broken, but my doubts were not strong enough to persuade me to examine that infected body more closely . . .' He spread his palms and shrugged. 'I fear the plague as much as any man here, so I chose to ignore my suspicions. That error of judgement has cost Nicholas Weaver his life.'

'Only King Solomon was perfect in his judgement, Osric,' Simeon told him gravely. 'What matters now is how we deal with this. If Brother David can break a man's neck as easily and as casually as any other might a twig, and if, as you say, he had no cause to kill the clerk, then not one of us is safe here. He must be restrained before he can recover from your narcotic. Since we have no cell in which to hold him here, we must take him to the hall garth and ask that he be imprisoned there.'

'I'll see to it.' Osric nodded.

'How long will the hemlock and poppy extract subdue him?'

'A day, perhaps even two.'

'Then first we must bury this unfortunate clerk. Over there by the wall, I think. Edwin, you are excused this chore, and boy . . .' He took Edwin by the shoulder and looked deeply into his eyes. 'Never, under any circumstances, are you to leave our compound again without first informing one of us of your intentions. Do you understand?'

'I understand, Father Simeon. I'll never let this happen again. You have my solemn word.'

'Good. Now go inside and show your sister that you are safe, and commend her for acting on her sisterly instincts, Edwin. You saw what befell Tobias. Edwinia saved you from a similar fate.'

Edwin left them in a mood of deep contrition, his head hanging and his steps reluctant, and the men set their backs to the task of digging a suitable grave for the clerk. Some moments later, Edwin came back at a run.

'He's gone, Father Simeon. He poured his beer into his night pot. He didn't drink Osric's sleeping draught. His stupor was a pretence and now he's vanished.'

Simeon's face was grim as he looked at the others. 'We have a killer loose among us,' he said flatly. 'This burial will have to wait. I want everyone warned, every woman and child guarded and every man armed to the hilt. David must not be challenged except by groups sufficiently large to overpower him. He must be found, and quickly, before his muddled mind prompts him to snap another neck.'

CHAPTER NINETEEN

In his cell beneath Figham House, Cyrus de Figham heard the distant bells announcing the closing of the Mass. He knew the voice of every bell and the familiar pattern of the ringings, so that the hours of the day were measured out slowly, from the first Angelus to the last, and then the long tolling of the midnight offices. In another hour the curfew bell would ring to mark the covering of all open fires, and an hour after that the final Angelus of the day. In a town of seven churches and a score of independent chapels, the pealing and tolling of bells was either a comfort or a torment, depending on a man's desire to be reminded of God's presence.

Father Cyrus crouched as still as stone against the far wall of his cell, one arm above his head, his long, thin fingers gripping a loop of iron set into the wall. Daylight was fading fast, but in the dull grey glow from the window the rats were clearly visible, humpbacked, dark and hungry.

The largest rat, the leader of the pack, he had named after Simeon, for although this beast was as glossy black in colouring as the priest was fair, he saw in its nature many of Simeon's qualities. It, too, was cunning and cautious, always alert to hidden dangers, ever present and yet always just beyond de Figham's reach. It watched him now with glittering black eyes, measuring the distance between them,

276

probing his stillness with a rodent's instincts. Rat and man surveyed each other in the semidarkness, natural enemies sharing the same cell, and only their cunning and a few small scraps of meat would determine which of them would gain the upper hand.

'Come, Simeon, a little closer if you please,' Cyrus whispered. 'Have the courage to take what you want from me. A few more steps and the meat is yours, vermin that you are. Come to Cyrus.'

Mesmerised by the sound of his voice and trained to associate the whisper with the meat, the big rat moved cautiously forward, its long snout twitching as it sniffed the air. It snatched one portion of meat and scuttled back, then approached again, more boldly, for the next. Slowly, Cyrus eased his fingers from the iron loop and stretched them upwards to give his bony hand a powerful cutting edge. His gaze was fixed on the rat, his eyes as gleaming black in the half-light as were its own. As it bent its glossy head to reach the meat, his hand came down with the fingers flexed in a swift and certain blow that found a yielding target. The rat died with the meat stuck in its throat, its spine crushed before it had any time to react.

'Got you, Simeon! At last!'

Father Cyrus wiped the edge of his hand on his robes, then picked up the rat by its tail and watched its lifeless body swing to and fro. With a snarl he tossed it across the cell and sat back, his arm raised as he waited for the next strongest rat to approach his store of meat.

'Come to Cyrus, Simeon,' he cooed hypnotically into the darkness. 'Come to Cyrus.'

At a sound from beyond the door he sprang to his feet and pressed his face close to the bars. The glow of a rush light was in the stair, and moving shadows played on the walls outside his cell. Cyrus pressed his back against the door, fearful that his brother had come to kill him. For all Hector knew, he might be lying dead in those filthy rushes, but if he had come to ensure his brother's death, he would lie in the rushes in Cyrus de Figham's stead. The rush

277

light moved back and forth, and then a face with indistinct features peered between the bars.

'Sir?' It was the voice of a common servant.

'Who are you, friend?' He used the same low, coaxing tone that had drawn the big rat to its death. 'Please identify yourself.'

'The yard woman, sir. Mary.'

Cyrus recognised the voice. 'Bless you, my child, I am in urgent need of comfort.'

'Who are you?'

He cocked his head in the darkness. 'Who do you think I am?'

'Not him,' she said, and spat on the ground. 'I heard you praying.'

'I pray night and day,' de Figham told her.

'He says you're Cyrus de Figham. The murderer.'

'Bless you, child. God will forgive your error. I am no murderer.'

'He's calling himself the curate, but I know it's him. I've seen him before, see.'

'What?' With a jolt, Cyrus realised what the woman was babbling about. One brother was a murderer and one was not, and this pathetic wretch could not tell one from the other. He gripped the bars and struggled to keep the soft tone in his voice. 'Listen to me, Mary. I am Hector, Curate of St Mark's in Lincoln. I came here to arrest my brother for murder and many other crimes. He had me flogged and thrown down here with the rats. I am innocent, Mary. God knows I am innocent. I am protected by His holy grace, despite my brother's attempts to procure my death. How else would I have survived three days and nights without food or water if not by a miracle?'

'A miracle?' the woman echoed.

'What else? Do I not live and breathe? And yet not a crust of bread nor a drop of water has passed my lips in all this time. You will have a purse of gold for this and full remission for all your sins. Go find the key.'

'Gold? A purse of gold?'

'Go quickly, Mary.'

'He's sworn to have the hand of anyone who helps you.'

'I can protect you from Cyrus de Figham. Trust me, Mary. Fetch the key.'

'I daren't.'

Cyrus sucked air through his nostrils and clenched his fists, holding his temper by a force of will. 'You must,' he told her softly. 'God sent you to deliver me, Mary. God Himself has opened your eyes to the truth and now you must do the Christian thing.'

'You said I'd have gold.'

'As much as you can carry in your skirts. Think on it. You will never go hungry again. Now do as God demands.'

'Oh, sir, I daren't . . . I daren't.'

As the woman turned and fled, de Figham raised his fists and stifled a roar of sheer frustration. The words he wanted to yell after her came out in a hiss through his clenched teeth: 'Idiot! Filthy swiller of shit! Worthless bitch!' He gripped the bars and, raising his voice, called out, 'Bless you, my child. God will be merciful.'

When the light was gone he paced his cell in agitated strides until, in a fit of unspent fury, he snatched up the body of the rat and dashed it against the wall.

He was dozing in his corner when the scratching came at the door. He heard the key turn and the lock snap free, and before the door swung open he was behind it. As the woman stepped inside he made a grab for her and flung her to the ground. The palm of his hand stifled her screams and his fist put an end to her struggles. A moment later he was up the stair and inside the house. He went directly to retrieve his hoard from the recess in the upper room, but the sound of many voices halted him. He crouched at the door to listen and heard the voices of the house steward and several others. He cursed through his teeth and retraced his steps. Without money his freedom meant little. His wealth was his power, and without it he was no better than any other man whose pockets were empty.

'Damn,' he hissed through his teeth, then clenched his

fist and struck it against his forehead. 'How will I survive with empty pockets?'

Hearing voices coming from the main room and the sound of wood being chopped in the courtyard, Cyrus crept along the corridor and slipped out through the kitchen.

The daylight was fading and patches of white still covered the ground. The pure, fresh breeze blowing off the pasture caused his head to spin. He could see the waters of the port and the sloping roof of St Nicholas. A small movement in the bushes startled him. A boy was crouching there, a skinny, ragged child with long black hair and rebellious eyes. He clutched a collection of items to his chest: horse leathers and decorative brasses, an earthen dish and a broom with a broken handle, all carelessly wrapped in a piece of filthy sacking. Here was a common thief caught in the act of robbing the stable of a nobleman, confronted by a fugitive making his bid for freedom. Each eyed the other in silence, both fully aware that neither would dare raise the alarm. Cyrus de Figham stared into those black eyes and felt old hatreds stir inside him. He knew this boy. His knew his swarthy features and his animal cunning, and he knew the look of pure hatred in his eyes.

The boy rose lightly to his feet, no trace of apprehension in his movements, then held the dark priest's gaze for one more moment and slipped away.

'Damn you for drawing breath, fishmonger's whelp,' de Figham muttered after him, then traced the line of bushes away from the house. While Bruno chopped and cursed at the wood in the courtyard, the canon made his way to the stables to saddle a horse. His branded hounds were tethered in a corner, and at his hissed command they crouched on their haunches, twitching their skinny flanks and whining softly. He intended to head for the port, where he could lose himself amongst the crowded warehouses and huts until the time was right for him to creep back to the house and take his treasure. One boot was in the stirrup when he heard the curfew bell. His face grew tight as he perched with one foot raised and the bridle leather already twisted around his fingers. In one more hour the last Angelus would sound and the boy would come to the window of his cell. Just one more hour and he would have the brat in his possession. Killing the rat that bore Simeon's name was not enough. He wanted that blue-eyed brat almost as much as he wanted the priest who sired him.

The curfew bell continued to toll and still Cyrus hesitated, his horse saddled and ready, his freedom right there for the taking. Not until the bell was still did he make his way round to the rear of the house and conceal himself in an angle of the wall. And there he waited, free but not yet free, for the last Angelus and Peter de Beverley.

It was dark and cold. The moon made fitful attempts to penetrate layers of heavy cloud, bathing the fields in temporary light, then slipping away as if exhausted by the effort. Passing-bells told him that corpses were being carted to the pits beyond the gates, and Cyrus hoped that Beverley, to a man, would take the plague and be no more. In the crook of the wall he waited, half convinced that neither he nor the swilling woman would be missed before he fled to the forest with Simeon de Beverley's bastard in his possession. He could not hope to pass through the port with Peter as his prisoner, but he knew those forests well enough to survive until some better plan could be found. Each time the moon found a gap in the clouds he peered across the meadow, and each time it slipped away he cursed the cold, the boy, the town and the long delay. At the pealing of the last Angelus he became alert, stamped the chill from his feet then crouched, as still as a stone, to wait for the boy.

Peter came as the last peals died away, a small, grey shape striding over sludge and snow to reach the window. He carried a small sack over one shoulder and wore his hood thrown back, and the sight of that mop of golden hair incensed the man who watched him from the shadows.

Reaching the high outer wall of the building, Peter set down his sack and dropped into a crouch over the window.

'Father Canon? Are you there?'

'I am right here, boy.'

When his wife could not be found and did not answer when he called, the ditch digger entered the house and searched the kitchen. He looked in the cupboard where she sometimes stole a sly sleep in the warmth, and in the dark under-shelf where she hid what bread or kitchen scraps she was able to pilfer. He searched the corridors and storerooms, the recess where the master left his waste, and the night-pot cupboard. When he saw that the door to the cellar was ajar he guessed the worst. The master was moving about and in poor humour, and if Mary was caught downstairs her hand would be forfeited. Resolved to give her a thorough thrashing lest he be held responsible for her disobedience, he took a rush light and hurried down the stairs.

'Mary? Where are you, woman?'

He found the cell door open and his wife collapsed inside, the key still clutched in her fingers and one side of her face an ugly mass of bruising. The prisoner was gone.

'Oh God, what have you done, Mary?'

The woman moaned as she began to recover her senses. 'The curate attacked me when I came to free him.' She cast about her, fingering her skirts and the straw all around her in a frantic search. 'Where is it? Where's my gold?'

The man began to pull her to her feet, where she swayed like a drunkard, still muttering about her gold. 'We've got to get out of here. He'll kill us.'

Husband and wife staggered up the stairs and reached the hall to be confronted by Hector, with Bruno and Paul beside him and two stout labourers behind him. Leaving his wife to slump against the wall, the terrified ditcher threw himself to the ground and dulled the polish on Hector's boots with his sweating palms.

'Be merciful, sir . . . in God's name . . .'

Hector dislodged and silenced the grovelling man with a sharp kick to his jaw, then stooped to snatch the key from Mary's fingers. 'Is he out?' he asked, and his face was growing pale. 'God damn it, answer me, woman.'

'He said . . . I thought . . .'

Hector signalled a labourer to check the cell. He stood with his fingers clasped and his head lowered, moving his lips in silent prayer. The atmosphere all about him was charged and tense, for this man had the authority to judge and punish without mercy. His hands were trembling when the man returned to confirm that the cell was empty and the prisoner lost.

'Out?' He asked the question in a small and petulant voice that grew by degrees to a higher pitch. 'How so? He should be *dead.*'

'He was saved by a miracle,' Mary said, holding her swollen face, still unable to stand without the wall's support. 'He said God would strike me down if I didn't fetch the key. He forced me to do it, Father Cyrus.'

'I am *not* Cyrus, you muddle-headed fool, I am Hector.'

'No . . . He's Hector and *you're* Father Cyrus.'

'The Devil take you for your foolishness. You have released a madman. When did he get out?'

The woman was unable to say how long she had lain senseless in the cell and looked to her husband for assistance. The ditcher struggled to speak through a bleeding mouth. 'No more than an hour, my lord. She was with me in the yard before the curfew bell.'

'And no horses are missing?'

'None, my lord,' Bruno answered, omitting to add that he had found de Figham's horse saddled.

'Then he cannot be far away. Get the horses and the dogs. Search the house, the grounds, and then the upper meadow. The man is half starved and weakened by the flux. Get after him.'

Hector turned with a flourish of his brother's wolf-skin coat, then raised his arm and felled the half-senseless Mary with a single blow. As her husband grovelled and sobbed for mercy, he nudged him with his boot and promised, 'Be sure I will deal with you and your damnable woman

283

when we have caught the fugitive and returned him to his cell.'

Cyrus was heading southeast towards the forest when he heard the dogs. Burdened by the struggling boy and hampered by pools of melted snow, he had made slow progress across the open meadow. Looking back, he saw that the house was still in sight. He counted seven searchers in all, four mounted, three on foot. His own hounds ran with them, their frantic barks betraying their master's route. They were trained to keep him in sight when following the hunt, and he cursed them now for their canine skills.

As the moon appeared through broken cloud he spotted a derelict well once used by pilgrims taking this country route from the forest to the town. He threw himself down behind the crumbling stones and cast about for a means of escape. The forest was still a mile away, and a running man was conspicuous in these open spaces with a bright moon above him and acres of snow below. Had the ground been hard, and had he not been so burdened, he might have hoped to reach the trees by now. His first task would have been to draw off the dogs and cut their foolish throats, for wherever he hid and however far he travelled those hunting hounds would obey their training and eventually find their master.

He knew he could not hope to reach the forest with four horsemen in pursuit, not with a ten-year-old boy to slow him down

'You have cost me my freedom,' he snarled at Peter. 'If not for you I would be safely away from here. I would be on a boat or riding for York, or hidden in the forest where they would never find me.'

Pinned to the ground with the priest's knee on his chest, Peter looked back at his enemy calmly. 'Father Simeon will hunt you down,' he said. 'He will find me.'

'He will find your wretched corpse,' de Figham sneered, then clamped his hands around the slender neck and pressed his thumbs over the soft flesh of Peter's throat.

284

'I will choke the life from you this time, priest's bastard, ditcher's whelp. As God is my judge, I will not be cheated a second time of the privilege of killing you.'

The hounds appeared from opposite sides of the well, barking and snarling as they ran this way and that, marking swift figures of eight in the mud and cornering de Figham as they were trained to corner a boar for the bowmen. Cyrus jumped up to call them to heel and the cry went up: 'There he is! Get after him!'

'Damn you, Peter de Beverley, I will not be made to give you up again.'

The priest grabbed the dazed boy by an arm and a leg, hoisted him chest high and, with a bellow of triumph, tossed him into the mouth of the derelict well.

'You will either smash your bones in the fall or drown in the mud,' he yelled. 'Here, take your pathetic food and medicines, and may they serve you well, priest's bastard, while you die.' He threw the sack of food and water after the boy, then turned and ran with the hounds at his heels, knowing his flight was futile.

The riders had him surrounded in minutes and he was taken without a struggle. Hector, mounted on Cyrus's favourite hunting horse and wearing his crimson robe, rode up at his leisure to supervise the binding of his brother's wrists.

'Well, brother,' He smiled at the glowering man. 'You have gained yourself an hour's freedom and a miserable mile of space. That is a noble achievement to ponder over while you languish in your cell.'

'You will pay for this, Hector.'

'I think not, *brother*.' Hector leaned down from his saddle, a crooked smile on his handsome face. 'It will take a dozen men with sharpened axes to get you out of that cell a second time.'

They bound his hands before him and secured the loose end of the rope to Hector's saddle. Thus he was hauled through mud and sludge, back towards Figham House and

285

his underground cell. Dragged along at a gruelling pace, he was hard-pressed to keep his footing, but as he lurched and slithered past the well, Cyrus de Figham wore a smile of satisfaction.

CHAPTER TWENTY

When Peter failed to join them for their early evening meal, Elvira set his bowl in the hearth and covered it with a linen cloth. She set his spoon and half-loaf beside it, then turned from the fireplace with a heavy sigh.

'Do not worry so,' Simeon told her, catching her hand in his. 'You know his ways.'

Much later, when the candles were snuffed and the clerks and scribes abed, she sat before the lowering fire, disturbed by the boy's long absence. When the Midnight Offices were over and still he had not appeared, she donned her warm cloak and visited, for the second time that night, every building and hut in the enclosure. Nobody had seen him since the last Angelus. A gateman recalled seeing him leave by the main gate with a bulging sack.

'Every evening at the same time,' he told Elvira, 'and he's always back within the hour with an empty sack and a blessing for us all.'

'Not this time,' Elvira reminded him. 'Did he say where he was going or which house he intended to visit?'

'Does he ever? "About God's work", is all he'll say to any who ask. He's mysterious, but a good lad, mistress Elvira. He goes towards the East Bar, that much I can tell you.'

Peter had not joined his companions in their search for

Brother David, as he had planned, nor had he shared his customary evening hour in the company of Canon Cuthbert. This fact alone increased Elvira's concern, for the pattern of their friendship, though seventy years divided them, had not altered in the whole of Peter's life. Her knowledge of that strange little boy told her that he would come when he was ready, but her heart insisted that something was very much amiss.

She saw the church door open and close and Simeon, always the last to leave after the later offices, walk slowly towards the bridge. There he paused to lay a hand on the heavy timbers, and she guessed that he was remembering Father Willard, impaled there during a storm ten years before. The water in the drain was higher now. The thaw had added to its force and it was at last creeping towards its natural level.

Simeon checked the lamps that hung at each end of the bridge, and when he turned he saw Elvira standing with her dark hair lifting about her shoulders in the chilly breeze.

'My love, you should be in bed at this late hour. Why did you wait for me?' One glance at her troubled face alerted him. 'Peter?'

She nodded. 'It has been ten hours. Where is he, Simeon?'

'Safe,' he told her with a reassuring smile. 'There have been other nights, Elvira, when Peter has not come home. He will be at the morning Mass tomorrow.'

He placed his arm around her shoulders and held her close as they made their way to the scriptorium. She was not fully reassured by his words and, had she glanced up and marked the grim expression on his face, she would have known that Simeon, too, was troubled by Peter's absence.

For Elvira the night was endless. She tossed and turned as any mother might who missed her only child. Her fears were weighted by the knowledge that Peter, innocent boy that he was, could count more enemies than most men might encounter in a lifetime. Long before dawn she heard sounds below that told her Simeon was already astir. She crept from her bed to peer over the timbers of the roof space. Simeon was warmly cloaked, well armed and carrying a staff, and as he left the scriptorium she saw that others, Osric and Antony among them, were waiting, similarly garbed, beyond the door. A sleepy clerk dropped the bar into its metal housing and returned to his bed as Elvira, moving quietly about in the rafters, gathered up her clothes and prepared to follow. She knew now that Simeon shared her fears for Peter's safety and that the sense of helplessness gnawing at her heart would make waiting intolerable. Once dressed, she shook the clerk awake and bade him bar the door behind her, then slipped into the darkness to join the search.

They returned in time for the Dawn Mass, weary and disappointed. None dared to voice what was already uppermost in Elvira's mind, that somehow Wulfric de Morthlund had trapped the boy.

Peter was to have borne the chalice in the Mass. When he failed to appear, Edwin was asked to take his place, with Father Richard standing by to assist him should he suffer a falling fit. Immediately after the Mass, Simeon left with Thorald for Figham House, for he now knew that Peter had come this way on at least a half-dozen occasions in the last few days.

It was Paul who admitted them to the house and showed them to a bench in the hall while a servant informed his master of their arrival.

'Peter has not been here,' he told them in a whisper, 'not since the night he stole the gems from the chapel.'

'But why would he come in this direction each night?' Simeon asked. 'The gate men confirm that he passed out and in within the hour on three successive nights. A family of turfers living near Flemingate swear they saw him come over the pasture.'

'Have you tried the tanning houses? The port? Did you search the dredgers' huts?' When Simeon nodded his head at each suggestion, Paul sighed. 'But he must be *somewhere*. Did you— ?' He broke off abruptly as the curtain at Hector's door moved and an ugly young woman stepped into the hall and muttered, 'Master'll see thee now.'

The curate received them with unexpected grace and heard

their story with no small measure of sympathy. The debris of a hearty breakfast was on the table, and already his bottle of wine had but an inch of its contents remaining. Bright-eyed and flushed, he demanded a full description of the missing boy so that he might employ his own men in the search.

'This high,' Simeon told him, measuring his hand against his chest. 'Very blond, blue eyes. He wears a light-grey robe with a matching mantle and he has . . .'

'Yes?'

Simeon held back from describing the puckered scar on Peter's throat. Already Rome had sought to investigate the boy's origins, his uncanny intellect and his talent for moving here and there in the manner of a will-o'-the-wisp. His enemies had put a price on his head, and the sword that had caused the scar could just as easily strike at him again. It had left a brand on Peter's throat for any enemy to identify at a glance. The fewer who knew of its existence, the safer he would be.

'He speaks briefly, if at all.'

'Nothing more?'

'Nothing more. I merely wondered if he had come here.'

The curate spread his hands and smiled. 'Why should he come here? Does he know me?'

'Children are inquisitive,' Simeon offered. 'We are inquiring at all the prebendal houses.' Despite the evidence that too much wine had sweetened Hector's humour, his agreeable manner aroused Simeon's suspicions. The curate was too obliging, too amiable. This prompted the priest to recall the many cells below the house, and to wonder if he now had a small boy interned there. 'How fares your prisoner?' he asked, and was surprised by the reply.

'I am delighted to inform you that he is quite recovered from his bout of flux. Do you wish to see him for yourself so that you might report his excellent condition to our provost?'

'You are most obliging, sir,' the priest replied.

It was Bruno who showed the two men down into the cellars. Simeon was able to check the empty cells and satisfy himself that Peter was not being held there. In the locked cell, Cyrus de Figham was but a dark shape crouched in a corner. The flaming torch illuminated their faces as they peered between the bars, but its flickering light barely reached into the cell. A voice they recognised spoke to them from within.

'You are a long way from St Peter's, Simeon de Beverley. Are you here to set me free or merely to gloat?'

'May God in His mercy turn your soul from evil,' Simeon said, signing the cross.

As he and Thorald climbed the stair, de Figham threw himself against the bars and yelled after them, 'Was it worth it, you sanctimonious priests? Was it worth it?'

'He thinks we revel in our victory over him,' Thorald remarked.

'We will,' Simeon promised. 'After the trial.'

The two priests went next to the house of Wulfric de Morthlund, where they were shown into a lower room while the message from St Peter's canon elect was conveyed to Wulfric's sickroom. They claimed to be observing the custom of the Church in visiting the house, paying their respects and assuring one of their number that he would be remembered in their prayers while in poor health. None but Daniel would guess that the duty concealed a deeper purpose and he, by whatever means he could effect, would find a way to speak to them in private. He appeared in the doorway almost immediately.

'My master sends his regrets that he is unable to greet you himself.' He kept his voice barely above a whisper as he lowered the door leather and stepped down two wooden steps into the room. 'How is Tobias?'

'Not good,' Simeon told him bluntly. 'His wounds reopen each time his plug is changed, and now his belly has become discoloured. His mistress, Martha, nurses him night and day, and we still hope.'

'Peter is missing,' Thorald told him. 'Is he here? Does Wulfric have him?'

Daniel bristled at the suggestion. 'Sir, in this house I am forced to endure many things that I abhor—'

'Aye, and you know that Nicholas Weaver was killed

291

because he tried to entice young Edwin here in your name.'

'Peter is not here. There are some things, my friend, that even I refuse to tolerate. Tobias was the last small boy to suffer at Wulfric de Morthlund's hands. So long as I draw breath, there will be no more.'

Thorald made a hissing sound of exasperation. 'Noble words, Daniel Hawk, easily spoken but impossible to institute.'

Simeon saw something in the young priest's eyes that caused him to raise a hand for silence. He held Daniel's gaze and knew that the limits of this unhappy man's endurance had been reached. He had shown no rage when told of Nicholas Weaver's attempts to make off with Edwin, nor anger when he had stood by Tobias's bed and soothed the weeping boy as his bloody plug was removed and another inserted. Something else had been in his eyes, something new and resolute. Simeon saw it now and guessed the truth.

'By the gods! You intend to bring charges against him!'

'I do,' Daniel confirmed.

'But you will incriminate yourself.'

'I know that, Simeon.'

'And he will not fall alone,' Simeon warned. 'He will accuse you of similar crimes.'

'I know that, too. My one regret is that my courage has been so long in coming.'

'Slow-growing plants often make the sturdiest vines,' Simeon assured him. 'God bless you, Daniel Hawk. Be sure that many good men will be prepared to speak out on your behalf. What brought you at last to this, my friend? Was it Tobias? Was it Edwin?'

Daniel smiled and answered simply, 'It was God Himself who brought me here.'

Before they left to continue their search for Peter, Simeon inquired as to Wulfric's health and Daniel informed him that the canon was still much weakened by the flux.

'Give him camomile,' Simeon suggested, 'and allow him neither wine nor rich food. He must drink water, lots of it, to replace the fluids the flux has flushed away. Let him eat only bread, either plain or scorched, and any good grains soaked in water.'

'Should I discontinue the blackthorn juice?'

Simeon was astounded by the question. 'What? You feed him blackthorn, *for the flux*?'

'For a bowel blockage,' Daniel explained. 'Did Brother David not explain all this? He persuaded Job to give blackthorn juice to Tobias so that Wulfric would think him infected and turn him out. Job told me to let my master drink it every four hours, for how long, I have no notion. He refuses to have it infused and prefers to sip the neat juice from a spoon. Simeon? Why do you look at me like that?'

'You feed your master a drastic purgative that will eventually corrode his bowel. Job has either forgotten his instructions or else cares not if your master dies and you are accused of his murder. Get rid of the blackthorn, Daniel, before his innards are stripped raw and his bowel becomes infected with ulcers.'

'Have I been *poisoning* him?'

'Little better,' Simeon said grimly. 'He must possess the constitution of an ox to take undiluted blackthorn juice in regular doses and survive.'

'I will not be responsible for his death,' Daniel assured him. 'Not like this, in the guise of trusted nurse. If I cannot face the man in strength and honesty, I will certainly not resort to anything so base and devious as poisoning him with medicines.'

'God give you strength, Daniel,' Simeon said, and Thorald added gruffly, 'Aye you're going to need it.'

'I'll pray for the boy. Send word when he is safely home.'

As they left the house Thorald shrugged his massive shoulders and lifted his hood against a fall of sleet. 'Will he do it? Will he charge his master in open court, knowing that he'll be judged as black as he, and in the certain knowledge that Wulfric will try to kill him for the betrayal?'

Simeon lifted his own hood, dismayed that the sleet would

hamper their search for Peter. 'I believe he will, Thorald, if he can keep de Morthlund from guessing his intentions in advance. I want you to return to your church and concentrate your search around the port. Peter must be hurt, or else someone has taken him. He would have sent word.'

Daniel Hawk stood at the window to watch them leave, then crossed to the kitchens to send a servant on an urgent errand. He paused in the hall to murmur a prayer for Peter's safe return before climbing the stair and drawing back the drapes from his master's door.

Wulfric de Morthlund lay on his bed with his hands clutching his belly, kneading the lardy flesh with his fingers as if to rub the pains away. Sweat lay in glistening patches on his face, plastered his thinning hair to his head and stained the front of his night robe. A team of servants swarmed about the bed, attending to his night pots and his linens. This mountainous man was fastidious in his person, and the constant fluxing offended him. He sat back, exhausted, on his mound of pillows, waved the servants out and reached for the hand of his priest and catamite.

'Am I dying, Daniel? Tell me the truth.'

'No, Wulfric. I have sent for camomile to help halt the flux, and the juice left here by Job must be discontinued. From now on, my lord canon, you will heed your priest in all things. Scorched bread and wetted grains will be your daily fare, and a full pint of camomile water every hour.'

'Bread and water? Wetted grains? Do you want to kill me?'

Daniel shook his head and placed a damp cloth across his master's sweating throat. 'Wulfric de Morthlund, I have served you well for fifteen years and saved your life on more than one occasion. I will not fail you now.'

'Dear heart, I am deeply touched by your loyalty.'

'All eyes will be on you at the trial of Cyrus de Figham, and I intend your part in it to be a spectacle neither priest nor clerk nor common man will ever want to forget.'

'I am overwhelmed.' Wulfric's brow creased in a frown. 'This sickness has given me ample time to consider my

294

position, Daniel. Certain aspects of this trial worry me. I know de Figham for the snake he is. He will speak against me.'

'Will it matter?' Daniel asked. 'The papal legate must be aware that men accused of serious crimes will often be vindictive and malicious in their efforts to avoid retribution.'

'Throw mud against a man's robes and those robes are stained for all to see,' Wulfric grumbled. 'He could damage me a thousand times over, just by speaking the truth. What will it matter to him if he incriminates himself in the process? What will *he* have left to lose? And he will do it, Daniel. He will take me down with him.'

'The trial is still several weeks away, Wulfric. Rest now. We will discuss all this later. A servant has gone for camomile, and when—'

Wulfric dashed his hand aside. 'How the devil can I rest with all these troubles to plague my mind? That brother of his will help him bring about my fall. He knows about my illegal arrangement with Cyrus for the lease of Antony's house in Keldgate, and we can be sure he'll not keep *that* from the ears of the papal legate. Geoffrey Plantagenet is about to offer him the provost's seat, so all my bribes and promises amount to nothing. What need has Hector of me with our damned archbishop in his corner?'

'My lord . . . Wulfric . . .'

'There is more, Daniel. My clerks were here while you were absent yesterday. That miserable curate has made complaint of me to Jacob.'

'Complaint, my lord?'

'On the grounds that I practise the sin of homosexuality. He quotes Leviticus and demands that I be put to death. He quotes the Council of London and demands that I be excommunicated. He seeks to trap me between the bible and the law.'

'I see. And how does he hope to prove such charges?'

'He will need no proof if sufficient witnesses can be persuaded to speak against me.' Wulfric screwed up his bulbous features as he kneaded at his belly. 'This papal legate, this Bishop Roberto, must be bribed.'

'They say he cannot be bought,' Daniel replied, shaking his head.

'Nonsense! Are we expected to believe that he has reached such a high position at the court of His Holiness the Pope without resorting to a measure of bribery on the way? Does this bishop take us all for idiots?' Another painful spasm sent Wulfric rolling from one side of the bed to the other. At the end of it he allowed Daniel to hold a cup of water to his lips, then fell back on his pillows and asked, 'Where is my clerk, Nicholas Weaver?'

'I have no word of him. Perhaps he has fled the pestilence.'

'Dismiss him. I want no cowards in my employ. Get rid of him. What news is there of Tobias? Is he dead?'

'Not dead, my lord, but injured internally.'

'And fit to tell a court how he came by his injuries.' Wulfric nodded. 'Damn him.'

While Daniel thought his master sleeping and crept to the window to let some cleaner air into the room, Wulfric de Morthlund was merely setting his mind to the task of avoiding appearing as one of the accused in the legate's court. He emerged from these thoughts with a start, his eyes as bright as polished beads in his fleshy face. 'No papers, no prisoner, no brat, no charges against me,' he declared.

'My lord?'

'Quite simple, dear heart. Papers can be stolen, prisoners can be moved and sick brats can die. I will petition Jacob to have Cyrus moved to my own cell, since only a canon should have the right to restrain a fellow canon. Hector cannot rightfully invoke our law of atonement, so his prisoner thrives and fears no tortures to cleanse his soul of its evils and prepare him for repentance. I must have him here, where I can set the matter to rights. Let us see how well he survives under *my* jurisdiction.'

'But my lord, what you're suggesting is—'

'What I am suggesting, Daniel, is a way out for us. I have men in my employ who can not only read and write well enough to identify the papers in question, but who can also steal them from under the provost's very nose. When the court convenes and the papers are missed, there will be no time to replace them, and I can claim that they were nothing but a fabrication all along. By God, it will work. With cunning, we can nip this little conspiracy in the bud.'

Daniel cleared his throat and kept his voice at a calm and steady pitch. He knew he must encourage his master to voice his plans so that, if necessary, Simeon could be warned. 'And what of the boy, Tobias?'

Wulfric shrugged. 'A pillow placed over his face? A little pressure on his throat?'

'I see, and who is to do the deed my lord? It will not be easy to put a man of yours within the walls of St Peter's.'

'Oh yes it will,' de Morthlund grinned. 'I do believe I feel better already. I see you are puzzled, Daniel, so let me enlighten you.' He caught the young priest by the folds of his robe, pulled him close and placed a wet kiss on his lips. 'Simeon trusts you, my handsome Little Hawk, so *you* are the obvious choice. *You* will kill Tobias!'

CHAPTER TWENTY-ONE

Elvira knew when she saw his face and the slight stoop of his shoulders that Simeon's search had been unsuccessful.

'Wulfric de Morthlund does not have him, we can be sure of that. He is sick in his bed and Daniel has the run of the house. He would know if Peter had been there.' He fell into step with Rufus. 'And here is good news for you, Father. Father Daniel is to bring charges against his master at the legate's court.'

'Will he dare? He is the man's catamite!'

'He will dare,' Simeon assured him. 'But let this go no further, Rufus. Wulfric will cut out his tongue if he even suspects Daniel's intentions.'

Fergus de Burton arrived an hour later, bringing his seven soldiers and a hooded man dressed in Christian clothes. They immediately set their backs to helping the labourers who were struggling to shift the massive timber bridge from its original supports. The sudden rising of the water, rushing against mortar baked by drought and then cracked by frost, had undermined several stones and rendered the bridge unsafe. Four masons were struggling to bolt a metal plate against the wall, a barrier between themselves and the flow of water, so that the work could be done without risk to their lives. Slotted inside this narrow metal cage, a man would work to repair the weakened mortar, and the plates would remain in place to prevent the current washing his handiwork downstream. Half the soldiers helped lever the bridge into its temporary position while the others, under Chad's direction, helped shore it up with a number of stout oak beams. When the masons had repaired the mortar the bridge would be returned to its ancient housings, and that vital access to the church across the drain would once again be secure.

'This is the worst of times for men to be making repairs,' Rufus said, watching a mason drop down into the narrow space behind the metal plate while water rushed by just inches from his head. 'If the water rises by another hand span he will drown in there.'

'Needs must,' Simeon answered gravely. 'We did not expect the thaw to come so early or so rapidly. The water still rises, so the repairs must be done at once, or the bridge will fall.'

He grabbed Fergus by the arm as the young man swung from one of the supporting beams to the area of solid ground at the safest end of the precariously tilted bridge. 'Your visit was well timed, young Fergus. Now come and dry your clothes before the fire.'

'*Shalom,* my friend.'

At the sound of that familiar voice, Simeon turned with a gasp. 'Aaron! *Shalom.*' He glanced at the robes and the conspicuous crucifix. 'We seem to have converted you to our faith.'

'My shirt, Priest, not my soul.' The rabbi smiled.

The reunion of friends was brief and laced with tension. Peter had now been missing without trace for nineteen hours. The weather was turning against them and every passing moment brought them closer to another night.

'We stayed over at Thorpe,' Fergus told Simeon, 'so I could show Rabbi Aaron my plans to transform that sorry place into my very own Ravensthorpe. He was impressed, as well he should be. Now, Simeon, give them but an hour's rest and my men are at your disposal. How can we help you?'

'You could visit all the churches and chapels in the

299

town,' Simeon suggested. 'Have them search their crypts and undercrofts and any wells on their property. Have your soldiers listen out for any rumours. Someone must know where he is, Fergus, so no scrap of information must be overlooked. And do not be too open with your purse. Men speak more truthfully when the coin is withheld until their story can be confirmed.'

'I will remember that.' Fergus smiled. 'My men will be dried off and ready to leave within the hour, unless they are needed to help lower the bridge. What am I to do with Aaron?'

'Leave him here. I doubt that chain and crucifix he wears will protect him once he is separated from your soldiers. Most people will be highly suspicious of a black-faced foreigner seeking an Anglo-Saxon boy.'

'Will Elvira also remain here in your absence?'

'She will.'

'With Aaron?'

Simeon had been hanging his wet cloak by the fire in favour of another. He turned to survey the young man with untroubled eyes. 'Could my lady be in safer hands, Fergus?'

'In less covetous hands, perhaps.'

'He loves her.'

'So I believe. Some men will take what they love by stealth, or even force, rather than lose it to another.'

'Not Aaron,' Simeon assured him. 'There are some, Fergus, who cherish that which they truly love above all else. Do not concern yourself on Elvira's behalf or on mine. Rabbi Aaron is an honourable man.'

'Aye, he is also thirty years old, wealthy, compelling to a fault and devilishly handsome. You dangle an exotic delicacy before your lady and trust she will not be tempted to take a bite.'

'I know my lady,' Simeon told him and smiled.

While the two men spoke inside the scriptorium, Aaron had found Elvira in the gardens. He drew her pale hand to his lips and she saw his heart clearly written in the black

300

pools of his eyes. '*Shalom*,' he whispered, and rarely had she heard such depth of feeling in a single word.

'*Shalom*, my dear, dear friend.'

'It seems we are destined to meet in tragic circumstances. I feel for you, Elvira, in this temporary loss of your foster son. I know how very precious he is to you.'

'Temporary,' Elvira echoed. 'If only I could believe it might be so.'

'Believe it. Have faith, Elvira, if not in God then in Peter and in Simeon.' They walked a little way in silence before Aaron said, 'Forgive my bluntness, lady, but have you considered the possibility that Peter's time with you is drawing to its close? Rufus has seen *the other*, apparently here for no purpose save to spend time with the boy. Perhaps it is time, my dear, for him to leave you.'

Elvira suppressed a shudder at the suggestion, for this was a possibility she had refused to contemplate. Beverley's blessed relics were safely hidden, its priceless treasures protected, its ancient books and scrolls retrieved. The gems stolen from the shrine of St John, missing for ten long years, had been restored, leaving the question she feared to ask herself: what more was there for Peter to do in Beverley?

'No,' she said at last. 'I cannot believe that. I *will not* believe it. Peter's place is *here*.'

Aaron's face opened in a smile, his big teeth flashing in dramatic contrast to the darkness of his skin. 'There are few things in this world more powerful than the will of a passionate woman, Elvira, especially one who—'

'Rabbi! Look out!'

Edwin's shouted warning came too late. Brother David sprinted from the trees with a bar of iron in his fist. Before Aaron had time to do more than shove Elvira out of danger, the bar swung down and clubbed him to the ground.

'Heathen! Debaucher! Slayer of innocent children!'

With a cry Edwin raced forward to assist the rabbi, received a back-handed blow to his chest and fell heavily on his back. Elvira was screaming for Simeon as she attempted to drag the dazed Aaron away, and all the

301

while the monk was lashing out and jabbing his club at the Jew.

'Arab! Infidel! Hanger of Christ! Spawn of the Devil!'

Simeon raced across the garden, followed by Antony and Rufus, and ran up behind the monk, then ducked and parried until he was able to grab the iron bar as David swung it over his head. He twisted it free and sent it clattering to the ground some yards away. A blow to the jaw sent David sprawling and, while the monk was so distracted, others were able to pull Aaron and Edwin to safety. The monk dropped into a crouch, his hands held out like weapons, his eyes boring into Simeon's.

Behind Simeon, Antony moved this way and that, anticipating David's next move. 'Watch out for his hands, Simeon. Remember Nicholas Weaver. This man's hands are strong.'

Rufus, too, had advice to offer his son. 'Talk to him, Simeon. Calm him.'

Glancing about him, Simeon saw the priest of St Nicholas running for the infirmary with Aaron across his shoulders, and Osric beside him with the breathless Edwin in his arms. The young priest, Richard, held Elvira by the arms, while others were running towards them from all directions. Seeing his opponent momentarily distracted, David lunged to his feet and, using his head as a battering ram, threw Simeon backwards and grappled him to the ground. In the skirmish that followed, many blows were exchanged. Then the onlookers saw a flash of steel as the crazed monk drew a dagger from his coat. Simeon rolled on the ground and sprang to his feet, gasping, one hand upraised to hold back those who would have come to his assistance.

'Stay back!'

'Simeon! Take my knife!'

Rufus withdrew his dagger and threw it, hilt first, towards his unarmed son. The heavy weapon arced through the air in Simeon's direction but caught the edge of his sleeve as his arm came up, and spun away. As Simeon wheeled to retrieve it the monk lunged forward and the priest went down with a crash. Winded, Simeon grabbed the wrist that held the knife, and only then, with that frenzied face so close to his own and the blade of a knife only inches from his throat, did he realise that he was fighting for his life. Grunting and gasping, the two men fought like devils, Simeon pinned down by the other's weight, David bent on piercing him with the blade.

'Listen to me, David!' Simeon ground words through his teeth into the other's face. 'I am not your enemy! Drop the knife!'

As if Simeon's voice had penetrated his madness, the monk relaxed his grip for just an instant, one brief lapse that was sufficient to give the priest the upper hand. He thrust his body upward and into a roll, and a moment later their positions were reversed. Now David was pinned to the ground and, with both their hands on its hilt, the pointed blade was pressing against the soft flesh under his chin. His eyes were clear, the look of frenzy gone, and suddenly his powerful hands were no longer resisting Simeon's battle for control.

'Do it, Simeon!' he hissed.

Simeon felt the knife shift forward and saw the blood spurt out as the pointed blade pierced David's skin. He saw the monk's eyes grow wide and heard his voice imploring, demanding, 'Do it!'

Like a splash of icy water in his face, those words cut through his vexation and his instincts drew him off. He tried to pull back, employing all the remaining strength in his arms to keep the knife from being driven home by David's own hands.

Unable to match the strength in those powerful hands, Simeon rammed his knee into David's belly and, crying a furious 'No!', managed to drag the knife away. It came free slowly, its blade slicing through the grasping hands of the monk so that every finger was left with a deep gash across its base.

'I am not your executioner,' Simeon declared, 'and I will not be made the tool of your suicide.'

He was hauling the bleeding monk to his feet when the cry went up that the bridge had shifted and a man was trapped below. David took full advantage of the distraction. His powerful forearm caught Simeon across the jaw, and as Rufus lunged forward to grab him he broke away and made a dash towards the bridge. They all gave chase, with Simeon right on David's heels as he reached the bridge and pounded over the timbers, then vaulted over the side and hung by his bleeding fingers from a crossbeam.

'What in God's name is he doing?'

Following Simeon's example, Rufus flattened himself face down on the bridge, hooked an arm through one of the side rails and stretched the other over the side. Father and son reached down as far as they dared towards the rushing water and the man who struggled to keep a grip on the crossbeam. A metal safety plate had been struck by a heavy log carried downstream by the current, wedging the mason against the bridge in the water. The log was trapped between the angled beams supporting the bridge. If it dislodged the beams, the bridge would fall, and the mason would be crushed beneath its weight.

The monk had not hesitated for a second. One moment he had been racing away from his pursuers, the next he was fighting the current in his attempts to attach a rope around the mason. Held fast by a metal plate, the frightened man battled to keep his head above the flow of water. David heaved on the metal, pulling against the water's weight as his broad back took the full force of the current. Inch by desperate inch the metal yielded, and as those above heaved on the rope, the trapped man was eased free. With a yell his legs and feet were released and he was pulled to safety, leaving David exhausted in the water.

'David! Up here!'

The monk looked up to see helping hands reaching down for him. Still clinging to the metal plate with one hand, he strained to reach his rescuers with the other. The current dislodged his grip and sent him crashing into the crossbeams, and the force of the impact shifted the massive oak by several inches. He saw the danger, the outstretched hands and Simeon's anxious face, and he stretched his own hand up for one brief moment.

'Grab my hand!' Simeon yelled.

Hanging from the bridge with Rufus clinging to his legs, Simeon felt the bloodied fingers brush against his palm. He closed his hand around them, felt them slide and pull free of his grip and the hand was gone. Below him, the trapped log swung around and broke away the beams that had hampered its progress. The monk closed his eyes and, resigned, waited for the bridge to fall.

Those on the bridge threw themselves down to protect themselves from the impact, while Antony and Rufus braced their bodies against the timbers to prevent the priest from being thrown into the drain. The drama was over in seconds. Simeon was hauled to safety and the rescued mason carried, bruised and shocked but otherwise unhurt, to Osric's infirmary.

'I let him go,' Simeon said. 'I had him for just a moment, but his fingers were limp and slippery. I could not hold on and nor could he.'

'Did he try?' his father asked.

'I do not know,' Simeon admitted. He stared down at David's body lying crushed and trapped between the great bridge and its housings, the arms outstretched, the face turned up to heaven. Ten years ago Father Willard had died like that, pinned to the bridge by a natural force too powerful for any mortal man to resist. With his father's arm about his shoulders, Simeon left the bridge, comforted by the knowledge that the troubled Brother David had died not as a suicide or a condemned murderer but during an act of selfless heroism. He had saved the mason's life. He was redeemed.

When the Jew opened his eyes Elvira was bending over him, her hair glowing in the light and her soft hand on his forehead, and it seemed to him that their first meeting was repeated.

'Must I be beaten half to death before you come to me, Elvira?'

305

'This time you were merely stunned,' she told him. 'The bar missed your skull but badly bruised your shoulders. No bones are broken. A little rest, some rubbing oil with chervil for the bruising, and Aaron the Ethiopian will be as new.'

'Who attacked me?'

'A poor monk who was suffering a prolonged bleakness of the soul. He is at peace now.'

'At peace?' the Jew asked. 'Did Simeon kill him?'

Elvira shook her head. 'Brother David died when the bridge collapsed. He saved a mason's life before it fell. You must rest now, Aaron.'

He drew her hand to his lips and kissed the palm, then reached into his shirt to pull out the token he wore on a thong around his neck. The length of hair had been neatly braided into a raven plait, pinned at one end with a clasp and at the other with a knot of gold thread. Aaron brought it to his face and his nostrils flared as he sniffed its perfume.

'You kept it,' Elvira said.

'Next to my heart.'

'And you came,' she recalled with gratitude. 'When I needed you, when Simeon's life hung in the balance and I was desperate, you kept your promise, Aaron.'

Aaron nodded as he replaced the twist of hair inside his shirt. His chest was muscular and very brown, with swirls of short black curls. A strong pulse beat in the hollow of his throat. 'Be warned, Elvira. If you ever have need of me again, I will serve you as before, but never again will I discharge a debt in the name of love, be it yours for Simeon or mine for you. Another time, another desperate situation, and you will be mine.'

Before Elvira could answer, Father Richard appeared with soothing oils to be rubbed into Aaron's bruises and with a message that Canon Cuthbert would visit the Jew in the infirmary.

'Where is Simeon?' Elvira asked.

'Gone with Antony and Rufus to the church.'

'Which church?'

'St Peter's,' Richard told her, 'to search for Peter.'

306

Elvira reached for her hood. 'I must go with them.'

As she hurried out, the Jew obediently rolled over onto his stomach to receive the oils. 'Another time,' he murmured as the bearded young priest applied the oil with care for the tenderness of the battered muscles.

St Peter's church was empty, as Elvira had expected it to be. They had crawled behind the panel near the altar. Elvira lit a rush light from the altar candle and shielded the flame with her hand as she drew back the panel. A cold, sharp breeze lifted her hair, a breeze as fresh as any that blew across the open pastures. She shuddered as she closed the panel behind her and made her way cautiously down the steps that curved their narrow way down to the tunnels lying below the town. For a while she kept her bearings with ease, moving west under the lower wall of the enclosure. She knew when she had reached St Peter's gate, for now she was between two waterways, St Peter's drain and the Eastgate ditch, and the sound of rushing water was all around her.

At the Minster, where several tunnels met or branched away in different directions, she suffered a loss of confidence and became confused. Here was a bewildering choice of routes. Should she select the wrong tunnel, or crawl by error into an unmarked shaft, she might wander for days and find no exit. Searching for a landmark in the darkness, she lost her footing on the rubble-strewn ground, tripped and fell against the wall and let her rush light fall. The darkness closed in around her. She listened for the sounds that would lead her back to the waterways and St Peter's gate, but in that cavernous place all sounds were carried here and there, and became directionless.

'Simeon,' she whispered, holding him in her thoughts so that she might draw upon his strength and not be daunted by her fears. As her eyes became accustomed to the darkness, the mouths of tunnels and shafts became detectable. Distant drainage holes and well mouths dropped shafts of pale light into the gloom, and her ears caught the separate sounds of water dripping down from the land above, where the snow was melting. With more caution than before, she approached the openings, selected one whose stones were smooth and scrambled inside. Inching her way along she saw a torch and shadowed figures move swiftly past its farthest end.

'Simeon!'

'Elvira? Is that you?'

The bright flame of the torch suddenly filled the hole and Elvira, almost weeping with relief, crawled on her hands and knees towards it. Simeon helped her out and held her briefly against him.

'How on earth did you get here, alone and without a lamp?'

'I dropped my rush light.'

'Aye, and you took a wrong turn,' he told her gravely. 'This shaft carries the overflow from the pond in Long Lane. If the levels rise much higher and the pond breaks over, the water will move so swiftly that anyone inside the shaft will be trapped. You should not be here, Elvira. The thaw and the rain make the tunnels dangerous.'

'I needed to be with you, Simeon,' she told him and he, knowing the torment in her heart, touched her cheek and whispered softly, 'I know, my love. Come, stay close behind me.'

'We're checking the main route from St Peter's to the Minster,' Antony told her. 'And from there to St Catherine's convent and St Thomas's chapel beyond the North Bar.'

As they made their way along the wider tunnel, Elvira fell into step with Simeon while the others walked behind. She and the monk were able to walk without stooping, but the two taller men were compelled to keep their heads bent down to avoid scraping them on the roof of the tunnel. Rufus was still amazed by his first venture into Simeon and Peter's underground domain.

'I saw the Beaver Lake,' he told Elvira, a tone of wonder in his voice. 'It was like a pool of gleaming quicksilver, with painted domes above it and ancient pillars rising up. There was a staircase with sculptured edges, going nowhere, and narrow shafts of light from above slanting down into the water like . . . like . . .'

'My father is so awed that he is lost for words,' Simeon told her with a smile. 'Now *there* is a miracle.'

'It was spectacular,' Rufus exclaimed. 'Who could imagine that such wonders were lying down here, right underneath the town. Will I see the treasure?'

'No, you will not,' his son told him firmly, 'but be assured that by the time we're above ground once again our journey will have taken you within mere inches of it. Let that suffice, Rufus.' He glanced back at the monk. 'Antony, we must speak to the masons about the tower foundations. They have shifted their position by another finger width. Not much awry, but if the current of the Minster stream increases with the thaw, that finger width will widen . . . Watch your step, Elvira, the ground begins to slope at this point.'

'Is the tower in danger of falling?' Rufus asked.

'It is indeed, unless its foundations are kept well planted. Do not be startled, Rufus. It might well stand for another twenty or thirty years. I had hoped to see it repaired by now, along with the Minster, but raising the money for all that work is proving difficult.'

'You'll do it, Simeon,' Elvira reassured him.

They moved on at a steady pace, their shadows jumping and twitching in the flickering light from Simeon's torch. When they reached a certain section of the tunnel where their voices were unlikely to be carried up shafts and wells to the streets above, they called out for the missing boy and strained their ears for his answering call.

'Peter! Peter!'

His name reverberated along narrow shafts and tunnels, and returned to them from the stones above their heads, then it fell silent. Water was running along the tunnel towards them, a shallow, fast-moving stream too narrow to reach the tunnel sides, so that where they put their feet the ground was dry. They moved in single file with Simeon in the lead and Antony bringing up the rear.

'Peter! Peter!'

For minutes they stood in silence, waiting for the echoes of their voices to give way to some other sound that would tell them the boy was found, but still they heard no answering call.

'No more calling,' Simeon instructed. 'Do you see that opening up ahead where the light is coming in? That is the cavern close to the Keldgate loop, and the area is densely populated. As we pass the wells you will hear voices, animal and kitchen noises in the shafts. Those families and traders go about their daily lives unaware that St John hears every word they utter and every sound they make.'

'Does the cavern have a higher roof?' Rufus asked.

'It does indeed, and we will need to climb a little way to reach the cross shaft Peter uses.'

'I will be happy just to be allowed to walk upright again,' Rufus informed him. 'My neck is as stiff as Cuthbert's from all this stooping.'

'Hush, everybody!' Simeon's voice was suddenly harsh. 'Listen!'

The big priest stood with his head cocked to one side, and soon the others heard what he had heard. A distant rumble, like confined thunder, reached their ears and, in the space between one heartbeat and the next, became a menacing roar that caused the very ground to tremble beneath their feet.

'What, in the name of God, is *that*?'

'Water!' Simeon grabbed Elvira by the hand and yelled a single word that chilled the blood in all their veins: '*Run!*'

CHAPTER TWENTY-TWO

'*R*un!'
       When Rufus turned to flee his path was barred by
Antony's stout staff.

'The other way!' the monk yelled above the growing din.

Rufus obeyed without hesitation and found himself running, against all his instincts, towards that thunderous and
terrifying sound.

Simeon reached the cavern first and all but threw Elvira
up to a stone ledge set in the wall above their heads. He
tossed the flaming torch up after her, then locked his fingers
and crouched to take the weight of Rufus's foot, straightening
his body with a jerk that hoisted his father high into the air.
The little monk came racing out of the tunnel and, without
even breaking his stride, made a leap for Simeon's hands
and was catapulted to the ledge so neatly that he landed on
his feet. As they stooped to grab Simeon's hands, the roar of
the oncoming water increased to a deafening pitch. Elvira
clamped her palms over her ears as Simeon was pulled to safety
with only seconds to spare before the danger was on them. A
great wall of water appeared from nowhere, erupted into the
cavern and hit the tunnel's mouth with such tremendous force
that the wall around it appeared to sag before the onslaught.
In an instant the tunnel was completely submerged beneath

the flood. They heard the thunder of rushing water retreating into the distance, rampaging like a wild beast into every open space. And then its roar was hushed and the beast became subdued, its fury spent.

'Where did it come from?' Rufus gasped.

'The Westwood,' Simeon told him. 'The snow has melted too quickly. When the streams and springs are overwhelmed, the water runs downhill to the town, breaking banks and boundaries as it travels.'

'Incredible! I swear I have never seen the like.'

'It would destroy our town but for the foresight of the monks who built these tunnels,' Simeon said.

'I thought to outrun it,' Rufus confessed.

Antony's laughter was without humour. 'A near fatal choice, my friend. Even a few inches of fast-flowing water can buckle a man's legs and render him helpless if it hits him from behind.' He paused to toss a large stone into the water. 'When such a surge as this is running loose, you either find a high place or you die.'

Elvira's voice was edged with fear as she spoke from the comforting crook of Simeon's arm. 'Does Peter know of this?'

'Be sure he does,' he reassured her with a smile. 'Our boy will not die by drowning, Elvira, not here in Beverley's tunnels. He knows them too well for that.'

He helped Elvira to her feet and retrieved his spluttering torch, then led the group along the ledge until they reached a cross shaft with a narrow mouth. 'We will be travelling on our knees and bellies for a good distance,' he warned them, 'but after that the going will be easier.'

They combed the tunnels for hours, calling where they dared to call, moving in silence where their voices might be heard in the streets above. At a cavern close by St Thomas's chapel, Elvira rested in a familiar chair and stared about her at familiar objects. There was the couch on which Aaron had lain for the better part of a week, recovering from the attack that had almost robbed him of his life. There was the stool where she had sat beside him, talking and coaxing

312

him back to health. Here in this pillared room Peter and Simeon, Cuthbert, Thorald and many more trusted priests had engaged the learned rabbi in deep conversation and often heated debate. And here it was that Aaron the Jew had come to love his gentle nurse, Elvira.

Simeon watched her now and knew that she, like him, was remembering that other time; a time when he had feared that he would lose her to another. She met his gaze and smiled. 'Was it really only three months ago?'

'It was. Have you any regrets?'

She thought of Aaron, holding her braided hair against his dark chest, and of Simeon, denied by his God the right to love her as a wife. Then she shook her head and answered, with a certain heart, 'No, Simeon, I have no regrets.'

They emerged from the tunnels weary and despondent, having made the homeward journey by a route that took them beyond St Mary's and close to the great North Bar. Richard had conducted the Noon Mass in Simeon's absence, and two of Fergus de Burton's soldiers had managed to free the body of Brother David from the bridge.

'They used axes,' Richard told him with regret. 'They had no choice. Too much of him was crushed by the bridge, and the current of the drain would have carried what remained into the beck.'

Grim faced, Simeon pushed his way through a crowd of volunteers preparing to join the search. Among them was Paul, so recently freed from his years of quiet sanctuary at St Peter's.

'The curate has sent me to help you in your search for Peter,' he explained. 'He has also sent a small party out to the pasture and the moor, to show his goodwill. I am to stay until the boy is found, if you will have me.'

'Gladly,' Simeon told him. 'Osric will tell you which group to join and where to search.'

In the infirmary Aaron was on his feet, helping the twins to crush the winter herbs and set them simmering in the pots above the fire. He drew Simeon aside and indicated the bed

313

where Martha sat with Tobias in her arms, singing softly as she rocked him to and fro with tireless care.

'I have heard some ugly stories here, my friend. Martha told me of her dead husband, and the poison that might have killed every innocent worshipper at the Mass. She speaks freely of Cyrus de Figham's violation of her, and that poor child's grievous injuries at the hands of Wulfric de Morthlund speak for themselves. And now your boy is missing. What is happening here, Simeon?'

'The Devil's work.'

'No, my friend, this is *man's* work.'

Simeon shrugged as he watched the liquid black of the rabbi's eyes. He saw compassion there and genuine concern for those at St Peter's whom he had learned to call his friends. 'Men we can fight,' he told the Jew. 'With the law or the sword.'

'Then speak to Fergus de Burton,' Aaron told him. 'He holds another weapon that can be placed at your disposal – politics. Use him, Simeon. Use the archbishop and the papal legate. Use the pope himself, if you must, but cut these festering cankers out before they destroy the body of your Church.'

'I am neither a soldier nor a politician,' Simeon reminded him.

'First a priest, and after that a man? I think not, Simeon de Beverley. Our God demands that we be both. Be sure you have a plan of action ready to be employed when it is time to put aside the priest's robe in favour of the sword.'

'Am I to smite my enemies, then, to murder them in their beds and settle everything by the sword?'

'In the hands of an honest man, *any* weapon can rightfully be called God's weapon. An eye for an eye and a tooth for a tooth, so our precious bible tells us. Remember this forgotten truth, my friend. From Genesis to Revelations, Jehovah was a vengeful God until you Christians made a priest of him.'

The Jew placed his palm on Simeon's chest and, either by accident or design, covered the golden brow piece. A little pressure and the disc's edges met the hard resistance

314

of his muscles, reminding him of its purpose and its history.

Those searchers who had returned to St Peter's were gathering in the long refectory building, groups of weary men and women who had tramped the streets and alleyways of Beverley in search of a boy no eye had seen. They came back to St Peter's with heavy hearts and saturated clothes. The sleet had turned to heavy rain and had been falling steadily since noon, and so they either stood or sat by the fire amid clouds of steam drawn by its heat. Baskets of bread still warm from the ovens were set about the room. The common pots around the fire were filled to the brim with good, plain fare with aromatic herbs and spices added.

Moving from group to group, Simeon heard of the plague pits opened by the rain and of the rats and crows that were feeding there. He heard of many cases where the pestilence had been controlled by sensible precautions and common-sense management of the sick, and of the frequent situations where panic and foolish superstition had cost many lives by cross-infection.

Fergus de Burton set aside his bowl of steaming stew as Simeon approached. 'There is a rumour in the town that Fergus de Burton has lost a nephew,' he told the priest, 'a fair-haired boy with blue eyes and dressed in a light-grey habit.'

'Your nephew?'

'Aye, and I am extremely keen to find him.' Fergus nodded. 'So keen that I offer a handsome reward for his safe return.'

'Oh? And is there some purpose to this lie, except to put a price on Peter's head?'

Fergus was disappointed by his response. 'You instructed me to have my men listen out for common rumour,' he protested. 'We came across talk in the town that the mystery boy of St Peter's, the lame priest's bastard son, has disappeared. Many are dredging up tales of the tempest and the fire, and your close encounter with death at the carting is still fresh in everyone's memory. We even heard that you were pierced right through with a crossbow bolt and survived the wound by magic.'

'Damn it, Fergus, I survived that wound because the bolt struck the brow piece.' He pulled the golden disc from his shirt to show the jagged hole pierced through its centre. 'It kept all but the point of the arrow from my flesh.'

'I know that, and I believe it, but do *they*? I judged it prudent to replace these rumours with a story of my own invention, before everyone knows that the boy we seek is Peter de Beverley. *Then* there would be a price on his head, and Wulfric de Morthlund would be the highest bidder.'

With a weary sigh, Simeon raked his hands through his hair and knew he had spoken hastily. 'Fergus, this business has dulled my wits. Forgive me. What you did was wise and very generous.' He extended his hand and Fergus shook it warmly. 'I will bear any costs incurred by your pledges.'

'You can be sure you will.' Fergus grinned. He handed Simeon a bowl of stew and tore a large portion of bread from his own loaf. 'Eat well. We need all our strength if Peter is to be found before another night is on us.'

Simeon ate despite his lack of appetite. Looking around the crowded room, he knew that every searcher would be out again when their bellies were filled and their bones warmed by the fire. This calamity had brought them out in their scores, and every man and woman here put personal safety in second place as they scoured the streets in search of the missing boy.

'Will you try to make peace with my father?' Simeon asked, and saw the pleasant face crease with distaste.

'I would, if he stopped making war on me. I never knew a man so argumentative or perverse. If I declared night dark, he would swear I lied.'

'He is anxious and frustrated, and with good reason. Make peace with him.'

Fergus pursed his lips and frowned thoughtfully. 'Very well, I will do my best, but I will not be your father's whipping boy to please you, peace or no peace. A truce is all I am prepared to offer, not full surrender. Speak to Rufus.'

'I will do that,' Simeon promised, then studied the young man's face as he chewed on his bread. 'I hear your generosity has extended beyond these walls,' he said at last. 'It seems you have a tender heart beneath that slippery exterior.'

'Not I.' Fergus grinned. 'My heart is cold.'

'I doubt the monks of St Dominic the Mailed will agree with that when they receive the carts you have dispatched on their behalf.'

'Ah, you've heard of that? Well, Simeon, the purchase of a few modest provisions does not prove me to be tenderhearted.'

'*Modest* provisions? I hear the shipment included meat and grain, blankets, fuel, sacks of salt, live chickens and pigs . . . Need I continue?'

'Look, in my defence let me tell you that the monks of St Dominic's own a certain relic left to them by a travelling priest many years ago. Since monks have no use for holy relics, and since my church at Thorpe has so little to recommend it, I hope to strike a bargain, nothing more.'

'But you know as well as I that those monks would trade a relic for a fraction of what you have given,' Simeon told him. 'Be man enough to confess your fault, Fergus de Burton. You are tenderhearted.'

'Spare me your priest's talk. I have a reputation to protect.' The young man's face grew grave as he drew Simeon aside and spoke close to his ear. 'Geoffrey Plantagenet is already travelling south to make the arrangements for his ordination and consecration as York's archbishop. He hopes to meet with the king in London, then ride with him to Canterbury, where the papal legate is lodged. He intends to have his future sealed by August.'

'So soon? Can it be done?'

'It can if Geoffrey wills it. Like the best of smithies, he will strike while the iron is hot, while legate, king and archbishop are at his disposal. If things go well for him, and I have no reason to suppose otherwise, he will travel here with Bishop Roberto to take first place at the provost's court. He intends to make this town his showpiece, Simeon,

317

and to use our courts to demonstrate his goodwill towards the Church.'

'Politics,' Simeon muttered, recalling the rabbi's recent advice.

'Aye, politics, and by the use of them we can play this ambitious man to our advantage. We must offer him priests and clerks who are willing to take their final vows, as many as we can muster, so that his reputation both here and in Rome is enhanced. We must give him a trial in which he can shine like a beacon as both judge and inquisitor. He seeks to impress the pope, the king and the people. We must help him do it, Simeon. We must help him dazzle the legate with his brilliance, and after that the Plantagenet will be our ally and Beverley's saviour.'

'*We?*' Simeon queried. '*Our?*'

'Did I say that?'

'You did, not once but many times.' Simeon caught sight of Osric at the door and knew that he was needed elsewhere. Before he moved away he touched the young man's arm and told him, with a mocking smile, 'Have a care with that tender heart of yours, Fergus de Burton, lest you find yourself amongst people who insist on calling you friend.'

Osric was waiting outside the door of the refectory with Simeon's dry cloak folded over his arm. 'We are ready to resume the search,' he said. 'Your father will join us in a moment, and Thorald has gone to fetch Antony from the scriptorium. Rufus has been with the rabbi since you came up from the tunnels. They are of a kind, those two, in many ways.'

'But are they in agreement?' Simeon asked, drawing the cloak about his shoulders. 'My father can be so argumentative as to tax the patience of a saint.'

'Aaron can cope with that,' Osric told him. 'I doubt even Rufus de Malham could touch a fuse to Aaron's temper.'

The two men stood below the eaves, watching the rain slanting down over the enclosure and falling in rivulets from the roof. The bridge across the drain was awash as the current carried the thawed snow and the rain towards the beck, the Hull and the open sea.

'God bless you, Willard,' he whispered towards the bridge. 'And God grant you peace, Brother David.'

Ten years before, Simeon's life had been secure and uneventful. His first sighting of the hooded figure, here in this safe enclosure, had changed all that. He had been transformed from a lame scribe and humble chantry priest into the focus of other men's hostilities and ambitions. That figure had come to Beverley with a raging tempest at its heels, bringing a newly born child to leave in Simeon's keeping. The priest would never know why he had been so chosen, why his crippled foot had been healed and his heart given over to a ditcher's wife who would be forever his and yet never could be his in truth.

'Where is he?' he asked, tight-lipped. 'Where is the Guardian at the Gate now that his Keeper at the Shrine is lost?'

'He comes when he is needed,' Osric told him.

'God's teeth! The boy is lost!' Simeon's anger stirred inside him. 'We need him now, Osric, *now*.'

'He will come when we face a situation in which we can no longer help ourselves. No matter how long and hard I ponder on it, I remain convinced of that above all else. *The other* comes when all seems lost. The answer to Peter's disappearance must be here within our reach, Simeon, and that creature won't help us . . . or perhaps *cannot* help us . . . while we still have the means to help ourselves.'

'So you still believe that Peter will be found?'

'I believe it.' Osric nodded. 'And if not, if time runs out for him, then *the other* will come to help us.'

'Our task is to protect the boy and we have failed. Our guardian has abandoned us. Unless we find Peter, how will we ever know if *the other* has withdrawn his charge and stolen him away?'

Simeon's own words struck at his heart, chilling him. Through the rain he saw Rufus appear at the infirmary door with Edwinia on hand to help him with his cloak, and the sight of that pretty girl with her ink-stained fingers gave him an idea as clear as crystal. He turned to Osric with hope burning afresh in his blue eyes.

'Any weapon is God's weapon,' he said. 'The Jew was right. God knows what He's about. Begin the search without me, Osric. I will join you when I can.'

He dashed across the muddy ground to grab the startled Edwinia by the shoulders. 'Where are your drawings? Get them for me at once, all of them.'

Minutes later he was sprinting towards the narrow gap between the infirmary and the storehouse. As he squeezed into the tunnel-like space, the breath caught in his throat. He had sheltered here with Father Willard when the tempest had been at its height, and then Willard had rushed out in a panic to meet his death head on, and Simeon had turned to meet the awesome gaze of that hooded figure. Shrugging off the memory of that terrible night, he raced along the gap and emerged in a wide strip of land lying between the buildings and St Peter's outer wall. Beyond was the ditch and the hovels lining Eastgate, and beyond them the fish markets, the heart of the town and Butcher's Row.

He knew that what he planned to do was an offence against the Church. He did not drag his foot, for his cripple's gait would slow him down, and should his haste result in public admission of his miraculous healing, then so be it. He must find the boy or lose him, of that much he was certain, and he had not loved young Peter as a son for ten long years to lose him now.

In her gloomy hovel in an alleyway just off Butcher's Row, Old Hannah saw a black-haired boy reflected in the gleaming belly of her copper fire pot. He moved with the silent stealth of a practised thief through the room at her back, peering and probing, feeling around every nook and cranny for something worthy of his interest and his skills. Without turning her head from the hearth she told him sharply, 'There is nothing for you here, Justin the fishmonger's son.'

The boy started in alarm.

'Ah yes, I know you, boy. Old Hannah knows *everything*.'

'But your back's turned to me,' he protested. 'How can you see me?'

'I see all things,' she said mysteriously, watching his tiny reflection in her pot.

'How do you know me?'

'By your eyes, Justin. And by your hatred. Beware lest your own fire consume you, boy. It is a big fire for so small a bucket.'

'You're a sorceress.'

'And you are a thief.'

'You're a witch.'

'And you are a pick-purse.'

Justin was edging towards the door when he spotted the rectangle of ivory lying face down near the hearth. He stared at her back and moved slowly towards her stool, his steps uncertain.

'Seen something that takes your fancy, Justin?' she asked in her rasping voice. 'A chicken bone, perhaps? A frozen rat's turd? A portion of cow dung?'

The boy darted forward, snatched up the ivory and made a dash for the door, leaving Old Hannah chuckling gleefully as she rocked before her empty grate and her glistening pot.

In the alleyway outside the hovel Justin collided with a big man in a saturated cloak. 'Have a care, boy. Why the haste? Well, well, our paths cross for a second time, you thieving rascal.' Simeon grasped the boy by his upper arms and lifted him up so he could see his face more clearly. 'Be warned, lad,' he growled. 'If you dare to spit at me again I will thrash you to within an inch of your life. Who are you?'

The dark eyes met Simeon's with defiance, and once again the priest was struck by their likeness to other eyes of such a deep and unusual colouring.

'Your name, boy.'

'Justin.'

'A noble name for a guttersnipe. Who is your father?'

'Gervaise the fishmonger.'

'I know him to be a widower. Who is your mother?'

321

'Don't know,' the boy said sullenly. 'And don't care. She died when I was born.'

Simeon set him down but kept a tight grip on his shoulder. He drew back the tattered leather and stepped into Old Hannah's filthy house, dragging the boy inside.

'Ah, the Special One, and with a snake-eyed thief in tow. Welcome, Simeon de Beverley.'

'Watch out!' Justin said in an anxious whisper. 'She has eyes in the back of her head. I think she's a witch.'

'Nonsense. She uses nothing more sinister than a high polish on her cooking pot.'

The woman turned suddenly on her stool to survey the priest from head to toe, nodding as if in approval. 'The Prophet.'

'My godson is lost.'

'Ah, the Lamb is lost. Pity the poor shepherd whose lamb has gone astray.'

'She's mad, she's . . .' Justin fell silent as Simeon shook him by the shoulder.

'I need your help,' the priest said, pulling the drawings from his coat. 'All you have said has come to pass. Why did you not warn Edwin of this?'

'He ran off in a panic,' she chuckled. 'He feared to draw the final rune.'

'Then draw it now.'

'No need. The rune is drawn.'

'Show it to me.'

Hannah laughed with an ugly cackle. 'Ask the thief. He has it.'

Simeon prised the ivory from Justin's fingers, then frowned as he turned back to the woman. 'Were you expecting me? Did you know I would come here.'

She nodded. 'You are a wise man, Simeon de Beverley, but make haste, the time is short . . .' she pointed a crooked finger at the rune, '. . . for him.'

Simeon stared down at the ivory in his hand. He saw a black circle with fine lines radiating out from a smaller circle set in its centre. Around it were solid bands of blue and green, some edged with gold, others with white, and others arcing like waves on moving water. Around the rune's edge was a narrow border containing runic signs and magical symbols, and entwined with them was the slender, slithering body of a serpent.

'I do not understand. This is meaningless.'

'Look again.'

He looked again and saw a smudge of colour in the centre circle, and, when he rubbed the grime away with a corner of his cloak, the tiny figure of a lamb, roped by the neck, revealed itself.

'Is this Peter? Is he the Lamb?'

'Read the rune,' Hannah told him.

'A pale circle within a black one,' Simeon muttered. 'A tethered lamb, an all-embracing serpent, and water flowing all around . . .'

'Well? What does it tell you?'

'Nothing,' Simeon said in exasperation. 'I see the lamb and I think it must be Peter. The serpent, too, is familiar to me, but the rest . . . the rest tells me nothing.'

Justin was hovering at Simeon's shoulder, his face intense with curiosity as his dark eyes searched the ivory.

'Does this black area represent a swamp?' Simeon demanded of the woman. 'Is it a bog? A boar pit? A lake?'

'It's a well.'

The old woman chuckled and clapped her hands together in delight at the thief's suggestion. Encouraged, he snatched the ivory from the priest to study it more closely, and a grubby finger crept over it, pointing here and there. 'See? These lines in the black are to mark the sheer walls of a well. The water's running under it, not over, but the lamb's lying on dry ground. Can't you see it, Father Simeon? We're looking down at the lamb from the rim of a well.'

'Where is he?' Simeon demanded, then took a threatening step towards the woman.

She grinned and raised her hand, cocking her head to one side as the pealing of the Minster bells became audible above the sound of falling rain. 'He hears them for the last time,' she warned, 'unless the rune is understood. The serpent has bitten you again, Simeon de Beverley.'

'Damn you, woman. Have done with your foolish games. *Where is my son?*'

'He's down the well!' She screamed the words so suddenly and so loudly that both he and Justin started at the sound. 'The rune is called the Sacrifice.'

Simeon flung the ivory aside, saw it strike the chimney wall and shatter into a thousand tiny pieces. As he strode to the door he heard Old Hannah's cackling laughter behind him, and as he ran through the streets towards St Peter's, he knew that the little ragamuffin thief was racing at his heels.

CHAPTER TWENTY-THREE

The bells were chiming out the afternoon offices and Simeon had just sped off with Edwinia's drawings when Elvira left the church as the first worshippers were going in. She had tried to pray. Kneeling at the altar, sick at heart and with her hopes dwindled to a numbing sense of dread, she had clasped her hands together and spoken her fears out loud. Above her head, the figure of the crucified Christ had stared down at her with unseeing eyes, and she had felt herself to be alone. Many years ago she had learned to accept Simeon's faith as part of the daily pattern of her life. The concept of an all-seeing, all-knowing God was not beyond her understanding. It was the essence of his faith that escaped her. She knew the words in English and in Latin. She had learned the services and the prayers, the words of the saints and the teachings of the Scriptures, but she had never believed that some vast, omnipotent being heard their prayers or cared a jot for their individual little lives.

Outside the church she turned up her hood and allowed Edwinia to take her arm.

'Is Simeon here?' Elvira asked.

'No, I think he has gone to Butcher's Row. Stephen Goldsmith was here seeking news of Peter, and the physician,

Job, has come to visit Tobias. You must come inside, before you take a chill.'

'The church was cold,' Elvira said, and the girl was saddened by the bleak look in her eyes. Without God to sustain her in hours such as these, her mistress had no comfort but the living, and Edwinia had learned that life was too contrary, and death too merciless, to endure without God's grace.

'The rabbi has been asking for you.'

'I must go out,' Elvira said. 'I cannot stay here, doing nothing, while everyone else is out scouring the town for Peter.'

'Father Simeon says you are to stay inside the compound.'

'But I feel so helpless, Edwinia.'

'I know, but you must be brave and ... What is it, Elvira?'

'Look! Over there, under the roof ...' She pointed to where a figure in a long black robe was standing beneath the overhang of the refectory roof, a man of extraordinary height whose cowl concealed his features. 'Do you see him?'

'Yes.' Edwinia's grip had tightened on Elvira's arm as she stared through the veil of rain towards that ominous shape.

'It is *the other*,' Elvira breathed.

'I know,' Edwinia said fearfully.

Hope sprang afresh in Elvira's heart. 'He has news of Peter.' She hurried forward and stepped below the eaves, feeling the rain from the roof striking her back. She peered up into the shadowed cowl and for one startling moment believed she recognised the eyes that locked with hers. 'All things to all men' was how Simeon had described him, and only now did she fully understand his words. She saw nothing but shadows within the cowl and yet, as those shadows held her gaze, she felt her soul uplifted. 'Have you found him?'

The cowled head lowered in a nod.

'Is he hurt?'

It nodded again and she caught her breath. 'The men are all out searching. Shall I come?'

326

Again the dark head lowered, then the figure turned and moved away with Elvira close behind.

'Elvira! Wait! You mustn't go with him!'

'Find Simeon.'

'You mustn't go alone.'

'*Find him!*'

As the girl ran off, Elvira hurried towards the gaping gate man. 'Let us through,' she said, and the astonished man obliged without uttering a word.

The figure led her to the Minster and across the rain-sodden lands beyond. She followed without hesitation, running at times in an effort to match its pace. From time to time it paused and turned, as if to make sure that she was close behind. She tucked her skirts under her belt and hooked the long folds of her cloak over her arm, then blundered on through mud and water, determined to keep the hooded figure in sight. It watched her struggles and beckoned her on as it strode with ease across the rough and muddy ground, but not once did it pause to offer her assistance.

At the south lakes she waded waist deep through icy water, her soft boots treading mud and silt. When they reached the Figham Stream she paused to catch her breath and to search for a safer crossing. The water was high and moving so fast that she could barely hear the chiming of the bells, now far behind her.

'I cannot wade through this,' she called into the rain. 'You must help me.'

The figure raised an arm and pointed upstream to where several rocks were compressed against the banks, making a rushing fall of water. The rocks were smooth and slippery, the gap too wide for someone of her size to leap from one side to the other. Elvira shrank from the water's force. 'No . . . I cannot. The gap is too wide.'

The figure pointed up ahead and beckoned again for her to follow. In a sudden flash of recollection she saw herself once again in the storm-battered rafters of the infirmary, too terrified by the killings she had witnessed down below to obey the gentle calling of the priest. And then his coaxing

327

voice had given her all the courage she had needed, and she had jumped to safety, and Simeon de Beverley had taken the half-starved ditcher's wife into his arms for the first time.

Now Elvira drew upon Simeon's strength again, called out his name just once and bravely jumped across the stream.

When they reached the well, she dropped to her knees and slumped against the stones, exhausted. The figure stood by in silence, its robes strangely still in the same wind that whipped her own clothes about her body like flapping standards.

'How much further?' she asked and, when the figure remained as still as stone, she understood and gasped, 'Is he down there? Is he in the well?'

As *the other* dipped its head and then was still, Elvira knew that she was alone and Peter's life was in her hands. She groped for the iron grips that would take her down, then swung herself over the side and began to descend into the darkness. As she looked up, the figure lifted a hand to sign the cross, and she found that brief and commonplace gesture strengthening.

'Peter? Peter?' Her voice reverberated in the shaft, then rushed away to a whisper down below. She counted the rungs as she descended, and by the time she reached the seventh the light was gone, leaving the inside of the well as black as pitch. The comforting circle of grey light in the opening high above her head grew smaller and more distant as she went down, as if the heavens themselves were deserting her.

'Fourteen. Fifteen.' The metal was biting cold against her hands, its edges sharp through the thin soles of her boots. 'Sixteen. Seventeen. Peter? Are you there, Peter?'

In the space beyond the twentieth rung her foot at last connected with solid ground. She dropped to her knees in the mud and began to crawl, sweeping her hands before her in the darkness. An icy draught blew from the tunnel that had once brought water to this well and she dreaded the possibility of having to search in there, not knowing in which direction to move or what her search might reveal. The pealing of the Minster bells was trapped down here in the tunnel, timeless echoes lost forever in the labyrinths of

Beverley's forgotten past. She could almost imagine St John's ghostly company of monks still moving through those ancient passageways, ringing their bells to the glory of God as they had done long centuries ago.

Elvira gasped as her groping hands encountered a small, cold hand and a limp body trapped beneath a fall of rock and timber.

'Oh, Peter, I have found you. At last . . .'

Fumbling in the darkness, terrified lest she had found the boy too late to save his life, she set the heavy rocks aside and then laboured to shift the timber. A heavy shoring beam had fallen across his body and jammed against a wall, protecting him from the rock fall. With a cry of relief she removed the last obstacle and pulled the limp form of her foster son into her arms.

'Peter? Can you hear me? You are safe now . . .'

She was weeping as she held him, hot tears that she had kept at bay since the hour he first went missing. Exhausted and almost sick with relief, she rocked him to and fro. Her gentle hands found a wound on his temple and crusted blood in his hair. His skin was clammy and he breathed in shallow gasps, but Peter was alive and Elvira knew that Osric's skills would cure whatever ill had befallen him. Close by she found his sack containing a dry blanket and several bundles and bottles. The bundles had been gnawed by rats for the meat and bread they contained, but when she examined his body and limbs she found no trace of bites. Those parcels of food had saved him from being eaten alive by rodents, for while the rats had easier meat to feed off, they had left the still-living food untouched. She found water in one of the bottles, still corked and fresh, and in the other a medicine of Osric's making. Tasting this, she recognised peppermint and anise oil. She gently poured it, drop by drop, into Peter's open mouth and wrapped the blanket around him, hugging him tightly against her, letting her body warmth drive away his chills. Elvira knew she could not hope to climb the shaft with such a burden in her arms, then cross that wasteland for a second time. She would wait and keep him warm, and give him a mother's much-needed comfort, until Simeon came to lift them from this hole.

'Hold on for just a little longer, Peter,' she whispered into the darkness. 'Simeon will come soon. I know he will.'

While Elvira rocked her unconscious foster son in her arms, Simeon scaled the wall of St Peter's enclosure and dashed along the main pathway, yelling instructions as he ran. 'Toll the bell! Get all our searchers back inside! Fetch ropes and irons! Fetch torches, as many as can be found! Move! Time is running out and every well in the town must be searched before dark!'

Antony, who had just returned to the enclosure with Paul and Osric, sprinted across to where the priest was barking orders near the infirmary door. 'What is it? What's happened?'

'He is down a well.'

'Where?'

'God alone can tell us that, but we must find him, and quickly.'

'Hell's teeth! There are *scores* of wells in Beverley.'

'Aye, and in this rain every one is in danger of flooding,' Simeon reminded him. 'They must all be searched. Osric, get the searchers organised so that none will waste precious time where others have already explored. We must begin right here, with our own wells, and then work in close ranks towards each town bar until—'

'Wait. I know where he is.' They turned to find the ragged young Justin at their elbows, still breathless from his attempts to keep pace with the running priest on his race through the town. 'Cyrus de Figham escaped his cell two days ago. I saw him. I came as close to him as I am to you now.'

'You saw him freed from his cell?'

'Aye, and when I saw him again, an hour later, he was carrying something heavy across the pasture, but when they caught him he came back empty-handed.'

Simeon made a grab for Paul. 'Is this true? Was de Figham out?'

330

'For an hour, no more,' the clerk confirmed. 'A serving woman stole the key and turned him loose. They found him on the pasture, but he was alone. Peter was not with him.'

'Simeon! Simeon!'

The rabbi came running with Edwinia at his heels. He was fully dressed and heavily armed and had a coil of rope slung over his shoulder. '*The other* was here. He took Elvira.'

'Dear God, no . . .'

'They left the town and went towards the south lakes, heading for the moor beyond the pasture. I was about to follow when you arrived. Come quickly. They have a good start.'

Justin tugged at Simeon's shoulder. 'Father Simeon, you mustn't try to go that way. The streams are flooded and the south lakes have grown too deep to cross without a boat. I know a better way.'

'To where, for heaven's sake?' Simeon demanded. 'Where has he taken her?'

'It's obvious,' the boy said, his dark eyes lit with excitement. 'He's gone as the crow flies, straight to the pilgrim's well.'

'That is where de Figham was recaptured,' Paul cut in, 'close by the old pilgrim's well on Figham Pasture, near the moor. But he was empty-handed, Simeon.'

'Aye, damn him to hell,' the big priest growled, recalling the twisting serpent in Hannah's rune. 'By then he had already thrown my son down the well.' He grabbed the startled Justin by his throat and lifted him several inches off the ground. 'You will guide us, boy, by your safer route, and know this, Justin, if you betray me, if my lady and son are lost because of you, so help me God I will track you down and cut your miserable throat!'

The Minster bells were still pealing as they left St Peter's with Justin running on ahead. They skirted the lakes and jumped the swollen stream and from its other side they saw the hooded figure in the distance, standing like a sentinel in the rain.

'Do you see him, Osric?'

'Aye,' the tough infirmarian growled.

331

The figure moved ahead of them, not striding out but moving nonetheless, so that each time their eyes focused upon it, the shadow-like shape seemed a little further away. When, on the slopes where the pasture met the moor, it stood still and the distance between them slowly began to diminish, they knew the pilgrim's well could not be far away. Behind them men and women were hurrying in their scores to join the search. As St Peter's bell called the searchers back, and as they learned that *the other* had come again, they grabbed what ropes and torches they could carry and set out for the southern pastures. In the vanguard were Thorald and Rufus, two powerful men who loved the missing boy for different reasons, one because he knew him to be blessed, the other because he believed him to be his grandson. These two moved swiftly across the muddy ground, determined to be on hand when the boy was found.

In the pitch black of the pilgrim's well, Elvira hugged Peter to her breast and drew comfort from the sombre echoes of the Minster bells. 'Simeon will come,' she promised the boy. 'Simeon will come soon.' Peter groaned and moved his head, and her fingers groped for the bottle to drip more medicine into his mouth. 'Hush, my dear. All will be well. Rest easy.'

She had no notion of the passing of time beyond seeing the pale orb that marked the top of the well turn to deepest black as the night drew in. Her fears had been dispelled by the certain knowledge that *the other* would soon guide Simeon to the well, and so she closed her eyes and crooned a cradle song to her child.

'What was that?' She heard a distant rumble of sound and her head came up in alarm. The rumble became a roar like thunder, far off but coming closer, and then the ground began to shake and she realised to her horror that the tunnel had flooded.

Dashing the bottle aside, she flung Peter's arms about her neck, pressed his face to her cheek and staggered to her feet. Her bearings lost in the darkness, she hugged the walls of the well and groped desperately for the ladder. She felt the tremors in the earth as the bellowing roar from the tunnels was intensified, and she knew that a deadly wall of water was bearing down on them. With her feet on the lower rung and one hand grasping an iron high above her head, and heavily encumbered by Peter's weight, she screamed up the shaft, 'Help us. For God's sake, *help us!*'

She felt the boy stir in her arms and begin to mutter, and the one word she heard above the din was enough to spur her on, 'Mother.' Steadying his limp body with one hand, she groped for a higher rung with the other, found it and lifted their bodies another foot from the base of the well. It was not enough. The tunnel mouth was as tall as she was and when that concentration of rushing water struck the opening, its force would push upwards and sweep them away.

'Hold on, Peter,' she begged, and hauled herself steadily upward. The metal scraped Peter's back as they climbed, but his arms held fast around her neck and his legs hung limply over her hips. Elvira's legs were trembling and her ears were filled with the thunder of the on-rushing torrent as she used every ounce of strength in her limbs to haul herself above the tunnel's mouth.

The water hit the arch of stones and bricks below with such a resounding impact that the force of it almost jolted her from her precarious perch. She clung desperately to the irons, trapping Peter's body against the wall and willing her numbed fingers and trembling legs to bear the crash. Her strength had all drained away by the time she heard the waters roar off along the tunnel, leaving a lapping flood within the well.

'Thank God,' she gasped, as the roar diminished to a rumble. 'I have no strength left to climb another step. Hold on, Peter. Help will be here soon.'

After a while she became aware of an icy chill invading the foot that bore their weight on a lower rung. The chill moved steadily upward, gripping her calf, her knee, her thigh, and suddenly she realised that the danger was not yet over. The flood water was creeping up the shaft. Somewhere along the tunnel it had met some firm resistance, and now the powerful surge was backing up and, seeking its freedom, rushing into the well.

'*God strengthen you, woman.*'

Elvira heard the words as if they came from inside her own head, gentle and reassuring, yet somehow just as empty, just as futile, as the blank gaze of the hanged Christ on the altar inside St Peter's Church. With a flash of fire in her eyes that echoed a sudden surge of anger welling inside her, she mustered every scrap of courage that remained in her and cried her answer in a voice that was clear and strong, 'God or no God, we will not die down here. By my will alone, I swear it, *we will not die down here!*'

With a strength she had not known she possessed, driven on by a mother's instincts to save her son, Elvira gripped the cold iron rungs one after the other and, as the bubbling, churning water dogged her every step, climbed steadily and obstinately ahead.

'*Elvira!*'

She heard his voice but was unable to answer it, for the water was now waist high, despite her efforts, and her lungs were labouring. Instead she reached her hand into the darkness and felt those strong, familiar fingers close around it. Seconds later, she was on firm ground and running with the others for higher ground. Those still streaming across the pasture to lend a hand now broke and scattered as Osric and the priests of St Peter's yelled out in frantic voices, 'Run for your lives! The well's about to overflow!'

Now just as ominous in its silence, the deluge broke over the rim of the well, scattering ancient stones in its path and then surging over the pasture. It swept down the slopes, dislodging stones and gathering mud and felling a dozen searchers as they fled to escape it. And then, like a beast exhausted by its charge, the water was subdued. The mouth of the well was reduced to a hole with a few bits of rubble strewn around it, and the scattered searchers looked to the task of pulling their half-drowned companions from the flood.

'I thought you were lost,' Simeon said, his voice hoarse with emotion as he held Elvira more tightly than he

334

had ever held her before. 'I thought I had lost you both.'

'I knew you would come,' she told him. 'We are not to be parted, Simeon.'

'Not in this world,' Simeon vowed. 'Not while I live.'

Standing to one side, Rabbi Aaron turned his head and stepped away, unwilling to watch this tearful reunion. He was content to see her safe, but he would not stay to see their love exposed in its unfathomable depths. He, too, needed to hold Elvira. He, too, needed to kiss her face and confess that he had died a little when he had heard that wall of water hit the well shaft from below. 'I thank God for your safety,' was all he said, and he knew that, with her lovely face pressed close to Simeon's chest, she did not hear him.

Osric made a swift inspection of the injured boy as he lay on his blanket on the ground, his pale face turned from the rain. His expert hands moved over Peter's body from head to foot, probing for any wound or broken bone that required his immediate attention. Finding none, he fashioned a neck brace using Simeon's leather girdle and Richard's mantle, so that any hidden damage might not be worsened by the journey home.

'What he needs is warmth, and quickly, and some decent food in his belly. Let's get him home.'

Peter was lifted into the arms of Thorald, the biggest and strongest man among them, and the huge priest of St Nicholas bore him home at a kindly pace, flanked by four priests to assist him should he lose his footing on the water-logged ground.

Some distance below, where the flood had carried the debris of the well down the slopes, many searchers were being helped away by others. While Chad bore a bruised man on his back, it was left to Rufus de Malham to assist the limping Fergus back to St Peter's. Thus a peace, of sorts, was established between them, and Rufus would never guess that the man he helped was feigning injury for just that purpose.

There were no shouts of celebration for the weary group

as it passed through the crowd that had gathered outside the gates of St Peter's enclosure. The whisper had passed around, 'Peter is found,' and all else was left to the wording of their prayers. As if to mark the solemnity of the homecoming, the single bell of St Peter's, tolled to call the searchers in, was stilled, and the Minster bells left off their joyful pealing.

Simeon saw the hooded figure standing beyond the massive gate supports, half hidden by rain and shadow. He gave Elvira over to Aaron's care and stepped into the dark recess where the figure waited. 'Who are you, friend?'

The answer came in a voice so deep in timbre that he felt the vibration of it in his breast-bone, a strange voice, neither within him nor without. '*You know me, Simeon.*'

'What I know cannot be possible.'

'*All things are possible, Simeon de Beverley.*'

'Amen,' the priest responded. 'Will Peter stay with us?'

'*He must. He is the Keeper at the Shrine.*'

'For how long? How long before we lose him?'

The figure raised a hand to sign the cross, and the Latin words *dominus vobiscum* were spoken with the blessing.

'God be with you,' Simeon repeated in English, then asked again, 'The boy, how long?'

He heard the words as if his own heart had spoken them: '*For a lifetime.*' Then the figure bowed its head and moved away into the rain-lashed darkness. When it reached the wall that marked the lower boundary of the enclosure, it joined the deeper shadows there and vanished where there was no opening.

CHAPTER TWENTY-FOUR

The enclosure was packed with people and alive with excitement when Daniel Hawk arrived. He had heard the bell tolling to bring the searchers back, and then the joyous pealing that told of Peter's rescue. He found Simeon alone in the porch of his church, still wearing his saturated and mud-stained clothes and with the strain of the last two days clearly visible on his handsome face. Daniel sat down beside him.

'Thank heaven the boy was found,' he said. 'This is a memorable hour, Simeon. With her courage, your lady has proved herself a jewel among women. Your son is safe. Why are you not with the others in celebration or at your altar giving thanks to God? Why so dejected?'

'I am tired, Daniel,' Simeon told him.

'Then find a bed and sleep.'

'I doubt I could. Did you hear that *the other* came again, that he led Elvira to where the boy lay trapped in the shaft of a well?'

'I heard it all.' Daniel smiled. 'I saw Peter a few moments ago and, apart from the wound on his head, he will probably be none the worse for his experience.'

'Aye, Daniel, God has smiled on us once more. The worst is over for us now. Perhaps tomorrow, when Peter is awake and

I am fully convinced that he has no hidden injuries, perhaps then I will offer up my thanks and believe them justified.'

'If you live that long,' Daniel said in disapproval. 'Those wet clothes will chill your innards and bring on a fever. Get them off, Simeon. Take a warm bath and allow your body to restore its natural warmth. Go inside and seek Elvira for your comfort. You should not waste the gifts God offers, Simeon.'

'And you should not be here, Daniel Hawk.'

'Wulfric intends to petition the provost for Cyrus de Figham's removal from Hector's custody. He claims the curate has no right to hold him and no powers to grant the benefit of atonement, and that while the prisoner is not required to repent of his sins through flagellation of the flesh, his soul remains in jeopardy.'

'And if Wulfric has him he'll insist on extreme atonement and accidentally kill de Figham with his brutal tortures,' Simeon replied. 'Is that his plan?'

'Exactly,' Daniel told him. 'He suspects that Father Cyrus will make counter charges that will sully his name before the court. In such an event there could well be a landslide of accusations aimed at Wulfric, not only by those who hate him or are in his debt but by those who wish to deflect any similar suspicions from themselves. So, if you intend to see de Figham stand trial before the papal legate, I suggest you take steps to keep him where he is, at Figham House.'

'I'll see to it at once,' Simeon assured him, 'but for now, Daniel Hawk, I am anxious to see you gone from here. If your master calls for you and finds you absent . . .'

'Father Wulfric sent me here as part of his plan to protect himself,' Daniel cut in. 'He has ordered me to remove the only witness to the crime that could be his undoing. I am to kill Tobias.'

Simeon turned his head to look Daniel in the eye. 'Has it come to this? Would he have you murder an innocent child?'

'He insists upon it, even threatens to engineer my excommunication should I fail. He frets and fumes that Tobias

338

will bear witness against him, on your instruction, before the papal legate.'

Simeon rose to his feet with a heavy sigh and stared down at the troubled young priest who all his life had wrestled with a dilemma. Only time would tell if, when it came to it, this divided man would stand his ground with courage and allow that beast to gore him to death.

'Go home, Daniel,' he said, signing the cross. 'Tobias died of his injuries an hour ago. Let your master fret on *that*.'

Cunning dark eyes watched Simeon leave the porch and make his way to his scriptorium. Justin was crouched in a dry spot beneath the overhang of a storehouse wall, a roasted chicken in his hands and a jug of ale beside him on the ground. He wiped a sleeve across his mouth where meat juices had dribbled, and he marked the progress of the priest as people touched his arm, his cloak, his hands as he passed by them. He liked this Simeon de Beverley, this strong, straight-talking man whom others respected but did not fear. And he liked this place. He had observed more casual acts of kindness here, within these walls, than he had known in all his life beyond them.

As if aware of the gaze that followed him, Simeon de Beverley turned his head, then stopped to watch the boy. He approached the storehouse and stood with a stern expression on his face, towering over the crouching boy, who neither rose to his feet nor left off eating his supper.

'Do not steal from us, fishmonger's son. Do not spit in anyone's face and take care to dip your fingers into no man's pocket but your own. Remember this and you will be treated well. Forget it and I will deal with you myself.'

'Yes, sir. There's talk that the canon, the one at Figham, will be brought to trial and made to answer for his sins.'

'If he survives his incarceration, and if no servant turns him loose, he will.'

'Is that why Peter took food to his cell?'

'Aye, Justin. Father Cyrus must live to face his punishment and repent of his sins.'

Justin nodded gravely, pushed the chicken into his coat and

squared his skinny shoulders in imitation of a grown man. 'I'll earn my keep. I'll feed the canon in Peter's place.'

'You owe us no favours, Justin. Go home to your family.'

'You said you wanted him to live so that he could be punished by God's law.'

'Aye, but not at the risk of another life. I forbid you to go up there.'

'Makes no difference.' Justin shrugged. 'I'll go anyway. Peter did, and he's smaller than me.'

'And Peter almost died,' Simeon reminded him. 'Now go home, lad, and forget about Cyrus de Figham. Good night, Justin.'

That very night young Justin slipped away and tramped across the Figham Pasture with his head bent into the rain. He found the priest's cell and pushed the remains of his supper through the window slit, then dropped a bottle of water after it.

'By the Devil! Who is that?'

'Peter de Beverley,' Justin whispered through the bars.

'Damn your lying tongue, that whelp is dead! You will never find him, and if you do, be sure you have his grave prepared. Who are you?'

'Peter,' Justin whispered again, then picked up his empty sack and hurried away, and when he reached the corner wall he laughed out loud and said again, 'I'm Peter, Peter de Beverley.'

In Simeon's scriptorium Elvira had hung a curtain of linen sheets across the corner where the little shrine was set. She had lit a candle and placed it on the altar, and its flickering light danced in warm reflections over the ivory crucifix. A tub had been set and water boiled to fill it, and the steam gave off a sweet scent of rosemary. Her hair hung loose in damp strands down her back, and her skin had the rosy glow of the newly washed.

'Elvira.'

As Simeon ducked to enter their private corner, she welcomed him with a smile that gave her lovely face the look of an angel. With gentle hands she helped him remove his sodden clothing, unfastened the thongs that closed his shirt and the drawstring holding his breeches. Unwilling and far too weary to offer resistance, Simeon watched her as she slowly slipped the garments from his body. Stripped of his clothes, his brow piece and his crucifix, he stood before her naked and unashamed. She touched his chest, tracing the dark-blond hair from breast to belly, and his body's swift response set bright lights dancing in her eyes. With a sigh she moved away from him and bade him step into the tub, then watched him slowly sink beneath the water.

Moving behind him, Elvira soaped his neck and face, wiped the wetness away with a perfumed cloth, then traced the contours of his chest with her palms. Her lips moved tantalisingly over his skin as she nuzzled close and whispered against his ear.

'Our bond is unbroken, Simeon. Our boy is restored to us.'

He felt her warm breath invade his body through his ear, and the touch of her hands on his chest made fires inside him. His lips met hers, and in that instant all else slipped away from him but her. He reached up to hook his arm around her neck and pulled her down, feeding his hungry senses on her mouth. And then he was standing in the perfumed tub, pressing Elvira's body to his while every barrier between them slid away with the water cascading from his skin. Her hands slipped about his waist and travelled down to stroke the hard flesh of his buttocks. Standing thus, with her breasts against his chest and his nakedness reaching out to claim her touch, they were no more the priest and the ditcher's wife, no longer the God-divided, sharing a love that was forbidden. It was as if God at last had turned his head and Simeon's vow of chastity was erased.

He came so close to taking her that his head swam with the wonder and the sweet surrender of it. Only the sounds beyond the curtains stopped him; the clatter of pots, the hum of a dozen separate conversations, the scraping of a spoon inside a bowl, the ring of laughter. Such love as theirs

341

was not a public thing, to be affirmed by those who would salute their union. It was their own, the link between his soul and hers, and it seemed to Simeon then that God no longer stood between them.

'Our bond does not begin and end with Peter,' he said hoarsely, and Elvira did not voice the words in her heart: *Nor with your God.*

She left him then, reluctantly but wisely, and stepped through the curtains, her shift drenched and her face serene, and went quietly to her bed amongst the rafters.

'Is he free?' Thorald asked, from his seat close by the corner.

Osric smiled the grimmest of smiles and shook his head. 'Not yet, my friend, but he will be soon.'

Stephen Goldsmith had spent the better part of the afternoon at the bedside of his provost. Every twitch, every groan or mutter of despair from the sleeping man had sliced across his heart with the cutting edge of a gutting knife. No man should have to live like this, helpless, dependent and wracked with pain. Jacob could neither stand unaided nor lower his back to sit, nor even bend his knees to kneel in prayer. His dignity was in the hands of servants, at the mercy of their whims and humours. Even sleep was no respite from the agony of wearing his brace or the torment of being without it.

Jacob de Wold opened his eyes as he always did, to pain, despair and hope in equal measure. 'Is the boy found?'

'He is,' the goldsmith nodded. 'Safe and well.'

'Thank God.' The provost attempted to clasp his hands in prayer, but the task defeated him. 'Help me, my friend.'

Stephen obliged and watched the visible play of pain on Jacob's features as he locked his fingers together in that simple gesture of submission. Even this small prayer of thanks exerted a terrible price from him, and when it was done Stephen tried to keep the pity from his eyes and voice as he spoke of the events already in motion.

'We expect the archbishop to arrive with the papal legate within the month,' he said. 'Church dignitaries and officials

342

are to gather here from York and elsewhere, much to the chagrin of certain men who are loathe to see our town honoured by such a concentration of princely persons. They would rather see this business transferred to York, but they will come to Beverley because they must. When Geoffrey Plantagenet is consecrated as archbishop, he will remember the name of every man who withheld his support during this, his grand demonstration for the benefit of the papal legate.'

'Such a show will strain Beverley's resources to their limits,' Jacob said.

'My friend, the Church can well afford the cost.'

'So Geoffrey must believe, since he will entertain this lavish company at Beverley's cost and not at York's,' Jacob answered wryly. 'Is his brother agreeable to his consecration?'

'I believe the king is delighted, since he will now claim credit for his brother's change of heart. This move on Geoffrey's part is timely, and must please King Richard well. There is word from Rome that His Holiness the Pope is failing rapidly in his health. Bishop Roberto is eager to return to Rome as soon as possible to cast his vote for the papal successor, should Clement die, and to that end he will not now travel on to York as originally intended. I suspect the outcome here is a foregone conclusion.'

Jacob stretched his neck and held his breath against the pain, then relaxed his muscles and said, 'Primed by Geoffrey Plantagenet, encouraged by King Richard, urged on by a dying pope. It seems this papal legate is being shuffled about the games board like a pawn.'

'Politics, Jacob. We are all subject to the intrigues of our leaders.' He cleared his throat and added, with some reluctance, 'You should know that Fergus de Burton has confirmed Geoffrey's intention to have Hector of Lincoln installed as provost in your place. The legate will require your resignation.'

'I see. Will Cyrus de Figham be convicted?'

'He will. Our new provost, among many, will insist on it.'

'Will he indeed? And see his brother condemned?'

343

Stephen smiled and spoke bluntly. 'This Hector of Lincoln displays his colours clearly. He will conspire to see his brother hang and then dance with glee on his coffin if he is not restrained.'

'What of de Morthlund? I believe another boy has died at his hands. The situation is grievous.'

'His days here are numbered. Hector plans to accuse him in court of homosexual practices and Simeon has vowed that Tobias will be the last child to suffer while the Church turns a blind eye to the debauchery of certain canons.'

'Good. Good.' With an effort Jacob nodded his approval. 'And what of Jacob de Wold?' he asked. 'What will I do with no counterfeit office to keep me on my feet?'

'You will rest, my friend.'

'Ah yes, *rest*. If only I could, Stephen Goldsmith. If only I could.'

The goldsmith lifted Jacob's hand, cupping the once-strong fingers in his own. Such agony looked back at him from Jacob's eyes that all his doubts and questioning blew away like wind-tossed leaves on an autumn meadow. A counterfeit office it was indeed, since this man held no power to do more than keep the peace with learned talk and tactful argument.

'God bless and keep you, Jacob.'

'God grant me mercy,' Jacob replied.

Stephen stooped to kiss the provost's fingers, signed the cross over Jacob's forehead with his thumb, then rose for the door. He paused with the curtain held aside and met the silent plea in Jacob's eyes.

'A man must be prepared at all times to die in a state of grace,' he said carefully. 'Are you so prepared, my friend?'

Jacob looked long and hard into his friend's face, suspecting a certain obliqueness in the question. Something passed between them, a quiet understanding that, with years of friendship for its conveyance, had no need of words. Hope sprang in his breast like a tiny flame. 'You will know when that is so,' he answered carefully. 'When I have sent for Simeon de Beverley and put certain matters of secrecy in order, and when he, rather than my personal priest, has heard my confession, then I will be fully prepared to meet my God.'

Stephen nodded solemnly, then dropped the curtain behind him with a muttered, 'So be it.'

With an effort Jacob signed the cross at his own chest. When he closed his eyes, tears squeezed out from between his lashes, and from his soul he whispered, 'God bless you, Stephen.'

It was a time of quiet celebration at St Peter's. The Sabbath dawned bright and clear and with it Peter, wakened by the bells, sat up and told his nurse that he was ravenously hungry. After a hearty breakfast he was carried to the Dawn Mass and held throughout the service in the arms of the towering Father Thorald. When he took the communion chalice from Simeon something passed between the two, an understanding only they could share, while those closest to them could do no more than touch its surface.

Looking down at his foster son, Simeon heard again the voice of the hooded figure, raised up against the thunder of the tempest at Peter's baptism all those years ago. '*Behold the Rock . . . Peter of Beverley. Behold, and pray for the Keeper at the Shrine.*'

'For a lifetime,' Simeon told the boy as he sipped the wine, and Peter raised his eyes to his and said, 'Yes, Father, for a lifetime.'

As Simeon raised the chalice, he met Elvira's soft, dark gaze and smiled, convinced that she, too, would be his blessing and his comfort for all their lives.

CHAPTER TWENTY-FIVE

Peter recovered swiftly from his injuries, though for a while he seemed confused by his surroundings and vague in his responses. Those early days following his return to St Peter's were especially worrying, for all who tended the boy and prayed for his recovery knew that his skull injury might lead to permanent damage. A thin, deep wound ran from his right brow to the top of his head, and from there across his scalp and down to the nape of his neck. Osric was anxious that the skull beneath it might be cracked, so he bound the boy's head in strips of cloth and packed straw under his pillows to keep all movement to a minimum. Only after four anxious days and nights were they convinced that his recovery would be complete.

'Your foster son and I have spent half the morning discussing the differences and similarities between your religion and mine,' the rabbi told the priest with a wry smile. 'His faculties are unimpaired and he hungers, as ever, for intellectual debate. The boy is returned to us intact. May I go home now?'

'You are more than welcome to stay with us,' Simeon told him.

'I know that, but my work and my responsibilities lie in York. Fergus has arranged for a small escort to travel with me if I leave today. After that I will be left to make my own way home.'

Simeon nodded and followed the Jew's gaze to where Elvira was drawing water from the well close by the scriptorium. 'Let me know when you are ready to leave, Aaron,' he said. 'Look for me in the church.'

Aaron shook his head thoughtfully as he watched the priest stride away. Here was a generous but cruel underscoring of his own love for Elvira, that the man who would not love her fully, as a husband, was prepared to leave her alone with one who would.

On the afternoon of Aaron's departure, Tobias was buried in that secret place near the eastern wall of the enclosure where Canon Bernard lay. They placed him close to Alice and hoped that, somewhere in the afterlife, the boy and the equally tragic young woman might find each other and share some mutual comfort. Martha wept as she saw him lowered into the ground. Nursing the boy had given strength and purpose to her shattered life. With his death she was free to grieve for her dead husband and mourn the shame of her experiences at the hands of Cyrus de Figham.

'You have your own child, your Alice, unharmed and dependent on you,' Elvira told her as she wept. 'Be strong, Martha, for her sake.'

'I will be strong,' Martha told her through her tears, then looked at Simeon and added, 'strong enough to see that black-eyed priest in *his* grave.'

The men of St Peter's were vigilant in their observance of every manoeuvre in the preparation of Cyrus de Figham's trial. Jacob de Wold resisted all appeals to have the imprisoned canon transferred to Wulfric de Morthlund's cell in Moorgate. He also turned aside the alternative appeal that he be housed instead in the provost's cells, where suitable means of atonement could be applied. While the courts at Hall Garth were being prepared for the archbishop and the papal legate, it was decided that Cyrus de Figham should remain in the custody of his brother and that the tortures of atonement should be withheld. Hector and his house steward were charged to feed the prisoner once a day, at sunrise, and both would be held responsible if he failed to appear before the court on the day of his trial.

So the world turned as the good Lord had intended, and with its turning the weeks progressed towards a kinder season. Little by little the brave town of Beverley began to reclaim itself, to shrug off the hardships of winter and recover from the ravages of disease. With that same spirit with which it had endured for centuries, St John's undefeatable *Beaver Lake* rose up from its misfortunes like a phoenix from the ashes, met the challenge of life head on and so guaranteed its own survival. The convent of St Anne was reopened and an abbess brought from York to help restore and replenish that vital source of goodness and charity. The port began to buzz with water-bound trade. The markets flourished and the pilgrims poured in. Every ambitious nobleman in Yorkshire, and every like-minded churchman in York's see, sent gifts of food, wine and cloth for the benefit of their archbishop and his party. Each was determined to stamp his name on the efforts to turn a hungry town into a venue fit for princes of the Church. In their extravagant quests for favour, trade in the town became brisk, and by that trade *Beaver Lake* would prosper.

As the mild weather continued, news reached the town that the Archbishop of York had arrived in Lincoln with His Eminence Bishop Roberto Madriosi of Florence, his coadjutors, lawyers, priests, secretaries, clerks and servants. Roberto and Geoffrey were equally wary of each other. One came as the personal representative of His Holiness the Pope, the other claimed to speak for the king. A promise of two thousand pounds to assist him in his crusades had convinced King Richard of his half-brother's change of heart. Now Geoffrey sought a swift and ostentatious victory with which to impress his king, his pope and his people. A mass ordination of priests had been arranged to demonstrate his power and popularity and to mark his change of heart, a gathering of souls that would be likened to Christ's claim to be a fisher of men. His judgement would decide which

348

canons fell and which were elevated. His seal would set a pliable man in the provost's seat and hold a dangerous one up as a fine example of this new archbishop's will to control corruption within the Church. It was a battle won, save for the collecting up of the spoils, and at the end Geoffrey would play his winning card by petitioning Rome to have the relics of Bishop John removed from Beverley and re-enshrined in his Minster at York.

Bishop Roberto also had a vested interest in this brief stopover at Beverley, for through it he envisaged his own triumphant return to St Peter's in Rome. At the start his appointment as papal legate had not pleased him, not while his pope was failing in health and this assignment was to be conducted during the long and arduous weeks of an English winter. He had also suspected that certain persons of higher rank had engineered his absence from the holy city at a crucial time. There were many who resented his closeness to Clement III enough to vote him into the wilderness and present him with a *fait accompli* on his return. He had abandoned his duties grudgingly, expecting hardship at every turn and resentment from those whose authority he was to investigate. Instead he had been received with great ceremony by these English bishops who, being so distant from the pope, shrewdly transferred their homage to his legate. The splendid gifts from Canterbury alone were sufficient to fill a whole cart and several pack animals. The bishops of Salisbury, Durham, York and Westminster had joined a host of lesser bishops to present petitions and beg an audience with him. The pope was dying, Roberto was his voice, and ambitious men would have him speak for them in the Roman corridors of power. He was party to Geoffrey Plantagenet's surrender to the yoke of holy orders, and by his close involvement, and his modesty, it might even be assumed that he had brought the matter about. He had spent no little time in private conversation with the king, which conveyed more than a hint of royal privilege. He also had an important role to play in the laying off of one pope and the laying on of another, and by the happy timing of these events he hoped to be recommended to a seat amongst the Roman cardinals. His presence in Beverley was vital to his plans, so long as he could return to Rome before his pontiff died and in the meantime prevent this pompous, insufferable Archbishop of York from plundering his glory.

At the end of February, Fergus stopped off at St Peter's on his way to Lincoln to escort his archbishop on the final leg of his journey north. The Church dignitaries who were to accompany him were resting at the bishop's palace between St Mary's and the market cross. The provost's courts and rooms in Hall Garth had, along with many other halls and houses, been transformed in order to receive the archbishop, the papal legate and their combined entourage. Those students and clerks who had stayed there throughout the winter had been found alternative accommodation, and those priests who lived there permanently were removed to other houses. Carts came and went in monotonous succession, stocking the kitchens and the cellars, bringing new hangings for old, extra seats and tables, additional beds and robe chests. The whole town was alive with preparation for the event as every merchant, craftsman, musician, cook, furrier, blacksmith, labourer, would-be servant and hopeful opportunist flocked to the bigger houses to offer their services.

The special envoy to Geoffrey Plantagenet clattered through the streets of the town like a fine young prince at the head of a royal company. He led an army of three score men, all splendidly garbed in fancy livery, and as he passed by the people of the town familiarised themselves with the colourful banners and bobbing plumes of Fergus de Burton.

He arrived at the gates of St Peter's with Chad, his friend and personal man-at-arms, riding in liveried splendour by his side. Fergus leaned down to speak to Simeon without dismounting. 'Are you fully prepared? It will begin within the week, and after that our lives are set to take a different course.'

'We are ready,' Simeon assured him. 'Jacob de Wold has sent for me, and I hope to have our case properly sealed and lodged with the court within the next few days. They are preparing to move poor Jacob to modest rooms in a house near the Keldgate Bar. His last act as provost will be to sign and seal our secret papers, thus ensuring that neither Cyrus de Figham nor Wulfric de Morthlund will survive to corrupt the new order of things in Beverley. Our Church and our town will have cause to thank you, Fergus, when the poison tainting both has been removed. All I ask of you is one thing. Steer Geoffrey from his interest in our relics. St John belongs to Beverley, and neither you nor the will of York, nor the might of Rome, will ever change that.'

'You are a stubborn man, Simeon.' Fergus smiled. 'I think you still doubt my powers of manipulation.'

'I doubt your scruples, not your skills,' Simeon admitted. 'You want your plans to work at any price, and Geoffrey wants our relics transferred to York. There will be no bargaining on that score, Fergus. Remember that.'

They were distracted from their conversation by the exit from St Peter's of a delegation of priests and clerks in holy orders. They had come to record the testimony of Rufus, who had travelled north with the merchant and his deaf-mute daughter. This man now claimed that St John had worked a miracle and that his chattering, laughing daughter was miraculously cured of her affliction. The Church was eager to gather what evidence it could to present before the papal legate, and Rufus, who had witnessed her erstwhile sorry state, was happy to swear his statement there and then. The delegation left in high spirits, for their evidence would be endorsed by many much-respected men of the Church who would be coming here for the trial. When Bishop Roberto carried their claim to the curia, it would be confirmed that the merchant's daughter could hear and speak as well as any other and that St John had touched her from the grave.

Fergus leaned down from his horse and shook Simeon by the hand. His smile was cynical when he said, 'While mortal men fret and plot over his final resting place, it seems your precious John has settled the matter for himself. A whisper or two from me to Bishop Roberto will do the rest. Help

351

prove this miracle, even if it be trickery, and no power on earth will shift your saint from Beverley.'

'I assure you that will be the case, miracle or no miracle,' Simeon told him firmly. 'However, if this cure is proven and the healing declared a miracle, we men of Beverley will know what we have always known, that St John belongs with us. God speed, Fergus. And may He lend a keen edge to that silver tongue of yours.'

The young man straightened in the saddle and touched his fingertips to his forehead as he met the steely stare of Rufus de Malham. His smile acknowledged the tentative truce between them, but Rufus bristled, despite his good intentions, at the dancing, twinkling mockery in the young man's eyes.

'May God speed you back to your country estates, Rufus de Malham.'

'May He speed you to the Devil, Fergus de Burton,' Rufus growled, but Fergus was laughing as he rode away.

'Will you stay for the trial, Rufus?' Simeon asked his father.

'I will, though I doubt my other son will thank me for my long absence,' Rufus told him. 'Thaddeus hates his life to be run by stewards and servants, however good their intentions. Still, I will see the outcome of the trial first-hand, meet your archbishop and witness the amputation of a few rotten limbs from this mighty oak you call your Church.' He turned then and clasped Simeon's shoulder, his face solemn behind his long, half-grey moustaches. 'And after that I will ask you one more time to leave this place, Simeon. When the dust is settled and all your present problems are set to rights, when Beverley is in safe hands and your Minister assured of its restoration, then I will ask you again, as a father to his son, to gather up your family and come home.'

As he moved away, Osric came from the gates, where he had been watching the dignitaries from York fall in with de Burton's splendid military escort. As the last banner, carried aloft by two stiff-backed riders, fluttered St Peter's crossed keys in a friendly breeze, the infirmarian shook his head and muttered, 'The pestilence has run its course and the

352

risk of flooding has passed. Peter is fully recovered and our dead are laid to rest in decent graves. What now, Simeon? What new troubles will beset us now that Beverley has all these powerful, ambitious men for her devotees?'

'The dividing of the spoils,' Simeon told him, resting his arm across his old friend's shoulders. 'And a safer future for Beverley and St John. Our time is coming, Osric, and ours is the stronger cause. We will endure.'

'Against York? Against Rome?'

'Aye, Osric, against the whole of Christendom, should it come to it.'

Osric drew back his head and scowled into Simeon's face. 'What did that hooded figure say to make you so sure? What did he tell you?'

'Enough,' Simeon told him simply.

That week saw the town become a hive of frenzied activity. The trial would coincide with St Oswald's feast day on the twenty-ninth of the month, and it seemed appropriate that this onetime Archbishop of York should be included in the festivities. At the mouth of the River Hull a ship was being prepared to carry Bishop Roberto and his entourage to Rome, and many local noblemen, including Sir Hugh de Burton, were making conspicuous donations to the bishop's comfort. Those absent canons who rarely saw the town that paid their fees or the hard-working priests who performed their neglected duties, now flocked back home to take up prominent residence. Once safely reinstalled, these canons surrounded themselves with clerks and proceeded to provide acceptable accounts of their absenteeism.

With a stroke of malicious cunning, and ostensibly with the full blessing of his royal brother, Geoffrey had appointed Bourchard du Puiset, the nephew of his vitriolic enemy, Hugh du Puiset, to prepare and submit the defence of Cyrus de Figham. This ineffectual man had employed every trick and ploy in his attempts to claim Geoffrey's office for himself. Now, as Geoffrey basked in the favourable spotlight of the Beverley trial, Bourchard would stand in the dark and plead his case for a lost cause. More than that, his name would be coupled with that of a man accused of heinous crimes against the Church. His reputation would be tarnished by association, and Geoffrey could henceforth hint that the one was influenced by, or acting in the interests of, the other. In retaliation, Bourchard du Puiset took to his sickbed with an army of physicians in attendance. Having extricated himself from his obligations, he dispatched an unaffiliated clerk to the Beverley cells, one with neither the experience nor the expertise to produce anything but a rudimentary defence. Bourchard planned a sudden recovery for the final day of the trial, having dissociated himself from de Figham's crimes without offering obvious resistance to Geoffrey's orders. This gave the archbishop a two-pronged satisfaction; he had left de Figham, through no fault of his own that would ever be recorded, with an incompetent defence against his accusers, and he had driven Bourchard du Puiset to his sickbed.

The trial was only four days away when Simeon arrived at Hall Garth to see Jacob de Wold. The provost was propped in a corner between two windows, encased in his cruel brace from neck to toe. Beyond him were the cloister gardens, and that small, enclosed area where Canon Bernard had been wont to sit on a bench beneath the spread of an ancient oak. Another tree had been planted there to replace the one ripped out by the tempest, a tall young sapling already ripe with spring buds. This was Jacob's window on the world, where he could watch the changing of the seasons and observe the flow of life, which barely reached him in the prison created by his metal and leather trappings.

'Jacob?'

He turned slowly, pivoting on his metallic heels and gripping a nearby robe chest for support. He looked exhausted. A shaggy growth of beard discoloured his cheeks and chin. His bald head bore livid scratches around the burn scars on his scalp, as if his fingers had tried to remove some irritation there. His eyes were bleak, and for a moment Simeon had the impression that this was a man who had given up, who had reached the end of his particular road and was unable, or unwilling, to travel further.

354

'You look tired, my friend.'

Jacob nodded. 'They are having me moved to Keldgate. I will miss the window.'

'Is there no view of the garden from your new rooms?'

'No garden,' Jacob smiled, 'and only a narrow window slit near the roof. However, we must be thankful for small mercies, and if my bed can be set on the opposite side of the room, I will still be able to see the sky.'

Simeon remembered the building work that had recently been restarted at St Peter's, the extensions to his library and scriptorium. If he set the masons and labours all to one specific task, they could have a room near the herbery completed within days.

'Jacob, would you consider living with us at St Peter's?' he asked with a smile. 'We would be happy to have you as one of us, and you can be housed at ground level, where you can walk directly into the gardens and—'

'Perhaps,' Jacob cut in, 'and I thank you from the heart for your generosity, but you have not come here to discuss my living arrangements. Tell me, do you recall what little time we had to protect ourselves when the fire began to spread?'

'Will I ever forget? In a few short hours our town was alight from end to end.'

'Aye, it was a terrible night . . . terrible. We should have been safe here, in this moated place, but the wind was fitful and I feared lest burning thatch be carried into our woodland. This brace is a constant reminder that my fears were justified. I took the precaution of concealing certain precious items that are the envy of many greater churches; treaties bearing the seals of Westminster, Rome and several English kings, rare maps and books, and little-known records of our Church activities. Dirt pits were dug many years ago beneath the floor of my lower chapel, all lined with lead and Roman tiles to protect such treasures from attack by flood, fire and plunder. You will find them beneath those tiles depicting the Expulsion from the Garden. Prise up the second red, between the hand of Eve and the tongue of the serpent, and the rest will follow.'

'And what am I to do with them?' Simeon asked.

'That, my friend, I leave to your discretion.'

'Thank you, Jacob. I am honoured by your trust.'

For a moment the provost closed his eyes and the knuckles of his hands whitened as he gripped the robe chest against a wave of pain. When he spoke again his voice was hoarse.

'Will you hear my confession?'

'Why me? Do you no longer trust your own confessor?'

'He has other duties.'

'Then I will be glad to oblige. I came prepared.'

'Ah, you are a wise man, Simeon de Beverley.'

'And you are transparent, Jacob. Are you nearing death?'

'I am.'

Simeon nodded, feeling a stab of deep regret. 'Do you fear what is to come?'

'No, nor do I fear the pain. I have learned how to live with that and so, God willing, I will bear it to the end with dignity.'

'You face a long and unfamiliar journey, my friend. You must fear to go alone.'

Jacob shook his head. 'All men must die alone, Simeon.' He smiled again and raised a finger to illustrate his point. 'But only once.'

Jacob refused to take confession on his feet as he had been compelled to do for two long years. Simeon unfastened the cruel braces at the knee, where the two parts were held rigid by buckled clasps. He lowered his friend to his knees and released the collar, so that Jacob could at last bow his head in prayer. In this position, sweating and racked with pain, Jacob de Wold made full confession and cleansed his soul of all his worldly sins. Without being asked to do so, Simeon recited the final rites and commended Jacob's soul into God's keeping, speaking his own farewells along with his prayers. This done, he left the provost to his private prayers and ordered two servants to wait outside the room to help Jacob from his knees when they heard his call.

He left the hall and, instead of walking directly to the gate, slipped into the cloister garden with its ivy-clad walls and pretty, quiet corners. Looking up at Jacob's window, he knew that brave, unhappy man would miss this leafy sanctuary. He prayed that God in His mercy would take Jacob into his keeping now, while he was resigned to death, absolved of his sins and in a perfect state of grace, or else allow him a little time to enjoy a peaceful retirement at St Peter's.

Beyond that high window, unable to rise unaided from his knees, Jacob reached inside his chest support and drew out a small glass bottle marked with a poppy. It was filled with many days' supply of the thick, sweet liquid that distanced him from pain, only this time the medicine was laced with rue and hemlock to produce a lethal combination of powerful narcotics. A few drops would be sufficient for his needs, and no one would ever suspect that so innocent and commonplace a bottle, identical to the many kept in his medicine chest, contained the blessed means of his release. None would know his secret save for the dear and merciful friend who had helped prepare him for his final journey.

'Forgive us, Lord, if mercy runs close to sin,' he prayed, forcing back his head to drain the bottle. 'God bless you, Stephen.'

He fell forward and came to rest with his cheek on his bible, and for one last moment he felt the sun on his face, heard the happy twitter of birds in the cloister garden, and felt no pain.

CHAPTER TWENTY-SIX

The provost's hall was a large, impressive building set in Hall Garth, that large area of moated woodland behind the Minster. It had three floors of splendid rooms, separate kitchens and a buttery, and a cluster of accompanying buildings to house its many priests and students, clerks and household staff. Its courts were set in the main hall on the first floor, with access via the public stair at one end and the provost's wing at the other. Rebuilt following the Great Fire of 1188, the building now sprawled to twice its original size, with its main hall extended to grand dimensions and ranks of new windows added. In preparation for the arrival of Geoffrey Plantagenet and the papal legate, this vast room had been hung with banners bearing pictures of saints and symbols of church authority, long, colourful strips of cloth which swayed and billowed with every breath of air that caught their tasselled ends. The walls were painted with scenes from Scripture and set at intervals with fancy metal sconces, each designed to hold a dozen candles. The polished oak rostrum was stepped so that those of higher rank might be seated above their lesser companions and so that each dignitary remained in full view of those gathered in the hall. The clerks and secretaries were expected to stand on the uppermost step with the top half of their bodies either lost in the gloom or hidden behind the banners, and their faces often shrouded in the clouds of tallow and wood smoke clinging below the rafters.

Geoffrey Plantagenet, no stranger to the discomforts and disadvantages of such halls, ordered his seat and that of the higher bishops to be set in a group in the centre of the lower part of the rostrum, leaving others to squabble amongst themselves in their haste to claim the supposedly better places. He had no intention of suffering the choking clouds of smoke that would surely become intolerable as the trial proceeded, nor would he allow himself to be veiled by hanging banners. His seat and Roberto's were draped with identical cloths and had fringed cushions at their backs and feet, and padded armrests. Geoffrey Plantagenet, Archbishop elect of York, was not to be overshadowed by this quietly commanding papal legate.

The bishop from Florence wore gold and crimson trimmed with white fur over an elaborately embroidered under robe. The archbishop was dressed in purple overlaid with gold, and the jewels of his over robe came alive in the flickering light to give this large, formidable man a shimmering, gleaming aspect. Only the robes of Wulfric de Morthlund, brilliantly worked in yellow, white and glittering silver thread, were equal to those of the bishops as he spread his bulk, and the copious folds of his robes, across seats designed to accommodate three men of normal size.

Seated close to the huge de Morthlund, the frail figure of Canon Cuthbert, clad in white and grey, was conspicuous in its lack of pomposity. He lowered his head and twisted his neck as if to admire the swaying banners hanging from the roof, but his keen eyes picked out the small shape crouched comfortably in the rafters, and he smiled to see that Peter was indeed fully recovered from his injuries. The lad had taken his place once again amongst those furtive creatures who could ignore locked doors and shuttered windows, the rats and mice, the spiders and the bats. Cuthbert nodded and did not look up again, for he knew the world was unfolding as it should.

The hall was packed from end to end with churchmen garbed in their finest and most colourful attire. Such were their numbers that they stood shoulder to shoulder, each with a man behind him and another before him. The rivalry between Beverley and York was displayed in peacock-like abundance as every ambitious individual strove to be noticed by his betters by claiming a more exalted position than that of his neighbour. When the doors at last were closed and the hourglass set, Stephen Goldsmith took his place as the provost's designated representative and addressed the court in a strong, clear voice that reverberated through the hall.

'This commission of inquiry is now in progress before His Eminence Roberto Madriosi, Bishop of Florence, Papal Legate, voice and conscience in these lands of His Holiness Pope Clement III, supreme head on earth of the holy Roman Catholic Church . . .'

'Jacob is dead,' Simeon whispered to Thorald, who had inched his way from the back of the room to join him close to the rostrum, his size and bulk enough to still all protests. 'I heard his confession and gave him full absolution, and his manner prompted me to administer the last rites. I thank God that I did, for he died soon after. He knew his time was near and he was brave right to the end. His face was calm and peaceful when they found him, still on his knees where I had left him after the blessing. I will miss him, Thorald.'

'God rest his soul,' the big man muttered. 'I will miss him too.'

'. . . and of Geoffrey Plantagenet, Lord Archbishop of York, son of King Henry II, brother of King Richard I,' Stephen Goldsmith intoned.

Simeon bent his head to whisper in Antony's ear. 'Note how our archbishop blows a fine trumpet for himself for the benefit of us all. The word "elect" has been conveniently omitted from his title.'

'Aye, the fault of a careless clerk if Rome should complain of it.'

'. . . and before these dignitaries here gathered, my lord

archbishops, my lord bishops, my lord coadjutors, reverend fathers . . .'

'These formalities are tiresome,' Thorald complained, and Rufus, standing on Simeon's left, folded his arms across his chest and nodded in grim agreement. Behind the trio stood Osric and Richard, with young Edwin, bedazzled by his grand surroundings, pinned firmly between the two so that no sudden falling fit could send him crashing to the floor and disrupt the court. He spoke only once when, his eyes fixed on the impressive figure of Geoffrey Plantagenet, he reminded his friends of Old Hannah's runes as he muttered, 'The Emperor!'

Simeon felt Osric's hand tug at his sleeve and heard him hiss, 'Look over there, between the sixth and seventh windows. Do you see what I see?'

'A group of foreign monks,' Simeon hissed in reply.

'But none you recognise? Look again, Simeon.'

As the priest turned his head, a certain monk lowered his cowled head so that his features were no longer visible, but not before Simeon had glimpsed a long nose, hooded black eyes and coil-like tendrils of hair behind the cloth.

'What? Can I believe my eyes?'

'Hush! You have seen nothing. Do not look that way again.'

The priests of St Peter's were grouped as close to the rostrum as their status would allow. The Beverley canons, including the already nodding Cuthbert, were packed into the rostrum seats on Geoffrey's left, the visiting bishops and coadjutors compressed together on Roberto's right. Those noblemen who were entitled to attend were grouped by the windows, with all remaining space claimed by priests and clerks, visiting dignitaries, secretaries, scribes and lawyers. Only a limited area had been roped off before the rostrum for the prisoner and his accusers. Here a slender table bearing a copy of the bible had been set on a wooden platform against which a block of steps was resting. The whole had been carefully measured so that the prisoner, when he took the stand, would not be elevated beyond the height of his judges.

At the end of his address, Stephen Goldsmith bowed and returned to his seat, leaving all further proceedings to be announced by the master secretary. His voice was less powerful, so that some strained forward to catch every word while others, impatient of the formalities, allowed their attention to wander.

'This commission inquires into allegations against Cyrus de Figham, Canon of St Martin's, Priest of the Chapter of the Holy Minster of St John the Evangelist at Beverley in the see of York.' As the master secretary read out the list of charges against de Figham, all eyes went to the door in anticipation of his final words: 'Bring up the prisoner.'

He came escorted by four armed guards, with the gaoler striding ahead of him and the lawyer, Bourchard's man, walking behind. He had been allowed to wash the grime of his incarceration from his body and change his filthy clothes for his canon's robes. His wrists were manacled across his body, his fingers intertwined, and despite his fetters Cyrus de Figham entered the provost's hall with the regal bearing of a prince. The collective gasp that met his entry became a hush as he climbed the steps and took the stand, lifted the bible in his hands, kissed its cover and pressed it to his chest. He appeared serene and pious, the very model of a priest in his holy office; except for his eyes. They were quicksilver in that room of streaming sunlight and flickering candles as he stared about him with a calm expression, resting his gaze momentarily on every face he recognised, marking this identity and that, measuring the opposition as the charges were repeated for his benefit.

'. . . that you abducted and branded the woman Alice and conspired to have her offend the sacred oath to the utter detriment of her immortal soul . . .'

Cyrus de Figham noted Bruno amongst the witnesses, unable to meet his master's eye for fear of being struck down for his treachery. And there, too, was a woman with her hood pulled low over her eyes, and he guessed that the cringing Martha would soon be made to speak out against him.

'. . . that you struck down and murdered Brother Thomas, the Minster bell-ringer, whilst instigating and perpetuating the Beverley riots . . .'

There too was the swarthy monk from Flanders who should have died with the bell-ringer but who lived to bear witness to that murder.

'. . . that you struck down and murdered Aidan, father abbot of the monastery of St Dominic the Mailed . . .'

Cyrus met the stare of Brother Gerard, whose crooked nose bore testimony to the rage that had resulted in his father abbot's death.

'. . . and attacked, without provocation and with clear intent to murder, your brother, Hector, Curate of Lincoln, whilst attempting to resist arrest . . .'

And there, on the rostrum close to the archbishop's seat, was the smug and supercilious Hector, dressed up in richly coloured robes and bejewelled at his younger brother's expense. Hanging conspicuously from his girdle were the keys to Figham House, its store cellars and its fortified barn, and on his face was a look of undisguised triumph.

'. . . by inciting the whole town to riot after bearing false witness against a fellow priest, one Simeon de Beverley, since proved innocent of your spurious accusations . . .'

De Figham's eyes found those of Simeon, and the animosity of a decade was revealed between them in that lengthy locking of their gazes.

'Who speaks for the accused?'

'I do, my lord.' Bourchard's clerk stepped forward, a lawyer of sorts yet barely confident of his letters and a nervous individual well acquainted with his own shortcomings. Uncertain as to whom his scribbled statement should be directed, he fixed his gaze on no face in particular and declared, 'The accused denies the charges.'

A rumble went around the room, mostly made up of comments from those most eager to hear the details of de Figham's crimes. Silence was duly restored when the gavel held by Stephen Goldsmith was soundly rapped on the wooden arm of his chair. The secretary rustled his papers, selected one and carefully read from it.

'Furthermore, you are charged with simony, in that you bartered certain church offices and privileges for your personal profit, and with sacrilege, in that you robbed the mother church of artefacts and relics for your profit and conspired to rob a shipment of goods belonging to the archbishop and intended for his holy church at York.'

As his crimes from the serious to the petty were listed for the benefit of the court, Cyrus de Figham faced his accusers with unexpected dignity. There was no sign of apprehension in his manner, neither dismay nor contrition on his handsome face. It was as if he stood apart from the proceedings, like a man observing the pieces on a games board, content to study the play and to measure the expertise of his opponent before making his move.

'Your Grace,' the lawyer began, then cleared his throat and looked at the sea of faces staring down at him from the rostrum. He picked out the face of the fat man in the brilliant yellow robes and, thinking him higher in rank than those seated around him, addressed his words directly to Wulfric de Morthlund. 'My lords ... Your Eminence ... The prisoner denies the charges.'

'No! I deny nothing!'

The distinctive voice of Cyrus de Figham rang out with perfect clarity. Beside him the startled lawyer allowed his papers to flutter to the floor and scrambled about on his hands and knees to retrieve them. When the room was silent once again, the prisoner raised his hands to heaven and cried out in passionate tones, 'My soul has seen the glorification of God. His grand purpose has been revealed to me. No earthly court is worthy to do His work. God alone will judge me.'

When the noisy response to these words had died away, Geoffrey Plantagenet leaned forward in his seat, his face dark with irritation. 'Is this court to understand that your lawyer is in error, that you do *not* deny the charges brought against you?'

364

When de Figham slowly turned his head to meet the archbishop's stare, his face was closed. 'God knows what He's about. I am at the mercy of my accusers. Do with me as you will.'

'We will do only as the law and Church require,' Geoffrey growled. 'How do you plead?'

'I am God's chosen scapegoat, selected by His hand to bear the sins of others. I make no plea.'

The archbishop drummed his fingertips on the wooden arm of his chair and watched the prisoner through slitted eyes. He had anticipated passionate denials from this dangerous, self-serving canon. He had expected malicious counterclaims, outlandish accusations to shift the focus of the court to the misdeeds of others. He had even suspected that Cyrus de Figham might fling himself at the mercy of the court, confess his sins and offer to forfeit most of his wealth in fines, but he had not for one moment anticipated this. The claim to a Christ-like sacrifice of himself in some godly cause would leave the court bewildered and its judges hanging neither one way nor another.

'Cyrus de Figham, this court receives your outrageous claims with the contempt they surely deserve. If you do not deny these charges then we assume that you admit them.'

'Not so, Your Grace, I admit only that I may not defend myself before this court.'

Here Roberto leaned forward to speak in his softly accented voice. 'Cyrus de Figham, the purpose of this court is to establish, according to the evidence presented, if you are innocent or guilty of the charges brought against you. You will confess your crimes or else deny them and set the burden of proof on your accusers.'

'Your Eminence, God Himself has directed me in this matter.'

'*God* has directed you?'

'By visions and signs, Your Eminence, and by the blessed words of His angels. I am denied the right to defend myself, since my doing so would provoke the guilty to further damn

365

their immortal souls by perjury. God knows the truth. He alone will judge me fairly.'

'And this court will not?'

'Your Eminence, mortal men, however just and honest in their hearts, are subject to the skilful play of fellow mortals. Only God is infallible. If martyrdom is to be my fate then I must accept it humbly and without complaint.'

Hector of Lincoln jumped to his feet, outraged by his brother's statement. 'You *dare* to bleat of martyrdom? You *dare* to use this court as a means of exalting yourself above all other men?'

'Silence!' Stephen Goldsmith's gavel rapped against the arm of his chair as Hector, spluttering and struggling to control his fury, was escorted back to his seat by attending clerks. Once again Roberto leaned forward to address the prisoner.

'Do you wish it to be recorded that you consider this court to be nothing but a sham, that it was convened with the specific purpose of making a martyr of an innocent man, that man being yourself?'

'Your Eminence, I have many enemies.'

'Indeed you have, Father Cyrus, and not one friend who is willing to speak out in your defence.'

'Alas, my friends are simple men who fear retribution should they speak out for me.'

A guffaw of laughter broke out beyond the crowd, followed by a noisy ripple of amusement after one man declared, in a loud voice, that if Cyrus de Figham's friends were afraid to speak on his behalf, then the Devil and his host of demons had all turned cowards.

'No matter,' Cyrus responded with an all-embracing signing of the cross. 'God's will be done. I forgive them.' He surveyed the room with a sad shake of his head. 'I forgive you all.'

'Ye gods! The man's insane!' Thorald spoke through clenched teeth. 'What manner of game is he playing?'

'A clever one,' Simeon whispered in reply. 'No witness will be called, since he has not denied the charges, and no punishment is due while he refuses to admit them. He has chosen God for his advocate, and neither criminal nor saint could have a better defence than that.'

'They'll never fall for it,' Thorald protested.

'No, but he hopes they will be confounded into passing a lesser sentence, and the records will show that he charged his accusers with perjury.'

Geoffrey Plantagenet folded his arms across his chest. His voice was a bellow as he reminded de Figham of the powers of the court. 'If you persist in offering no defence this court will find you guilty by default.'

'So be it,' de Figham answered humbly, and bowed his gleaming black head as if in prayer.

Amid a cacophony of jeers and stamping feet, the court was adjourned to consider the prisoner's stand. In an anteroom attached to the provost's wing, Bishop Roberto pondered quietly in an armchair while the Archbishop of York paced the room in restless fury. Lining the walls, bishops and coadjutors, clerks, priests and lawyers wrung their hands and shook their heads in the face of Geoffrey Plantagenet's displeasure. The priest who had heard Cyrus de Figham's confession before he had been brought up from the cells was ushered into the room and given special dispensation to waive the holy seal of confession. Reluctantly, he repeated the words supposedly sacred to the holy seal.

'Father Cyrus spoke of his conversion, Your Grace, of his innocence and his gullibility in mortal matters. He spoke of his blindness to the faults and unholy conspiracies of others, of plots and wickedness within the Church, but as to these charges . . .' the priest shook his head, 'he said only what I have heard repeated here, that God in His wisdom has chosen him to be publicly raised to martyrdom by the court.'

'Damn his impertinence!' Geoffrey exclaimed. 'He's guilty. We have sufficient proof of his guilt to hang him six times over. By heaven, I'll not have him tarnish the integrity of my court by—'

'*My* court,' Roberto corrected in a firm voice. 'Let us view the matter calmly. It seems to me our options here are clear, Archbishop. We can call every witness individually and have all twenty-two charges against him substantiated despite his silence or we can find him guilty by default. A sorry result in either case, since the first option will surely delay my ship for several weeks, and the second will leave some doubt as to his guilt.'

At a signal from Fergus de Burton, Geoffrey waved his emissary forward and gave him leave to speak.

'I am Fergus de Burton, Your Eminence,' the young man said to the papal legate, since few were aware that the two had spoken at length, and in strictest privacy, during the journey north. 'In the trial of Father Mullen some years ago the second option was taken and the court was applauded as merciful when it waived the anticipated execution in favour of a lighter sentence.'

Geoffrey exploded. 'I'll not hear of it! I'll accept nothing less than his total removal. I'll not have my future plans overshadowed by this thief, this murderer, this corrupt priest, this persistent offender against the Church, this . . . this . . .'

'My Lord Archbishop,' Fergus said in soothing tones, 'the law requires that he be punished and the Church requires that he be free to sin no more in its name. Any verdict of the court must satisfy both. Give him the statutory eight days to quit the country or be outlawed and made the subject of every good Christian's wrath. Send him out as he stands, penniless and friendless as an excommunicant deprived of all human rights and privileges. The people will call it just, Rome will call it merciful and the court will be applauded for its wisdom. The legate's ship will sail on time and you'll be rid of this devil in priest's clothing.'

Bishop Roberto, concealing a smile, signalled the young man to leave the room and lifted up his hands as if in submission. 'I compliment you on your choice of counsellor, Archbishop. That young man speaks exceedingly well.'

'He speaks as I think,' Geoffrey snapped. 'He speaks for *me*.'

'Of course,' Roberto smiled. 'And now I will leave you to rest while I retire to sign some papers. Tedious stuff, but best attended to without delay. The court will reconvene in half an hour ... er ... if you are agreeable, that is, my Lord Archbishop.'

'Half an hour? Very well, I am agreeable to that.' Geoffrey bowed, still scowling, and watched Roberto leave the room, not sure if he had detected a measure of mockery in the Italian bishop's manner.

Roberto was standing by the window of a storeroom hung with vestments when Simeon entered. He heard the door open and close and a deep, rich voice inquire, 'You sent for me, my Lord Bishop?'

Simeon de Beverley was all Roberto had heard of him: tall and powerfully built, as handsome as a painted saint and elegant of speech and movement. One glance confirmed what he had already deduced from the conflicting stories told about this blue-eyed priest, for no man could move so gracefully with a crippled and useless foot. There was, however, something about this striking young priest Roberto had not anticipated. His presence seemed to dominate the room and his steady gaze, like his voice, had a strangely compelling quality to it. Such charisma belonged only to the rarest of individuals, and Roberto had no doubt that this priest was a man among men.

Simeon was untroubled by the bishop's scrutiny. He sensed neither malice nor censure in it, only a frank and open curiosity.

'You are the prisoner's primary accuser,' the bishop said at last. 'Is he guilty?'

'He is.'

'And has he been touched by the hand of God as he claims?'

'God reaches out to the worst of men,' Simeon reminded him.

'Indeed, but has He touched Cyrus de Figham?'

'No, my lord.'

'Are you so certain of that, Simeon de Beverley?'

The young priest nodded. 'His tongue and his manner speak of God's intervention, but his eyes do not.'

'I see. You are a man who reads the eyes of others as clearly as some might read the pages of an open book, so I am told. Tell me, would you accept de Figham's banishment, or do you seek nothing short of his execution?'

'His banishment might serve to purge him of his sins,' Simeon said with a shrug. 'I will not contest it.'

'So, you are not a vengeful man?'

'I am a man, my lord,' Simeon said with a smile, 'and therefore prone to such faults as God considers manly. I have much to hate de Figham for. It would not pain my heart to see him dead, but neither will it plague my peace of mind to see him banished.'

'Indeed.' The bishop nodded thoughtfully. 'It has been brought to my attention that Geoffrey Plantagenet will seek to gain possession of the holy relics of St John for his church in York, and that you might be the main obstacle to his plans. Will you release the relics?'

'No, my lord.'

'He might prove a formidable enemy if his plans are thwarted. Will you resist him?'

'I will, my lord.'

'How if he petitions Rome and, in the light of his present favour, is successful in his petition?'

'St John will remain in Beverley,' Simeon told him.

'And if this cunning archbishop offers the full restoration of your Minster as his price for the relics?'

'Even that would alter nothing,' Simeon said, shaking his head emphatically. 'If our church was reduced to rubble, God forbid, St John would continue to rest where he belongs, here in Beverley.'

'You are uncommonly frank, Simeon de Beverley.'

'I am not to be shifted,' Simeon insisted.

The bishop seated himself on a stool and gathered his heavy robes about his legs. 'Do you believe in miracles, Father Simeon?'

'I do. Each day is a miracle. God Himself is a miracle.'

370

The bishop fell silent for a time before asking his final question. 'Should I hang this prisoner and risk making a martyr of him, or excommunicate him and risk offending Rome? It might be whispered that I executed a man whom God has ear marked for Himself and, if I don't, that he bribed my court with gold and silver to purchase a lesser sentence.'

'You have a dilemma, my lord.'

From his low stool, Roberto surveyed Simeon with a closed expression, searching the clear eyes for some hint of spite or political strategy. Finding none, he sighed.

'Thank you, Father Simeon. I hope one day we might meet in less grievous circumstances.' As Simeon bowed and moved towards the door, Roberto called him back and lowered his voice to ask in a conspiratorial whisper, 'Are you aware of a Father Mullen who was given a lesser sentence after offering a similar performance at his trial?'

'I know of no such case,' Simeon told him. 'Is it significant?'

The bishop chuckled and waved the matter aside with a delicate flourish of his fingers. 'No, Simeon, only the silver tongue of a certain young nobleman who has the archbishop's ear is significant here.'

In the great hall, Martha had been standing amongst the witnesses with her head lowered and her thoughts in turmoil. She had come prepared to reveal her shame to the world in order to bring this blackhearted canon to account, but now she feared her courage would come to nothing. Amid the hubbub in the hall, she saw her rapist and her husband's killer raised up above his peers, his face turned to heaven and his manacled hands held fast in prayer, all evidence of his evil veiled by the folds of his priestly robes. The court proceedings were at a standstill, the bishops retired to rest, and here and there she heard the whispers of conspiracy, doubt and martyrdom. It seemed to her that Cyrus de Figham was safe in the silk-clad bosom of his own kind, and that these priests would rather lay claim to a martyr than to a transgressor.

'The witnesses will not be heard,' she heard a man say.

'The charges will be dropped,' another speculated.

'This is surely a genuine conversion,' insisted another.

Martha approached the raised stand where Cyrus de Figham stood in saintly composure. He towered above her and, though his eyes seemed closed, she caught a glimpse of silvery black between his raven lashes and knew that his gaze was on her.

'Rapist!' she hissed, then raised her voice for all the room to hear and cried out, 'Rapist! Vile abuser! Murderer! Listen to me, all of you. This man killed my good husband, abducted my child and made me a prisoner to satiate his obscene appetites.'

'You there, clerk. And you. Get this woman out of here.'

Martha ducked and dodged to avoid the grasping hands that reached for her. 'Don't listen to his lies. He's the Devil's tool. He's evil.' A laughing guard caught her from behind and propelled her back from the stand, but not before Martha had spat on de Figham's robes and screamed into his face, 'Filth! The good Lord will punish you, Cyrus de Figham, even if these cowardly priests will not.'

As the guard dragged her off, she came face to face with the kindly Italian, Bishop Roberto, as he re-entered the hall by the anteroom door. Geoffrey Plantagenet and several bishops followed him. She looked at them with contempt. 'Let your clerks write this for your pope to read,' she told them all. 'Cyrus de Figham used me for his depraved and filthy practices and would have used my child in the same way but for the intervention of Simeon's priests. I saw him strike the blow that killed Abbot Aidan, saw it with my own eyes, and while you priests close ranks to protect your own, you prove yourselves equally guilty of his crimes.'

Roberto raised his hand and gently signed the cross close to Martha's tear-stained face. 'Go home, child, with the blessing of your bishop and your God. Your testimony has been heard and duly noted by the court. Guard, take her out and treat her kindly.'

Martha shrugged off the guard's hand and walked stiffly towards the door, ignoring the sniggers and ribald comments. As she passed the stand she paused and raised her right hand with the first and last fingers extended and jabbed it at de Figham in the ancient sign against the forces of evil.

When the bishops had reclaimed their seats and the order of the court had been restored, all twenty-two charges were again read out by the clerk, and once again de Figham responded with, 'God is my only judge. Do as you will.'

The sentence was read by Stephen Goldsmith in a voice that reached every corner of the hall.

'Perpetual banishment,' he declared. 'The prisoner will be stripped of all his worldly assets and accoutrements and sent from this place at the closing of the gates. He will have safe conduct for eight days, after which he will be declared an outlaw, deprived of shelter, fire and succour, and banished from all holy sacraments. If he be found on English soil beyond the eight-day limit, any Christian man who loves his God will have the right and the duty to hunt him down like a wolf and deprive him of his life. So be it.'

All who heard the sentence were horrified by its implications. Even those who had hoped to witness Cyrus de Figham's execution were chilled to the bone by the prospect of perpetual banishment and the severance of all connections with the Church.

'Speak your piece, damn you. *Speak your piece!*'

Bourchard's clerk started in alarm at de Figham's hissed instructions, then struggled to recall the words with which he had already been primed.

'Your Grace . . . Masters of the court. The prisoner humbly requests that he be permitted to return to his house at Figham in order to lay aside his vestments with due ceremony.' A glare from de Figham prompted him further. 'And that he be allowed to kneel for the last time before his own altar in the chapel of his house.'

Heads bowed and nodded as those gathered on the

rostrum murmured together. Hector shrugged his shoulders in assent, and the bishops agreed to allow the condemned man his simple and commendable request. Only those standing closest to de Figham saw the faint smile playing at the corners of his mouth as he lowered his head and murmured, 'God bless you for your generosity.'

'You will be put outside the gates at sunset,' Geoffrey Plantagenet told the prisoner, 'and in eight days your excommunication will be complete and no man will be bound to stay his hand against you. Do you understand the sentence?'

'I do, my Lord Archbishop.'

'May God have mercy on your soul. Guards, take the prisoner away.'

As Cyrus de Figham was led out, he sought and found the face of Simeon de Beverley, and the words he mouthed across the room were easily read by those who saw them shaped: 'Damn you to hell!'

While the court moved on to other matters, de Figham was led through the jeering, gesticulating crowds that had lined the streets for hours in anticipation of a spectacle. For the most part they were disappointed and confused by conflicting rumours from the provost's hall. Even those who had come prepared to pelt the prisoner with stones and rotting vegetables held back as the group passed by on its way to Figham House. Here was a powerful canon known for his cruelty making his stately way home with a tightly formed escort. Few could see the manacles at his wrists, and none was prepared to strike a blow against him lest he'd been found innocent. On the fringes of the crowd a darting figure kept pace with the group as Justin, knowing nothing as yet of the court's decision, determined to keep the dark priest in his sights.

At the house, now guarded by liveried staff and a score of newly appointed household servants, Cyrus de Figham was permitted to enter his vestment room alone. The room was first searched and the window irons latched in place, then the canon was handed a simple pilgrim's robe and left to discard his priestly accoutrements in private behind a heavily guarded door. He immediately ripped off his clothes and tossed them over a robe chest with a snort of contempt for all they represented. He snatched the crucifix from his neck and hurled it across the room, then rummaged in a cupboard for the pouches and body purses that would conceal his treasures beneath his pilgrim's robe. He could carry enough from this supposedly empty room to buy his immediate safety and lay down a new scheme for his future, and one day soon, when Beverley least expected it, Cyrus de Figham would return to reclaim his wealth and exact revenge on this cursed town.

Working slowly and loathe to make the slightest sound, he inched the heavy chest from the recess and crouched to remove the loose stones from his hide hole. Groping blindly in the darkness, he found a simple wooden cross, an earthen cup with a strap and nothing more: the hole was empty.

The guards came in to subdue him when his screams and roars had echoed through the house for several minutes. They half dragged him to the lower chapel and, as the court had instructed, flung him inside to kneel before his altar for the last time.

'Pray for a swift escape from England's shores,' one grinning guard advised him. 'There'll be dogs and horses on your scent before you've gone a mile from the Beverley gate.'

Cyrus made a lunge for him and the guard struck him a neat blow with his elbow before stepping back and closing the door behind him.

Enraged by the loss of his hidden wealth and knowing himself reduced to little more than a homeless beggar, de Figham paced the floor of the chapel, cursing to hell his brother, his fate, his God, his Church and every living soul in Beverley. He cursed the saint depicted in the faded icon on the altar table and, with a furious flailing of his fists, sent icon and cross, chalice and candles crashing to the floor. It was then he spotted the small, familiar pouch lying amongst the debris of the altar. He stooped to retrieve it, dipped inside and held a brilliant blue stone before his face. 'The shrine stones! By the gods, they have not beaten me yet, not while I still have these. Enjoy your smug victory while you can, Simeon de Beverley, and your enemy will steal his survival from the very lap of your precious St John.'

The court concluded its business for the day shortly after vespers. By six o'clock every man had dined to his satisfaction, and when the curfew bell began to toll, half the town was at the gates to see the disgraced canon officially expelled. It was announced that anyone found outside when the gates were barred would be arrested, for the court was bound to ensure that the prisoner received the full advantage of his eight-day stay of execution. His death within that time would be judged as murder.

'"Let him be damned at his going out and his coming in."'

Father Richard quoted the words with heartfelt passion, being little relieved at the outcome of the trial. He had wanted the murder of Canon Bernard added to the list of Cyrus de Figham's crimes. He knew the truth, as Simeon had certainly proved it at the time, but one man's word against the denials of another in the aftermath of that unholy and unnatural tempest had concealed the murder then as it did now, a full decade on.

'Let it be enough,' Simeon told him. 'Let Bernard rest in peace.'

A scaffold of wooden beams and dining tables had been erected against the high wall of St Peter's. Simeon stood with Elvira nestled in the crook of his arm and Peter by his side. Osric and Thorald, Rufus, Richard and Edwin shared their vantage point and watched the gates of the East Bar and the deserted stretch of Flemingate beyond. When the guards dropped back after symbolically striking de Figham on the shoulder with a priest's staff, the watchers saw that the prisoner was not alone. A boy was with him, a skinny, black-haired boy with a pilgrim's sack slung over his shoulders.

'Justin!' Simeon spoke the boy's name in dismay, then snapped his fingers and muttered, 'Of course . . . How could I have been so blind?'

'Call him back,' Elvira entreated. 'He mustn't be allowed to follow that monster into banishment.'

It was Osric who silenced the sudden babble of consternation on the scaffold. 'Listen to me, all of you. Gervaise the fishmonger had a daughter, Maud, a mere child of twelve years old when her father allowed a priest to use her in order to pay his debts. She was brutally ill used and died in childbirth.' He shook his head, the memory of Maud still bitter in his mind. 'The priest's fee was not equal to the midwife's fee.'

Elvira's eyes were wide. 'Maud was delivered of a boy before she died.'

'Aye, lady, a healthy lad of Norman colouring.'

'Justin,' Simeon added coldly. 'And the priest was Cyrus de Figham. They are father and son.'

'Dear heaven,' Elvira gasped, 'but the boy despises him.'

Simeon touched Elvira's cheek. 'He does indeed, and such loathing becomes an obsession with careful nurturing. Perhaps the boy is incapable of letting go. It might be easier for him to share his father's suffering than to stay behind and have done with his obsession.'

Osric nodded his head and reminded Simeon of the forces that had driven de Figham for a lifetime. 'He hates you and Beverley in equal measure, Simeon. I wonder how that devilish priest will let go of his *own* obsession?'

They watched the two figures until they were lost beyond the curve taking Flemingate towards the port.

'Is he really gone from Beverley?' Elvira asked as Simeon helped her down from the scaffold, and he could only hold her close and pray that it was so.

When the court reconvened on the second day, the new hierarchy of the Beverley chapter was officially established. Jacob de Wold had died peacefully at his prayers, thereby relieving all of the task of announcing his removal from office. Hector of Lincoln, having gained the dispensation of his bishop, was duly sworn in as provost and declared to have assumed the title de Figham for his own use. Daniel Hawk was recommended to the canon's seat in the service of St Martin, and both would be confirmed by holy rite at Geoffrey's mass ordination of priests in a few days' time.

Simeon was called to take his place before the rostrum and was sworn in as Canon of St Peter's, and it was recorded that Canon Cuthbert, who was without fault, had willingly stepped down in favour of his priest. When the brief formality was concluded, Canon Cuthbert was helped from his seat on the rostrum and, begging the indulgence of the bishops, bade his priest kneel and receive his blessing. With his gnarled, veined hands on Simeon's head he whispered, 'You have been my charge, my protégé and my priest, and now I will be honoured to call you Canon. Receive this blessing, Simeon de Beverley, Canon of St Peter's, and may God inspire you with wisdom, mercy and compassion in your Office.'

Witnessing the moving scene, Rufus glanced at Elvira and saw his own misgivings reflected in her eyes. Could he be a husband now that he was Canon? Could he be a dutiful son and heir while so committed to his Church? In theory his robes would weigh no heavier than in all the years he had helped shoulder the burden of his mentor's Office, but in practise they might well shackle him more tightly to his altar and his vows.

Three other canons were replaced that day on the grounds that their prolonged absence from Beverley had reduced their overworked priests to a state of hardship, and that they had left their prebendal mansions in ruinous condition and effectively stripped their altars of faithful souls. When worshippers were discouraged their regular offerings were diminished, and so the Church lost the means of its upkeep and its priest the means of his personal survival.

On the third day following his death, Jacob de Wold was buried quietly in the grounds of St Peter's enclosure and his crucifix was hung on the newly plastered wall of the small stone building that might have been his last sanctuary. Elvira had supervised the roofing and the hanging and bracketing of the door. The Little Sisters of Mercy had brought the linens, the hangings for the windows and the embroidered drapes that would enclose the bed. Although the intended tenant would not now enjoy this hastily completed place, with its wide, glazed windows and easy access to the herbery, Simeon had been asked to perform the rites to secure God's holy blessing on the house.

Rufus stood in the doorway, watching Elvira laying fresh rushes on the floor and sprinkling twigs of rosemary amongst them. 'We have been discussing the matter of yourself and Simeon,' he told her gravely.

'Oh? and who are "we"?'

'Osric, Thorald, Richard and myself ... and certain others.' He shrugged his big shoulders and met her gaze without embarrassment. 'You have been without a husband for ten years, Elvira. Nobody knows if he is alive or dead, and none would censure you for considering yourself a widow, free to marry or not, as you choose.'

'Rufus de Malham, what lies between your son and myself will not be decided by a council of our friends.'

'Forgive me if I have offended you. We meant only to—'

'I know you mean well,' Elvira told him with a smile, 'but we have no need of your assistance, Rufus. What will be will be.'

Rufus cupped her chin in his palm and looked at her closely. There was a delicate flush on her cheeks and a brightness in her eyes that made the deep-brown colouring glow like freshly turned soil.

'I believe we are of like mind,' he suggested.

Her flush intensified and she dropped her gaze. 'Yes, Rufus, I believe we are.'

On the following day the Beverley miracle was officially recorded when the merchant's daughter who had received the cure offered a brief song of praise which brought a tear to many an eye. When Rufus made a brief appearance as a major witness to her transformation, the Archbishop of York studied his face with unconcealed curiosity. 'Who is this man?' he asked Wulfric de Morthlund, who preened himself at being so singled out by his archbishop and hastened to apprise him of the witness's identity.

'He is the father of Simeon de Beverley, Your Grace.'

'What age is he?'

'Not yet fifty. I understand he was married at a tender age to secure his inheritance and that his sons were born soon after.'

'He's a fine figure of a man,' Geoffrey conceded grudgingly. 'I would have taken him for a soldier.'

'Your Grace, from what I hear . . .' Wulfric's attempts to engage the archbishop in conversation were thwarted when a ringed hand waved him down.

On the fifth and final day of the legate's inquiry the court was convened at a much later time to allow Bishop Roberto to travel to the River Hull, a distance of almost two miles, to inspect his ship and supervise the loading of his chests. The captain hoped to catch the evening tide, and Bishop Roberto could see no pressing reason why the good man should be disappointed.

The business of the day might well have passed with little interest had not rumours begun to fly that yet another canon was to be called to answer charges of serious crimes against the Church. Those spectators who had drifted away to find entertainment elsewhere now flocked back to the provost's hall with renewed interest. So shrouded in mystery and ripe with speculation were these final proceedings that the hall was crowded to capacity and undignified scuffles broke out amongst those who could advance no further than the door but considered themselves entitled to better places.

An obedient silence descended on the hall as the Bishop of Florence and the Archbishop of York appeared from the passage dividing the rostrum from the provost's wing. Roberto was elegant in crimson and black while Geoffrey, a full head and shoulders taller than the bishop, was magisterial in gold and green. For the last three days Wulfric de Morthlund had worn his canon's robes with a rich cloak draped over his massive shoulders, but now, as

380

on the first day of the inquiry, he was magnificently dressed for the occasion in brilliant yellow and white, edged with wide borders of glittering silver embroidery. He expected to be in the procession that accompanied Roberto and his bishops to their ship, and with those who later sat down to dine at Geoffrey Plantagenet's feasting table. For these concessions he had paid out vast sums in bribes, and his swaggering self-importance declared his confidence in the power of his purse.

The archbishop was well pleased because the inquiry had so far progressed to his satisfaction. He had managed to put several pompous noses out of joint, not least the elegant appendage of Bourchard du Puiset, who had only now arrived from his so-called sickbed and could find only a small space at the door amongst the less than privileged spectators. Such small slights and petty humiliations, finding their mark in this public place, gave Geoffrey a sense of gratification as he took his seat beside the papal legate. To tease the court, he had left one matter over from the previous day's proceedings. He had the master secretary read out the petition.

'The Vicar of St Jude's at Thorpe petitions on behalf of his church, which is much dilapidated for want of endowment. He pleads that—'

'Granted,' Geoffrey snapped. 'Two thousand pounds.'

'But my Lord Archbishop, the petition begs only *one* thousand pounds.'

'Two,' Geoffrey confirmed. 'While I'm archbishop no church will fall to ruin for want of funds.' He glanced at Fergus de Burton, who gave no inkling of his interest in St Jude's, then dismissed the matter of the petition with a flourish of his hand. 'Have the figure altered and the money paid over without delay. St Jude is much in need of it.'

Bishop Roberto leaned over the arm of his chair. 'You are generous to your churches, Archbishop, even those that have been in disuse for several years.'

'I'll have no derelict altars in my see,' Geoffrey told him. 'This Minster you so admire will soon have similar sums, and

381

more, towards its restoration. You may inform His Holiness the Pope that Geoffrey Plantagenet will be a diligent and generous archbishop.'

Roberto smiled and tapped his steepled fingers against his lips. He had the full measure of this ambitious man. Geoffrey would assist the church at Thorpe for the benefit of his clever young advisor, Fergus de Burton, and restore Beverley Minster as compensation for making off with Beverley's relics.

The master secretary was preparing to address the court, and now all eyes were on the rostrum and all ears straining to catch every syllable. He cleared his throat and announced, 'Hector, newly elected Provost of Beverley, along with Simeon de Beverley, Canon of St Peter's, and with five others of impeccable standing, here accuse a canon of the Beverley chapter of abduction and homosexuality and of causing fatal injuries by his unnatural and lewd practices.'

As a murmur of astonishment went round the hall, Wulfric de Morthlund stiffened in his seat. The look he flashed at Simeon said, *You would not dare!*

Simeon bowed to the glowering canon and held a sheaf of papers aloft before handing them to the master secretary. Wulfric realised with a jolt that all those documents he had caused to be pilfered from the provost's clerks had somehow found their way into his enemy's hands.

'Seven witnesses will be called,' the secretary continued, 'and the charges will be substantiated by the sworn testimony of our provost, Hector de Figham. Wulfric de Morthlund, Canon of St Matthew's, priest of the Chapter of St John the Evangelist at Beverley in the see of York, I charge you to admit to or deny these charges.'

'What? This is an outrage!'

'Please take the stand, Father Wulfric.'

'But this is preposterous . . . how dare they?'

'The stand, Father Wulfric, if you please.'

'I refuse . . . this is an outrage . . . a pack of vicious lies,' Wulfric blustered.

Geoffrey signalled to a guard.

382

'Your Grace, I will not tolerate this.'

Roberto rose to his feet and Geoffrey, not to have his authority overshadowed, did the same. Several others, attentive to protocol, rose up likewise, so that Wulfric de Morthlund found himself confronted by the full force of ecclesiastical authority.

The fat man, ungainly in his extravagant robes, was helped to his feet and escorted to the defendant's stand. He clutched at the little desk before him, furious and astonished as the master secretary described the charges in detail. Those in the hall hung on to every word as a boy known only as James described how, two years before, his father had been robbed of his living when a cart had overturned and crushed his legs. Destitute and unable to feed his family, and with nothing to offer a surgeon to mend his legs, this man had been persuaded to sell his son to Wulfric de Morthlund. James had been obscenely used before Simeon of St Peter's had given him refuge.

'I was ten years old. My father died,' James finished in a brave voice.

'Lies!' de Morthlund raged from his precarious perch on the stand.

Simeon was called to give evidence concerning Tobias, then Osric described the boy's horrific injuries and his own attempts to save the eight-year-old's life.

'All lies!' De Morthlund screamed, but his protestations lost their edge as Job, the physician, swore that he had been called to examine Tobias in Father Wulfric's prebendal house, and found the boy issuing blood from internal injuries inflicted by the canon.

'But he had the flux . . . the pestilence,' Wulfric insisted. 'He was a servant, nothing more, and he passed his filthy infection to me. I was close to death and God, knowing my innocence, spared my life.'

The physician told the court how he had prescribed syrup of blackthorn, in large and regular doses, to be administered by Father Daniel to cure his master's constipation and to convince him that both he and the boy were suffering from the flux. As he described the canon's 'pestilence' in detail, guffaws of laughter echoed round the courtroom. They were silenced by Stephen Goldsmith's gavel and by de Morthlund's bellows of protest.

'It was the pestilence!'

'It was constipation, cured by blackthorn juice,' Job countered.

Wulfric stared about him, his face and neck purple and his flabby flesh aquiver. 'All this is hearsay and wicked supposition. You have no witness to the crime. No man can say I touched that boy . . .'

'I can!'

There was a collective gasp as Daniel Hawk, wearing the over robe of his new office, stepped forward to confirm what the court had heard. He told his story simply, beginning with his own corruption by de Morthlund at the age of fourteen and ending with the sodomising of Tobias, touching upon several incidents between that had involved the defiling of young boys. He finished with the last order given to him by his master, to murder Tobias before the court convened.

'Snake! Betrayer!'

'I confess to being party to my master's sins these many years,' Daniel finished. 'May God forgive my cowardice. I knew no other way of life.'

Roberto signalled his secretary to have Simeon returned to the rostrum. 'I believe Father Daniel has made several attempts over many years to make amends. Is this the case?'

'It is, Your Eminence. He has on several occasions begged my help in keeping certain boys from the reach of his master. It will be found that no tongue in Beverley can honestly speak of any fault in Father Daniel, nor make any claim that he is guilty, of his own free will, of any unnatural practices.'

The bishop nodded and glanced at Geoffrey Plantagenet, who shrugged his shoulders as if Daniel Hawk's admitted involvement was of little or no importance. 'The whipped cur will obey its master in fear of another whipping,' was all he said.

As provost in all but holy rite, Hector dared to add his protest. 'The Book of Leviticus demands the death of men who lie with men. The Council of London demands their excommunication. I say that he who shares the mattress also shares the fleas therein.'

Once again the bishop nodded his capped head. 'Daniel Hawk, do you repeat your oath that what you have told these present is the truth?'

'I do, Your Eminence.'

'Traitor! Back stabber! By God, I will see you in your grave for this!'

'The witness will be silent,' Geoffrey ordered, pointing a warning finger at the stand.

'God's teeth, I should have killed you years ago,' de Morthlund shouted, too purple with rage to heed the words of his archbishop. When Geoffrey half rose in protest, Roberto touched his arm and said, 'Allow him to continue, if you please.'

Wulfric de Morthlund gripped the desk with one hand and pointed at Father Daniel with the other. 'I warned you, Daniel Hawk. I told you how it would be if you ever dared to speak against me. I will order your tongue and ears clipped. I will have your throat slit from ear to ear.' With his fury now running beyond his control, he leaned precariously from the stand and shook his fist in Daniel's handsome face. 'God damn you, Hawk, you will pay for this betrayal. I will destroy you. I will have you cast amongst the wolves. So help me God, I will have you *excommunicated!*'

'Enough!' The voice was Geoffrey's. He had shaken off Roberto's hand and now leaped to his feet in indignation. 'How dare you call upon God in such a manner? How dare you, a mere canon, threaten this witness with excommunication in the presence of all these princes of the Church? Tongue clipping? Throat slitting? *Excommunication?* Who are you, sir, that you dare to speak in such a manner before this court?'

'He is my priest, and he dares to betray me with wicked lies,' de Morthlund protested.

'It seems he is your prisoner, sir, your chattel, but I doubt he is your priest.' Geoffrey turned to Daniel Hawk and demanded, 'When did you last hear your master's confession?'

'Your Grace, I have never heard my master's confession.'

'What, never? But are you not his priest and confessor?'

'I am, Your Grace.'

'Are you telling this court that a canon of this chapter does not confess his sins?'

'That is so.'

'And who is your own confessor, Father Daniel?'

'Father Simeon.'

'What?' de Morthlund shrieked. 'God damn you both for this deception.'

'Silence the prisoner,' Geoffrey bellowed. 'Strike him with your staff if you must to still his tongue. Simeon de Beverley, when did you last hear Father Daniel's confession?'

'This morning, after the Dawn Mass,' Simeon answered. 'He takes the sacraments and makes confession regularly.'

Now Geoffrey paced the area before the rostrum, his indignation in full flow as he felt his authority as archbishop publicly challenged. He rounded on Daniel Hawk and jabbed a finger in his face. 'Why did you tolerate such a situation? Why did you not approach your archbishop? You should have come to *me* with your dilemma. One word of this and I would have stepped in to put an end to his reign of terror.'

'But Your Grace, my master claims to have your friendship.'

'What?' Geoffrey heard the mutter of speculation and knew there would be many, Bourchard du Puiset first among them, who would hasten to repeat the lie elsewhere. 'Let the court record that I barely know the accused, and that I, Geoffrey Plantagenet, would never, under any circumstances, extend the hand of friendship to such *slime.*'

At this point Bishop Roberto had his secretary strike the gavel and announce a brief adjournment. He spoke with Geoffrey and his bishops for half an hour, and when the court reconvened it was to find Wulfric de Morthlund lying prostrate on the floor with a clutch of physicians in attendance. He was hauled to his knees, sobbing loudly.

'We find the case against Wulfric de Morthlund proven,' Bishop Roberto told the court. 'He will submit a fine of six thousand pounds to his chapter, surrender his prebendary, along with the prebendal mansion, and forfeit his canon's seat.'

'No! Damn you to hell. *No!*'

'The court will note the prisoner's response. Furthermore, Wulfric de Morthlund will make a pilgrimage to the tomb of St James at Compostela. He will report at specified churches along his route and receive sealed proof of his obedience so that Rome might be fully apprised of his progress. At Compostela he will make atonement for his sins at the tomb of St James with a bishop in attendance. He is not to return to the see of York for a minimum of three years, and then only with the Archbishop of York's permission. Let the sentence be recorded and the prisoner removed.'

Now Wulfric faced the full horror of his predicament. 'Have mercy,' he begged. 'The roads are crawling with thieves and vagrants, footloose monks and wicked opportunists. I am not a well man. Such a journey will kill me. Have mercy.'

'Be sure this sentence is carried out to the letter,' the bishop told him coldly. 'Until proof of your pilgrimage is received in Rome, you may consider yourself an outcast of society. You are infamous, sir, and Rome will know if you default in your punishment.'

'Oh, have mercy,' Wulfric pleaded. 'I swear to change my ways . . . take regular confession . . . marry.'

'Marry? What woman would have you, sir?'

'Then I will shave my head and wear a hair shirt. I will atone . . . flagellate my flesh, eat bread and water . . . anything. I will make full restitution . . . I swear.'

'Make no false oaths to further damn your soul, Wulfric de Morthlund. The sentence will stand.' He turned to Daniel and surveyed the young man with compassion in his eyes. 'As for you, Father Daniel, Canon of St Martin's, you will submit a fine to your chapter of five hundred pounds and make atonement before your own altar on each Sabbath for a year and a day. You will love God and sin no more, and be thankful for the mercy of this court. I understand you wish your prebendal mansion to be allocated to the monk, Antony, for the continued shelter and succour of the homeless?'

'That is my wish, Your Eminence.'

'So be it. You are dismissed.'

Seeing that his priest had been treated more leniently than himself, Wulfric de Morthlund shuffled on his knees to kiss the feet of the bishop and archbishop in turn, sobbing and protesting as many hands reached down to restrain him. 'Have pity on a sick man. I repent. I am a wealthy man. Let me make amends.'

Geoffrey crouched and grabbed de Morthlund by his hair, glaring in disgust at the flabby face with its tear-stained cheeks and dribbling mouth. 'Quit York while you can or do your penance at the hands of Geoffrey Plantagenet,' he growled, then left the fat man sobbing on the ground. Willing hands hauled him on his belly to a door behind the rostrum. Once again it was Stephen Goldsmith's powerful voice that called for order in the courtroom.

'We are asked to hear one final petition,' the master secretary began when he was capable of being heard. 'That of Geoffrey Plantagenet, Archbishop of York and—'

'Archbishop *Elect*,' Roberto corrected.

Geoffrey stiffened in his seat at this unexpected reminder of the papal legate's authority, but he offered no protest as the secretary continued with his reading of the petition.

'Archbishop *Elect* of York, son of King Henry II, brother of . . .'

'Yes, yes, get on with it.'

Now Geoffrey voiced his chagrin. 'My Lord Bishop, I protest—'

'Come, come, do not be tedious,' Roberto cut in, leaning

388

close to the archbishop. 'Remember the evening tide and the vital papers I am to carry back to Rome with me. Time is too precious to squander on unnecessary formalities. We must get on. Continue, master secretary.'

'. . . petitions His Eminence the papal legate to sanction the removal of the relics of St John, one-time Archbishop of York, from his shrine at Beverley to the Minister of St Peter's in York, there to be—'

'Denied!' Roberto cut in.

'What? You deny my petition? On what grounds?'

Roberto used his fingers to count his points as he answered Geoffrey's question. 'On the grounds, Archbishop Elect, that mine is the higher authority here. On the grounds that another miracle has been proven in association with these relics and that the curia alone will decide what, if anything, is to be done with them. On the grounds that the removal of St John will signal open warfare amongst the people of Beverley, and that I, its instigator, would be standing in the thick of it. And on the grounds that neither Pope Clement III nor his successor will thank me for leaving riots and ill feeling in my wake. Your petition is untimely, Archbishop.'

'By the gods, you have misled me, sir. I took you to be favourable to my cause.'

'On the contrary, sir, you deliberately kept me in ignorance of your intentions. Come, Geoffrey, this latest miracle happily coincides with your mass ordination of priests and your lavish celebrations for St Oswald's feast day. Let Pope Clement think on it. You will be travelling to Tours for your consecration as archbishop. Petition Rome directly from there, with the full weight of your Office in your favour, and you might be successful.'

Geoffrey's scowl was fierce. 'Will you speak of me to His Holiness the Pope?'

'Oh yes.' Bishop Roberto smiled, and once again Geoffrey suspected a glint of mockery in his eyes. 'You can be sure I will speak of you to him.'

The papal legate reached out to take Geoffrey's petition

from the hands of the master secretary, acknowledged Stephen Goldsmith with a bow and signed the cross over the heads of all those gathered in the provost's hall. 'This court is dismissed.'

CHAPTER TWENTY-SEVEN

The sailing ship bearing the papal standard slipped out to meet the evening tide in brilliant sunshine, the gold of an early sunset touching lightly on its half-furled sails. The landing and river shores were awash with colour as every man of status, richly clad for the occasion, lent his presence to the papal legate's departure. The bells of Beverley were pealed for over an hour, and a flotilla of little boats, dressed with banners and hastily decorated, escorted the greater ship downstream like ducklings paddling after a mother bird.

Bishop Roberto Madriosi of Florence would not forget his visit to this far-flung see of York. He carried home a cargo of wines and cloths, precious altar plate and delicately perfumed candles, fancy chests and heavy rolls of exquisite tapestries. The Archbishop Elect of York and his Beverley chapter had plied their guest with gifts to rival those already received from Canterbury and Westminster, but the gift Roberto held most dear was now gracing the forefinger of his right hand. It was a ring fashioned by the goldsmith, Canon Stephen, made from the gold of a simple candlestick and bearing the figure of a beaver in relief. Below the animal were curving lines depicting the ancient lake, and under these was carved, in English, the legend *Beaver Lake.* Here was a fitting reminder of this extraordinary town, where good and bad existed on equal terms, and where a long-dead saint was still capable of inspiring men to every extreme of passion devised by God.

'Rest easy amongst your good priests, St John of Beverley,' he said, signing the cross towards the fire-blackened timbers of the Minster now receding into the distance. 'And may God, in His infinite mercy, bless and keep your precious *Beaver Lake.*'

The mass ordination of Beverley's priests and the rites of installation of its new canons were performed at the Evening Mass in the Minster. Amongst those taking their final vows was Paul, the one-time sanctuary man, now firmly established in Hector's employ and hopeful of becoming the new provost's personal priest. This splendid ceremony was followed by a procession through the streets led by Geoffrey Plantagenet in his ecclesiastic cart, a magnificent vehicle hung with a tasselled canopy and bedecked with the banners of saints and holy sees. After that the archbishop elect prepared for his evening feast, and the provost's hall was once again the venue of a memorable occasion.

At the curfew bell Wulfric de Morthlund made his stately exit through the East Bar. He had secured no less than seven carts for his private use, and these were attended by thirty riders hired to protect his person and his possessions. Each member of this makeshift guard had struck a hard bargain for his services, claiming the wages of a qualified man-at-arms, a good horse and a suit of clothes, leather boots and a well-cast weapon. Any one of them might rob his benefactor once the town was behind them, taking for himself what he had been paid to protect, and not one of them had agreed to act as any kind of servant for the personal comfort of the exiled canon. De Morthlund was alone, for in the whole of Beverley there was not one soul who called him friend or cared enough to share his exile. He went amid jeers and taunts from those who had just cause to despise him, and with mocking jibes and laughter from those who bore no personal grudge but were content to see a mighty man brought down. He wore the clothes with which he had hoped to impress his lord archbishop, now stained with dirt from the boards of the provost's hall, and as he passed from Moorgate to the East

392

Bar, children flung themselves down and crawled on the ground beside his cart, wailing his own words back at him in cruel mimicry. 'Have pity on a sick man. I repent.'

'I pity him.' Daniel Hawk was standing with Simeon on the scaffold when he spoke the words, and his eyes were moist with tears as he watched the huge carts trundle over the great bar's timbers. 'He will be forced to sleep on the open road, friendless among strangers, prey to thieves and villains. Simeon, he cannot unfasten his own girdle or reach his feet to lace up his boots.'

'Then he must learn such simple skills,' Simeon replied. 'Pray for him, as I will, but do not distress yourself with imaginings and futile pity. Let him go, Daniel Hawk. He has held you by an unholy force for too many years. Let him go, and be forever free of his influence. Look, here is Edwin come to beg a lesson, and that, I believe,' he grinned as he pointed to the gate where a group of monks was arriving, 'is a certain monk with whom I am acquainted.' He jumped lightly from the beams and strode for the gate, where he stood with his fists on his hips and declared in his sternest tones, 'Sir, your effrontery is equalled only by your courage.'

The monk flung back his hood and revealed his huge teeth in a grin. '*Shalom*, my friend.'

'*Shalom* indeed! You dull the ring of truth in my Beverley journals, Rabbi Aaron. Will posterity ever believe that a Jewish rabbi was present at our historic Beverley trials?'

'We Jews are unpredictable creatures,' Aaron reminded him. 'If you thought for one moment that I would miss the raising up of a friend and the expulsion of his enemies, then you sadly underestimated me.'

'You do not seek a place at the archbishop's table, then, in your arrogance?'

The Jew wrinkled his nose. 'I have no taste for your Christian fare. The horror of being confronted by a pig's carcass arranged on a platter with plums and apples vomiting from its mouth is only surpassed by the disgusting sight of men actually devouring it. I'll dine with you, on more acceptable fare, if I might beg an invitation.'

'You are more than welcome, Rabbi. We have much to celebrate and a great deal to be thankful for.'

The rabbi brought his forefinger to his nose in that peculiar way he had of indicating some matter just recalled. 'You need not concern yourselves with scrimping through your purses to meet the cost of Father Daniel's fine. It is fully paid, with my compliments.'

'You have paid it?' Simeon asked, amazed, then scowled and folded his arms across his chest. 'For a moment I forgot your flair for usury. Tell me, at what rate of interest does the debt accumulate? Daniel has nothing of his own. Even his clothes and boots were confiscated by de Morthlund before he left. How are we to repay you, Aaron?'

The rabbi bowed his head and explained gravely. 'There will be no interest, since no transaction was ever agreed between us, and there can be no repayments where there is no loan.'

'Then let me thank you on Daniel's behalf. It was most generous of you, Aaron.'

They took their evening meal in the refectory, long after night had fallen and the labourers, clerks and scribes had eaten their fill. They gathered together as friends united in a victorious cause, and they drank good wine and unwatered ale in celebration of the week's events. Fergus de Burton joined them for a short time, so stuffed with stewed beef and roasted pork that he shook his head at every platter offered.

'We thank you for your timely words to the papal legate on our behalf,' Simeon told him, 'and for your handsome contribution to our Minster fund.'

'I can well afford it,' Fergus grinned, 'since Geoffrey Plantagenet is now fully and publicly committed to the restoration of my humble church at Ravensthorpe, as it will be known from this day on. I shall have my village, my wealth, and my altar dedicated to the saint whose name I bear. I too am a happy man today, Simeon.'

'Congratulations, my lord of Ravensthorpe,' Simeon offered with a respectful bow. 'However, let me offer a word of caution, Fergus de Burton. When next you quote a legal precedent to the legate's court, be sure the man you speak of is not just a hasty fabrication on your part. Father Mullen does not exist and never did.'

Fergus laughed out loud. 'The name tripped so lightly off my tongue that even I was convinced I spoke the truth.'

'But the bishop was not, though he chose to accept your story.'

Rufus wiped his mouth and grumbled loudly. 'A slippery tongue to serve a slippery mind. When will you leave for York?'

'Still eager to be rid of me, Sir Rufus?' Fergus asked without offence. 'I leave when my Lord Archbishop has had his fill of revelling in self-inflicted glory. He is to be consecrated in late August by the Bishop of Tours, and after that he will have so many problems thrust upon him that Beverley will be free of him for a while. In fact, if all I hear is true, his enemies will do all they can to prevent him setting his feet back on English soil, despite his consecration. He'll not return as gloriously as he sets out, that much is practically guaranteed.' He glanced at Aaron, winced and heaved an exaggerated sigh. 'Am I to suppose you need a safe escort back to your house at York, Rabbi?'

'Your offer is most kind, sir. I accept.'

'Was that an offer?' Fergus quipped. 'If you insist on it, you can be sure I will have your baggage searched for Christian artefacts before I agree to escort you as far as the nearest street.'

'It seems we have a deal,' the rabbi answered with a smile.

Simeon was still in easy conversation with his friends when Elvira came up behind him and, smelling of anise and rosemary, slipped her arms about his neck and pressed her cheek to his. Her breasts were firm against his back and her breath hot in his ear as she whispered so that only he could hear: 'I will wait for you in Jacob's house. Come soon, my love.'

Her words were so inviting and her closeness such a torment to his senses that Simeon felt a flush rise to his cheeks and a sudden tightening in his belly. It was Rufus who saved his blushes.

'Tell me about this place called Compostela where Wulfric de Morthlund is to beg forgiveness at the tomb of St James,' he demanded cheerfully. As the topic was taken up with much enthusiasm, Simeon was more than grateful for what appeared to be a spontaneous distraction.

Later, as he walked alone through the grounds with much to fill his thoughts, he heard the soft murmur of voices in the church. Perplexed, he passed through the porch and found that the door, kept secure at night while so many strangers were passing through the town, had been unlocked. It stood partly open, though the heavy drapes beyond were lowered and drawn together. From there he heard the unmistakable sounds of chanting priests led by a single voice that was so deep and rich in timbre that it set up vibrations in his breastbone and caused his scalp to prickle. *The other*!

His fingers drew a gap in the curtains through which he saw the hooded figure, clad in black from head to toe and with its features hidden, standing at the altar with its arms raised up. In its hands it held two golden keys crossed in the emblem of St Peter, the symbol of their Church, their faith, their hopes of entering God's kingdom in the afterlife. Light played upon the gleaming swirls and curves that were a representation of the strength and purity of Peter, Christ's own vicar, keeper of the sacred keys of heaven. It was an awe-inspiring sight, and Simeon felt himself moved to his very soul. A dozen cowled priests were kneeling close by, their voices little more than an echoing whisper in the church. The only light came from a single altar candle which threw the shadow of the crucifix, greatly enlarged, across the walls. On a bench by the altar sat the frail old Cuthbert, his face lit with rapture as his lips followed the chanting of the hooded priests

'Whose ordination?' Simeon whispered against the curtain.

For an instant *the other* seemed to pause and look in Simeon's direction. The priest was concealed from view by the heavy hangings across the door, and yet that unseen gaze locked with his own and he knew *the other* had sensed his presence. It was then that he saw the small, grey-clad figure of his foster son kneeling before the altar with his head bowed and his hands clasped in prayer, and only when the hooded figure lowered its raised hands to his head did Simeon realise that the boy's hair had been shaven to create a crown.

'Oh, dear God, he is still a child.'

Simeon sank to his knees by the curtain as the sweet, familiar tones of the service rose and fell in hypnotic waves. He closed his eyes and added his own voice to those of the choral priests, and when he opened his eyes again, the chanting had stopped and Peter was alone in the flickering candlelight.

'God bless and keep you in your Office,' he muttered with a heavy heart. 'I have witnessed your ordination into the priesthood, Peter de Beverley. May I live to see your destiny fulfilled.' Leaving the boy to his prayers, he rose from his knees and left the church as quietly as he had entered.

He was still brooding on this unlikely ordination of a ten-year-old boy when his steps brought him to the tiny stone house that had been prepared for Jacob. There were chinks of light around the window shutters and a thin tendril of smoke snaking up from the smoke hole in the roof. He drew back the curtain from the open door but did not step inside. Instead he leaned against the door frame to watch Elvira brushing her long black hair. Her eyes were as dark as midnight as she looked back at him, and in her lovely face was all the love and comfort he would ever need.

'You never change,' he told her, his voice hoarse with emotion. 'Ten years and you are still the same, as beautiful and as dear to me as ever.'

Elvira set down her hairbrush. 'I love you,' she told him, sliding the shawl from her shoulders and moving her head so that her hair cascaded over her creamy skin. 'Come inside.'

He shook his head. 'My thoughts are in turmoil, Elvira. I feel . . .'

'Vulnerable?' she suggested. 'Must a canon be invulnerable,

Simeon? Can a canon not be a man, neither first nor last, but simply a man?'

Simeon touched the golden brow piece hanging behind his unlaced shirt. 'Elvira, when you were trapped in the well and I heard the floods approaching, I thought . . . I feared . . .'

'That your God sought to divide us,' she finished for him. 'It will never happen, Simeon. We have His blessing. Do you not see that now? We have God's blessing on this love of ours. We have *always* had His blessing.'

'My dear Elvira, if I could only believe that.'

'Have faith,' she told him, she who had no faith in anything but him and love itself. 'God gave us His blessing ten years ago, but we were both too blind to see it then. Open your eyes to the gift, Simeon. Come inside.'

Gathered together in the shadows beneath the slanting refectory roof, the men of St Peter's saw Simeon framed in the lighted doorway of the house. They stood in silence, each with his own hopes, his own prayers for the times ahead. At last their vigil was ended when they saw the priest stoop to enter the house and the rectangle of light vanish as the door swung closed behind him. Aaron the Jew lowered his dark head so that none would see the moistness in his eyes.

'God grant them happiness,' Osric sighed and Thorald, in his deep growl, added, 'May God grant them each other, as man and wife.'

Rufus de Malham, stroking his long moustaches in satisfaction, glanced at the grinning Fergus and said, with a smile, 'Amen to that!'

The conspiracy shaped by the men of St Peter's did not end with the closing of Elvira's door behind Simeon. They were convinced that, had the good Lord slept or turned His head for just a moment, Simeon would not have kept his vow of celibacy for a decade. Now they prayed that God would not intrude upon this moment, that He would be kind to one who had found true faith and cherished love above all else, and to the lady who had proved her constancy. As Peter emerged from the church and signed the cross in their direction, the men of St Peter's heard the soft sound of bells from distant churches, discrete and unobtrusive in their pealing. For the first time in living memory, Great John, the deep-toned Minster bell, and Peter, the sweeter-voiced prayer bell of their own church, were silent at the ritual ringing of the last Angelus of the day.

POSTSCRIPT

When Geoffrey Plantagenet refused to hand over the two thousand pounds promised for the crusades, King Richard sent the Bishop of Bath and Bourchard du Puiset to Rome to get his election as archbishop quashed, at the same time forbidding all archbishops in his dominions to consecrate his brother. Pope Clement III, however, confirmed the election, and Geoffrey promptly excommunicated the Bishop of Bath and Bourchard du Puiset. Both were later absolved by Clement. King Richard was persuaded to withdraw his prohibition and Geoffrey was consecrated at Tours in August 1191. Geoffrey was arrested and imprisoned on his return to England and was not enthroned at York until All Saints' Day in November of that year. He assumed the title Primate of England.

The Book of Leviticus, Ch.XX v. 13 states: 'If a man lie with mankind as with womankind, they shall both surely be put to death. In 1102 the Council of London pronounced excommunication on all homosexuals. Although the mediaeval Church claimed to demand that offenders be beaten with rods, buried alive, plunged into marshes, given seven to fifteen years penance, banished, starved or excommunicated, no record exists of any such punishments ever being enforced.

Aaron the Jew became Archpresbyter of York from 1236 to 1243 and, despite being one of the most powerful Jews in the country, died ruined and penniless. His father, Josce, the wealthiest of all York's Jews, was slain during the 1190 riots, his assets confiscated and his debts collected by the Crown. The stone house he built in York was Aaron's home throughout his life and stood on the site of Leake and Thorpe, now Ernest Jones, in Coney Street.

Despite centuries of dispute, the relics of St John of Beverley were never acquired by York. St John was born at Harpham in Yorkshire and educated at Canterbury, later to be ordained Bishop of Hexham and Archbishop of York. He founded Beverley Abbey, to which he retired before dying of old age in 721. The present Minster is the result of the abbey's growth over the last twelve hundred years.

Following the Great Fire of 1188, the relics of St John remained hidden until 1197. His casket, including four iron nails, three brass pins, six beads, several scraps of bone and hair, and a much corroded dagger, vanished again when the church tower collapsed in 1213 and was not located for another hundred years. The relics are now believed to rest beneath a commemorative tablet in the centre of the nave of Beverley Minster.

In 1213 an elaborate extension was added to the Minster tower, resulting in the collapse of the tower and the destruction of the entire east end of the Minster church. The original octagonal chapterhouse was not rebuilt following the Great Fire of 1188.

In 1221 Stephen Goldsmith, master craftsman and a canon serving Beverley Minster, gifted all those enclosed lands east of the Eastgate ditch (St Peter's enclosure) to the Dominicans, known as friars preachers, thereby keeping his vow never to allow his lands to fall into the hands of the Archbishop of York.

Only traces remain of the mediaeval village of Ravensthorpe, close to Bygot Wood, near Beverley, though the Burton family name is still evident in several villages in the area.

As recently as 1960 the water in the well to the right of the high altar of Beverley Minster was found to be pure and sweet, more than a thousand years after the documented blessing of the Keldgate stream by St John of Beverley.

Excavations undertaken between 1960 and 1983 at the site of the Old Friary enclosure (St Peter's) in Eastgate revealed the foundations of a mediaeval church, much of which lies in the trench of the present railway station. Also found was evidence of twenty-six burials, some grave slabs, tiles, masonry, cooking pots, jugs, spouted pitchers, fragments of painted window glass and pieces of leather shoe soles, all dating from the eleventh and twelfth centuries. Many skeletal remains were also uncovered. Details of these excavations can be found in *Excavations at the Dominican Priory, Beverley* by P. Armstrong and D. G. Tomlinson (Humberside Heritage Publication No. 13).

Master of the Keys is the third book in the Beverley Chronicles inspired by, and dedicated to, the unknown priest whose tomb stands on the east side of the North Transept of Beverley Minster.

Keeper at the Shrine

Domini Highsmith

A freezing winter's night, a mysterious hooded rider; a sudden storm of sinister and devastating power: strange forces are unleashed on the Minster town of Beverley in the see of York . . . and worse is yet to come.

It is December 1180. At the height of the tempest the hooded figure brings a new-born child for baptism . . . a child whose divine task it is to defend the sacred shrine of St John of Beverley. In the great Minster Church a crippled priest is healed of his affliction and made the boy Peter's guardian when the figure vanishes.

United with Elvira, the beautiful young woman engaged as wet-nurse, Father Simeon is driven to unforeseeable lengths to protect the child from the evil elements within the church. Together they become both catalysts and scapegoats in a game with ever-changing rules, a game in which the priestly players are capable of anything, even murder.

The church is divided, the shrine of St John besieged, the town itself in danger of destruction . . . and then the hooded figure reappears.

Guardian at the Gate

Domini Highsmith

September 1190. Drought and pestilence threaten the town of Beverley in the see of York, still struggling to recover from the worst fire in its history. Its great Minster Church lies half ruined and its powerful canons are divided in their loyalties.

At the core of the conflict are Simeon de Beverley's beautiful lover, Elvira, and their godson, Peter, the mysterious boy responsible for saving the treasure and the precious relics of St John from the fire. As the double-dealings of its priests push Beverley once again to the brink of disaster, so there begins a gathering-in, a drawing together of those who serve the Minster and St John, as Simeon and his loyal companions are slowly driven into the trap devised by his enemies.

All are pawns in the deadly games of corrupt and ruthless men. Pitted against impossible odds, their lives hang in the balance until, from the fire-ravaged timbers of the ancient Minster, the mysterious black-hooded figure reappears to redirect the course of Beverley's history . . .

Other best selling Warner titles available by mail: